LE

LETTERS TO LINZI

Edited by Linzi Drew

First published in 1993 by
Nexus
332 Ladbroke Grove
London W10 5AH

Reprinted 1994

Copyright © Linzi Drew 1993

Typeset by TW Typesetting, Plymouth, Devon
Printed and bound in Great Britain by
Cox & Wyman Ltd, Reading, Berks.

ISBN 0 352 32860 6

This book is a work of fiction.
In real life, make sure you practise safe sex.

CONTENTS

INTRODUCTION

Over the past decade I have been the recipient of thousands upon thousands of letters of a wild and wanton nature. They arrive from all corners of the globe from both men and women, whose common interest is to divulge their most intimate sex secrets or to reveal their dirtiest dreams and desires. The mucky masterpieces started to arrive when I worked as a columnist for *Club International* magazine. My mail bag continued to bulge when I was appointed editor of *Penthouse* magazine. And now that I'm editing a glossy magazine entitled *Eros* incorporating *Men's Letters*, as you can well imagine, my kinky correspondence has reached an all-time high! In *Letters to Linzi* I found the perfect outlet to compile the best collection of all these sexually explicit, randy revelations.

But I'm frequently quizzed on the authenticity of my correspondents. Do they really exist or are these lewd letters just the hand of some sordid hack tucked away in a sleazy office who spends his every waking hour conjuring up sexual scenarios and fantasies? Well let's get this one cleared up once and for all. They're all genuine letters! There would have to be an entire army of hacks to have the stamina and the weird and wonderful imagination to come up with this lot!

No, my contributors are the real McCoy. They sit down at home on a quiet night when there's nothing on the box and write to me. Or they put pen to paper when they're on the train on their way to work and drop me a naughty note. Or they seize the time during their lunch break to pour it all out. Who else are they going to tell about that unbelievable hand job on the back of the number 49 bus; or how they've been having some fabulous fucks with the horny housewife next door; or about the time the gasman got the best blow job of his career; or how they'd like to smother my bouncing breasts in sticky, strawberry jam?

They say that confession is good for the soul – and well it might be – but it also makes for a bloody good dirty read. One small complaint, however, before I let you loose on this sizzling collection of lusty letters. Although I am truly grateful and greatly indebted to the excitable bunch who write to me and have made this saucy book possible, I just wish they could manage to do so without becoming so stimulated and orgasmic that their handwriting becomes totally illegible! It really is enough to make a girl go blind!

Linzi Drew 1993.

1. ALL DRESSED UP

Do you like to get all dressed up in order to slowly and seductively strip off again? Or perhaps you prefer to indulge with your clothes on? Check out what this horny bunch of correspondents get up to with and without their clobber!

A Tight Squeeze

Dear Linzi,

Last night I had the wettest dream! You were in a totally empty room with white floor and ceiling with absolutely nothing else in the room except you. You were totally and utterly naked except for a pair of sheer black nylon tights. Nothing else at all. No knickers, no shoes, nothing.

I suddenly entered the room and saw you there, lying on the floor with your head resting back. You spread your luscious, long black legs as wide as you could, stretching them in the air so that I got a distorted glimpse of your juicy slit through the black nylon material. Moist patches appeared in the crotch of the tights where your hole had leaked. I knelt down between your legs and placed my nose up to the soppy spot and took a long, hard, gorgeous sniff of the deliciously sweet female sex smell. It sent my pole sky high. With my eyes shut I began to lick at the gentle, soft, wet nylon material stretching across your leaking crotch. The sweet juicy taste tickled my taste buds as my tongue teased your pussy lips through the tights. I ate your pussy for an age making you cry out in orgasm, your body quivering in excitement. Then, after one more good sniff and lick, I raised my head, and lifted one of your legs up so that your exquisitely smooth, black-tighted foot was in front of my face. I began to stroke this incredibly sexy footsie, holding it to my face, kissing the toes, heel, and sole before I took another gorgeously long sniff of the sexy aroma of your feet, savouring the lovely smell. I licked and sucked the soles of both of your feet with your tights still on, my velvety tongue gliding over your silky smooth skin. Finally you wiped your wonderful tootsies all over my face as I bit your toes playfully.

The best part of all was when you wrapped your feet around my throbbing tool and began to push my thick, pink foreskin back and forth over my shiny purple helmet, using just your delicate toes. It was such an erotic sensation to feel your toes wriggling around my stem that I couldn't hold back and a creamy splurge of thick spunky come exploded out of my spunk gun onto your lovely feet. It was then that you took the spunky tights off and placed the part where your feet had been into your mouth, so you could lick the spunk off.

Next you turned over on to your knees and thrust your lovely peachy bum into my face. I just couldn't resist the lovely sight of your arse beckoning me. So I leant over, clutched a creamy cheek in each hand and slowly peeled them apart to reveal your lovely fleshy pink pussy. I proceeded to lick delicately and slowly, digging my tongue right in.

I stood up, gripped my stiff tool in one hand, my creamy helmet bulging, purple veins pulsing, my balls dangling heavy in my scrotum as I started to guide my purple end into your hole. Slowly, ever so slowly, I forced it in. It was a struggle. You were screaming in ecstasy as I rammed my long, thick knob into your juicy slit. It was so tight, your pussy walls gripping my penis and almost squeezing it to death. I felt myself coming. The spunk began to flow as I pulled my knob out. As it exited your creamy cunt, a jet shot over your fleshy bum cheeks and up your back. You groaned a final cry of ecstatic pleasure.

The fun still wasn't over! You took my wilting willy, still dripping with come and sucked it into your mouth. Slowly you licked up and down the length of the stem with your pink tongue, until my limp prick started to stir again. You took the whole length of my enormous prick in your mouth until a third fountain of come spurted down your throat. At one point you couldn't handle the flow and spat the spunk out. But afterwards you laughed, lay back on the floor rolling and writhing around in spilt spunk and cunt juice. It was smeared all over your body, your face and in your hair, but we didn't care. And the fun still wasn't over!

Out came a tin of thick golden syrup and I started to trickle the gooey, yellow treacle into your deliciously fuzzy pubic forest. What a mess! The syrup trickled out of your soft, fuzzy bush around your clit and pussy lips. I dug my head in and started to lick it out, first concentrating on your pubes and then moving lower to your fleshy lips and clit.

3

And finally no dream would be complete without the ultimate fuck. And it came! I slowly buried my bulging rod into the dark, wet depths of your spunky, syrupy cunt and slammed it in and out until you were moaning with delight, and I shot the last load of come from my spunk-drained balls deep into your raw slit.

And then I woke up, stuck to the sheets . . . If only!

Anonymous.

Wet and Wild

Dear Linzi,

Oh the joys of wet sex! My girlfriend and I love nothing better than an evening of washing and fucking. I get her to dress up in stockings and suspenders and then we go into the bathroom. There, on my hands and knees, I get a really soapy flannel and wash her up-turned breasts and blonde hairy pussy. I squeeze the bubbles right into her hole and lick the warm water as it mingles with her juices.

Then it's my turn. I sit on the edge of the bath and she slowly lathers up my balls and cock using a flannel and her soapy fingers until I can stand the suspense no longer and we plunge into a hot bath and fuck. Sometimes she likes me to wank her with the shower hose turned up to its highest pressure. She lays on her back in an empty bath tub, spreads her legs wide, and while I fingerfuck her, I aim the warm, gushing water at her clitoris. I love her all dressed up in stockings and suspenders getting very wet in the bath!

Barney. Cornwall.

Lewd Nurse Luna

Dear Linzi,

My girlfriend, Luna and I, went to a fancy-dress party. She dressed up as a nurse in a short, pale blue tunic, with a white belt, a white hat, white high heels and a large navy cape draped over her shoulders. Underneath she put on white lingerie and stockings. She looked smashing. I dressed as a vicar in a white collar and a long black robe. Beneath my clerical frock I wore only my socks and shoes, and a pair of jazzy Union Jack boxer shorts.

The party was held in a large country house owned by some rich friends that Luna knows through her work as a fashion designer. Most of the guests were in fancy dress and I was quite taken with some of the sexy outfits worn by the women. But, not as taken as I was by Nurse Luna. She is a living doll with a figure to put a 'Page Three' girl to shame. She has enormous breasts, tipped with pink whoppers of nipples, a tiny little waist, lovely round bum cheeks and a pussy that is constantly wet. She looks exotic because she is Italian and has long black hair, big, brown eyes and huge lips that work wonders on my dick!

All evening I couldn't take my eyes off Luna and neither could most of the other men at the party. She's a bit of a flirt, but I don't mind because I know it's always going to be me that she ends up going home with. All night Luna and I were both so hot and horny for sex that we couldn't wait until the party ended.

About halfway through the evening, Nurse Luna and the Reverend Phil had a smoochy dance together. The nearness of Luna's glorious body made my cock start to swell. It stood bolt upright like some majestic flagpole poking her in the middle.

'You vant to fuck?' Luna asked in her heavily-accented voice.

'Yeah, but where?' I answered, gripping hold of her arse and pulling her towards me so that she could feel the full benefit of my excitement. She kissed me deliciously on the mouth and we started knecking so passionately that her nurses cap nearly fell off. She pulled away breathing rapidly and said, 'Come, we find somewhere!'

She took my hand and together the nurse and the vicar disappeared upstairs. In the room that was being used for coats, Luna lifted her skirt and flashed me her white panties. They had a big, damp patch around the crotch.

'Leek my pussy?' she offered, pulling her knickers off to one side to give me a look at her moist black bush and pouting pink lips. Grabbing hold of her stocking-clad legs, I squatted on my haunches and went to play on her dangly, shiny clit.

5

She thrust herself forcefully onto my mouth, squirming and wriggling until I could feel her body tensing, and then I tasted the sweetness of her come.

'Now, Mr Veecar, I am going to suck your cock,' she breathed as she lifted my gown, got rid of my boxers and slipped a warm hand to my swollen member. I lay on my back on the bed as she used both hands; one to grip at the base of my shaft, the other to cup my balls as she took me in her mouth.

After much slurping, she paused and said, 'I vant to deep throat you!' So we swopped places. This time Luna lay on the bed with her head hanging off the edge, getting the position exactly right, so that I could sink my cock all the way down her throat. It went down like a dream. My whole cock being swallowed up by her wet mouth made me feel out of control. I was coming in no time. My hot spunk whooshed down her throat.

Luna had me hard again almost immediately. She took off her panties and lay down on the bed. She opened her cunt and started to frig her clit. Within a minute or so I was inside her, fucking her for all I was worth, my black gown hoisted up around my waist, my dog collar skew-whiff, as I rode my lover to the gates of heaven!

I didn't believe that sex with Luna could improve, but that night, naughty Nurse Luna really gave me the special treatment!

Phil. Oxford.

Temptress in Tights

Dear Linzi,

I fantasize about you wearing tights. Perhaps you don't find them sexy. Let me explain my point of view.

Your gorgeous lovely legs are just right for tights. What turns me on is the thought of you wearing black fishnet tights or smooth, black, silky tights that are a size too small for you. When you wriggle into them, you really have to stretch the hot nylon mesh over your firm thighs and red hot pussy. It really is a squeeze as you pull the gusset up tight over your pussy, making you moan with ecstasy.

6

My fantasy is that you are a business woman, sitting behind your desk watching your new secretary bend over the filing cabinets in a miniskirt and seamed tights. Like you, she has no panties on. Your naughty secretary knows that she is turning you on by showing you her tights, and you just have to pull up your short skirt and finger yourself through your tights. Seeing this, your secretary lifts up her tiny skirt to reveal her tights-encased pussy and bottom. She stretches the nylon fabric tight against her pussy and you can't control yourself as you come in your tights, soaking the nylon mesh.

J.P.

Panting for Plastic

Dear Linzi,

I like to see girls dressed up in PVC and leather. Plenty of thigh-length kinky boots with spiky high heels, crotchless, shiny panties and peephole bras. Whenever I fancy a really good time, I get my girlfriend Janie to dress up in PVC pants and a front fastening bodice that finishes just below her round, heavy tits. I play around with her pushed up globes and squeeze her brown nipples hard, before moving down between her legs to rub my fingers up and down the open slit of her shiny plastic knickers. Plastic panties make her cunt so wet and sticky that I generally end up fucking her two minutes after I've got my tongue in her hairy twat. Plastic panties make me pant for sex!

Billy Edgeware.

Park It Here For Pleasure

Dear Linzi,

You may not believe the tale I am going to tell you, but honestly it's true! I can hardly believe it myself.

Last week I had to go to Kensington High Street to get my mum a birthday present. I knew exactly what she wanted, and as I was having awful trouble parking, I thought I'd chance parking on a single yellow line, rush in and get her gift and be

7

back before any harm was done. So I parked in this quiet mews and hurried off to do my shopping.

Barely ten minutes later when I returned, I noticed with dismay that a traffic warden was standing by my car. As I got a bit closer I realised just how good looking she was; short blonde hair, a pretty little face and only about twenty years old. I ran back to my car all flustered and saw that she had a wicked smile on her face.

'Who's been a naughty boy then?' she giggled, flashing a wonderous smile and tapping her pencil on her notebook.

I had this strange feeling that she was really enjoying the situation. If I apologised, I wondered, would she let me off? It was worth a shot, and besides I have a fascination for women in uniform, especially ones that are damn attractive, so I took the bull by the horns and said, 'You know I am very sorry. What if I was to invite you out for dinner? Would you forget about the ticket?'

She crossed her legs and leant back against my car. I could hear the russle of her smooth stockings as she rubbed her slender legs together. 'You've got an awful cheek, but you've also got a deal!' she smiled. She wrote down her address and told me to pick her up that evening.

When I called at her flat that night, I couldn't believe it when she answered the door still dressed in full uniform.

'Have you only just got off?' I asked innocently.

'I haven't got off yet, but with your help I intend to!' she laughed, lifting her skirt to reveal, slim stocking-clad thighs and no knickers!

Wow! I couldn't believe my good fortune as she led me into her bedroom and told me to sit down beside her on the bed. She hiked her skirt up around her waist and took my hand. Well I'm not backwards at coming forwards, but she seemed to like doing all the running and I loved playing it her way. 'You know men who leave their cars where they shouldn't in my parking zone have to pay a forfeit,' she whispered naughtily, whilst running a hand across her hairy fanny.

My mouth was watering, I knew just where I wanted to park my prick. I asked her, 'And what is that?'

'They either pay a ticket, or I have the sole use of their body

8

until I am completely satisfied,' she breathed, now manipulating her fanny and pulling her lips slightly apart.

I needed no more games as I bent my head to her lips and stuck my tongue right up inside her. She smelt beautiful as I drank her sweet juices. She lay back and opened her jacket and blouse to reveal a gorgeous pair of boobs with big, swollen nipples that I reached out and kneaded. I left her fanny for a moment and moved up to her ecstatic face and pouting lips and kissed her long and hard. Tasting her own lovejuice made her even randier. 'Come on and screw me, you naughty boy!' she screamed as she rolled over, thrust her bum in the air, pulled her cheeks apart and helped me in. I grabbed her fat arse and thrust right into her. She was wet and slippery and she clung to me with her fanny, squeezing my cock, thrusting with me and then sucking every last drop of come from me as I came in an enormous judder.

We never did make it out for dinner. I spent the entire evening screwing a traffic warden in full uniform and none of my friends will believe a word of it. You believe me don't you, Linzi?

T.D.

Leopard-skin Lust

Dear Linzi,
One of the things I find most exciting when having sex is to do it with clothes on. I love to feel my wet knickers being dragged off to one side, or adore the sensation as a hand creeps up under my skirt. The other week I had a great quickie fuck and I did it with all my clothes on.

A girlfriend and I went out on a boozy girls' night out. We ended up at about midnight in a small club in the West End. Instead of all the usual, awful rap music, the DJ was actually playing some great records. My mate Ruth and I got on the dance floor and we were really giving it some. I was wearing a tight, stretchy leopard-print dress and matching high-heeled calf-length boots. Underneath, I was only wearing a tiny leopard-skin G-string. As I gyrated around on the dance floor

9

my dress wriggled up my body showing off almost all of my long legs, which really are my best asset. I noticed the good-looking DJ watching me, his eyes hungrily looking me over. He was around thirty, just a couple of years or so older than me and he looked very sensual, with an oval face, big green eyes and his hair scraped back in a ponytail. I was feeling very horny and wondered just what it would be like to fuck him.

I slinked over to him smiling and pulling my dress down just a little. The music was so loud that to make a request I had to lean right over and talk in his ear.

'All I want to do is make love to you,' I said. Then after a pause, I continued, 'The record by Heart!'

Our eyes locked and I knew I could have him.

'Come round the back here and I'll see if I can find what you want,' he said knowingly.

He must have put on an extended-play record because just a few seconds later we were in the back of his booth, his hot lips crushed against mine. He didn't care about changing the disc on the turntable. The loud music throbbed as I unzipped his jeans. He pushed up my leopard-skin dress, eased aside my leopard-print panties and slipped a finger inside my juicy pink pussy.

'Do you want fucking?' he mouthed as I worked his foreskin back.

His fingers squelched in and out of my drippy puss. I shook my head and groaned, 'Oh Yes! Yes!'

We wasted no time. In the same position, with my back against the wall, I guided his hot rod between my puffy pink lips. I went up on tiptoes as he entered me, his prick pumping hard and fast. My back slammed against the partition wall, my nails raked into his back as he fucked me wonderfully. One of my tits bounced out of my dress and he bit it savagely; he behaved like a wild animal as he built to orgasm. His behaviour excited me immensely and I screamed out that I was about to come. With that he filled me full of cream. Then, I straightend up my G-string, pulled down my leopard-skin dress and went off to the bar and ordered a stiff drink!

Jo. W. London.

It's A Fair Cop

Dear Linzi,
I thought you would like to hear my fantasy about you.

I was walking home from the pub one Friday at 3 p.m., just as the bar had closed for the afternoon, when I saw you dressed as a WPC. You were leaning over the bonnet of a car looking at the tax disc on the windscreen. The split up the back of your skirt opened just enough to show the tops of your seamed, black, silk stockings. That was too much for me. The drink had taken effect, so as I passed you, I 'goosed' you. You moaned with delight, then spun around and slapped my face. Then it was out with the handcuffs and my wrists were clamped behind my back. You said nothing, just grabbed my tie and led me down an alleyway between the pub and the betting office.

Quite a long way down the alleyway you stopped and asked me if I had any reason to do what I had done. I was so shocked I couldn't say anything. Then you said I would be searched for weapons. You looked me straight in the eye as you took off my belt and unzipped my trousers. They fell down around my ankles. You slid your thumbs inside the elastic of my pants and slowly pulled them down to my knees.

Your eyes opened wide as you looked up from your kneeling position. 'What's this then?' you asked, as you put your leather gloved hand around my ever increasing cock. The moment had been as good for you as for me, so you lifted your skirt and forced those leather-clad fingers deep inside your cunt as my rampant cock bounced in front of your burning eyes.

Seconds later the hand, wrapped around my aching cock, brought me to climax. We came almost together and I collapsed in a heap. You took a few seconds to compose yourself and straighten your stockings. You licked your ruby red lips then removed the handcuffs.

'Now let that be a lesson to you!' you said, before walking off down the alleyway, your bum swaying from side to side as you slowly disappeared from sight.

Jack. Herts.

Suzanne Is So Good Around the House

Dear Linzi,

I am writing to tell you about a marvellous night of lust that I had a couple of weeks ago. I have been going out with my girlfriend for four years now, and although our sex life is good, sometimes it can be a little samey. So we decided to liven it up a little. We decided that instead of screwing in our bed, or on the couch, we'd dress up in our sexiest undies and fuck in different places around the house!

Suzanne got all dressed up in her favourite raw silk, pale pink teddy with an open crotch. She wore it with white stockings and high-heeled shoes and I put on flame-red silk boxers. Suzanne wiggled her way into the kitchen with me in hot pursuit. She lay on her back on the table, opened her legs and offered herself to me. I pulled back the lacy sides of her pants, revealing her pink, inviting pussy and poked my tongue inside her. She was sopping wet as I sipped her lovejuice and lapped away at her lovebutton while she screamed and hollered to climax.

She told me to lay down on the table and stood beside me, playing with herself with one hand, using the other to rub my prick through my silk boxers. I was rock hard when she lowered my shorts and took hold of my prick. It started to grow even bigger as she wanked her hand up and down, now and again brushing my tip against the lace of her teddy.

Soon we were both in a wonderful state of sexual intoxication. She climbed onto the table and squatted down on top of me. Her pussy all open and gaping in readiness for me. When I slid inside her she jerked up and down, impaled on my cock, riding faster and faster until I shot my load into her clenched cunt. That was the first of the evening.

Next we moved on to the bathroom where I sat on the toilet and asked her to sit on my lap. A few minutes of snogging and her writhing her beautiful arse on top of me had my cock at the ready, and I was shoving it up her once again. I grabbed her around the middle and thrust her up and down on top. All the time one of her hands was squeezing my balls until they felt ready to burst.

We had a little rest after that. Suzanne lay down wet and sticky in front of the fire and I started to casually stroke her tiny, bud-like tits. She's got these fabulous big nipples that grow gigantic after a good fingering. Her tits are very sensitive and I can make her come just by playing with them. I lay beside her gliding the flat of my hand over her erect nipples and gradually I felt a stirring in my loins. Her hand reached down between my legs and gently tickled the head of my prick. I was erect in no time and soon I was sliding my hardness over her nipples, massaging them with my cock until they stood out firmly and her breathing was hard and heavy.

This time I rolled her over onto her tummy. She arched up her arse, with her pouting pink pussy lips positioned perfectly for me. I slipped two fingers inside her and she begged for my cock, so I gave it to her. I knelt behind her, grabbed her arse and slowly squeezed inside her hot hole. Her muscles gripped me like a vice and she kept her head low on the ground, growling, 'Fuck me! Fuck me!' I held her tight and pulled her on to me harder and harder, shafting her to the hilt until we jerked to a mighty big O together.

Three times was all I could muster, Linzi. I'm sure you've probably had studs who can perform half-a-dozen times, but I say it's quality, not quantity that's important. Suzanne and I had a great night of sex, we didn't actually do it in many unusual places, but it was different for us. This weekend we're planning a day of it, and if it's not too cold in the evening, we're thinking of dressing up in warm overcoats and little else, and trying the phone box on the corner!

Robert. Doncaster.

A Dressing Down

Dear Linzi,

In this particular fantasy about you, you and I are due to go to a fancy-dress party together, but as luck would have it we never manage to make it to the party.

The evening begins when you get all dressed up in a Wren's uniform from the second world war that you have hired. It's

13

fantastic: an airforce blue colour, with a tailored jacket that hugs your waist closely and a tight skirt that accentuates your beautiful round arse. It looks really authentic. As you are standing admiring yourself in the mirror before we are due to leave, I can see in your eyes that you are becoming aroused just by smoothing your skirt over your hips, and imagining that you are a different person.

You then strip off your jacket and fondle your breasts through your blouse. As you stand before me I too am becoming really turned on, especially when I notice the way your nipples are hardening and pushing through your tight blouse before my very eyes.

'That's made you feel horny!' I say.

You reply, 'I know, but do you want me to take it off?'

That question needs no reply. And so gradually you strip for me, slipping out of your blouse, and skirt, right down to your stockings and suspenders. You're wearing those seamed stockings, the old-fashioned ones, and I love those. I run my fingers up the back of your legs, and then I kneel down in front of you and start to stroke your buttocks. My nose is right by your pubic mound and I am able to smell your sweet lovejuices. The heady aroma makes my cock grow another inch. You are panting as I continue to rub the cheeks of your arse, and nuzzle my face in your silky pubes. You reach down and pull your lips apart with your fingers, to reveal how wet and pink the inside of your pussy is.

I start to rub your juices all over your lovelips, and also lap away at your labia, flicking my tongue against your clitoris before plunging my tongue deep inside your pussy. I tease your clitoris out of its hood and start to frig you off. You look so abandoned, really passionate and sexy too.

We lay down on the bed's satin sheets and you position yourself on top of me. You slip your hand between your legs to test how moist your pussy is.

'Are you ready?' I ask.

You shut your eyes and guide my hand to your wet slit. You allow it to rest there momentarily, then push it away. I shut my eyes and lay quite still for a moment, not really aware of anything, then I feel a gentle rhythmic movement where your

14

thighs touch mine. I crack open my eyes and have the pleasure of the most erotic sight I've seen in years; your hand is rubbing at your pussy, your crotch jerking forward with each rub, your big, squashy, hard-nippled tits swaying together, and all the time, your eyes are shut tight in concentration, your mouth gaping and emitting tiny gasps of breath. All at once I can stand it no longer, I just have to be inside you. You sense the moment, open your long legs and welcome me inside that heavenly haven of love. My head and spunk explode simultaneously and I am lost in a reverie of sexual exultation.

Aaron.

2. CUTE KINKS

Like to play at being cute and kinky? Whether it's PVC panties, short sharp spanks, pretty, pink toenails or muckspreading that you've a penchant for, I'm sure you'll find something to tickle your fancy in this chapter!

Teacher's Pet

Dear Linzi,

I thought I'd drop you a line to tell you what my wife, Joanne and I have been up to lately, as we had a bit of a kinky experience the other night. Two days ago, to be precise. Instead of our usual Friday night routine of going out to a club or to the pictures, we decided to spend the evening at home. Well it was Joanne that made the decision and she was also the one who decided that we would spend the night having one hell of a sex session.

We went upstairs to the bedroom and got changed into our uniforms. I was playing the part of a naughty schoolboy and Joanne was my headmistress. I put on my grey shorts, grey socks, black shoes, white shirt, my black tie with yellow stripes and a grey sweater. Joanne put on black underwear, dark stockings, a white blouse, dark skirt, a black robe and a black hat. We went into the spare bedroom which we had previously rearranged to look like a classroom. I sat at my desk and started to work with Joanne on some maths. When we moved on to human biology, I started to act stupid by using filthy words to describe different parts of the human anatomy. The headmistress warned me to stop using filthy words or else she would have to reprimand me. So I became even more abusive and the headmistress told me that she was about to teach me a lesson I wasn't likely to forget!

She ordered that I stand in front of her desk, then she disappeared from the room, returning a few moments later with one of her own, size seven slippers. She told me to bend over the desk as she was about to give me six of the best as punishment for my outrageous behaviour in her class. She pulled my shorts and undies down with one sharp yank and gave my bare arse a few light slaps with the palm of her hand, just to warm it for the main event with the slipper.

After a minute or so, when I suspected my arse was turning pink because it was beginning to smart, the headmistress picked up the slipper and started to thrash me with it. She raised it high above her head and brought it down hard and fast. I could feel my bum cheeks getting hotter and hotter as she whacked me viciously time after time.

When she had hit me six times with the punishment slipper, she told me to stand up. As I turned to face her, the headmistress noticed that my cock was starting to grow. She instructed me to strip off and after I did and stood before her stark naked, she took hold of my hardness and started to wank my cock for all it was worth. She knelt on the floor and took me in her mouth. Her wet tongue wriggled up and down my shaft and she chewed gently on my knob end. I was becoming very excited. I said I was ready to shoot my load quite soon, so she started to suck faster on my tool fetching me to a wonderful orgasm seconds later.

Now it was Joanne's turn. She got up off her knees and asked me to punish her. I removed her hat, and as I took off her gown, I saw that beneath it she had on a very sexy blouse and a leather miniskirt. The skirt was about eight inches above the knee. I told her to take off her blouse and show me her tits. She has big tits with tasty nipples. When she released them from her bra, I tweaked them hard and watched as her red nipples got bigger and bigger. Then I sucked on them for a while until they were really swollen.

With her big tits hanging free, I told her to bend over the desk, then I lifted her miniskirt above her hips to discover that she had no panties on, only black nylon stockings and suspenders.

'No knickers! What a naughty girl!' I shouted, and started to slap Joanne's fleshy buttocks to warm them. They soon turned pink with the force of my blows. She was squealing with excitement as I smacked her again and again. Her fat bum cheeks wobbled and through the gap in her legs I could see her thick black pubic hair. I stopped beating her and opened her cheeks with both hands. Her pink cunt was wet and glistening. Swiftly I unzipped her miniskirt and let it drop to the floor. With her bum towards me I parted her legs a little more so I could gain access to her beautiful hairy cunt. I started to manoeuvre two fingers in and out of her and rub my tongue up and down her cunt lips, teasing her clitty, nibbling and sucking on her swollen lovebutton which made her moan and squirm. Joanne was soon so fired up she had a noisy, jerky orgasm and her warm juice shot out on to my face.

Joanne remained in the same position, bending over, her back arched, her squashy tits flattened against the desk and her cunt looking fucking amazing, all juicy and ready. Steadily I eased my erect cock inside her soaking wet lovehole. My balls slapped hard on her slit as I rode her hard, ramming my cock in her as far as I could. I watched as my stiff cock penetrated her time and time again, then I leaned forward and took one of her titanic tits in each hand and fingered her nipples as I banged her.

All of a sudden Joanne was coming. She began to squeeze at my cock with her pussy muscles. Her hole was so hot and so tight that I couldn't hold out. The next thing I knew I slipped my cock out, grabbed it and aimed it at her splayed arse cheeks. I watched with delight as my creamy white spunk splattered all over her fleshy bum. I licked off every last drop of jism, then was ready to fuck her again.

Mike. Manchester.

Housewives' Choice

Dear Linzi,
I have discovered a fantastic new way to bring myself to tumultuous orgasmic spasms – wanking myself off with a cordless electronic toothbrush! My husband thinks I'm sex crazy and he's probably damn right! But he's off at work all day, so I have to amuse myself the best way I can. It started off when I was doing the washing, and the machine programme went into a heavy spin. I was standing nearby waiting for the cycle to finish and I suddenly wondered what it would feel like to thrust my fanny up against it. It felt bloody great! The movements of the shuddering machine had me coming before the two minute spin was completed!

I soon tired of rubbing myself off on the hotpoint, and

discovered a toy more satisfying than any vibrator – my toothbrush. Those soft bristles do things to me that only the most expert tongue can master. The only problem is that on full-set wanking, the batteries only last six minutes and I need a full eight minutes to reach my peak. Any ideas!

Gloria. Hayes.

Death by Chocolate

Dear Linzi,

I had a late business meeting in the West End, so enroute to my flat in Chelsea I decided to stop off for a bite to eat. It was pretty late but I managed to find one of those American-style hamburger and ice cream parlours open. As it was a weekday, the place was pretty empty, and two extremely good-looking waitresses attended to me. They both wore their long, blonde hair pulled back in ponytails, and had their names pinned to the bodice of their flared, pink, gingham minidresses. Susie, the taller of the two was a big, buxom girl with firm, jutting tits, whilst her associate Gina, was shorter, a little more petite, with the most sensational pair of legs that were tanned and naked, aside for white ankle socks.

Seated in a cosy little booth at the back of the restaurant, I ordered a cheeseburger, fries and all the trimmings. By the time I'd washed that down with a Budweiser, the place had emptied. I fancied a big, gooey slab of chocolate fudge cake, but thought I might just be out of luck as the girls seemed to be clearing up, so I thought maybe they had stopped serving. But I motioned for their attention and both girls hurried towards me attentively.

'Could I possibly order a portion of chocolate fudge cake?' I asked politely.

'Sounds delicious! Coming right up!' Susie said, licking her glossy pink lips.

Little did I know what those two horndogs had in mind for my dessert!

A few moments passed, then both girls returned to my table – Susie, with an enormous wedge of gooey chocolate cake on a plate, and Gina carrying a jug of warm chocolate sauce. They

21

sat down on either side of me, then Gina very sexily dipped her forefinger into the chocolate sauce and when her finger was completely smeared, offered it to my mouth. I was confused, but nevertheless I sucked on it greedily. As I gorged, I felt fingers unzip my flies. Holy shit! I thought as both girls took hold of my flaccid cock, which began to get stiffer and stiffer by the second. I was dumbstruck, but feeling very horny!

'Ooh what have we got here?' Susie breathed, taking me in hand and gripping me firmly.

'I reckon "Death by Chocolate" is what you'd really like, isn't it big boy?' Gina teased.

I thought I'd died and gone to heaven, but I merely nodded as the girls got the game underway. Together they pushed the table away from me, crawled onto the floor and taking the jug of sauce proceeded to trickle it gingerly over my prick! Wow! the sensation of the warm sauce dribbling over my genitals, closely followed by contact from two eager tongues, which squirmed and slobbered all over my balls and shaft, was a real mindblower! Within seconds I felt my seed rising. In wild ecstasy I spunked all over their pretty, girly faces.

It was a wonderful, once in a lifetime experience, but I did feel a prat leaving the restaurant with chocolate stains smeared all over my crotch!

Bob. Chelsea.

What We Want!

Dear Linzi,

You give myself and my workmates a great deal of pleasure and excitement. To start with we are five rampant and sex-hungry guys, and just for your reference one of us is hung like a donkey! We would now like to tell you what each of us would like to do to you.

John would like to give you a really good titty fuck and shoot his load in your fluffy blonde hair. He has mentioned this to the rest of us, several times.

Dave would like to dress you up in a school uniform, with stockings, suspenders and frilly knickers, and he would play the part of the strict headmaster. You have been a naughty girl and he will punish you for it by getting you to bend over his knee and spanking you, whilst fingering your pussy.

Tony would love to cover your tits with peach melba yogurt, fill you up with aerosol cream and then eat and lick every inch of you until you are screaming out for a good fucking.

This brings us nicely to the man known to his friends as King Dong. He would get you to kneel on the floor so that your tits swayed from side to side. Pretty soon you would be ready to take his weapon. He would slip it in to you inch by inch, so that by the time you got the lot you would be screaming with joy. You might of had some big pricks before, but I guarantee that you've never had one like this before!

Last but not least, there's myself, Ian, who wrote this letter to you on behalf of myself and my workmates. I fantasize that you lay me down on a bed naked, and then start to play with my cock and balls, sucking me until I am fully erect. Then I would tell you to put three ring doughnuts on my cock and top it off with whipped cream. You suck and chew until this luscious dessert is gone before finishing me off with one of the most sensational blow jobs ever. Naturally I'd shoot my load straight down the back of your throat.

These are just some of the things we want. I hope they get you all juiced up.

Ian. Chobham.

Coffee Compliment

Dear Linzi,

I have been with my girlfriend Jane for a couple of years now, and I'm a very lucky bloke. She's a gorgeous, intelligent blonde with a cracking figure and she loves sex. The story I'm about to tell happened last weekend, when Jane suggested that I help her best friend Allison move house.

Alli is twenty-four, she's tall and slender with big brown eyes and bobbed dark hair. She wears very sexy gear, has great legs and I've always had a bit of a soft spot for her. On the day of the move, Jane was working so it was just Alli and I who organized the removal. We hired a van and it took us the best part of the day to load up, drive to her new house in Weymouth, then unload. As it was already dark by the time we'd finished unpacking her stuff, Alli insisted that I stay the night, and as a big thank you invited me out to dinner.

We had a lovely meal and Alli was great company. She really opened up to me and talked about herself frankly, even telling me how frustrated she was because she didn't have a boyfriend at the moment. Glancing down at her lovely legs, I thought to myself that I could sort her out, but I didn't really think about it seriously. She's Jane's best mate, and besides I had no idea that she was hinting that she wanted me to fuck her!

In the taxi home she put her head on my shoulder and told me I'd been a real gentleman – if only she could have read my mind, her legs would have been wide apart. I offered her a coffee once we were inside her house. She asked for it with cream and would I be so kind to take it up to her on a tray.

When I got upstairs, she was undressed and in bed. She asked me to stay and talk a while. When I eventually made a move to leave, she asked for a goodnight kiss, so I leaned over and lowered my lips to hers. When they mct, my head exploded, and a bolt of electricity ran through my veins. The next kiss was longer and fuller, our tongues battling for supremacy as I fell on top of her. We explored each other's mouths and Alli tugged at my clothes.

'Please take them all off,' she sighed.

She sat up as I got undressed, our lips not separating, as if glued to each other. As I got out of my boxer shorts she held my very hard cock and pulled me to her. Then, with an evil glint in her eye, she poured cream all over it, and began licking it off. She licked my balls and the length of me as she took me in her mouth. Seeing her suck me ever so slowly was such a turn on, and it wasn't many minutes before I had to stop her because I knew I would come. I motioned her to the middle of the bed and poured the cream over her breasts and fanny. Then I traced a line to her fanny and licked my way down to it gradually. I told her there wasn't much left for her coffee and she just smiled, and said, 'Drink it out of me!' Then she opened her cunt lips.

She shivered as I poured it in and around her already very moist opening. I began to lick it up and she shivered again. The mixture of her juices and the cream was lovely and I made a real meal of it, teasing her outer lips, then her inner lips before sliding my tongue in her vagina, then working on her clitoris, licking it until she shook with orgasm.

I eased my way back up her body, tracing a line with my tongue, then asked her if she wanted me to do it again or if she wanted me to make love to her. My penis was squashed between us, but my balls were covering her cunt, and she felt very hot and wet. Without saying a word she took hold of me and eased me inside her. I just lay there feeling her warmth as we kissed. I pulled myself almost all the way out, and her hips moved up to meet mine. I went back inside her hard and fast, finishing with a little wiggle. She moaned, so I did it again, waiting longer at her entrance this time. The third time I came all the way out and rubbed my head around her lips. She got panicky and wrapped her legs around me, so I went back in. She now retaliated by flexing her cunt muscles and holding me inside her. She said she wanted to watch me enter her, so we adjusted ourselves on the bed and both touched where I penetrated her. A few hard thrusts and that did it. She shook and her face clouded over. I kept fucking her a little while longer before I had to let go. And when my mind cleared she was sobbing, so I kissed her tears away as she told me she had never had an orgasm that intense before, and that she envied Jane.

'Jane taught me,' I said.

'I know, she told me!' she replied.

It suddenly dawned on me that I'd been set up, but what the hell! Before I went home the next morning we fucked about six more times, and we both felt tired and pleasantly sore at the end of it. Back home, Jane not only insisted on me telling her every detail, but also re-enacting it, as she said the thought of it really turned her on. Allison is due to visit us in a couple of months, and I can't wait, I've already ordered the cream from the milkman!

Richard. London.

A Spanking Good Secretary

Dear Linzi,

I decided to write to you in the hope that firstly, I will get a reply, and secondly, that you don't feel too scornful. I am a normal guy with a family, kids and a mortgage – the whole catastrophe, but I have this dreaded secret, which I obviously keep to myself and a certain lady friend of mine. I love to be spanked over the knee of a tall, leggy, beautiful woman – it turns me on so much. After the spanking, as my bottom sizzles in blessed relief, I always come. When you have picked yourself up off the floor from laughing, please read on and tell me what you think of my favourite fantasy.

Linzi my fantasy is about you, particularly when I am being disciplined by my lady friend in London. I see you in suspenders, high heels and sheer stockings. All black, so wicked! You are sitting on a chair with your knees together and laid across you is your lovely blonde secretary. Her skirt is pulled up, her panties are pulled down to her knees, revealing her pert little bottom, and you are administering a light spanking.

T.D.

Chocoholic

Dear Linzi,

I've got this incredible food fetish. Lately the wife has had to buy rubber sheets because we get into such a delicious mess in bed. I just love having her smear my dick with aerosol fresh cream, then greedily gobble it all off. She loves sweet things and she loves my dick, so my missus is more than happy. Lately I've moved on from poking her pussy with a big soft banana. Now she likes to have a bar of chocolate shoved up her hot twat to wank her off before we both devour the juicy chocolate bar. It's delicious – you should try it!

William. Northants.

Full of Spunk

Dear Linzi,

I'm a very naughty girl, but I just can't help it. I just can't stop picking up men. I literally pounce on complete strangers that I fancy and ask them if I can wank them off.

I have this fascination for penises. I just like to watch them grow, love to feel their hot flesh in my hand, and adore seeing them spurt their cream. I never let these men fuck me because that wouldn't be safe, but somehow or other I manage to persuade guys to let me take their penises out and wank them until they come!

Only last week I did it at the pictures, and then I did it on the back seat of the bus, but the best I've had for ages was in the fancy-dress shop. I had gone to the shop to hire a period costume for a party that I was due to attend. Anyway, there was this very sweet, young assistant who was helping me. I put on this frilly Victorian frock which needed lacing at the back, so I invited him in to my cubicle to do it up for me. Straight away my eyes focused in on the bulge in his trousers, and before very long I started on him. I began by stroking him. His eyes nearly popped out of his head as I slowly started to unzip him. He hurriedly turned to make sure that the curtain was fully covering the naughty goings on inside the cubicle, then he leaned back against the wall, let out a tiny moan and closed his eyes.

On my knees I took his stiffening prick in both hands. I have very long nails and I gently ran one talon-like fingernail along the underside of his prick. I cupped his balls with the other hand, and then started to wank him steadily. He had a lovely fat cock and he felt very hot as I slipped my hand up and down his shaft, faster and faster, gripping him tighter and tighter, waiting excitedly for that wonderful moment when he would spurt. That's my biggest turn on, watching this wonderful jet of spunk fly forth from their pulsating pricks. I hadn't bargained for this spunky man though!

When he finally let out a stifled groan to tell me that he was about to come, I jerked him faster and faster. Then all of a sudden a torrent of spunk erupted. I've never seen so much cream, it was all over my face, up the walls, all over the mirror, the curtains and it covered my party frock. This man had so much spunk that just seeing it shoot out of his prick made my legs turn to jelly and my cunt tremble in a wonderful orgasm. I left him to clear up all the sperm. That must of been some job!

Lynette. Essex.

Kinky Collection

Dear Linzi,

I am writing to ask your opinion on something. I would value any advice you can give me very much. A few months ago there was an article in our local newspaper about a local pub which collected women's bras and displayed them above the bar. I would like to start a similar kind of collection as I think it is an unusual and different kind of hobby. I would like to say that I am not perverted in any way and would not want to offend women. However, I am a bit shy and I am finding it hard to start my collection as I am too embarrassed to ask women for their bras. I would be most grateful if you could give me your views on my intended hobby. I'm telling you this because I'm a great fan of yours. If I was to start a bra collection I would give anything to have one of your bras.

Simon.

World's Biggest Wanker!

Dear Linzi,

There are some lovely models, but for me you'll always be special. You can keep your teenage nymphets (but if you've got one going spare, let me know!). As for big bosomed beauties, well I'm sure that with my imagination and an extra large carton of strawberry yogurt, I could have some nice, sticky fun! But what I really prefer is a sexy, sophisticated blonde, especially if she has the initials L.D.!

Of all the fantasies I have enjoyed about you, my favourite is the one where I go down on your golden-haired pussy. You

28

lie naked beneath me and I gently slide a cushion under your lovely firm bottom. Then I press my mouth against your bushy, blonde mound as you lift your knees up and part your smooth brown thighs. My phallus throbs and pulsates as your warm, wet mouth encloses it, and in response I push my tongue between the succulent lips of your pussy. I lick your clitoris, slowly at first, then more rapidly, pushing my tongue in and out of your tight wet hole until I can taste your luscious pussy juices oozing out. In my fantasy, I slide an ice cube of the finest champagne into your tunnel of love, and as it fizzes and melts inside you and mingles with your tasty juice, I lick and lap away lasciviously, until you squirm and cry out in orgasmic ecstasy, your screams stifled only by my twitching prick as it fills your mouth with it's hot creamy stream.

So, Linzi, darling, what do you say? Shall I nip down to the off licence or not? I've heard of bubbles getting up one's nose, but this is ridiculous! I'm so frustrated at the moment that I'm thinking of entering myself for the Guinness Book of Records, but on second thoughts, who wants to go down in history as 'The World's Biggest Wanker'? Anyway I'll go now before my trousers catch fire!

Kevin.

Mud, Mud, Glorious Mud!

Dear Linzi,
I want to tell you what me and 'her indoors' get up to out of doors on our farm. My wife Ann, who measures 34-24-33 adores romping in muck. For instance, one day we had just finished feeding the animals and then started mucking out the stables. I was just wheeling out a wheelbarrow full of muck, when suddenly I felt a huge clod of mud land on my back. I turned around and Ann was standing there with her hands on her hips grinning at me. So I ran over to her, picked up some mud, shoved it down her shirt and rubbed it into her tits. She screamed with delight and started to massage a large handful of muck into my groin. I took her into the corner, ripped her clothes off and began to smooth the soft mud all over her body. She loved

29

it. When she was completely covered in muck she walked off and got the hose. She turned it on herself before directing it at my trousers. She then undid my flies and sucked on my cock. Soon I laid her back on a bale of straw and really gave it to her. Now every weekend when it's warm, mucking out the stables usually results in a good, grungy sex session.

Sam. Devon.

Dominatrix Required

Dear Linzi,
I am a submissive male who loves to see you dressed up in leather playing the bitch. I saw you on the James Whale Show and was impressed with your mind as well as your body. I want some advice. I have asked quite a few women to play the dominant role with me. Some have obliged, but obliged is the predominant feeling. I didn't feel that it was their choice of pleasure. Do dominant women exist or am I condemned to a life of fantasy or prostitutes? I am reasonably intelligent and articulate, loving and caring. I feel there should be more to life than a quick jerk over Skin Two mags. Any advice on meeting a woman who likes to be obeyed would be greatly appreciated.

Bob. Fulham.

Tempting Tootsies

Dear Linzi,
I love to see bare feet in magazines. In front of me now I have two of my favourite pictures that really excite me. One is of a beautiful brunette on a deserted beach. She is showing off her quim with her legs drawn up, with her bare feet positioned right next to her pussy. Even better is the photo of a busty blonde lying on her tummy on a lilo at the edge of a pool. Her legs are splayed so it is possible to glimpse her golden minge, back view. As I glance down her shapely, bronzed legs, her soft bare feet are revealed, and this time it is the underside.

Oh what fun to take my stiff prick and rub it along those smooth soles! She'd just feel a little tickle as my swollen member nuzzles against her. I could spend hours of bliss just tickling her pretty feet, letting my balls rest there against her soft, moist skin. I'd love to turn her over and play with her feet, covering them in kisses, perhaps painting her toenails with shiny, pink polish. This time I'd rub my cock all over her tiny toenails.

All this rubbing of my cock and balls would arouse a great lust within me and so the blonde would open her legs for me and exhibit just a bit more of her golden minge, which is now glistening and wet. I can see the sweat on her curvy arse as I slide my cock all over it. She moans and arches herself up as I kneel down and plunge my prick in. I start off slowly, building up a rhythm. Her pussy seems to suck in my cock and I can feel her squirming as I drive it home. I lean back and grab at her feet which are lifted from the ground, and as I shoot huge spurts of come inside her, I am holding on tight to her sweaty, bare feet.

So you see, Linzi, I'm not a foot fetishist, yet within a good screw, I love to be in touch with a woman's feet. So do us a favour please, try to get all the ravishing models to do just one or two shots without their clompy high heels!

F.M. Scarborough.

3. DIRTY DIALLING

Are most of your telephone calls no more stimulating than keeping in touch with the in-laws, or placing a bet with the bookies? If that's the case, then you certainly are no match for these dirty diallers who use British Telecom to add that extra dimension to their sordid sex lives!

TALK DIRTY TO ME
FOOLING AROUND IN THE
    PHONE BOX

TELEPHONE SEX AFFAIR
HOT CROSS LINE
HOT LINE TO HEAVEN

Talk Dirty to Me

Dear Linzi,

My husband works as a bouncer in a night club, so for six nights a week, I've only got the dog and TV for company. As you can imagine I get pretty bored, but last night the situation changed when the telephone rang. I let the answerphone click in. It was a wrong number, but the male voice at the other end of the line sounded interesting, so I picked up the phone. My answermachine recorded our conversation. No way will I let my husband hear it, but I've written it down in its entirety and recreated my sensual mood.

It began when I interrupted the machine, picked up the phone and said: 'This isn't Judy, my name's Sue. I'm sorry you must have misdialled.'

'Sorry to have troubled you then, Sue.'

'It's no trouble, I was just sitting here watching the tele,' I said sweetly. I was bored and fancied someone to talk to, and besides he had such a sexy voice.

'My name's Pete,' he offered. 'Fancy a chat?'

'Why not? There's nothing on the box!' I laughed.

'Tell me what you look like, Sue?'

I giggled and wondered if I should make it up. I thought what the hell! I'm a good-looking woman, even if I say so myself. There was no need to lie. I picked up the remote control and switched off the TV. I plumped up my pillows on the floor and drew my skimpy kimono around my body, before describing myself to a complete stranger on the telephone.

'I'm twenty-three years old, I've got very long, dark brown hair, big green eyes, a tiny nose, big lips.' At that point for some reason I blew him a wet kiss. I felt a bit ridiculous afterwards, so hurriedly added, 'How about you?'

'I'm thirty, stand six two tall. I work out, so I'm well built.

34

I've got longish, black hair, dark eyes and I get off on talking dirty on the phone!'

'Have you done this before?'

'Done what before?' he answered, an element of humour in his voice.

I laughed, knowing instinctively what was going to happen, deciding that I might as well get the ball rolling. 'Got a big dick have you, Pete?'

He paused for just a second and then whispered, 'A good nine inches when it's nice and hard. Probably just the right size to slip between your big lips.'

His words sent a shiver up my spine, made my nipples stiffen and my pussy start to throb. Just as I was about to answer, Pete said, 'What are you wearing, Sue?'

I started to tremble and one hand crept beneath my robe and cupped my bare breast. Stroking my pink nipple with my fingertips, I breathed: 'Not much, not much at all. I'm lying here on the floor of my living room wearing a shorty kimono and white panties.'

'Are you playing with yourself?'

His question made me quiver and squeeze my nipple hard. 'Ooh, I'm playing with my nipple. You're making it all big and swollen.'

'Tell me what you're doing, Sue, describe your tits to me, I want to be able to imagine them, I want to be able to taste those strawberry nipples!'

I loosened the tie on my robe and slid one hand down between my legs. I realised there was no going back, my panties were moist around my crack as I gently fingered my clit through the silky fabric.

'My tits are big, 36C's, lovely and round and I've gorgeous nipples. Huge pink buds that I know you'd love to suck.'

'I'd love to let my tongue wriggle all over them. I want to gently bite each nipple in turn,' he gasped.

'Ooh, Pete, I've got a confession to make. Thinking of your mouth slobbering all over my tits, well it's making me wet. I'm playing with my pussy. I've got my legs wide open and I'm rubbing my cunt through my panties.'

'Tell me, baby, tell me!'

'I'm pulling my knickers off to one side to show you my cunt. To show you my hairy pussy. Look at all those lovely soft, black hairs. My cunt is very hairy on top, but I shave my lips. Let me show you, let me spread my bald pussy lips wide open so you can imagine rubbing that big dick of yours all over them.'

I cradled the phone between my shoulder and my neck, pulled my damp knickers off to one side, opened my cunt with both hands and spread my lips wide.

'Ooh, I'm so wet, Pete. You're making me so wet. I've just got to sink my fingers inside. Ooh you don't mind, do you?'

I lowered the phone to my cunt and gasped ecstatically as I slipped two fingers in my hot little hole. I squelched them in and out, using my other fingers to stroke my clit. I put the receiver back to my ear, but still kept two fingers embedded knuckle-deep in my pussy. I used my thumb to caress my clit.

'Take your knickers off, Sue,' Pete instructed.

I placed the phone on the seat of the armchair and wriggled my knickers down my legs. I propped my back against the armchair, my knees raised and wide open as I picked up the phone. I looked down at my engorged nipples and then at my cunt. My juices were dribbling down my inner thighs. 'My cunt's dripping,' I said, my fingers between my legs as I spoke.

'I want you to imagine that I'm licking your cunt, Sue. I want you to feel my tongue on your clit.'

'Yes, yes!' I gasped, finding my clit and stroking it. 'I want you to lick me, Pete. I want you to bury your fingers in my cunt and push them in and out, squelch them in and out while you suck my cunt, lick my clit, eat me, ooh yeah!' I plunged three fingers in my pussy and continued excitedly, 'Come on Pete let me feel that tongue lick me long and hard. Mmm, I can feel it slipping into my hole, salivating all over my clit. You're going to make me come, keep licking me, keep sucking me, finger me Pete, that's it! Oh yeah! Oh yeah!'

Suddenly words failed me as a shuddering orgasm hit me. My cunt started to tremble and I squealed into the phone. I was still shivering as I listened intently to Pete, who was wanking to climax. His breathing came hard and heavy, 'Oh baby you make me spunk so much. Oh yes, I'm coming. Oh that's so good, so good! I bet you'd like to lick the cream from my knob. Come on lick it up, lick it all up!' he grunted.

I slid my fingers inside my mouth and sucked greedily on my juices. All the while imagining that it was Pete's spunky cock that I was sucking on.

'Baby have you got something there to play with? A vibrator or a dildo or something? Something big and hard to stick in that hot little cunt of yours?'

'Oh yes, so I can watch it spread my hot lips and pretend it's your fat, spunky dick filling me up,' I answered, my fingers slipping from my mouth back to my cunt, my other hand kneading my erect nipples.

'Hang on a minute, I'll be right back,' I said as I stood up, discarded my robe, opened a cupboard door and took out a huge rubber dildo.

Grabbing the phone again, I said: 'I've got a big, thick dildo here and I'm going to stick it in my cunt. Stick it right up my hot twat and imagine that it's your nine-inch prick, Pete.'

'That's good, baby. Now bend over a chair and let me take you from behind. Bend right over and stick that lovely big arse of yours right up in the air, so I can squeeze your fleshy cheeks and get a good look at your pink slit.'

I knelt up and bent over the seat of the armchair, jammed the phone in the crook of my neck and used both hands to spread my buttocks and pussy lips. I breathed into the phone, 'I want to feel that huge meat of yours splitting me wide open, penetrating my crack, inch by inch.' As I spoke I guided the rounded head of the plastic prick to the entrance of my cunt. Still holding myself open, I teased the dildo against my clit. 'Fuck me, fuck me!' I gasped.

At this point I was so rampant that I dropped the phone onto the arm of the chair and in one hard thrust rammed the slippery sex toy all the way in, until my eager cunt had swallowed its entire length. I could still hear Pete's husky voice, 'I'm fucking you, baby. Feel my dick pumping inside you, eh?'

'Your cock is stretching me wide open. I'd like to feel your hands all over my arse. I want you to grip my buttocks and slap it hard into me, go on bury your huge cock in me, ride me! Let me feel your hot, hairy balls slapping against my clit.'

'Oh yeah, I'm fucking you baby, giving you every inch. Ooh let me grab those beautiful tits as they hang down and bounce around every time I bang my cock in you!'

'Squeeze my nipples and fuck me, fuck me, Pete!' I cried out as I jerked the dildo faster and faster, harder and harder until the whole of my body started to spasm.

'I'm coming, I'm coming!' I screamed in ecstasy as a tumultuous orgasm sent me into near delirium.

A few moments later my body had stopped trembling, I eased the dildo out of my twitchy twat, sat back down and picked up the phone. 'Wow!' I said.

No reaction.

All of a sudden I realised that in my frenzied passion I'd cut him off! However, on the up side I had experienced two great climaxes and now I didn't have to face the embarrassment of wondering what to say after it was all over!

Chrissie. Croydon.

Fooling Around in the Phone Box

Dear Linzi,

Letters, books and magazines always seem to feature correspondents who boast their sexual conquests in all manner of outrageous places, but I think I'm correct in saying that I've yet to read about sex in a phone box. Which is exactly where I had the most out of this world, frenzied first fuck the other night.

I'd gone out with a couple of mates to this new wine bar that has just opened. I was pleasantly surprised that it was full of tasty looking crumpet. One little corker in particular caught my eye. She was a petite little thing around eighteen or nineteen. She had tightly cropped bleached blonde hair, a sexy little face and a gorgeous body squeezed into a tight red dress.

We got chatting and at the end of the evening I asked if I could take her home. She said that would be nice and gave me a coy little grin. The wine bar was far too rowdy to use their phone to ring for a taxi so we set off to the red phone box just a few hundred yards away.

I dialled the local cab company and was knocked out by the

fact that as I waited for the cab firm to answer, the randy little bitch was busy unzipping my jeans. By the time the call was answered she was already peeling back my foreskin and running her hands up and down my length. Trying to keep cool, I just about managed to order a cab without grunting and groaning and making a complete arse of myself. I told them not to hurry. By the time I replaced the receiver she was on her knees chewing on my stiff prick!

I love having my prick sucked, but the whole scenario was such a mindblower that I thought I might spurt too soon and I wanted to be in her. I wanted to feel her hot cunt surrounding my pole, so I grabbed hold of her and pulled her to her feet. While I kissed her sexy mouth I raised her dress and slipped my hand into her knickers. Her pussy was so wet!

Just a few seconds later I lifted her up and set her down on my rigid prick. She wrapped her legs around my waist and screamed as I entered her puffy, pink pussy lips. She was so juicy that I didn't even have to work it inside her, my prick just plugged straight in. Using both hands to control her hips, I jerked her up and down, up and down, until she cried out that she was coming. That brought on my climax and I jetted huge amounts of sperm right up inside her hot hole.

I took her home and fucked her again and again, but fucking her in the phone box was the best!

Andrew. Nottingham.

Telephone Sex Affair

Dear Linzi,

I want to tell you all about my wonderful sexual affair that started off over the phone. I'm twenty-one years old and had only been married for six months when it all began. My husband was called away to the Far East on business for a full three months. At first I kept myself sexually amused by spending the long, cold winter evenings listening to music and masturbating in front of my open fire. But after a few weeks I was becoming increasingly bored and longed to feel the warmth of companionship and a cock between my fanny lips.

39

I was soon to be lucky enough to have both. It started quite accidentally one evening while I was lying on the hearth, my legs spread, a large, golden vibrator buzzing away inside me, when the telephone rang. Without removing my sex toy, I crawled over to the telephone and answered it whilst laying on my tummy. It was a wrong number, but the voice on the other end of the phone was such a turn on that I didn't want to let him go.

He seemed quite interested in me too, and we started to talk for several minutes. His voice was making me feel very randy, so I rolled over onto my back and started to push the vibrator in and out of my fanny. When he asked what I was doing, I simply told him! He immediately got very excited and asked if we could meet. I wasn't yet ready to answer, I continued playing with myself and told him to do the same.

I'd never had sex this way before, not even with my husband. I've always felt a little bit embarrassed about saying rude words, but to this faceless stranger on the phone I poured it all out, telling him how hot I was, telling him how wet my cunt was, telling him that I wanted to feel his mouth on my nipples and his cock inside me.

Within a few minutes we had both reached a climax. Seconds later he was asking me to describe myself to him. I told him the truth, well almost. I suppose I did glamorize myself just a little. I told him my age, my marital status, that I had long brown hair, brown eyes, large boobs and long legs, and was a housewife. He, in turn, told me that he was thirty-five years old, worked as a gym instructor, was almost six feet tall and was of Italian descent so had a swarthy complexion. Then he asked my address. As it happened he lived about an hour's drive away. He told me he would be there as soon as he could.

When I put the phone down, I wondered what I was letting myself in for, inviting a man I'd never met into my home? He could rob me and leave me for dead. Somehow I didn't think that was what he had on his mind! I hoped he would come over and fuck me until neither of us could take it any more. I waited for him in a weird state of anticipation. I wanted to stroke and play with myself, but as soon as I started, I stopped, because I wanted to save it all for him!

As good as his word he turned up about an hour later. His red MG pulled into my drive and I peered out through a gap in the curtains to catch a glimpse. As he climbed out of the car, I felt my knees turn to jelly. He looked fabulous. Even wearing heavy winter clothes; tight jeans and a jumper, I could see that his body was a delight. I hurried to the mirror and checked that I looked okay. I had slipped into a rather tight black dress and was wearing my slinkiest red undies underneath. My stocking tops showed just slightly as I answered the door.

I thought this moment might be somewhat embarrassing, but it wasn't at all. No words were necessary as he put his arms around me on the doorstep and kissed me hard on the mouth. 'Whatever will the neighbours think?' flashed through my head as his body pressed against mine and his hand travelled up my thigh. Still with our bodies clinging together, I backed through the door and naturally he followed. As we stood in the hall, I could feel the warmth of his cock pressing against my groin. I was becoming very moist in my panties as we clung together kissing, his mouth and tongue exploring mine.

Things started to get even hotter when his hands finally worked their way into my panties. I pulled off his jumper at this stage so I could feel his chest and play with his nipples while he stroked my cunt. His chest was tanned and covered in fine black hair, and it felt wonderful. I rubbed my hands all over it, tweaking his nipples and sucking on them, between kisses.

By now his hands were inside my panties and he had zeroed in on my clitoris. His gentle stroking with thumb and forefinger was bringing me to boiling point. I desperately wanted to touch his cock, so as he drove me wild to orgasm I fumbled with the buttons and released his magnificent cock. Just as I was about to come, I pulled it to me and rubbed the engorged head all over the lips of my cunt, which made me wail in rapture.

With my cunt still hot and twitchy, we moved into the lounge. There, we feverishly stripped each other until he stood before me naked, his muscular body and rippling muscles a real picture, his cock stiff and pointing skywards, and coming to rest somewhere past his bellybutton. I kept on my high-heeled shoes, my suspender belt and silky stockings.

I sat down on the sofa and spread my legs. He knelt before me and parted my pussy lips with his tongue. As his tongue explored the folds of my cunt, he probed with two fingers into my lovehole. I told him I wanted to feel all his fingers inside me, and he duly obliged by sliding all four fingers up me. This seemed to get him very excited, and he worked his fingers in and out feverishly as he lapped and sucked at my sodden cunt with unbelievable enthusiasm.

Seconds later I was wrapping my legs around his head, drawing him right into me as another wave of orgasm washed over my body. He'd given me so much pleasure that I now wanted to work on him. I wanted to taste the sweetness of his cock, so we positioned ourselves on the hearth rug and manoeuvred into a 69 position. I was on top as I took him in my mouth. With one hand I softly stroked his balls, the other was busy working up and down his stem, while my tongue tickled all around his knob.

Below me he was very busy too. One hand was gripped tight on my splayed thigh, while the other massaged the uppermost part of my cunt. His tongue was deep inside me moving in and out, like a tiny prick. He nibbled and sucked my clit and had me writhing around in sheer ecstasy.

In this position we rolled over until he was on top. His cock was now in a wonderful position for me to deep throat him, a technique I practised regularly on my husband. This seemed to excite him no end. He seemed no longer able to concentrate on licking out my cunt. He just lay above me massaging my big, squashed tits, fingering my nipples and grunting and groaning. His cock felt wonderful and I could feel it hotting up even more, until the warm cream rose in its glands and shot into my mouth with such a force that I couldn't swallow it all. It burst out of my mouth and dribbled down either side of my chin.

We clung together in that position for some time. Then I got out a bottle of baby oil that I always keep handy for my wanking evenings. He lay flat on his back on the floor, and very gradually I let a little of the greasy liquid trickle over his sleeping cock. It twitched back to life immediately it made contact, especially when I started to rub the oil into his cock and balls. I lay on my tummy between his open legs with my face resting just by his cock and started to play with him. As I wanked him my tits were nudging against his cock and soon he was pushing it between my big tits and thrusting backwards and forwards, the slipperiness of the oil making them squash together deliciously.

We were now getting to fever pitch all over again, and I really did need that cock inside me. I told him as much in no uncertain terms as I crawled back to the sofa and leant over it, my face buried in the cushions, my arse thrust out towards him, so he could see my swollen pinkness through my legs. Moments later he was clinging to me. His arms around my tummy clutching me to him as he plunged his cock inside me.

I leaned back as his hands moved up to play with my tits. He took me on my knees on my living room carpet, his wonderful cock pumping in and out of me. He fucked me slowly at first, building up to a speedy rhythm until I begged him to fuck me harder and harder, so I could enjoy the firm slap of his greasy balls against my burning slit.

We didn't stay in that position long. Soon, still thrusting together, we were rolling around on the floor, fucking on the side, and then with me on top with my back to him. Suddenly we couldn't hold it back any longer and we shuddered to an unbelievable mutual climax on the hearth.

That first evening seemed to go on and on. We hadn't finished then. This man I had discovered was something of a sexual athlete. My husband has often told me that he believes me to be insatiable. Sometimes I would really wear him out because I really can go on and on fucking and sucking, quite simply because I'm so happy when I've got something, or somebody, playing with, or fucking my pussy! In fact I'm never happier than when I've got a hard cock installed in my hot snatch!

That night we just didn't stop! We moved up to the bathroom next and had a lovely, soapy fuck in the shower stall. I ended up on the floor wet and happy as he spurted his come all over my tummy. Then we moved into the bedroom. I have a wonderful four-poster bed and he allowed me to tie him hand and foot to it. Then I spent about an hour playing with his cock, sucking it and stroking it, until finally I had to have him once again. I straddled him, lowering myself down on top of him, taking him inch by inch into my excited wet cunt.

43

We finally fell asleep in each other's arms at about seven o'clock in the morning. That was fine by me, but a little more difficult for him as he had to be at work by ten. I lay in bed for most of the day and wrote down everything I could remember about the wonderful night of sex. No doubt that's why I've managed to send it to you in such detail!

Anyway the situation is that my husband will be back in just under two weeks. My lover, Tony, and I have been meeting almost every evening since our first incredible sexual encounter. I really don't know what I'm going to do. What I'd really like is to have two fabulous lovers, but that way I'm sure I'll get into big, big trouble! I'd better close now as I've got to get ready for another night of lust. Tony has promised to stop in a call box a few miles from me and get me going by talking dirty to me on the telephone. I love it!

K.I. Tonbridge Wells.

Hot Cross Line

Dear Linzi,

I want to tell you about a cross line that I dialled into the other night. I was ringing a colleague to discuss some business with him and I couldn't get through. All I could get was a cross line. At first I hung up a couple of times, but on the third try, I heard a woman's voice say the word 'fuck' in an incredible, breathy manner. So bugger business, I thought, and started to listen in.

It soon became apparent that this man and woman were having some kind of illicit affair. From what I could gather, the woman's husband had just popped out and she had got straight on the phone to her lover. The conversation, as far as I could remember went something like this:

Her: I've got my bra off and my nipples are so hot.

Him: I want to suck them. I want those cherries in my mouth. How many fingers have you got in your pussy?

Her: I'm sliding two fingers in and out. Mmm, can you hear how wet I am?

With that she must have placed the telephone receiver near her pussy because the line was silent aside from the sound of a juicy cunt being fingerfucked. Well by now I had my cock in my hand!

Him: I've got my cock out. It's bursting out of my trousers, Sonia. You really are a horny bitch. Can't I come over and see you for just five minutes? Just five minutes so I can fuck you?

Her: He'll be back by then, so we'll just have to do it over the phone. Come on Lee take your cock out and imagine that I'm holding it, stroking its purple glans. Let me run my long red fingernails up and down it. You'd be sucking my pussy by now, wouldn't you?

Him: Yes, yes! Let me tongue that clit. Let me spread your lips and rub my face all over that pink heaven of yours, Sonia!

Her: Lick my clitty, Lee. Lick it fast with the tip of your tongue.

Him: I want to feel your hot cunt surrounding my dick. I want to feel you riding on top of me, sucking me dry. I'm coming, Sonia. I'm coming!

At this point in the proceedings Lee gave out a loud groan and Sonia started to squeal. A few more strokes of my cock and I was right there with them!

I was curious to know what would happen next, but it got less interesting as all they did was arrange their next meeting and then rang off. My evening got much less interesting then as I finally got through to my colleague to sort out that business!

Laurie. London.

Hot Line to Heaven

Dear Linzi,

The other evening I dialled my brother's telephone number and was somehow misconnected. The telephone was answered by a youngish sounding woman with a soft, West Country burr. I apologised for the inconvenience and was about to hang up when she told me that it really was no trouble, she was needing someone to talk to anyway. I groaned inwardly thinking that this young lady was about to bestow on me all her troubles and woes, when she surprised me by saying, 'I'm feeling horny, you see!'

45

She started by describing herself. She told me her name was Dawn, she was single and twenty-two years old. She had auburn hair, big green eyes and sexy lips. She went on to reveal that she was just over five feet four inches tall, and had smashing legs. Then she started getting very explicit. Maybe she was exaggerating, but I didn't interrupt as she began describing her voluptuous body.

'I've got very big, heavy tits, with huge brown nipples – 38DD's!' she informed me with obvious pride. She went on, 'I like to wear nice tight sweaters to show them off. I can turn a few heads in the high street!'

'Quite,' I mumbled. Being a bit of a tit man myself, I was becoming quite aroused. 'Go on,' I urged.

'Would you like me to tell you what I'm wearing?' she asked, her voice now seeming more of a whisper.

I could tell that she was becoming turned on, so I said, 'You know you're getting me all excited, don't you?'

'Oh yes,' she said with a nervous giggle. It's getting me all het up as well.'

'Good, then let's both enjoy it. Come on tell me what you're wearing,' I coaxed.

'Right, well I'm sitting here in my kitchen. It's very warm, so I don't have much on.'

'Are you naked, Dawn?'

'No, I'm wearing a loose fitting button through dress, and matching pink panties and bra. My panties are getting a bit sticky.'

'You're giving me the horn,' I grunted.

'Well you'd better take your cock out and stroke it,' she invited. 'Hey, I don't even know your name!'

'It's Brian and I've already got my cock in my hand!'

'So you don't mind if I play with my fanny?'

'Be my guest!' I rasped as I steadily stroked the length of my shaft.

'I'm pulling my panties off to one side now and looking at my fanny. It's covered with lovely ginger hairs, and I'm sinking a finger in. Wow! Listen I'll put the phone down between my legs so you can hear me fingering myself.'

There was little I could do except wank furiously and groan

46

nonsensically as she carried on, 'I love the taste of my ginger fanny. Listen I'm sucking my fingers and smearing the juice all over my huge nipples. I'd love you to lick it off!'

'Please! Please!' was all I could manage.

'Sorry, but I'm too excited now,' she wailed. 'I need my fingers back in my fanny. Listen how wet it is as I finger my clit, squeeze my clit, until . . .' she hesitated, her breathing becoming uncontrollable as she screamed, 'I'm coming, I'm coming!'

And yep, you've guessed it, so was I!

By the time I finally finished spunking I said, 'Hello' into the telephone, but it was dead. So there ended a beautiful relationship! Perhaps in her euphoric state she had accidentally replaced the receiver? Or perhaps embarrassed by her noisy orgasm, she had done it on purpose? I'll never know. Shame, eh!

Brian. Baldock.

47

4. FANTASY FUN

Why does a grown man crave to slide ice cubes of finest champagne up my hot little pussy? And what on earth comes over a naughty housewife to make her feel so horny that she dreams of having two pumping pricks, simultaneously stretching her cunt to the limit? Find out all you want to know about outrageous fantasy in this chapter because, believe me, in fantasyland anything goes!

Can I Help You, Madam?

Dear Linzi,

You know I always say there's nothing like a good stiff poking to start the day off proper. That's always what me ol' man gives me before he goes off to work. It's supposed to last me until he gets home around six o'clock. That's a bloody long time! If I'm busy about the home with a big wash or a large pile of ironing (yuk!), I don't usually have the time for daydreaming about all kinds of mucky things. But, sometimes if I get all the housework done, I'll take myself off for a bath with one of me husband's dirty books and fiddle with myself, rubbing my hairy fanny till I go all twitchy. Time he gets home for tea I'm as horny as a bitch on heat and before he can wash his hands, I'll make him shag me over the kitchen sink, pinny and all!

I like being a housewife, now the kids have left home and aren't under my feet any more, I please myself. Let me tell you about me. I've just turned forty and you could say I'm well built. My measurements are 42-26-38. I'm five feet two inches tall, have long strawberry-blonde hair, green eyes and I always wear orangey lipstick on my pouty lips. I've been married for twenty years and during that time I've messed around with other fellas now and again, but nothing serious. Still I do get a bit bored sometimes and dream about wild sex with other men. I fantasize about being shagged by three men, one after the other.

In my fantasy I get all tarted up on a Friday afternoon to do my weekly shop. When I've finished in the supermarket I pop into this little boutique that has just opened up in town. It's a ladies shop but strangely enough the staff are all blokes. They sell everything from posh evening frocks to sexy underwear. The three blokes who work there are all from London and right sexy looking. The owner is called Paul and he's a real gentleman, who dresses in nice suits and has short, black hair. He's probably

50

only about twenty-five and right good looking. He has two young assistants that work for him and they're only in their late teens, early twenties. One of the lads is called David and he's my favourite; a right cheeky lad with long blond hair and flashing eyes. He's really tall and broad shouldered with it. I often think about him when I'm playing with myself in the bath! The third lad in the shop is Simon. He's a little darling, always trying to chat me up. He looks like a real gypsy with long, dark hair and an earring. He's always poking his head into the cubicle when I'm changing. Just to see if I need anything he always says. I reckon he wants to get a look at my big tits!

Well in my fantasy the boutique is just about to shut when I get there, but as it's me, Paul welcomes me with open arms and tells me to come in. Simon locks up, but tells me not to rush. David comes over to say hello, bringing with him a big bundle of brand new undies that have just arrived. I pull the curtain across and start to strip off my clothes. When I am down to my knickers, the curtain is pulled back and there's Simon peering in asking if I want anything. I tell him a toy boy would be nice, and with that he reaches in and cups my big tits. His warm hands lift them gently and start to squeeze. I stand there enjoying the feel of his hands on my nipples. I reach a hand down inside my knickers and pull them up until they are cutting into my fanny. He moves inside with me, drawing the curtains behind him. One of his hands disappears into my knickers and strokes my hairy fanny, finding my opening and sliding his fingers in, while his other hand is grabbing my tits. His dick is getting bigger in his trousers, I can see the shape of it and reach out for it and stroke it in his pants. I undo his flies and his meaty cock flips out. He is fingering my fanny while I start to wank his dick. His lovely young dicky gets bigger in my hands. He takes his fingers out of my fanny and with one quick movement tears off my knickers, then pulling me towards him, he lifts me off the ground and his dick slides right inside my open fanny. I wrap my legs around his middle and he shoves it in me time and time again. My mammoth tits are jumping all over the place and he crams one in my mouth, shagging me up and down, up and down, till we collapse together on the floor of the cubicle, his spunk filling my fanny.

Moments later Simon has gone. He must have told David what had happened because in less than a minute that randy bugger David is there in the cubicle with his dick sticking right out in front of my face. I get up on my knees and put his dick between my orangey-painted lips. I kiss the end of it, leaving lipstick all over his helmet, then suck it right back in my throat. He tells me he's fancied me for ages and that he's always wanted to fuck me. I have my mouth full, but I squeeze his balls gently as if to say yes, he can fuck me!

I suck his dick for a while, loving every bloody minute of it. Then he tells me he wants to tit-fuck me. Lovely! His slippery dick slides a treat between my huge tits. I push them together and hold them as his pelvis moves back and forward frantically, my tits rubbing up and down his shaft until he comes all over them. I feel bloody disappointed for a minute, but he soon puts a stop to that, when he tells me to stroke him for a few minutes, then he'll be ready to fuck me.

When he's nice and hard again, I tell him that I want to move to the big changing room so I can watch the action in the big mirror as he shags me. He agrees and we hurry along there.

I get down on all fours, sideways to the mirror, and watch his cock as he holds it out in front of him, then aims it right into my slit from behind. I can't take my eyes off it as he rams it in and out, his balls slapping about wildly as I reach back to play with them.

Soon I am crying out at the top of my voice as I start to go all twitchy. David holds on to my hanging tits as we shudder together in seventh heaven. It's just at this point that Paul walks in. He looks bloody amazed at first. David, looking quite sheepish, takes his dick out and hurries out of the room. I roll over on to my back and lay with my legs spread. David's warm spunk is dribbling down from between my thighs. I put my fingers to my fanny and touch my clitoris. It is massively swollen and I stroke it gently with my fingertips. Paul stands there stuck to the spot as I start to moan loudly and wank my clit faster and faster. One moment he is watching me, the next thing he is down there with me, his mouth on my fanny, licking me and drinking my come. I beg him to fuck me and he takes out his dick. Very soon my fanny is filled with its third dick of the day! As Paul shags me there on the floor of the changing room, his two assistants creep back in to watch us. Paul bangs me hard and fast in the missionary position, and I reach up to grab two more cocks, one in each hand, wanking them in a complete frenzy until Paul announces that he is about to come, and suddenly David and Simon are shooting too. Spunk fills my raw fanny and splashes all over my face. Now that's what I call a fantasy!

Elizabeth. Southend.

Fat Chance!

Dear Linzi,

I am quite sure that you get a lot of fan mail that is sexually orientated, with you as the focal point and recipient of their dreams and fantasies. This letter is of that type. I wanted to meet you and give you a good shafting ever since I saw your nude photographs. If you wish to be shagged by me, it could happen quite easily, if you are agreeable to do so. My wanting to shag you must take place in a public park. It would also involve another blonde lovely – one with 38DD breasts. I'm sure you could think of someone to fit the bill.

You would be wearing a short, white, denim miniskirt with a back zip, a red lace suspender belt, red fishnet stockings, a red silk blouse, a Levi 501 jacket, a red half-cup bra and red stiletto shoes. No panties! You would be leaning on your blonde friend with your fingers up her pussy. She would be wearing a dark gymslip, hold up, fifteen denier, black stockings, a quarter-cup basque in white with black lace trim and laces, black stiletto sandals, a white blouse and a brown suede jacket.

Your blouse is undone and your young blonde friend is sucking on your left nipple. I see you and walk up to both of you. I unzip your skirt and lift it at the back exposing your sexy bum, then shove my rampant cock up your sopping pussy. I undo your mate's blouse and tweak her tits while I'm shagging you!

I could meet you both one day soon to talk about it. I'm six feet six tall, fair haired, brown-bearded and wear glasses. I usually wear a Dutch army combat jacket. If you won't meet me, I'll just have to fantasize about it!

Henry. London.

Strawberry Delight

Dear Linzi,

I thought I would write and tell you about my sexual fantasy. In my fantasy I dream that glamour model Lisa Remzi is a cookery teacher at an adult education centre that I attend. The busty blonde dresses in a white hat, white overall, white bra, white cotton panties, white, nylon stockings and a pair of white high heels.

We are alone together in the domestic science room. I get a bit pissed off and start throwing food around everywhere. Then I walk over to the blackboard and draw a picture of my stiff willy on it. By this time lovely Lisa is very annoyed and announces that she is about to teach me a lesson. She takes a cane from the stockroom and quite matter of factly strips down to sexy underwear. She strides over to me and informs me she is going to give me a good thrashing. She orders me to unfasten my trousers and drop them, and lie over her knees. I comply with her wishes immediately. Lisa strokes my arse with the thin wood of the cane and then reaches between my legs and grabs my balls. When she has both my balls in her hand, she asks me if I intend to behave. Naturally I promise her that I will, so she says I will be rewarded.

She tells me to stand up and face her, which I do obediently. She goes down on her knees and gives my prick a few good, long strokes with her hand before forcing it into her mouth. Almost at once I shoot my creamy, hot sperm down the back of her throat. This seems to displease her and she wipes her mouth in disgust, gets up, and angrily tells me that I have misbehaved. She drags me to a chair, bends me over her knee and spanks my bare buttocks until my bottom burns fiery red.

This seems to get her really turned on, and when she has finished slapping my arse, she allows me to remove her white bra to expose her wobbly tits and huge suckable nipples. I grab a pot of sticky, strawberry jam and spread it all over her squashy tits. Very slowly, I start to lick it off, squeezing and eating her sweet buds. I move down her body dotting it with tiny kisses until I reach her hairy cunt. I pull aside her white cotton knickers and gently part her pussy lips, sliding my tongue up and down her beautiful lovetunnel. I bury my tongue right inside her as she has an orgasm.

To finish off I would give her a good shafting and perhaps give her round arse a good spanking!

Bruce. Staffordshire.

Fantasy Photo Shoot

Dear Linzi,
My fantasy!

After a photo session you've still got your last outfit on. A nice tight-fitting miniskirt with hold-up stockings, leaving nothing to the imagination. I come towards you and kiss your neck and ears; I grip your arse with my rough hands.

'I want you,' you whisper.

You stand before me as I nuzzle against the material of your blouse. Your nipples are standing erect as I unbutton the blouse and strip it from you. I curl two fingers around your nipple and squeeze and roll it vigorously. I put my other hand between your legs. You push your legs together, trapping my hand, but as I touch your button you slowly spread them. I can smell your musky aroma as you pull the mini down over your stockinged thighs. My hand, between your legs is joined by yours, as you help me find your lovebutton again, rubbing it from side to side. Little moans escape from your mouth as I stroke your red hot pussy.

You take charge and pull me over to the bed. You sit on the edge and unzip my jeans, pulling them off quickly with my undies. My cock bounces to attention as you wrap your hand around my shaft, bending your head forward and kissing the pre-come away. I push you back onto the bed and say, 'Lay back and enjoy what I'm about to give you.'

Immediately I go to your tits again, kissing them, licking

them all over and grabbing and squeezing them. Sucking first one into my mouth, and then the other. Your head sinks into the pillows as my tongue licks between your cleavage. I use long sucks to keep your nipples fully erect.

After a good time spent feasting on your tits, I slide my head down your body. I move gradually, kissing every inch of your glorious tummy on the way down to your hairy mound. I kiss and rake my tongue through your golden hair until I find your slit. Your lips slightly apart, your legs well spread, I position myself between your open legs. I put your legs up around my shoulders and open your lips as wide as possible, smelling the sweetness. Your clit stands up between the lips as I touch it with my tongue, licking every gorgeous inch, licking each side, left to right, and top to bottom.

Your arse lifts off the bed as you come slightly. Not a full blown climax, but almost there. You pull my head into your pussy as you reach another orgasm. This time it's the real thing. You shout, 'Go faster.' Then your legs tremble and quiver as you come. Holding my head on your pussy, you whimper and cry softly, telling me how good it was!

You are anxious to repay me. Your hands are on my cock as I hold your face and kiss you long and hard, driving my tongue deep into your mouth. You suck on it, fighting it with your tongue. Then I tell you to take your time. I shudder as you start to work on my body. You kiss my neck, my chest, and then suck on my nipples, staying on them as I groan with pleasure. Soon you move down to my cock. You grab it at the base, making it throb and stiffen, then bend down to kiss it. You deep throat it until I feel my cock touching your tonsils. You release me, licking my knob end, kissing the shaft, playing with my balls. You position yourself so my cock is touching your tits, your bullet-like nipples flicking against my bell end. Seconds later you have me greedily in your mouth, deep throating me again.

Switching from tongue action to brushing your hard nipples over my knob is driving me crazy! Suddenly you move around and straddle me, not letting go of my cock, positioning yourself over my throbbing member until your fanny is directly on top. You ease yourself down so slowly, gasping as my length enters you. Then in one delicious thrust you sit up. I begin to jerk my cock inside you, thrusting upwards in slow rhythms, sliding juicily in and out as my hand cups your buttocks. Your head is rolling from side to side as you come again and again, engulfing my cock deep inside your trembling body, loving the slurping, sucking noises our two ecstatic bodies are making. I grab your shoulders pulling you to me, kissing your face as I explode my spunk deep inside your slippery wet pussy.

Anonymous.

A Touch of the Orient

Dear Linzi,
My name is Jessica. I'm twenty-two and a blue-eyed blonde. Since holidaying in Thailand I have a thing about Oriental women. I'm heterosexual, but have taken to dreaming about a beautiful Thai girl licking me out! My most recent fantasy is this:

I am at a luxurious hotel at a charity function and I find to my delight that I am seated next to a stunning Oriental girl. She looks gorgeous in a strapless, black dress that exhibits her smooth skin. As I am listening to the rather dull speeches I feel a warm hand rubbing up the inside of my leg. My evening dress is slashed right up to the thigh, and little by little her nimble fingers climb higher and higher. I ease my legs open as she starts to stroke the area of flesh just inches away from my cunt. I look into her eyes and she smiles at me devilishly. I am beginning to pant a little now and squirm in my seat.

The other diners are completely oblivious to the situation as she strokes my burning clit through my lace knickers. I find difficulty in refraining from squealing out in ecstasy as she slips my damp panties off to one side and fingers my wet slit. Her butterfly touch drives me wild as she gingerly strokes and feels around my slippery crack, before pushing a couple of her tiny fingers inside my hot, hot pussy.

'Shall we go to the ladies room and do this properly?' she whispers to me.

'Ooh yes!' I whimper. The fingers buried knuckle-deep in my pussy are sending shivers of delight throughout my entire body.

Moments later we are standing in the middle of the deserted ladies room. Grabbing a velvet-covered stool, the Oriental nymph asks me to sit down and spread my legs for her. I do so willingly, thrusting out of my bottom to give her plenty of cunt to lick. She slips her tongue gently between my lovelips and gradually parts them with slow, deliberate sweeps of her tongue. My pussy quivers as she eases four fingers inside my gaping hole, and works her hot tongue on my clit. Wanking my erect clitty with her flickering tongue, makes me feel so good that I am swiftly building to orgasm. I can feel my fantasy lover's long, soft, black hair tickling my inner thighs as she fingers and sucks me, slurping, teasing and wanking until I am shaking and shuddering in raptures, a tumultuous orgasm traversing my body.

Jessica. Belfast.

When I'm Cleaning Windows

Dear Linzi,
This is my fantasy involving me and you. I know this sounds corny but I would be cleaning your windows, and just as I begin to do your bedroom window, I am treated to a full display of nudity as you prepare to take a shower. The sun glistens on your shapely body as you disappear into the bathroom, leaving me up a ladder with a great big hard on!

Five minutes later upon finishing your windows I knock on your front door to collect my money, only to be greatly surprised when you answer it in the buff. You invite me in for a cuppa, and leave me sitting in your lounge.

I await your return, then almost faint with excitement when you enter the room in your black, bondage gear: satin waspie, leather miniskirt, seamed stockings and suspenders, spiky, patent stilettos and a pair of long, satin opera gloves complete the outfit. I immediately follow you to your boudoir where I remove your miniskirt to reveal your gorgeous muff. You sit on the end of the bed and begin to unbuckle my belt and release my cock from its temporary torture. I shudder with ecstasy as you take my cock in your mouth and begin the best blow job imaginable. Then just as I am about to shoot my load right down your throat, you take it from your mouth and grip it firmly with both gloved hands and demand a hard fucking.

I don't need a second invitation and as you lie back and hold on to the brass headrail I thrust my rod into your awaiting lovebox. What with the heavenly combination of your fanny sucking on my tool, the feel of your stockinged legs against my skin and your stiletto heels digging into my backside, it's not long before I begin to erupt inside you and deliver what feels like gallons of spunk!

Michael. Tyne and Wear.

So Hot It Burns!

Dear Linzi,
I feel I must write and tell you about my fantasies about *Sunday Sport* model Tara Bardot. Her pictures in a recent copy of *Penthouse* magazine were so hot that they were almost in danger of constituting a fire hazard! She has fired my imagination with some right juicy fantasies, which crept upon me when I was enjoying a leisurely shower yesterday morning.

The warm water falling on me was making me feel rather dreamy and I closed my eyes. I imagined that I was the photographer taking the pics of gorgeous Tara, and she was having a fantastic effect on me. Blondes are my favourite, but this one is something special. My tool is painfully hard. As I struggle to focus my camera for the final shot, she looks back over her shoulder and says, 'You know you can't just tease me in this state.'

She is on all fours, her arse towards me, her mound looking ripe and ready. I can't take much more of her teasing, so I quickly discard my T-shirt and jeans, and step out of my underpants. Taking a step nearer, I'm ready to drop to my knees and enter her from behind, but Tara rolls over onto her back, closing her legs.

'Uh huh,' she says. 'Not quite so fast, baby. You've got to make me wet first,' and then licks her lips slowly.

I get down on the floor next to her and kiss her deeply, before placing my mouth on her left nipple. She moans softly and squirms as I suck and lick her pert breasts. The feel of her tits is driving me wild with lust. They feel so firm and warm, but I leave them for a while and let my tongue trace a path down her stomach into the soft hairs of her bush. Tara gasps as I reach her pussy, and dip into her. She's hot and wet, the musky smell of her juices filling my nostrils.

Suddenly she struggles away from me, and kneels down a couple of feet in front of me. Looking around, she drops to all fours again.

'Now, I think!' she breathes.

I'm determined to have her this time, and grabbing her by the hips I press my cockhead against her pussy lips. Tara pushes back, letting my thick shaft sink deep into her. The pleasure is so intense that I cry out, and begin to rock to and fro. There's not much finesse to our coupling as I screw Tara as hard and deep as I am able. She shudders and moans in ecstasy, and I know it's not going to last much longer, so I surrender to the aching in my loins. My cock swells as the pre-come starts to squirt out, and I manage to gasp, 'I'm coming!' just before my body is wracked by a severe spasm.

A sudden spray of cold water made me open my eyes. I was coming hard all right. I looked down to see that I wasn't buried in the delicious Tara, but my jets of sperm were splashing all over the bathroom tiles! It was still a wonderful orgasm, though, and I felt utterly drained after it. What could happen, dare I ask, if you and Tara teamed up for a shoot? Never mind a fire risk, Linzi, we're talking highly explosive material here!

Adrian. Watford.

Best of Both Worlds

Dear Linzi,
My husband works away a lot and for the last few weeks while he's been away, I've embarked on a full-blown affair. What I'd

really like is for Kevin, my lover, and Martin, my husband, to fuck and suck me both at once. It's my ultimate fantasy, but I'm sure Martin would never agree to it!

My fantasy would be for Martin to arrive home early from a business trip and to walk in on Kevin and I while we are in mid-fuck. Instead of being angry with me, he is incredibly turned on, when he sees my pussy stretched to capacity, filled with Kevin's big cock. So while Kevin pounds his cock into me, Martin would strip off quickly, releasing a monster erection. I'd take him in my mouth and feel him grow even bigger. I think I'd like to have Kevin fucking me doggy fashion while I suck my husband to orgasm.

Naturally it wouldn't stop there and I'd get them to swop, so I could get my dear husband's cock back inside me. It's been such a long time, and although I've had Kevin poking me regularly, I still miss it! You know what I would really enjoy would be to try to take them both in my pussy at once. I just can't understand how that must feel, although I know it's possible because I saw Traci Lords do it in a porno movie once!

I think my fantasy threesome would come to a mind-blowing climax when I lay spread-eagled on a four-poster bed. My arms and legs would be tied to each of the four corners. Kevin and Martin would tease me with their cocks, allowing me the merest taste of their secretions. I would soon be desperate for them. Then one by one they would fuck me for a few minutes, and keep withdrawing and changing over until the three of us are ready to come, then they would wank themselves all over my swollen nipples. Wow, I'm getting hot just thinking about it!

Elaine. Clacton.

Ice Cold With Alex

Dear Linzi,

Don't you get incredibly bored by some of the unimaginative, semi-literate drivellings of some of your so called fans? There seems to be an incredible trend to take what used to be quality soft porn more and more down-market. Linzi, darling, I don't blame you. You can only respond to what your readers write and request. And at the end of the day you have a business to run! But when is the last time you really enjoyed a sexy letter? Whatever happened to sophisticated, powerfully erotic entertainment? Well, Linzi, in the next few pages I hope to prove to you that it's alive and well and living in south west London! So if you can spare me the time, let me show you what sort of letters I think you deserve! And of course, let me see if I can turn you on!

I see you lying here in my warm, cosy flat stretched out on a soft duvet. You are naked, relaxed and ready for love. I want to watch you reading one of my stories, I want to enjoy the look of pleasure on your face. I savour each moment that you wet your lips. I gaze at your fabulous boobs and firm behind. When you glance up at me you see me undress, you watch how I stiffen before your eyes, and as you read on you hear me gently rubbing myself.

Now and then we smile at each other and as the story becomes more and more arousing I see you slide your left hand between your legs. When the story is finished, you roll over on to your back and begin to work your hand expertly between your thighs. You tell me how hot and wet my story has made you, and the word 'hot' gives me an idea. I tell you just to lie there with your eyes closed and your legs open and to frig yourself sensually. I slip out of the room and when I return, I tell you that we are going to play a game called 'hot and cold', and that the only rule of the game is that you keep your eyes shut. Then I join you on the duvet.

As I press my body against you I can feel just how hot you are. A lush warmth emanates from your soft flesh. Your stiff nipples seem to glow with desire. Your pussy is like a furnace, almost too hot to touch. But touch it I do, and for a little while I just lie there frigging your fiery cunt and pressing dozens of kisses on your lips and your face, your neck and your breasts. And when I suck your golden brown nipples into my mouth they seem so hot they almost burn my tongue. You are so hot Linzi – hot, wild passion! Hot with desire. Hot with lust! So now it's time to cool you off.

Out of the blue I spread something so cold on your boobs

that it makes you gasp out loud, but more in pleasure than anything else. With your eyes tightly shut you can only guess what it is, but you feel your nipples expand, almost as if they will explode, and you feel the heat of your burning flesh melt whatever it is on your boobs.

When at last I let you open your eyes, you are faced by the sight of pink ice cream melting over your breasts. Rivulets of strawberry ripple running down from your stiffened nipples to form a little pink pool in your navel. Then you lie back while I lick it all off you!

My tongue follows the line of your strawberry stream back to your nipples until your boobs are clean again, but glistening from the attentions of my wet tongue. I quickly straddle you and start to rub my phallus between your glistening titties, and in this game of 'hot and cold' you know only too well that hot is the next sensation you will feel. You smile up at me and let me rub myself between the flesh of your breasts. And when I explode into orgasm you grasp my twitching prick and let my hot come splash all over your face, sucking the tip of my tool between your lips to lick up the last droplets.

I tenderly wipe your face clean with your panties, then set to work thinking of how to subdue the fiery heat still oozing from your cunt. Again I make you close your beautiful eyes and when I return from a second trip to the kitchen, you hear me giggle mischievously. I tell you to open wide, but I'm not a dentist and I don't mean your mouth! I make you part the lips of your pussy with your fingers and I can see the succulent flesh of your pussy pulsating with heat and desire. I slide against you on the bed and you can feel my phallus already semi-stiff. Then suddenly, unexpectedly, you sense cold again, ice cold against your breasts. Something hard, and oh so cold! And it melts, but a lot more slowly than the ice cream and you feel me tease your nipples with it. What can it be?

I slide it slowly down your body, rubbing icy circles on your tummy, pausing when I reach your mound, then moving it on to where your fingers still hold your pussy lips invitingly open. I press it against you and the pink flesh of your hot wet hole is chilled instantly and there's a sensation like you've never felt before. I ease it into you, not deeply, but far enough for you to feel its icy hardness stretching you. And then you feel the ice cube melt!

But then this is no ordinary piece of ice, Linzi, my love, for when it melts, it fizzes. And when I press my mouth against your pussy, what I taste trickling out of you is champagne – Chateau Drew 1989! I taste sweet champagne and even sweeter you! And very tenderly I lick all of the champagne and all of you, bringing you right to the edge of a wonderful climax with my tongue before rolling between your thighs and plunging my hot, stiff prick into the cauldron of your cunt. There's no need to hold back and no chance of doing so because we are both so totally aroused. And when we come, we come together, magnificently so, and when I press my mouth to yours you taste the champagne too!

Alex. London SW11.

5. GIRLS ON TOP

When we women like to take charge, dominate or clamber on top – you guys had better beware! Especially you toy boys! In this chapter the lewd ladies calling the shots are mature females: a Lady of the Manor, a physiotherapist, a schoolteacher and *femme fatale*. No doubt you'll find all of them equally downright dirty and debauched.

YES M'LADY   PROFESSIONAL TOY BOY
FEMME FATALE   SUN, SEA, SAND AND SEX
HELP AT HAND   PLEASE TEACH ME

Yes M'lady

Dear Linzi,

My name is Lara, I'm twenty-seven years old and a native of Holland. I'm tall, quite curvy, with long, blonde hair, green eyes and a few freckles scattered across my nose. A few years ago I married an Englishman and moved to the beautiful Berkshire countryside. I have a great marriage, although my husband can be a little stuffy at times. Sometimes he thinks me a little outrageous, but that's the kind of girl I am. He likes to think of me as his little sex kitten and I love it. I really do purr when we make love!

When my husband is off in the city making pots of money, I try to keep myself amused, and what I've always thought is, what he doesn't know won't hurt him. He'll never spot my confession if you should choose to print my letter, Linzi. He never has time to read anything other than the *Financial Times*. I'm the one who reads all the sexy material in our house. To occupy my time I spend plenty of time in fantasy land. I lay on our huge brass bed and play with myself before the maid serves my early morning tea. She's quite a little cutie and I wouldn't mind getting her slender fingers involved with my hot pussy! I think she'd be shocked, though, so I haven't suggested anything of the sort!

One of the staff who doesn't seem so easily shocked is our chauffeur. He is very good looking, and looks a proper darling in that uniform of his. He's thirty-two years old and very tall and well built. He has piercing blue eyes and thick black hair. I've fantasized about him screwing me on several occasions, but I never thought it would really happen. But it did when my husband was away for a few days on an important business trip. Actually I must confess I planned it all. I just couldn't stop myself. I woke up so horny that I just wanted him so much. I longed to feel his strong body next to mine, to feel his hands

66

spread my legs and most of all to feel his dick right inside my juicy pussy.

We live about forty miles from London, so that morning I told Tom, the chauffeur that I wanted to go to Knightsbridge to do some shopping. We left at 10 a.m., Tom all preened and pressed in his dashing uniform, and I too looked pretty good in a chic silk suit in flame red. To add the finishing touch, my long legs were sheathed in 10 denier silky, black stockings and I wore them with high-heeled court shoes. As Tom opened the door to let me in the back of the Bentley, I made sure he had a good eyeful of my legs as I let my skirt ride up my thighs. I wasn't wearing any panties, but I don't think he was aware of that at the time.

I instructed him to take the scenic route to avoid the traffic and to turn the stereo on. Then I closed the glass partition and sat back to listen to the smoochy rock ballads filtering through all four speakers. This morning I'd only had minimal time to play with my pussy, so I was feeling very horny. I spread my legs and let my skirt ride up to my arse. I started to run my fingers through my golden pubic hair. I didn't glance up at Tom to see if he was observing me in the mirror. But it gave me a little kick to imagine that he was. I was becoming very moist as my fingers moved lower and came to rest on my clitoris. I squeezed it gently between my thumb and forefinger. I couldn't help squealing with excitement at that, and as I cried out, I glanced up in the driving mirror and realised immediately that Tom was watching me intently.

I leaned forward and pressed the button to release the glass partition. 'Hey, Tom, haven't you ever seen a girl turn on before?' I mouthed to him. He adjusted the volume on the stereo and said, 'Sorry, Madam.'

'Don't be sorry, it makes it much hotter for me with you watching, but maybe you'd better slow down a bit. Then you can enjoy watching me finger myself without crashing the Bentley!'

He looked at me open-mouthed for a second and then obediently slowed to a snail's pace. I lay back on the seat and went to work once again with my fingers. I spread my lips and pushed my fingers in and out, removing them completely now and again to suck on them. My juices tasted so good that I leaned forward and offered my juice-soaked fingers to Tom. Driving very slowly, he turned his head to one side and sucked sensuously on my outstretched fingers, not saying a word, just working his tongue around my knuckles and fingertips and inhaling deeply. Oh, just the thought of him savouring the smell of my cunt started to make me come. I stuffed my fingers back into my cunt and with my other free hand, exposed my breasts and started playing with my nipples. My climax was very soon in coming.

But naturally now I wanted more. The idea of a shopping trip to London was pushed to the back of my mind, so I told Tom to find a quiet place to stop. Within ten minutes he had pulled into the entrance of a deserted field. Leaning through the gap in the glass I kissed him forcefully on the mouth, before groaning, 'I want to suck your cock!'

I heard him unzip his trousers and I gasped as I saw his cock. It was thick, very big and already hard. His hand started to move along his length, and I reached for him, but was able only to stroke him with my fingertips.

'Come around the back Tom!' I urged.

With his cock sticking out of his pants, he hurried around to the back door, while I pulled down the roller blinds on the window. Together we took off my skirt and then I eased myself back on the seat and brought my legs up to meet his chest, exhibiting my pink pussy which was soaking wet. Tom found my clit with his thumb. His hands were big and soft, and his technique wild! He bent his head to me and gave my slit one long lick. His tongue felt so good, especially when his wriggling tongue made contact with my clit, then tickled its way into my open hole.

'Want to fuck?' I asked in a voice as shaky as hell.

'Yes please, Madam!' he almost shouted between slurps of my hot pussy.

I took a condom from my handbag, and just seconds later it was in place and he had my legs straight up on his shoulders and his cock was driving into my pussy. When he finally made the thrust that connected, I groaned in ecstasy. He felt so big and I just adore big cocks! He started to pump me, gently at first, his full length slipping in and out, the speed increasing with each thrust, until he was banging me so hard! He was so horny that within a few minutes he was coming.

That was fabulous, but we were still only a matter of ten miles from home and I wanted him at home, in my bed, to finish what we'd started. With his cock resting on my tummy, our arms around each other, I told him, 'Take me home to bed, Tom!'

Twenty minutes later he was knocking on my bedroom door, dressed in full uniform as instructed. I was wearing a crimson silk gown that was unbuttoned, a matching garter belt, stockings and high-heeled mules. Tom looked a little uneasy when I first let him in, but I reassured him by unzipping his flies and taking out his cock. It was hard once again and I knelt and ran my tongue over its delicious helmet.

'You like that?' I teased.

'Yees, Maam!' he grunted.

I reached over to the bedside table and grabbed a bottle of cold champagne. 'You like champagne, Tom?'

He nodded his head.

'Like to feel it on your cock?' Not waiting for an answer I dribbled a little over his bell end and then sucked hard on it as the fizzy liquid trickled through his thick pubic hair.

'Take your pants off and pour some over me!' I demanded.

Hurriedly he whipped off his boots, socks, trousers and pants. He was still wearing his shirt, jacket, tie and hat as he shook up the bottle and let the golden liquid spray over my near naked body. I lay across the bed, my back arched, my pussy aimed towards him. He began to lick me all over, starting with my breasts and tummy, then moving down towards my honey pot. He spread me wide with his fingers and dipped his tongue deep. Just as I was starting to come, he inserted the neck of the champagne bottle and very gently shook it. The sensation as the frothy liquid entered me was wonderful and I fizzed to an almighty climax.

I wanted to feel Tom naked, so I stripped him out of the rest of his uniform and ran my hands all over his taut, muscular body. He looked even better without clothes. I told him to take off both of my stockings and to use them to tie me loosely by my legs to both corners at the foot of the brass bed. He did exactly as he was told, making me tremble with delight as he rolled my silky stockings agonizingly slowly down each leg. Then I was well and truly tethered and helpless with my legs wide apart, my cunt open and throbbing. I helped slide a condom onto his prick and then gripping my legs, he mounted me. His cock felt even bigger this time as he screwed me very hard, pounding in and out, in and out, squeezing my breasts and fucking me harder and harder until we brought each other to orgasm.

That was just the first time. These days if my sweet husband is away, Tom is always on hand and more than happy to keep me amused. We play some very exciting sex games, but what really turns me on is the fact that I'm totally in charge. I'm not like that with my husband, oh no, I let him do the dominating. I'm his fluffy little pussycat. But with Tom, he seems to like me to take the lead and that suits me perfectly. I'm just like a tiger and when we fuck, I don't purr, I roar!

Lara. Berks.

Femme Fatale

Dear Linzi,
As a twenty-year-old student in London, money is obviously very tight, so I took a part-time job in a west London wine bar. It's great, it not only gives me the opportunity to earn a bit of well-needed cash, but it's just the job for picking up women.

Before starting my job at the wine bar, the only girls I dated were other students. Most of them quite fun but inexperienced in bed. The type of women I meet at my job are often sophisticated, older, and know exactly how to drive a young man crazy in bed!

I'm seeing two of them at the moment. Deborah is thirty-five, married to a managing director and bored. When I'm not studying, I often pop round to her Chelsea flat in the afternoons for long, exotic lovemaking sessions. And my other mature love, Gaynor, is even more fun. Gaynor is probably well over forty – old enough to be my mother, but she is absolutely gorgeous and a raving nymphomaniac! When she came into

70

the bar, she literally picked me up. She bought a round of drinks for herself and her two girlfriends, handed me her card and demanded that I telephone her at a specific time that afternoon.

Of course I did, and as soon as I finished my shift I went round to call on her. It was four p.m. when I arrived at her sumptuous house in Kensington. She answered the door with her face exquisitely made up, her golden-blonde hair piled on top of her head, and she was wearing a slinky, black, full-length, chiffon gown decorated with boa feathers at the collar and cuffs. It was very see-through. On her bare feet she was wearing high-heeled black satin slippers and aside from those two enchanting pieces of attire, she was entirely naked! Talk about a *femme fatale*!

She informed me coolly that her husband was in prison for a few years for a big fraud, and then asked if I'd like to fuck her on a regular basis! I just stood there gulping, and then she opened her gown completely to reveal small firm breasts and a totally hairless cunt as if to show off the goods on offer! I shook my head up and down to answer in the affirmative. She smiled seductively, drew her gown around her nude body and then told me to follow her upstairs.

She led me into a bedroom featuring an ornate, antique bed with a sunken bath full of soap suds which bubbled away in the far corner of the large room. As she dropped her gown to the floor, she invited me to strip and join her in the Jacuzzi. Naked, she kicked off her shoes and climbed down the marble steps into the tub. My mouth watered as I devoured her body with my eyes and tore at my clothing.

When I joined her in the swirling, steamy water, she washed my body all over, paying particular attention to my young cock, lathering up and down my shaft, her soapy fingers squeezing my bollocks until my penis was enormous. She slid over onto my lap and guided me into her. The smooth feel of her hot pussy was like suede on my penis, and the added delight of the gushing water surrounding my body was mind-blowing.

And after that things got even better. After fucking her in the bathtub, she dried me in a large, soft towel and told me to lie flat on my back on the bed. She sat on my face and rubbed her bald pussy all over me. Her perfumed, hairless pussy tasted fantastic as I ate her, my tongue exploring every inch of her sex. I was soon dying to fuck her again, but she kept me waiting for what seemed like forever!

She sucked whipped cream off my penis, she smothered me in oil, she even let me nudge the tip of my prick up her arse for just a few seconds before she jumped off and told me that, maybe, she'd let me do it properly later. Then she made me suck her pussy again and again. By the time she allowed me to fuck her bald minge again, I was fit to burst. That was the first day in her bedroom. I felt like some kind of sex slave, but it was fucking brilliant!!

Vernon. Battersea.

Help At Hand

Dear Linzi,

It is a relief to tell someone about something I have done lately and not keep it bottled up inside me. I am a married woman with a good husband and two nice children. I work as a physiotherapist. My job involves calling at people's houses and administering any necessary treatment to get their limbs back to fitness after an accident or illness.

A couple of months ago I started visiting a man in his early thirties, a bachelor, very good looking with a nice body. He was recovering from two very badly broken legs which he received in a car accident. He was manging to get about quite well under the circumstances, on his sticks or in his wheelchair.

On about my third or fourth visit, the fella seemed a bit depressed. He told me he was missing the active life he'd been used to prior to sustaining the leg injuries. The more we talked, the more specific he became. He told me that what he was really missing was sex. I was a little taken aback when he asked me to kiss him. I don't know if I felt sorry for him or if I really wanted to, as in the past I've always been totally faithful to my husband. I was unsure of my motives, but as we kissed, I felt an extreme sense of power over this poor, helpless chap, who wasn't in a position to move or do anything. It really turned me on knowing that this masculine creature was totally at my mercy.

I managed to manoeuvre him over to the bed, where I laid him down flat on his back, his arms reached out for me, but I withdrew tantalizingly. I honestly don't know what came over me, I was a woman transformed. Slowly and sensuously in front of him I stripped. I was only wearing a white smock over my bra and panties, so I took that off and danced around before him in my underwear. When I took off my bra, I noted that he had acquired an erection of monster proportions. Very gently I touched the tip of his prick with my fingers, stroking it up and down until he cried out in ecstasy.

The feeling of power seemed to be growing all the time, and as that feeling grew, so too did the need to get my partner's outstanding working feature – his prick, inside me! He kept yelling for me to straddle him, but I was intent on running the show myself.

Eventually when the man was reduced to a virtual state of tears due to sheer frustration, I moved closer and knelt over him, slowly lowering myself down on his stiff prick. Gradually I allowed him to penetrate me, bit by bit. I could feel my pussy filling up until I was fit to explode. All the time I was so engrossed in my own personal pleasure, my friend was screaming and shrieking. God he really was frustrated, I thought, as I reached my second fever-pitch orgasm.

My new found sexual power and my visits to this particular patient on Wednesdays are now the highlight of my week. Now he only has four more weeks of treatment left and I fully intend to make the most of it!

S.L.

Professional Toy Boy

Dear Linzi,
Just had to write and tell you about a wonderful sexual experience I had recently. I am eighteen years old and a bit shy with women. I've had a few girlfriends, and a few one night stands, but basically I'm a bit of a beginner with sex, although I glean a lot from your sexploits, Linzi!

Anyway last week I met this woman at my local. She was

73

standing alone at the bar, a stranger – a very attractive woman in her late thirties, early forties. I went and stood alongside her, not meaning to chat her up or anything, but to my surprise she struck up a conversation with me.

Before too long we were getting on very well. She told me she was in town on a business function and mentioned the name of a very posh hotel that she was staying at. She was dressed well in a pinstripe business suit, a white blouse and black high heels. I felt rather a scruff in my jeans and T-shirt. She had long, dark hair pulled back in a ponytail, deep brown eyes and lips painted bright red. She was very sexy, so when she invited me back to her hotel for a nightcap, I was absolutely delighted.

She took me straight up to her room, where she kicked off her shoes, sat on the edge of the bed and ordered room service – a bottle of wine. All on the company, she boasted. While she was talking on the telephone, she started to undo her jacket. I couldn't help but notice how big and firm her tits looked. I was really staring, I suppose. Still talking on the phone, she looked me straight in the eyes, concentrating more on me, as she started to unbutton her blouse.

She put down the phone and beckoned me nearer as she revealed her lovely tanned flesh and these lovely big breasts crammed into a half-cup bra. She teased one bright red nipple over the top of her brassiere and told me to suck on it. At once I was there with my trembling hands cupping her bra and sliding a juicy nipple between my lips. As I sucked her she started to wriggle around undoing her skirt. Very soon she was just dressed in frilly undies and stockings. I'd never had sex with a woman wearing stockings before!

She lay back against the headboard and pulled her knickers off to the side. They were soaking wet with her juices. I placed my tongue inside her fleshy pussy and started to rotate it, trying to find her pleasure spot. She guided me to her clit and told me to slide three fingers in her, while I nibbled her clit quite hard. She tasted wonderful, her sweet smell made my cock ready to erupt. It was poking into the bed like some huge flagpole. I tongued her to orgasm as she raked her long fingernails through my hair, panting and grunting loudly, thrusting herself up from the bed as she came.

As she lay there recovering she slid her hand into my flies and started to stroke my cock. She told me to stand up on the bed so that my cock was in line with her face. She welcomed me in her mouth and her tongue danced all around my prick head, one hand wanked the length of my sword, while the other, fondled my scrotum.

Just as the cream began to rise in my glands, she'd remove her mouth and decrease the speed of her wanking motion. Time and time again she brought me to the brink of orgasm, but every time, she would stop and look at me, getting immense pleasure from the tease.

Soon it was too much for either of us to bear. It was just at this time that there was a knock on the door. It was room service. She shouted to them to leave it outside the door, but unfortunately it had to be signed for, so this guy came in while I struggled to cover my ginormous erection with a towel!

As soon as she got rid of him, she pulled me on top of her demanding that I screw her. I pulled down her knickers and raised her knees up as I penetrated her hairy cunt. She held me inside her in a grip of iron as I thrust into her, time and time again, fucking her steadily at first, and then banging her hard when she told me she wanted it hard and fast. Moments later I was in heaven, my whole body was in shock as I reached my peak, and she raked her nails down my bare back, screaming blue murder. It was wonderful!

I haven't seen her since. It was just a one night affair, but from now on I reckon I can learn a thing or two from the older woman. Perhaps I should become a professional toy boy?

Gary. Winchester.

Sun, Sea, Sand and Sex

Dear Linzi,

I have just returned from my summer holidays, which I spent in Menorca. Although I am eighteen years old, I went with my parents who generally give me a free rein and pay for everything into the bargain, as I am still at school. I've had my fair share of girlfriends, mostly about my own age or younger, but it was in Menorca that I was seduced by a mature woman.

Sophie is in her early thirties. I met her one day when I'd gone off on my own and was sunning myself on a fairly secluded beach. As you surely know, Spanish resorts are well known for the fact that nudism is widely accepted, and the beach I was on had its fair share of naked bodies. Young and old, male and female. Actually I wasn't naked. I didn't want to burn my cock for one thing. That's one sure way to put a damper on any holiday romance!

It was on this beach that I first laid eyes on Sophie. I happened to glance up just as she was emerging from the sea. Her magnificent mature body was sparkling with oil, and droplets of water ran from her large, naked breasts and trickled down onto her bronze tummy. She was wearing a tiny G-string which struggled to cover an obvious batch of bushy hair that was sneaking out from both sides of her bikini briefs. Her blonde hair was tied up in a bun, and her pearly white teeth dazzled against her tanned skin.

I must have been staring at her open-mouthed because she really was a sight to see. Suddenly our eyes met and she changed direction, headed towards me and asked if I minded if she shared my towel. I was mesmerized by her beautiful breasts before I managed to avert my eyes to her pretty face. I noticed a smattering of freckles across the bridge of her nose, and that she was perhaps only a few years younger than my mum, but she was so sexy! I was all of a tremble. I smiled nervously at her and actually answered her by saying, 'Yes please!' I felt such a complete twit, but she grinned and lay down beside me, making small talk whilst rubbing her hands briskly over her body to get rid of excess water.

We talked for hours and the time just flew. Suddenly I realised that it must be getting quite late as the beach was now completely deserted apart from Sophie and I. She seemed to sense it too, and after looking around to see that we were all alone, she came close to me, took my face in her hands and pressed her warm lips against mine.

Moments later our tongues were squirming around like electric eels. She laid down on top of me and pressed her fabulous tits against my chest. We rolled around a bit, our bodies entwined, her pussy mound grinding into me. I could feel my cock swelling in my trunks as it rubbed her greasy body. It wasn't long before it popped out over the top of my pants and Sophie gripped it tightly and guided it to her quim. As I slid easily in and out, in and out, she was on top and I buried my face and mouth in her beautiful tits.

Of course I came in about three seconds flat. But Sophie just smiled, laid down on her tummy, told me to lie on my back while she went to work on my cock. The way her tongue slithered up and down my tool was a brand new experience for me. Many's the time I've had a good blow job, but this was a superb one. A real tongue expert, she got me hard in seconds, then she forced her big, bare tits onto my cock and I splashed another lot of cream all over her brown buds.

But it didn't stop there! She knelt up in front of me and with one hand opened her pussy and wanked herself, all the while giving me a filthy running commentary. She told me in a husky whisper how she was sliding her long red fingernails in and out of her cunt and telling me how hot her clitoris was. Her cunt was bright pink and glistening and her clit was bulging, I ached to taste it. I crawled on my tummy and lay directly beneath her big arse and dribbling cunt. I was frantic as I tasted her. The smell of her almost made me dizzy as I pushed my tongue inside. She kept talking dirty to me. Telling me just what she wanted. Telling me how good it was. And finally telling me she was about to come.

Then I was in her again. Holding her firmly by the buttocks, I slammed it inside her hot crack, letting my balls slap against her open lips, squeezing her wobbly boobs as I fucked her. We made it together this time. Her, still mouthing obscenities. Me, wailing and whining like an animal in pain. But oh no, it was sheer pleasure that made me scream! With my cock still tucked snugly inside her luscious lovetunnel, we fell back on to the sand and hugged each other tight, exchanging, hot, passionate kisses.

As you can imagine, Linzi, telling this story has brought it all back to me. I've been writing this letter with my pen in my right hand, my cock in my left, slowly, and sometimes frantically, rubbing my cock to several orgasms. Do please excuse my writing!

Micky. Middx.

Please Teach Me

Dear Linzi,

I am writing to tell you of my fantasy about making it with my teacher – Mrs Finney. I'm a second year student at polytechnic and have always been attracted to women that are older than me. I feel that women of my own age are generally immature, or the ones that I meet up with are anyway! Well, one of my teachers, Mrs Finney, is very sexy. She's probably thirty, thirty-five, with long dark hair and a mouth that I'd just die to prise open with my tongue. She's got this great body with lovely upright tits and a tight little arse. She doesn't exactly hide her shapely figure and always seems to wear clothes that show it off. I'm sure she even wears stockings, because her legs make that wonderful russling sound when she walks up and down the classroom. I'd love to be a teacher's pet, and find out what's between those tempting thighs of hers. I don't think it's very likely because I've heard she's happily married, but she does like to flirt.

Most evenings when I'm at home studying, my mind wanders back to Mrs Finney in the classroom. So now I've set the scene, this is my fantasy that always brings me to a sticky climax and makes an awful mess of my duvet if I'm not fully prepared with a box of tissues!

It's a Friday and Mrs Finney is looking particularly sexy in a tight yellow sweater and a black fitted skirt. Her long, lean legs are encased in sheer black nylons and she is wearing the highest heels I've ever seen her in. As the lesson is drawing to a close, she comes to my desk, leans over, her pert tits thrusting at me, and in her lovely clipped accent she asks me to stay behind after class as she'd like to go through some of my work with me. I agree, happy to have a bit of time with her on my own, never guessing that she wants to get me on my own just as much.

The rest of the students filter out and I go and stand beside her desk. She takes hold of a text book and as I lean down to look at the page she turns to me and kisses me. I can't believe these beautiful lips that I've wanted to kiss so much are there for me. Her mouth is open and we are really kissing passionately. Her French kiss has made me spring into action and my feverish hands wriggle all over her; smoothing her tits, caressing her neck and then finally reaching down and stroking her ankles and calves. My hand moves steadily upwards, until bingo, they're between her legs, and she is wearing stockings! That fact alone makes my cock grow another inch. I find that delicious area of flesh between her knickers and stocking tops and gently stroke her there. She hoists up her skirt, thrusts her cunt forward and pushes my hand towards her tight black knickers. On my hands and knees I crawl between her legs and rub my face into her dampness. She is so horny by now she is fingering herself through her knickers, and with her other hand she is frantically massaging her tits.

I reach up and pull up her jumper. She is braless and I use both hands to play with the cherry-red tips on her tits. I pull down her panties and breath pure cunt. She has such a sweet smelling lovehole. With one hand I spread her petals, then stick my tongue in as far as I can. She grabs my hair and moans loudly as I find her clitoris and lick at it. Her lovejuice is dripping out as I slide my thumb all the way in and she comes all of a sudden all over my face.

With half-open eyes, she tells me to fuck her. She gets to her feet and quickly unfastens my flies, releasing my desperate stiffy that has been cooped up too long in my pants. Then, climbing on the desk, keeping one leg stretched out to the floor and bringing the other up into a kneeling position, she offers her wet pussy to me. I need no further enticement and my thickness slides deliciously in her hole. Her cunt is tight and grips me fiercely, sending a shiver up and down my pole. On tiptoes, I thrust in and out, starting slowly then building up, accelerating until I am pumping her quicker and quicker and depositing copious amounts of spurting come inside her!

Of course it's at that stage I need the Kleenex handy!

Todd. Scotland.

6. HORNY HOLIDAY ROMANCE

Have you ever been fortunate enough to meet that very special someone on your travels? Someone new and exotic who drives you crazy with desire? I've had my moments, as have the guys and gals who've put pen to paper to contribute to this erotic chapter.

Easy Riders

Dear Linzi,

It was from one of those holiday TV shows that I got the idea for a weekend away mountain biking. 'Enjoy the beauty of the highlands and get fit into the bargain,' Anneka Rice suggested. Well if it's good enough for Anneka, then it's good enough for me! So I headed for my local travel agent, booked my ticket and two weeks later I boarded the train, with my flashy yellow and black bicycle and bulging haversack.

The weekend hotel was set amidst mountains and embellished with lavender and purple heather. The offer of spectacular, panoramic views was certainly substantiated. My room was cosy and warm and boasted a large, bay window. I sat on my bed and observed as the other energetic weekenders arrived in dribs and drabs. It was with great pleasure that I noted an abundance of healthy, robust young women turning up.

At a welcoming dinner that served up an appetizing spread, I mingled with the other guests. Two in particular especially caught my eye. Both were female, in their early twenties and Swedish. One blonde, the other brunette. I managed to wangle it so we were all sitting at the same table. I remember when I hit puberty, 'Swedish girls' translated to 'promiscuous, easy sex partners'. But that evening as I enjoyed their company, aside from fleeting lascivious thoughts, I had no such preconceptions. The erotic experience that began with a mountain top *ménage à trois* and continued throughout the remainder of the wild weekend served to prove that as a boy, I had a pretty good grasp of sexual matters! I didn't have to try hard to impress. The girls, Icke and Sacha, warmed to me naturally. They spoke good English, made extremely amenable dining companions and flirted outrageously with me. That night when I returned to my room alone, the sexy Swedes sent me off into fantasy land, my hot dick in my hand as I

82

dreamt about what those two Swedish strudels could do for me.

At the crack of dawn, the spring sun was shining and I was raring to go. There were twenty-four cyclists and an expert guide embarking on this morning's vigorous mountain ascent. Directly after breakfast we set off. Once again I palled up with Icke and Sacha, the two fresh-faced beauties looking even more delicious in skintight, knee-length lycra shorts and singlet vests that emphasized lean, trim figures. The going was pretty tough, but I'm fairly fit so I managed to keep in the middle of the pack with my two attractive companions. Icke was riding directly in front of me and I had difficulty with the gears when being constantly distracted by that edible, round arse of hers bouncing around in the saddle. Luckily it was all a bit too much like hard work, or else a massive great erection might have proved somewhat embarrassing in my snug fitting cycling shorts!

By late morning we had lost a few stragglers and it was decided that we would stop to regroup and for refreshments. I laid my mountain bike down on its side on the stony ground, sat down beside it, and gulped back some water from my flask. 'You want to walk with us?' Sacha suggested, abandoning her bike, smiling profusely and gazing around at the bewitching mountain scenery.

'Yes, lovely,' I answered, somewhat knackered but keen to keep these beauties within my line of vision. I didn't intend to have them nicked from under my nose.

We walked for about ten minutes until we reached the hillside peak and stood quite still to admire the breathtaking view. I inhaled deeply and felt clean, fresh air rush into my lungs. A satisfying feeling, but that sensation was swiftly followed by another of even greater magnitude. Icke and Sacha were stroking my prick through my cycling shorts. I could hardly believe that my fantasies were starting to come true!

While maintaining constant contact with my swelling prick, the girls stripped off their T-shirts to reveal glorious breasts. Icke was quite buxom, her breasts were full, upturned with pale pink nipples. She cupped them and offered them to my mouth, as Sacha, proudly exhibiting her beautiful, pert breasts, knelt down and lowered my shorts.

Soon my pants were around my ankles and both girls were on their knees – on the top of a hillside – my dick alternating from one hungry, greedy mouth to another. Never before having sampled two sensual women simultaneously, I put myself completely in their hands. They were undoubtedly the experts. Sacha used one hand to pinch my nipples, while her other hand gripped my cock at the base as she lapped at my balls, every now and then allowing her salivating tongue to traverse the length of my shaft, encircle my knob and suck my swollen, purple head between her warm lips. Icke's delicate fingertips stroked my shaft with enthusiasm, using her mouth and applying tiny nips with her teeth at every opportunity. She enterprisingly used the moments when my cock was engulfed in her friend's mouth to crouch down and manoeuvre between my legs, tickle my balls with her tongue, and between mouthfuls of my genitals inform me how good my cock tasted.

It was time to take off my restrictive shorts and to get my first glimpse of their sexy Swedish slits. The girls discarded my shorts, then their own, pushed me back down on the ground, and while Icke slipped my cock into her open mouth, Sacha squatted above my face, rolled her hips and teased me with a delicious looking cunt covered with soft, honey-coloured hair. My pelvis jerked vigorously upwards as I thrust my cock hard into Icke's mouth. I grabbed Sacha by the outside of her thighs and eased her bulging cunt lips to within easy reach of my tongue. Tentatively licking her wet slit and gradually opening her cunt wide with the continued efforts of my tongue, I savoured her sexual aroma. Her juice was pure nectar, and it flowed freely as my tongue whipped her into a frenzy. I could feel her hips shuddering as I licked faster and faster.

All of a sudden her come oozed onto my tongue and dribbled down my chin. She squealed ecstatically and thrust her cunt all over my face, drenching me in her juices. I was beginning to think that I'd died and gone to heaven, but even better things were yet to come as I felt a hot pussy slide over my dick. Icke was straddling my cock. While Sacha still writhed on my face demanding more tongue action, Icke was driving my prick in and out of her lovehole. The sight of a swollen, dribbling, pink pussy just inches from my face while an equally delightful cunt swallowed up my prick was rapidly bringing me to the point of no return. I thrust my hips hard and fast and used one finger to stroke the clitoris that dangled invitingly above me. Moments later it was all over, my cream spurting out in torrents as Icke jumped up off my cock, and finished me off with her hands. She bent over to catch my stream of flying spunk as it splattered over her large hanging tits and bare belly.

After that I needed a rest. However, the two sexy Swedes didn't. While I lay panting on a hilltop, suddenly realising how uncomfortable a bed of scratchy shrubs and heather had become, I watched their lesbian action. Icke was still drenched with my come and Sacha wasted no time in massaging it into her friend's body. She commenced by spreading the cream over Icke's belly and brown bush of pubic hair, slowly moving her hands up to her friend's breasts and fingering her nipples before clamping her mouth on to one sweet, pink bud. Icke responded by whimpering with delight, and finding Sacha's wet cunt, she gingerly probed a manicured finger into her lover's slit. I could hear the wet squelch as she inserted one finger, then another, and another. As Icke fingerfucked Sacha with three fingers, both girls started to sex up even more. One swift glance at my prick and I knew it was time to get in there, time to fuck the arse off beautiful Sacha.

Sacha was in complete agreement with my unspoken proposition. The beautiful Swede knelt on all fours, her friend Icke standing before her, her moist, hairy cunt on offer for licking, as I pointed my prick between Sacha's creamy arse cheeks. Her pussy was so wet it gleamed, the golden fluffy hair that covered it seemed to be attracting the sunlight. Her puffy, pink pussy lips trembling as I guided my prick for home. Still guzzling greedily on the magnificent muff before her, she reached through her legs and gripped my swollen head. Before allowing me entry, she used my prick to stroke the length of her wet crack. Almost awarding me entrance to this hot tunnel of love several times, but calling a halt each time I dared to squeeze my knob between her hot lips.

After a few tantalising moments I wanted in, so I thrust my hips forward and felt the sizzling walls of her cunt welcome me. I grabbed her arse and fucked her to the hilt, my strokes long, hard and speedy. As I gave her every single inch of my prick, Icke used her hands to spread her cunt lips wide, enabling me to view a sensuous lesbian spectacle as I picked up my rhythm and slapped into Sacha's cunt faster and faster.

This time I had a little more control. I wanted these two hot bitches to come before I did. It didn't take long. Icke mouthed Swedish obscenities as her pulsating pussy was sucked and wanked ferociously by her bisexual lover. She climaxed first, her ample tits bouncing up and down as Sacha's omnipresent tongue and fingertips finally sent her over the top.

Then it was Sacha's turn. I spanked her arse lightly and shoved my prick in her so hard that she screamed out loud and quivered like a jelly, the upper half of her torso flopping forward. Her beautiful round arse wobbled erotically before me, as I withdrew my throbbing prick and watched my cream splatter over her bare buttocks.

And would you believe that afterwards I still had a thirty-mile cycle ride ahead of me? I made it though and that evening I was making it again and again! The girls suggested we take an early dinner in their bedroom and Icke started off a lewd night of sex by using a peeled banana as a makeshift dildo. Amazingly resourceful these Swedish girls! Sacha and I proceeded to strip each other naked, then shared a banana delight from between Icke's well-splayed thighs. That kind of got the ball rolling! I hardly got a wink of sleep, the randy pair kept me fucking and sucking all night long. The following day's cycling really put my stamina to the test, but I managed to survive and managed to have the most unbelievable sexual weekend of my entire life, courtesy of two sensual Swedish easy riders.

Max. Reading.

A Perfect Climax to a Perfect Holiday

Dear Linzi,
I want to tell you the story of my beautiful holiday romance. Well actually it was just a one-night stand on the eve of my departure, but it surely made my entire holiday! Just for a week

86

I travelled to the beautiful Greek island of Zante. It was fabulous: gorgeous weather, nice food, friendly people and watching all those hunks in their tiny posing pouches got me at it every night. I slept very soundly! I was determined that I wouldn't spend every night alone playing with myself, so I hung around the tavernas trying to meet an attractive man. I didn't meet with much success at first, although I had some very pleasant evenings, but it was on my last night that I got lucky.

I was standing sipping an ouzo when I noticed this lovely man come into the bar alone. As if it was the easiest thing in the world, we got talking and we were soon getting on like a house on fire. He originated from Manchester, had a lovely tan and was working as a tour rep. He was gorgeous, tall and blond, and was wearing denim shorts that showed off his strong, tanned legs.

After a pleasant evening drinking and chatting, he suggested we go for a walk along the beach in the warm dark night air. Soon I was to realize that if you haven't been fucked by a well-endowed man on the shimmering shore, doggy fashion, with his round balls slapping against your bum as you pant away, well then you haven't lived! A perfect way to end a perfect holiday.

Rowena. Glos.

Spread Those Legs

Dear Linzi,
I thought that I must write to you to inform you of a fantasy of mine. You are on holiday somewhere in Greece and you have chosen a quiet resort so that you won't be recognized by all those holiday-makers who turn on the charm just so they can give you a good fuck. As you are the kind of girl who likes to get an all-over tan you decide to be a naturist for the week.

Just by coincidence I am at the same deserted beach that you are on. The sight of you on that beach baring all to the sun starts my heart pounding. You are asleep in the sun and haven't realized that you're being watched by an admirer. I move in closer to get a better view because I'm a randy bastard. To my satisfaction I am rewarded with a full view of your golden pussy, but now you have woken up and seen me. I am surprised however to find out that you don't mind and to give me an extra special treat you open your legs wider and extend your vaginal lips so that I can now see the whole of your honey pot.

You see that by now my penis is bulging to get out of my trunks, so you help it out and whisper to me that you haven't had a good fuck in weeks and can't go any longer without one. Quickly I put you out of your misery and thrust my hard penis into that golden lovebox of yours. I begin to ride you long and hard and you respond by wrapping your legs around my waist to achieve full penetration. I play with your brown nipples and grope your fat bottom cheeks as my thrusting begins to get deeper and faster inside you until you cry out that you are coming. My big dick is fucking you into a frenzy as we fuck faster and faster until we finally climax together.

P.N. South Yorks.

Monte Carlo or Bust

Dear Linzi,
Set high in the hills just north of glamorous and glitzy Monte Carlo lies Roquebraune, a sleepy tenth-century village complete with a crumbling medieval castle. My lover and I were holidaying in the south of France and came upon this captivating part of the French Riviera quite by chance.

It was late afternoon when we parked our hire car at the perimeter of the village and ascended the ancient stone steps that spiralled through the hillside and alongside a myriad majestic old houses that jutted out at odd angles. The Côte d'Azur was experiencing a wet spell and fine rain fell gently. As we gained height I noticed that the exotic trees and shrubbery appeared juicy, their leaves a vibrant green, damp with moisture; a hazy mist hung heavy in the air.

After a steep climb that left us slightly breathless we arrived at the ornate arched entrance to the antiquated castle. We gazed in awe at the vision that surrounded us. Stretching away into the distance behind us lay the magnificent Monte Carlo coastline, and ahead was a mystical step into the past. I felt exuberant, exhilarated and very sexy!

I had not really dressed to sightsee an ancient monument. I was wearing white denim shorts, a skimpy sleeveless T-shirt, white socks and pumps. My tanned body was quite exposed and was wet from the constant drizzle of light rain. My long blonde hair was damp and tousled and my nipples were hard as bullets. They nuzzled firmly against the thin material of my vest, a spectacle my boyfriend, Kim, noted with delight.

After paying an entrance fee of twenty francs we started to explore the castle. The roof of the building had been worn away with age in parts, so as we wandered hand in hand the rain continued to fall upon us and my nipples maintained their erect status. There were few other visitors around so Kim reached out and caressed my breast through my vest. My nipples were burning with desire and I could feel a hot flush between my legs. Hooking my breast out of the T-shirt, he teased my nipple with his fingertips. We embraced and kissed passionately as he used both hands on both breasts, cupping them and squeezing them lovingly. I could feel his hard cock pressing against my hot mound as we feasted on each other's delicious mouths. Our kisses became more urgent, more hungry as Kim's warm hands released my breasts and travelled down my trembling body towards my inner thighs. Just as his fingers were slipping inside the leg of my shorts we heard voices behind us. We pulled away quickly and I popped my breasts back in to my T-shirt. We turned away from the approaching tourists and wandered off hand in hand.

'Kim, we just have to find a place. I want you and I want you now!' I told him huskily.

He grinned naughtily, kissed me hard on the mouth and said, 'Just you wait, in only a matter of minutes you are going to get well and truly fucked young lady!'

He was as good as his word. In a crumbling corner of a tiny room that measured no more than six feet by six feet, we found our perfect lovenest. Our chosen spot was tucked away neatly off of a large cave-like room that was adorned with various interesting wall coverings. Although the larger room would probably draw a trickle of tourists, we considered our place would hold little interest to other visitors. We hoped we could have the privacy we desired without unwanted disturbance or intrusions. And we did!

The tiny cave was dusty, yet romantic, and was lit by some beautiful natural light that poured through the one small window. It also featured a stone step at seat level on which I parked my arse and said breathily, 'Now where were we, darling?'

I unbuttoned Kim's jeans and took hold of his cock. He was still semi-hard as I took him into my mouth. My lips engulfed his knob, and my hands stroked his shaft and fondled his hairy balls. As I sucked him long and hard, his hands kneaded my breasts and gently fingered my swollen nipples. I looked up at him and saw that wonderful sensual expression on his face. With saliva dribbling from my mouth, I flicked the tip of my tongue all around the head of his cock, then paused to ask, 'Do you want to lick me or fuck me first?'

'Get those shorts off, Mandy!'

Together we stripped me naked and, facing the window, I knelt upon the stone steps and thrust my bare arse high in the air. Kim squatted and stared at my pink crack from behind before slipping an inquisitive finger up and down the length of my creamy crack.

'Lick me!' I begged craving his tongue.

Seconds later his hot, smooth tongue parted my golden fur and slipped easily into my lovetunnel. He lapped me faster and faster until I was squealing noisily. I heard voices in the outer room, but I still kept whimpering as a sensational orgasm sent me to delirium.

Still quivering in climax, I felt Kim's engorged knob slide up and down my open, twitching slit.

'Push it in!' I whispered.

Agonizingly slowly Kim entered me. As his hot cock was thrusting deeper and deeper inside me, he reached forward and grabbed a handful of my swaying breasts. He used the other hand to grip one of my buttocks as he pumped me full of his meat. Each long stroke of his cock made me cry out with ecstasy. His grip on my buttocks and breasts became firmer and I knew he was building to orgasm. His obvious excitement got to me, I screamed out that I was about to come. Moments later we peaked simultaneously. We came together beautifully, my lovejuice mingling with the hot cream that whooshed deep within my sex.

When we exited our lovenest, there were a few visitors standing around observing the natural beauty of the ancient castle. Not one of them batted an eyelid, although they must have known what we were up to. Without a doubt they couldn't have been prudish Brits, they must have been sexually liberated French or Italians!

Mandy.

Good Deed for the Day

Dear Linzi,

Last week I did my good deed for the day, and got duly rewarded in the most pleasurable way imaginable. I set off in my car to drive from London to Devon to visit my old mum for the weekend. I've got quite a decent car, and plenty of good music to listen to, so I wasn't bothered about the long drive.

It was around eleven o'clock on Friday evening when I turned off the A38 towards the village of Rattery, where my mother lives. As I approached the T-junction I spotted someone standing by a red Mini Metro. The bonnet of the car was up and the person was bending under it. I slowed alongside, and realized that it was a woman who had broken down. It always puts a bloke in a bit of a predicament, but I stopped the car, got out and went over to her. She was dressed in tight jeans and a thick mohair sweater. She had short, brown hair, big green eyes and she wore a big frown on her face.

'Trouble?' I asked rather unnecessarily.

She sighed heavily and said, 'Yeah, don't suppose you have a phone in the car, do you?'

'No, but my mum only lives about a mile away. I could call for help from there if you like?'

'Yeah, I suppose so,' she answered hesitantly. 'I was going to call the AA, but I'm a bit scared about being here on my own.'

'Well we could lock the car up, and I'll drive you to where you're heading, then you could sort your car out in the morning when it's light,' I suggested.

'I'm going nearly all the way to Plymouth.'

'That's okay. Hop in.'

Her name was Judy and I dropped her at a small cottage in a village near Plymouth. I gave her my mother's number and told her to call me if she needed any help in the morning. I didn't really expect to hear from her again, but at twelve o'clock the following morning, Judy rang me and told me that she had sorted everything out with the car, and by way of a thank you said that she would like to invite me over to her house for dinner. I told her I'd be delighted and agreed to see her at eight.

That evening Judy was a changed woman. No longer the helpless hitch-hiker in need, she was dressed in a sexy red dress that showed off her fabulous figure.

When we finished eating a superb dinner, I couldn't resist giving her a kiss – by way of a thank you. To my surprise she responded by sticking her tongue halfway down my throat and starting to unbutton my shirt! I slipped the dress from her shoulders and got my first glimpse of her magnificent boobies. I sucked on her round, dark nipples as I felt her fingers on my fly.

Not only was she a good cook, but she was a marvellous cocksucker as well. She'd only been gobbling me for a few minutes when I spunked all over her face. I've never seen a girl lick up my jism so greedily.

Then of course I fucked her. On a sheepskin rug in front of a roaring log fire, I lay on my back while she climbed on top of me and opening her slit wide, sank down onto my stiff cock. Her hips rolled around ecstatically and her beautiful pussy gripped me until she'd squeezed out every last drop of come. What a night. We were fucking till daylight!

My horny hitch-hiker is one hell of a woman and I'm hoping to see her again soon. And of course my dear ol' mum will be happy to see her loving son spending more time in her neck of the woods.

Paul. London.

Love in the Hayloft

Dear Linzi,

I thought I'd drop you a line in my lunch hour to let you know what me and my boyfriend, Carl, have been up to sexually. We've just come back from our holiday in St Helier, Jersey.

On our first night we went to a nightclub. Neither of us drink alcohol so we didn't get drunk. We had a good time and left about one o'clock. We went off to find a quiet and deserted place for a good long necking session. We found a perfect spot after only a few minutes searching, somebody's old barn shed. I took my jacket off and so did Carl, and we both lay on the floor and started French kissing. Carl lay on his back while I got on my knees and started to unfasten his trousers. I took his shoes off, then lifted his legs in the air and slipped off his trousers and red undies. I knelt between his legs and started to tickle and fondle his balls with my long, slim fingers. Within a few seconds his prick was erect.

Carl undressed me. Firstly he removed my white blouse and put one of my pink nipples in his mouth. He gave it a good long chewing and sucking session, and then he did the same to my other tit, until both of my buds were hard and tingling. He unzipped my miniskirt and pulled it from my body. He was even more turned on because I wasn't wearing panties, just light blue stockings, blue shoes and a very sexy white garter. Carl parted my legs slightly and gently eased his middle finger into my hairy lovehole, fingerfucking me to a noisy orgasm.

We had a rest for a few minutes then I lay on my back on the rough hay and opened my legs as wide as I could. Carl placed his dick at the entrance to my wet hairy pussy and ever so slowly, he pushed it inside me. I wrapped my blue-stockinged legs around his back as he got his rhythm going, thrusting harder and faster in my tight fanny.

A couple of minutes later I was screaming as I was about to come. Carl was building to orgasm as well, so he quickened his pace and the power of his thrusts brought us both to a wonderful climax.

Sarah.

Turkish Delight

Dear Linzi,

I'm quite sure that you get a lot of fan mail which is sexually orientated. But what about fan mail from Turkey? I am twenty-two years old and going to university in Cyprus. Last month, by chance I found a copy of *Penthouse*, and as I went through the pages I was amazed by the quality of it – no need to say about the quality of the hot babes! But damn, when I got to Linzi Drew, I saw the most gorgeous, sexiest, hottest chick I've ever seen in movies or magazines. I was shocked by your beauty, by your sexy look. Then I read the fantasies written by you, and by the time I had finished my cock grew really hard and I masturbated and came four or five times just thinking about you. Now I want to write a very hot fantasy about you – I hope you find it hot too!

I see you at the beach. You're wearing a very small, topless bikini that allows me to see almost every fantastic curve of your very fit body. Your long, curly, blonde hair is caressing your soft shoulders and falling down your back. You start walking towards the sea and I can't take my eyes off your beautiful body and swollen pussy. I can't even blink my eyes. You catch me looking at you. Our eyes meet and you just attract me towards you like a magnet attracts a pin. You give me a sexy look and smile in such a way that makes me desire you very strongly. When I get close to you, you give me that sexy look again and start walking towards the sea. I follow, hypnotized by your beauty. Your lovely arse cheeks swing from side to side as you walk to the sea.

When you get into the water up to your tits, you turn back and raise your hand and call me. I hold your hand and you pull me towards you. Our eyes meet again, but this time our lips meet too. I start sucking your full lips and try to discover every corner of your mouth with my tongue. Then I start kissing, licking and sucking your earlobe. You start to moan as I rub your very firm breasts. Then I lower my right hand to your love triangle. I can feel its wetness even in the water and I untie your bikini strings and start to stroke your cunt. Very gently I press my rock-hard manhood against your thighs. You scratch my back with your long, red nails. I lower my head and this time I kiss, lick and suck every square inch of your flesh as I go downwards. When I get down to your gorgeous tits, I squeeze one gently, and I suck on the other's hazelnut-sized nipple. I lightly bite your nipple and make circles around it with my tongue.

Your moanings turn into long gasps and then into little screams by the time I get to your bellybutton. I take a deep breath and go on kissing and licking my way down to your cunt. Your hands are curling my hair and pressing my head down to your hothole. I take my head out of the water, take a deeper breath and go down once more. This time I lick your inner thighs and I can't believe the speed that your hips move as I lick your outer lips. And then you have your first orgasm. I go on licking your volcano-hot clit after taking yet another deep breath. After two more divings you have your second and stronger orgasm.

You whisper in my ear that now it's your turn. Still gasping we kiss a little while longer and then you make your way down to my manhood, licking every square inch of my skin. You take my steel hard, twenty-two centimetre cock in your hand and start doing circles around its head with your tongue. I feel like I'm in heaven.

When you take your head out of the water, I lift you up and take you in my arms and carry you to the beach. As we walk we kiss like hell. When the water gets to my ankles I lower you into the shallow waves. You kneel down and start kissing my cockhead again. Soon my whole shaft has disappeared into your mouth. I can't stand it any longer and I have to fuck you.

You kneel on all fours in the blue, trickling waves and I guide my manhood between your sweet outer lips. The feel of your cunt surrounding me is dreamlike. I slide it into you slowly and you scream wildly, toss your head from side to side and rake your long fingernails in the damp sand.

The waves crash over the lower half of our bodies as we are riding in ecstasy. Your moist paradise starts to quiver and I too come, shooting my hot milk inside your lovely cunt.

Janni. Cyprus.

Four Hours of Foreplay

Dear Linzi,

I visited London about four months ago and purchased a *Penthouse* magazine. I think as an editor you do a great job. I decided that my recent experience, although it didn't actually involve full sex was maybe good enough to get printed. So here goes . . .

On my summer vacation, like always I went to San Diego with my family. Usually I take a friend, but not this time. Anyway, one day I was up in my room looking down at the beach. I saw two of the most gorgeous girls I've ever seen outside my building. I rushed down to the beach to talk to them. I had butterflies in my stomach as I sat next to them. They were real friendly and we sat around and talked. Soon I found out that they were sisters. I'll call them Lynn and Lisa. After a while they had to go and eat dinner with their parents. So they told me to meet them back on the beach after it started to get dark.

I was terribly prompt, when I returned to the beach to meet them. After a while Lynn left me and Lisa alone and took off with some guys. Lisa and I walked hand in hand along the moonlit beach. She told me she had to get back but showed me where her window was in the hotel next to mine. She was on the first floor.

At about one o'clock I went to their hotel. Lynn saw me and came out on to the balcony. She invited me in, so I climbed up the wall to join them. They were both getting ready for bed. Lisa was in a robe and wasn't wearing a bra. She went into the bathroom and changed into a cut-off shirt and shorts. Lynn was tired and went to bed. Lisa and I stretched out on the floor to watch a movie. I knew I had to make my move, so I rested my head on her shoulder. My mouth was right next to her succulent tit, so I pressed my tongue against her breast. She just had to have felt it! When I looked up, she was looking at me. We stared at each other for about two seconds before we started kissing. I lay on top of her and started to play with her tits. She obviously liked it because she took off her shirt. I immediately began to suck her tits. I nibbled and sucked for what seemed like an eternity. As I sucked her tits, I watched her watching me. She was so beautiful.

She took off her shorts and I rubbed her pussy lips with my fingers and she got really excited. Although she liked it much better when I bit her nipples. She got orgasmic over that. So I bit her tits and played with them for about twenty minutes.

Any time we didn't have our mouths other places, we were kissing. She started to explore down my shorts and began to jerk me. It was so good. She slid down and unbuttoned my shorts and pulled my dick out of my pants. She sucked on my dick and it was one of the best blow jobs I think I'll ever get!

We ended at 5 a.m. after four hours of playing. My mouth was raw from her kisses, and my dick was swollen from her tongue. She lives in California and I live in Arizona, but we keep in touch. I've planned a weekend with her soon. Maybe I'll get to screw her next time around!

David. Arizona. U.S.A.

Fellatio as an Art Form

Dear Linzi,
Just had to write to tell you about my holiday romance. Don't worry it's not going to be all sentimental and romantic. It was downright dirty!

You see, I've just got back from spending a couple of weeks in Ibiza. I'm sure you've probably visited there on your travels. Well the sun shone all day long, and most of the bars and discos were open all night long. And as it happens, wide open and willing are exactly how I found the randy ladies holidaying there!

Well it was on the fourth night of my holiday that I met her. The lads and I were just downing a few drinks, when in she walked. My eyes nearly popped out of my head, she was just my type. A tall, leggy blonde with a gorgeous tan and a tight, white dress split up to her thigh. When she got comfy on a bar stool, just a few feet from me along the bar, I stared at her cute, rounded arse, realizing with great excitement she had no VPL – visible panty line. The horny little bitch wasn't wearing any knickers!

I watched her as she sat with her girlfriends and ordered a jug of sangria. Her pouty lips, painted in bronze gloss, seemed to embrace her glass as she sipped her drink. I really must have been gaping at her because all of a sudden, her eyes met mine and we sort of clicked. She smiled a great smile, flashing off pearly, white teeth, and I was hers for the taking.

An hour or so later found us walking along the beach. We sat down at the water's edge and began to kiss deeply. Her lovely tongue explored my mouth, as her hand started to massage the growing lump in my trousers. That was my cue to slide my hand along her smooth, silky thigh and come to rest on her inviting quim. As my fingers probed her open lips, I discovered she had very little hair on her pussy. The whole front of her lips had been trimmed short or shaved. When I asked her why, she told me that it was because it made her more sensitive, which she immediately proved by shuddering and jumping to a noisy climax as I slid my fingers in and out of her.

She lay back in the sand, raising her knees up, spreading her legs and pushing my head down to meet her twitchy lips. I needed no more urging and seconds later I was laid flat out on the sand, my tongue slopping in and out of her wet slit as she clung to my hair and thrashed about.

The taste of her pussy was so good that I thought my cock was going to burst through my jeans, or at least make a bloody great hole in the sand. Just when it was all getting a bit too much, she slid her hands to the buttons of my 501s and took me in hand, gently stroking my purple helmet, bending over and kissing the head of my by now throbbing member.

She seemed to treat fellatio as an art form, bringing me to the brink of climax several times, her mouth enveloping my cock, drawing it deeper between her soft lips. All the time her beautiful eyes looked into mine, enjoying my pleasure immensely.

Just when I thought I could hold back no longer, she straddled me, raising her knees high up and sliding my stiff cock between her hairless lips. I groaned in ecstasy and started to squeeze her nipples through her tight, white dress. She squirmed and wriggled on top of me, bouncing up and down as our sweaty bodies slapped hard together. I pulled her dress off her bronzed shoulders and took her full breasts, one in each hand. Her nipples were enormous, sticking out like bullets. She leaned forward towards me and changed the angle that my cock penetrated her. She kissed me frantically as her tits slammed against my chest. I tried to get one sweet nipple in my mouth as she grabbed me, clawing at my back and we both reached an exhilarating climax.

As you can probably imagine, Linzi, that was the beginning of a beautiful friendship. While my mates screwed around with different girls every night, I stuck fast to my little lady, Julie, with her amazing cocksucking techniques, wonderful body and her great sense of adventure. I knew I'd got myself one hell of a catch. We still keep in touch by letter. Actually it was one of her letters that got me thinking of writing to you. She describes in explicit detail what she wants me to do to her the next time we meet. I'm planning a trip to her hometown of Wigan very soon, my tongue is hanging out at the prospect of that musky, sweet-smelling pussy of hers. Perhaps I'll let you know how it goes!

G.L. Luton.

7. LESBIAN LICKS

Lusty lesbians. Every man's fantasy? Every girl's secret dream? In this chapter you can read letters from first timers, seducers, the seduced, bisexuals, and a guy who hides in the closet to peep at his naughty girlfriend enjoying some hot lesbian licks!

Ripe for the Picking

Dear Linzi,

Sex with another woman is a subject that has never really interested me greatly. Oh sure, I'd had the odd sexy dream about meeting up with a lesbian who'd show me the ropes as it were, but I never seriously thought it would ever happen. It just goes to show how wrong a girl can be.

I suppose timing has a lot to do with the awakening of my bisexuality. A couple of months ago, my male lover of two years decided he'd had enough of me and went off and found himself a newer model. Actually it was the best thing that could have happened to me. I've got to admit it, we were both in a sexual rut. So for two long months I'd gone without. Just my trusty silver-bullet vibrator and my fingers to keep me happy. Until last week, of course, when I met Cheryl.

Cheryl is a stunning looking woman. She has huge brown eyes, naturally blonde hair that's fine and golden and hangs halfway down her back. She's twenty-five years old (just a year my senior), and has the sort of figure that looks wonderful in business suits, but even better naked. Before I met Cheryl, other women's breasts were something that I gave little thought to, but now I think of Cheryl's breasts all the time. They are so beautifully shaped, upturned with the sweetest pink nipples. Oh and they're so sensitive! The way she squeals with delight when I start to suck on them makes my cunt drip with desire. Talking of cunts, Cheryl has a beauty. Covered with a silky layer of flaxen hair, trimmed a little shorter around her lovelips. I adore the way it swells up when I lick her. The smell of her cunt is so delicious, I just love to rub my nose right inside her. I suppose from my letter you can gather that I'm quite smitten with Cheryl! Until last week I had no inclination to poke my nose inside another woman's cunt, but now I seem to think of little else.

I'm the complete opposite to Cheryl's Nordic looks. While Cheryl's hair is blonde and flyaway, mine is thick and dark brown. Our bodies are basically quite similar though, both being quite slim and leggy. Being so dark of course, I've a fine batch of black pubic hair, which Cheryl has great amusement finding her way through. That is until she persuaded me to shave all the hairs off one night!

But I digress. I wanted to write this letter because my first time with Cheryl was so unbelievably exciting that it has to be told. I work in the City on the stock exchange. One day last week after I'd had a very hectic working day, I set off to meet a few colleagues in a wine bar in the West End. I couldn't face the tube so I hailed a taxi. Just as I was climbing into the cab, the other door opened and I came face to face with Cheryl. I remember thinking what's this woman doing in my cab, before Cheryl smiled at me and asked me where I was heading. I told her I was going to Oxford Street, and as she was heading in the same direction, we agreed to share the taxi.

Well if you know anything about rush-hour traffic in London, you are aware that a trip from the City to the West End can take a while. The next half hour was about to change my sexual perspective. Two whole months going without, and then fate hands me a firecracker like Cheryl. I really didn't stand a chance!

Cheryl was very subtle at first, introducing herself, making small talk and telling me about her work as a travel executive. I was sitting opposite her on the long bench seat, while she was seated on one of the pull-down chairs. Every few minutes she'd cross her long, slender legs and reward me with a flash of stocking tops. I couldn't for the life of me understand why I was so attentive, but I could feel my eyes drawn to her hemline, hoping that her navy, pinstripe skirt would ride just a little higher to give me a glimpse of her panties. I was fascinated by her manicured hands that she used expansively when she talked. She brushed them against her pouty lips, stroked her throat with her fingers and seemed to be tracing a line from her neck down to her breasts. I was mesmerized by her, and for some reason completely alien to me, I wanted her to be as interested in me as I was in her.

103

I could feel a dampness seeping into my knickers as I leaned back in my seat and opened my legs a little. She spotted it at once and for a full ten seconds or so stared hard at my parted knees. Then slowly she leant towards me, placed a hand on my knee and asked me if my appointment could wait. Afraid to answer, I just nodded my head, and with that she sat alongside me.

Her hand never left my knee, it just began to climb. The sensation of her talon-like fingernails snaking up my leg made me quiver. Her face close to mine, she told me, looking me right in the eyes, in a slow, even voice, 'I'm going to take you home and eat out that sweet little pussy of yours.'

'I'd like that!' I gulped, my heart pounding. I could actually feel my cunt twitching. Her fingers crept around to the inside of my thigh and continued to travel upwards. By this time I was thrusting my crotch to meet with her fingertips, but she kept me waiting.

'Touch me!' I pleaded, desperate to feel those butterfly fingers on my tingling pussy.

She leaned towards me and kissed me. And as her tongue probed my mouth, her fingers made first contact with my knickers. I started to come immediately, even before she pulled my knickers away from me to expose my swollen cunt lips which she caressed lovingly. Between suffocatingly deep kisses, I gasped ecstatically. As her fingers very gently opened my hairy cunt, I was still coming. My intense orgasm just went on and on!

Still transfixed in a kind of sexual trance, I felt the cab come to a halt and flickered my eyes open to glimpse Cheryl sucking her fingers and smiling mischievously at me. She pulled down my skirt, paid the driver and helped me out. On my way up to her apartment I explained that I'd never been with a woman before. Cheryl just giggled naughtily and said, 'I know, but you are going to love it, Vanessa. When I get you out of your business suit, spread those pretty little legs of yours and let my tongue go wild on your pussy, you are going to go crazy!'

I knew she was right. Just by talking dirty to me, she could make me go weak at the knees.

Once inside, she undressed me incredibly slowly. One by one

she slipped the buttons on my shirt, caressing my bare shoulders as she removed it, nibbling my earlobes and kissing my neck. Her fingers spread, she softly squeezed my breasts, her forefinger flicking my nipples through the lace of my bra. I was standing, but as she tweaked my nipples I sank to my knees. Cheryl unclasped my bra and let my breasts swing free.

My nipples were so hard they were almost painful as she drew them one by one into her mouth, gripping each nipple with her teeth. Kneeling together on the floor of the lounge, she thrust her knee between my splayed thighs and nuzzled it firmly against my cunt. As she gorged on my tits, I rubbed my hot cunt against her stockinged knee.

It all got a bit wild then as we both tore at each other's clothes, desperate to abandon all that was inhibiting us from exploring. I distinctly recall seeing Cheryl's breasts for the first time. She has nipples that point skywards and are pert and pink. A perfect mouthful is how I would describe the first time I covered them with my lips. Saliva dribbled from my mouth as I ran my tongue all over them. All the while I feasted on them, Cheryl fingerfucked me, sliding two fingers in my juicy cunt.

Particularly sweet was when Cheryl bent me over the sofa, so my bottom was hoisted high in the air. Her long fingernails tantalizingly fondled my buttocks, creeping nearer and nearer to my creamy crack, until finally one warm hand reached through and grabbed handfuls of my hairy cunt, before zeroing in and fingering my clit. She used the other hand to smooth away my thick thatch of dark pubic hair and to peel back my outer lips to make plenty of room for that slippery, soft tongue of hers. By this time I had lost count of the number of times I had come, and I had not yet tasted her cunt.

It was in her bedroom that I first got to sample her sweet nectar. Still dressed in a navy garter belt and stockings, she made herself comfortable on her king-size bed, and with one hand pulling back the top of her slit, in a breathy voice she invited me to taste her. A little nervous at first, I lay between her knees and came face to face with her glorious golden pussy. Unlike mine, it was covered with feathery, silken hair and was very neat. Her lips were bulging and her cunt simply dribbled with sexual juices. I lowered my face to it and breathed in its heavenly aroma. Grabbing me by the hair, she raised my head and said in a gutteral groan, 'Now, Vanessa, you are going to learn how to lick a cunt. My cunt! But not yet. First I want you to have a good look at it. I want you to watch while I finger myself until I come. Then you'll know exactly how I like it.'

Staring at this beautiful blonde cunt while the flashy, red nails went to work, was truly unbelievable. As her fingers pumped in and out of her, I couldn't resist sliding my tongue on to her clit. Her fingers and my tongue were a blur as she peaked, clawing at my hair and calling out my name as she thrashed about ecstatically.

We lay in each other's arms for a while. But only a short while. As I rested my head on her breasts, I couldn't help but nibble on her strawberry nipples, and it wasn't long before her fingers were smoothing down my coarse, damp pubic hair. She kissed my mouth breathily and I rolled on top of her. I grabbed at her hair, pulling her towards me, opening my mouth, enjoying her breath that reeked of my juices. She started to grind her hot cunt into mine and I began to tremble with sexual excitement as I savoured another new sensation.

Seconds later she had swivelled her delicious body around so that our legs were in the position of scissors, and so that her cunt was right up against mine. I grabbed hold of one of her legs and pulled her into me. We were just hot pulsating cunt against hot pulsating cunt. The softness of her hair and the rigidity of her clit rubbing against me sent a shiver throughout my entire body. Gripping firmly together, we rode each other's squelchy pussies until Cheryl clamoured, 'Vanessa, that burning hot pussy of yours is going to make me come!'

The sound of her pleasured screams triggered my own orgasm and for the first time we reached our sexual zenith together.

Since that amazing night of lust last week, things have got even better. Cheryl talked me into letting her shave my pussy and now when she sucks me I'm even more sensitive. The feel of a drippy wet pussy when it's completely bald is something else, believe me! We've also played around with a huge strap-on cock that Cheryl wears and rams into my cunt just as she knows I'm about to climax. And then last night she slid a banana into my pussy, then licked it out. Now that was fun! The thing I like most about Cheryl, aside from the fact that she is an extremely attractive, intelligent woman, is her inventiveness. She just loves to try anything new. And after going without the pleasures of the flesh for two whole months, I was just ripe for the picking and she was just what I needed. I've not gone off men, though. I'm still on the lookout for a good, solid dick, but even when I find one, I'm sure I won't give up my Cheryl!

Vanessa. London.

Amorous Allison

Dear Linzi,

For ages now I have fantasized what it would be like to make love with another woman. I'm not a lesbian, I love men, it's just that I wanted to try it. I've never had anyone particular in mind, but when I masturbate I sometimes concentrate on female movie stars, but mostly on my girlfriends, especially the ones that I know have had the odd fling with another girl.

One afternoon, my friend Allison called round to my flat. Now Allison is married and only twenty-one years old, five years younger than me in fact. Not exactly the type I'd imagined being seduced by. But I had fantasized about her all the same. She really is very pretty – petite, long, rich brown hair, big, brown eyes, and she has the most beautiful, shapely breasts I've ever seen.

When she arrived I was under the sunbed, so I wrapped a robe around me and let her in. My sunbed is one of those tops that you slide over the bed. So I left Alli sitting on the bed while I went off to get some fruit juice. When I returned with her drink, she had stripped off and was lying under the sunbed.

'Come on, we're both really slim, we can tan together while we have a natter.'

'Okay,' I grinned, trying not to stare at her pussy. It looked gorgeous; very neat, with fine brown hair that was straight and smoothed to meet in the middle of her slit.

I'd only been naked, lying next to her for a matter of minutes, when she reached over and laid her hand on my pussy. I turned my head and stared at her. She reacted by kissing me full on

107

the mouth, her tongue parting my lips, all the while her nimble fingers were slipping up and down the entrance of my pussy. I was very wet. We pushed the sunbed canopy from over us and Alli climbed on top of me. She sat astride me, her pussy spread. With one hand I squeezed her bud-like breasts, and the other I used gently on her clitoris. By now we were both so sexed up.

We manoeuvred into the position that I had dreamt of so often – sixty-nine. I'd never licked a pussy before, but the musky sex smell of Alli's pussy coupled with the delicious aroma of her juices was so sweet that I couldn't wait. As Alli dipped her tongue deep in my honey pot, I gripped her thighs firmly and lapped at her open lips for all I was worth. I think I came three times in that position. Alli's tongue was soft and gentle and so wet, and I was so turned on by the taboo of lesbian sex that it took mere minutes to make me multi-orgasmic!

We finished our delightful afternoon of hot lesbian sex when Alli wrapped her legs around me, scissor-fashion, so that our pussies were touching. Then grinding her pussy into mine, Alli worked her swollen clitty on mine. It felt like my whole pussy was on fire as I had my most intense orgasm of the afternoon.

P.L. Kensington.

Fantasy Strip Poker

Dear Linzi,

I am a horny lesbian bursting to lose my virginity! I find magazine pictures of naked girls like yourself, exciting and beautiful. One of my favourite fantasies is about a famous model who often graces 'Page Three' of the tabloid newspapers. My fantasy goes like this:

I am in a hotel bar in London on a visit to the capital, and I see my dreamboat at the bar. I introduce myself and say that I recognize her, and we begin talking. Uneasily at first, but then we become much more friendly. She explains that she is staying at the hotel because she has a photo session early the next morning. We get on very well and she invites me for a drink in her room.

When we get there we play a game of pontoon.

'First to win five games wins £10,' she ventures, and I notice that although she isn't drunk she is pleasantly light-headed.

We sit opposite each other as she deals the cards. I can't help but notice how beautiful she looks. She is wearing a white, plain blouse (I can see her black, lacy bra beneath), and a short black skirt with sheer, black stockings. She removes her shoes casually and crosses her legs – this gesture being enough to consume me with waves of lust. It's then that I realize that this night has to be more than a game of cards.

'How about a game of strip poker?' I suggest bravely. 'The first to lose their clothes wins £20.'

I expect her to call me a pervert, but to my surprise she agrees and laughs, 'You're not funny are you?'

I laugh with her and we begin the game. I feel a blush rise to my cheeks and I start to shake slightly with sexual anticipation.

The game commences. I win first and reach across to remove her blouse, saying, 'The winner must remove the loser's clothing.'

'Oh my goodness,' she giggles, 'you do like girls!'

To my relief I realize that she is laughing and does not appreciate my feelings for her.

She wins the next few games and removes my dress. As she is removing my stockings (how lucky I was to remember to wear them), I become aware of how much I want her. Every muscle in me seems to be shaking. My panties feel damp, but it doesn't show because they are black. I wonder how much longer it will be before she realizes that I fancy her. Her soft, gentle hands caress my legs as she removes my stockings and she giggles girlishly as she unfastens my bra. My breasts tingle as they are bared and I laugh to hide my lust.

'This isn't fair!' I exclaim, looking at her sitting there still almost fully dressed.

Then I begin winning again and get to remove her skirt. I stand behind her and undo the button and zip. She steps out of her skirt to reveal a tiny black G-string. I gaze longingly at her perfectly shaped bum.

'Come on, let's get on with the game,' she says wiggling her bum playfully and breaking my trance.

I win again and she sits on the edge of the nearby bed, legs out, so that I can remove her stockings. I struggle to unhook the suspender belt, finding it hard to conceal my shaking hands. I drag my long nails along the insides of her thighs as I remove her stockings from her delightfully fleshy legs.

I win again and approach her to remove her bra, my excitement rising. As I reach for the clasp on her front-fastening bra, she says, 'God, you're shaking like a leaf!'

'Well I've never taken off another girl's bra before,' I laugh. I reveal her small but beautiful, sweet breasts. I tear myself away from their inviting pertness.

'This game to win £20,' I breath.

She wins the decider and despite my half-hearted protests I collect £20. She squats in front of me to remove my knickers. She pulls them down slowly and I am suddenly aware that she can smell my lust for her. Her giggling subsides and she stands to face me. Her eyes sparkle and flash, her gorgeous nose twitches and she licks her lips. I almost faint.

'Do you find me attractive?' she purrs.

'Of course,' I croak.

'Bloody hell! You fancy me, don't you?' she says, now giggling playfully and sitting down on the bed.

Suddenly my passion takes over and I reach across and try to remove her G-string. She screams frantically and spins on to her stomach. I leap on her back, my damp pussy pressing against her firm buttocks. She is still giggling, her face pressed into the pillows. I rub myself gently on her bum and stroke her back and hair lovingly. I fondle her breasts, and as I kiss her neck, her giggling subsides. I turn her over and we stare at each other for a full twenty seconds. Her mouth is open and she is panting quickly. I move down and our lips meet for the first time. To my delight she responds and we tongue kiss hard. I move down her delicious body and kiss her breasts. Soon her tongue is working marvellously over my aching nipples.

Finally I move down and remove her G-string. I gaze at her gorgeous pussy longingly, a sweeter sight even than I imagined. I explore her first with my fingers and then my tongue, drinking, her hot, but deliciously fresh juices. She grunts and groans and squeals to an almighty, throaty orgasm.

She starts to use her tongue on me, and I delight in the sight of her gorgeous face between my open legs. Her long, honey-coloured hair feels like silk on my inner thighs, as she gently pulls open my lips and delves her tongue inside me. I am so overcome by passion that within seconds of her slippery tongue sliding in and out of my pussy, I am coming in gushing jerks.

Linzi, this is the point in my fantasy when I do come in gushing jerks. I hope you've enjoyed reading this letter as much as I've enjoyed writing it.

Wendy. Newcastle.

Unobtrusive Spectator

Dear Linzi,

My girlfriend has just discovered bisexuality, so I get the best of both worlds. I get to fuck a very beautiful, insatiable woman and I get to watch when she brings her girlfriends home for lesbian sex sessions. She is only nineteen years old and has a figure that is out of this world. She has big tits, with huge, amazing nipples, a tiny waist, a wonderously wet pussy and long, slim legs. Her hair is brown and she wears it long and full, she's got blue eyes and freckles. Some of her lovers are pretty good looking too!

The first time she let me watch her at it, I had to hide in the louvred wardrobes at the end of the bed. It was a bit difficult but I didn't mind because it was well worth it. I got myself comfy and peered through the slatted wood as Margaret stripped a very sexy blonde. I had my dick in my hand and was wanking steadily as my horny lesbo girlfriend started to run her hands over her lover's naked body. Their tongues were mingling as the blonde helped Margaret out of her clothes. When they were both nude, they embraced and their tits and hairy cunts rubbed against each other. That seemed to turn them on immensely, and naturally it excited me all the more!

The rampant pair lay down on the bed in a sixty-nine position. By now my dick was throbbing and I was wanking furiously. I had a great view of the blonde's open legs and Margaret's face. My naughty girlfriend used both hands to spread the blonde's cunt wide open and started to tease her clit and slide her fingers in and out of the lovely blonde muffhole. My right hand was in a frenzy as I watched Margaret's tongue enter the sopping quim. Both girls were talking with their mouths full, licking and sucking, yet talking dirty and whimpering with pleasure at the same time. Soon they were rolling around in ecstasy, shouting out loud that they were coming, time and time again. So was I, but I managed to do it quietly in my cupboard!

Now that Margaret is aware that I can be an unobtrusive spectator, she allows me to watch all the time. One of these days perhaps she'll let me join in!

Richard. Surrey.

Lick Me, Linzi

Dear Linzi,
I am writing to you because I am jealous. My wife once read a letter in *Penthouse* in which you implied you are bisexual. Anyway my wife wrote to you and you kindly replied with a signed photo. That was almost three years ago now and my wife still has the hots for you. In fact she often has that photo of you by her side, looking at it while she makes herself come with her fingers. She lubricates her fingers so well from her juices, then licks them clean, wishing it was your lovejuice she was licking! Not just from her fingers, if you get what I mean!

Of course I don't really mind my wife having a crush on you, or I wouldn't be writing this letter, Linzi! In fact I really enjoy watching her play with herself, and while she is doing that and thinking of you, then that's fine by me. On some occasions I have gone down on her and she moans as she is coming, 'Lick me, Linzi!'

Then afterwards we make love until we both come. It can take between three to five hours because I never like to rush. No 'Wham bam thank you, ma'am' for me! I like to please my lady in any way she wants, which is why I don't mind her having the hots for you. I'm thinking of trying to find a girlfriend for her. She'd have to have a great body just like yours.

Linzi, my wife has just read this letter and is getting very hot, so I'm going to have to finish now. Getting back to the point about jealousy, I'm only jealous because I haven't got a signed picture of you. Could you please send me one? I must close now as my wife is showing me her pussy and sliding two fingers in and out!

Tony.

Lady Boss

Dear Linzi,

Seeing all the letters that I read from people getting up to all sorts of dirty tricks, I thought I'd add my bit. I've been married to John for about eight years now and we've got a pretty good sex life. We did use to hang around on the swing scene, but of late haven't been bothering. I was quite happy shagging John and fantasizing about all sorts. That was until my boss propositioned me. Firstly, let me tell you I'm a secretary and my boss is Irene, a stunning woman, a few years older than me, probably in her late thirties.

We were working late together, just the two of us to get some figures done for the auditor. It was a very hot evening and I was wearing a thin cotton top. I've got very small tits, with very big nipples and somehow or other I sensed that Irene was staring at them. Under her gaze, I could feel my nipples swelling. I was becoming quite red in the face, when she came over and stood next to me. She used the flat of her hand to caress my pointy nipples through my blouse. Immediately I felt an electric tingle in my pussy and I knew exactly what was going to happen. Irene took both of my nipples between her thumb and forefinger and started to squeeze them.

'You've got beautiful nipples and I want to suck on them, Janie,' she told me as she massaged them quite hard and lowered her face to kiss me. Her lips were hot on mine, kissing me open mouthed, all the time manipulating my huge nipples between her long thumbnail and fingernail. She broke away from our kiss and pulling my top off over my head, she told me to take off my panties.

'Now I want to suck your pussy,' she groaned as she moved forward and started licking at my nipples.

I wriggled my knickers down. They were damp. My pussy

113

was so wet. With one hand she squeezed my tits, her mouth still nibbling at my nipples, the other hand she plunged between my legs. She moved her forefinger up and down my slit to open me up. The feel of her long fingernail made me shudder and as her hot mouth closed in on my burning nipples, I felt myself building to a climax. As she found my clit and eased it out of its hood, I was there!

As I squirmed and cried out in orgasm she lowered her face between my legs and inhaled deeply. The air was full of the smell of sex, and she made my orgasm go on and on, by sliding her tongue right up in me as I was still shaking with orgasmic delight. She didn't let up at all, she just kept on sucking and licking at my throbbing clit. In my ecstatic state I fumbled with her clothes. She had big tits and I grabbed them eagerly. She moaned out loud as I kneaded the cheeks of her arse. I don't think I can go on much more as I'm getting so turned on writing this letter. Needless to say we had a great time and I'm still Irene's executive secretary, and as she's bisexual I'm thinking about taking her home to meet John.

Janie. Worcester.

The Ladies Room

Dear Linzi,

For several years I have been a great fan of yours. The image of you gently sucking on my large pink nipples as you run your hands through my long, straight, blonde hair is always in my mind as I gaze at pictorials of you. However, my most recent fantasy about you is one that I would like to share with you and your countless fans.

We are at a posh do at a luxury hotel and to my delight I am at your dinner table. You look absolutely stunning in your strapless black gown that shows off more cleavage than it conceals. Between courses I startle you by running my hand lovingly up your left thigh. When I finally reach my destination, I find to my delight that you are wearing no panties. With a trembling hand I caress your pussy until your hand grasps mine. No, I say to myself, please don't take it away, but guess what?

You don't! Instead you push my fingers deep within your lovebox and gently lean in my direction to expose even more cleavage for my viewing.

'Shall we go to the ladies room?' you whisper to me in a wonderfully husky voice.

The ladies room is covered in majestic pink wallpaper and fitted with wall to wall carpets. In a minute you are out of your gown and standing naked aside from sexy black suspenders and stockings. Your beautiful blonde locks on your shoulders and your rich mound of golden pubic hair make you look fabulous. I feel as if I am staring at a goddess of human sexuality.

Within seconds you move over to me and pull down my sopping wet knickers. As you push your fingers deep into my lovecanal, which is rapidly overflowing with my sex juices, a tall stranger walks in on us. With a mischievous grin you bend over, and gripping your buttocks you pull your fanny hole wide open and offer yourself to the man. The long-haired stranger unzips himself and plunges his thick, erect prick into you as you cry out, 'Give me a good fucking!'

You haven't forgotten to keep me happy. You push me back onto a stool and spread my long legs wide apart. With your moist tongue, Linzi, you caress my aching fanny as I close my stockinged legs around your head. Your pleasure-giving tongue starts to slide in and out and then you suck on my tiny clitoris until I shake to my climax. The stranger is banging you hard and fast as orgasm upon orgasm racks my body.

For hours the three of us make mad passionate love in our private retreat in the hotel. I certainly hope that left your knickers as wet as it left mine!

J.L. Ireland.

Love Thy Neighbour

Dear Linzi,

I've been happily married to the same man for sixteen years. I'm thirty-six years old, reasonably attractive and highly sexed. Since I've been with my husband, I've always found the need to fuck other men. That doesn't mean I think any the less of him. None of my sexual activities could have been classed as a full-blown affair. I used to meet one bloke regularly in the woods for a nice outdoor shag. Another bloke used to shag me in the front seat of his old, classic sports car, and from time to time, I played around with my boss.

Anyway that was all in the past. I've now met somebody who I seem to have a kind of obsession with, and it's a she. Sometimes I just can't concentrate on anything. All the time I'm daydreaming about sex with this wonderful woman. Until recently I'd never even thought about lesbianism. I've always been the kind of woman who likes to feel a nice, stiff prick between my legs. What started me off was one evening when I was browsing through an erotic magazine and came upon a feature about lesbians.

All of a sudden I could feel my cunt go all twitchy, so I slid my fingers inside my knickers and started to play with my clit. As I read on the wetter I became. An hour later I felt absolutely exhausted and had come six times! I tell you my husband got a right good seeing to when he got in from work!

After that night I started to fantasize more and more about making it with a woman. I thought fantasy is all it would ever be because the thought of going out and consciously trying to meet up with a lesbian . . . Well I just wouldn't know where to start! So I got myself a few naughty lesbian videos to keep myself happy.

That is until John and Sheila moved in across the road. Now John is just the kind of guy that normally I would have been desperate to get inside me, but not this time, no it was Sheila that I wanted. She has just turned twenty-two and is a real stunner: long, dark hair, a great figure with lovely firm, big tits and a curvy arse. I wanted so much to strip her naked and lick her body from top to bottom. So I made it my goal to seduce her.

It was a piece of cake. Being neighbours, I started by inviting her over on a Saturday for coffee. One particular Saturday afternoon when the guys had gone to football. I invited her over for a chat. Well that's what I told her anyway! We sat next to each other on the sofa and as the film on the TV was very old, I asked her if she'd like to watch a video. She agreed and I put on the dirtiest lesbian video I could find.

On screen two very pretty girls started to kiss each other. I looked at Sheila out of the corner of my eye and noticed she was blushing a little. Her big, dark eyes were wide as I reached over and put my hand on her knee. To my surprise I realized that she was into it straight away. She pushed her crotch forward and sighed loudly as my hand disappeared beneath her skirt.

She was wearing tight panties and I started to rub her on top of them. Very quickly I found her clit and massaged it with my thumb, while hooking my other fingers inside her pants. As I slid my fingers into her juicy crack, she slumped down on the sofa and thrust her pelvis wildly as I fingered her to orgasm.

After her first climax we started all over again, but this time much more slowly. Neither of us had been in a lesbian situation before so we took it steady, gradually stripping off our clothes before we lay naked on the living-room floor. I climbed on top of her and we rubbed our bodies together, nipple on nipple, cunt on cunt, sliding around, kissing and caressing until we both started to come.

Then of course there was the licking. I'd never tasted another female's cunt juice before. Sheila's tasted beautiful. We got into the sixty-nine position and I buried my face in Sheila's hairy cunt. I could feel her exploring me with her fingers, sliding her forefinger over my clit. I sucked her pussy and then moved around to her arse and gave that a good tonguing too. We had so much fun and so many orgasms!

I tell you, Linzi, that afternoon was electric. Now we meet up every Saturday afternoon when our husbands go to football. We haven't told them. It's our little secret, and we restrict our sex to once a week, so that we both really look forward to it. All week long I dream of that juicy cunt of hers. It's always worth the wait!

Tina. Essex.

Lesbian Casting Couch

Dear Linzi,
The reason I am writing to you is so as to enable me to at last express my sexuality to someone. I do hope you will read this,

so at last someone will appreciate my feelings. I am an eighteen-year-old girl, and although I have had several boy-friends, I am a lesbian. I don't know any other lesbians and it's taken me a long time to come to terms with my feelings. I have tried to force my brain and desires to what is 'normal', but I find that my fantasies only concern other girls, and I'm only attracted to girls. I live in a clichéd 'normal' family at home with my parents, and only one very close friend has even the slightest knowledge of my sexual preferences.

I first bought *Penthouse* magazine when I noticed Linda Lusardi on the cover. I must say I find *Penthouse* exciting, laughable and beautiful depending on my mood. Anyway, Linzi, your letters pages are my favourite. I love to hear you say rude things and talk about any of your own lesbian or bisexual exploits. One of my main fantasies would be to be auditioned by you for a photo session. I am blonde, five feet one inch tall and slim.

You would start by rubbing your hands all over my body to feel my shape and firmness, then you'd kiss my mouth and start to play with my breasts, before taking off my pants and stroking my pussy, playing with my clit and licking me out.

I would love to know if you really do enjoy lesbian love with the models?

Lucy. Brighton.

The First Time

Dear Linzi,

I'm twenty-one, work as a secretary and have a woman for a boss. She's competent, in her thirties and very attractive. She seemed to take to me immediately we met, and sometimes after work we'd go out for a meal together. We'd got to the stage that I'd drop in to see her at her flat for a coffee or a gossip.

Well one night I had this really bad row with this bloke I was seeing and was very upset. On the off-chance my boss would be in, I called on her. She was and she was lovely about it. She gave me a big drink, comforted me and let me cry on her shoulder. But as we sat together on the floor cushions, the atmosphere somehow seemed to change – subtly, smoothly, but unmistakably. Instinctively I knew where it might lead if I made the right signals. So I did just that, by eye contact and moving my body as she touched me.

It was quite different from making love to a man. Just stroking each other very softly, our lips meeting in a warm tender kiss. We undressed each other slowly and then she pulled me close. I felt our breasts crush together, and her long, freshly-washed hair brush across my face. For a long time we just lay together enjoying the embrace, letting our thighs mingle, kissing and caressing.

She gently rolled me onto my back and began to move her fingers all over my body. At each touch her light stroke moved lower and lower until I could hardly wait for her to touch me there! I felt my thighs opening in anticipation and when I thought this is it, she started running her fingertips along my inner thighs. No man had ever made me wait so long and by the time I felt her fingers brush against my pussy, I was ecstatic. She did exactly what I wanted, finding my clitoris instantly and fingering it with great finesse. I wanted to do the same to her, so I plunged my hand between her legs. She felt warm, wet and wonderful.

She gently parted my lips with her fingertips and very lightly teased my slit. Then she started to rub her nose all over my pussy, breathing me in, savouring my smell. Her hair tickled the insides of my thighs as she started to lick a little harder and a little faster. I was clinging on to her head, moaning and crying as she feasted on me, before deliberately inserting a long, manicured fingernail inside my pussy which made me cream and cream!

Gina. London.

8. LOCATIONS OF LUST

The weird and wonderful locales that we select to engage in frantic fornication are terribly important to good sex. Where and when we make love can be almost as important as who we do it with! Some varied and vulgar venues get tried out by the randy ravers who make up this chapter.

A First-Class Ride

Dear Linzi,

Of all the places to get picked up by a man, I suppose a speeding train is as good a place as any. A business trip to Scotland was a bit of a bore, but a good excuse to get out of the office for a few days. I've got quite a high-powered job, so I always insist on travelling first class. It's not that I'm a snob, but the differences in service is noticeable and for a lengthy journey a necessity.

As I boarded, I noted with pleasure that it was one of the older style trains. The type that has individual first-class carriages. Luxury, I thought. With a bit of good fortune, I'll be able to put my feet up, do a bit of work and enjoy the ride. Not exactly what happened but it certainly was an enjoyable trip.

For the first part of the journey, the first-class compartment was fairly busy, but as the journey progressed, I found myself alone in the carriage. I slipped off my shoes, put my feet up and must have dozed off.

When I awoke I was at Crewe station and there was a man sitting directly opposite me, my stockinged feet were propped up on his lap, and to my astonishment he was stroking them lovingly! I blinked my eyes thinking I was in the midst of a sexy dream, but it all seemed so real. That's because it was!

Naturally my first instinct was to remove my feet, but this rather attractive looking man clung on to them and said, 'Go on admit it, you adore having your feet tickled. Pleased to meet you, my name is Gerry. Are you going all the way?'

There seemed an underlying meaning to his question, and I was lost for words for a few seconds before I blurted out, 'Edinburgh, and my name's Sabrina.'

As the train rolled out of the station I made no further move to displace my feet from his lap. He was dead right it did feel pleasant. It suddenly dawned on me why it felt so nice. My toes were resting on the bulge in his trousers which was growing harder by the moment. I gave him an embarrassed smile and his soft hands started to massage my calves. He really did have sensual hands.

'Ever made love on a train?' he asked suddenly.

'No,' I answered quickly and honestly.

'Ever felt like it?' he went on.

I looked at his face. He was very handsome and extremely sexy. Just my type in fact. About forty, a good few years older than me, which is how I like my men. He was immaculately dressed in a grey double-breasted suit and he did have the most wonderful hands.

'Are you propositioning me?' I laughed.

'Yes!' he answered immediately. 'Can't you feel what your lovely tootsies have done to me? You've been stroking and tormenting my cock for quite some time.'

'I haven't!' I blushed.

'It's the truth!' he said. 'I came in this carriage and sat opposite you. You were curled up in a ball asleep. I'd only been sitting here a few minutes when you plonked your feet on me and have been driving me crazy ever since!'

Naughty old me! I removed my feet from his crotch, stifled a giggle, pulled down the blind and went to sit beside him. Bending my head towards his dick, I unzipped him. I squeezed my hand into his boxers and found his short, fat cock.

'Lovely and fat, just the way I prefer them,' I groaned as I dropped my wide-open mouth upon it.

Gerry grunted and caught hold of my hair, jerking my head up and down as I gobbled him. His short fat cock soon became a long, fat cock. And by now I was feeling deliciously decadent and dying for a fuck. So, still holding his cock in one hand I grabbed my bag, found a condom and stretched it over his big dick. Then I dragged my tight skirt up around my hips, while Gerry assisted by pulling my French cut panties off to one side, and we had the all clear.

Facing him, I began to kiss his lips as I straddled his cock, slowly easing myself down onto his bone-hard prick, while he held me around the waist. It felt so satisfying as he sank into me, penetrating me deeply while he gripped me firmly and thrust me up and down on it.

I came very quickly but Gerry kept on fucking me. Up and down, all the time his hands groping my breasts, stroking my face tenderly as he slammed his hard cock into my slit. He told me he was about to come and that got me quivering all over again.

All in all it was a first-class ride. British Rail, they're getting there, don't you think?

Sabrina. London.

Class

Dear Linzi,
The other night I was bored, at home watching TV, when something came on my screen that got me wanking. Yes, believe it or not on TV! I don't know if you happened to see this film, it's called *Class*. The scene that got me really excited was when Jacqueline Bisset seduced a young college boy in a lift. She was taking the lead and the lucky young guy, who was a virgin was fumbling about as she kicked off her clothes and screwed him in this glass lift! It wasn't very explicit, but enough to get my imagination and my prick going crazy!

Guy.

Moist Paradise

Dear Linzi,
I had the privilege of being able to visit your beautiful country last month where I saw your photographs for the first time. They blew my mind! My image of you is that of a very gentle girl, with a latent sexuality that lurks under that graceful exterior. Thus my fantasy of you goes something like this:

We meet at this dinner party. You are wearing a long black gown with a very low back. Your long, blonde hair caresses your bare shoulders. As you move, flashes of your tanned thighs can be seen through the high slit in your gown. I know

124

instinctively that you wear only pure silk underwear. Salmon pink.

By some incredible luck you are seated next to me at the table. As you sit down the slit of your gown opens to reveal your gorgeous inner thighs. You see me looking longingly at them, but you make no move to cover them up. You smile softly. Your long, red nails scratch your leg and this sends shivers through my whole body, by now my cock is threatening to break my zip.

We talk a little during 'starters'. In between courses I suggest we go outside for a little fresh air. We walk for a while around the large grounds, laughing a lot. We finally stop at a large fountain. We sit down on the grass and I look into your eyes. I am drawn to your lips, they open instantaneously and your tongue comes out fighting for position. My hand goes down between your dress slit. Your legs open as I run my hand up your inner thigh. As I touch your silky mound it is as if I am hit by 10,000 volts. Your panties are soaked with your honey lovejuices.

My mouth moves to your mound and soft whimpers can be heard. Your hips begin to gyrate, slowly but with a definite purpose. Your hand is on my head, giving direction and pressing my tongue deeper inside your red hot volcano. Your body erupts and you shake uncontrollably as your volcano glows white hot.

Your hand goes to my zip and you stroke my cock, rubbing my hardness against the smooth skin on the inside of your thighs. Then you simply slide me inside your moist pussy. I move in and out very slowly and feel myself coming. The sensation begins in my toes and moves up my legs as I explode within your moist paradise.

Dave. South Africa.

Mile High

Dear Linzi,

I'd like to tell you about a wonderful experience that happened to me recently. I know that you've got such a dirty mind that you'll love to hear all about it in juicy detail.

I'm a business man, fairly successful (if I say so myself!), who does a lot of travelling to and from America. Well, a few weeks ago I had an important business meeting in Chicago and had to take a night flight, so as to arrive bright and early for my meeting. The company always sends me first class so naturally the cabin staff paid me quite a lot of attention. More than I'd ever dreamt of in fact!

There was this gorgeous American stewardess looking after the passengers. She was dressed in a smart red uniform complete with shortish skirt, enhancing her beautiful legs, and she wore high-heeled, red court shoes. I couldn't help gazing at her as she served me a brandy. She had shortish well-cut blonde hair, big brown eyes and a wide slash of a mouth smothered in glossy red lipstick. Her figure was slim and petite, yet her tits seemed to thrust themselves against her tight blouse. Just staring at them, I found myself licking my lips and imagining what it would feel like to slip those pert, strawberry-bud nipples between my teeth.

I actually got to find out! During the night when the movie was over, and most of the passengers were dozing off, I wandered up to the loos. As I approached, I saw her standing just by the entrance and she was dazzling me with a gloriously sexy smile. When I was standing right next to her, her breasts fairly poked into my chest, she continued with her sexy smile and asked, 'Is there anything I can assist you with, sir?'

'I don't think you should make offers like that!' I joked.

'You know it's quite a serious offer, sir,' she said smiling wickedly, and with that she took hold of my hand, and glancing over my shoulder to see that we hadn't been observed, she led me into the loo. She turned and locked the door behind us, and then with a savagery, I never expected or dreamt of, she was on me. Her tongue probed my mouth, French kissing me like I'd never known before. Her delicate, manicured hands slid all over me, expertly unzipping me and squeezing my cock between her fingertips. My trousers dropped to my ankles as I positioned myself on the sink. She took my cock greedily in her mouth, guzzling my knob, whilst wanking her hand up and down my shaft. As her tongue ran up and down my cock, I fumbled with the buttons of her blouse, eventually getting them undone, hoisting up her bra and taking her beautiful pink buds between my fingers, squeezing and stroking them before nibbling on her perky pink nips.

Pretty soon we were in such a state of excitement, the only route to relief was a good hard shafting. I pulled her up and kissed her long and hard on those sticky red lips of hers, then my hands slipped up her skirt and into her panties. The horny bitch was wearing stockings and just a tiny G-string. As my finger slid inside her, I could smell her heat. It was sensational. Her big, swollen clitoris trembled as I fingered her. She started to move her body and ride my fingers, moaning and biting my neck. I couldn't take it any longer. I pulled her panties right down, turned her around and rammed my thick cock between her slippery lips. She seemed to have me in a grip of iron, as her pussy muscles grasped me and sucked me into her. We fucked together, slowly at first, getting our rhythm going in such a confined space, until I could hold my creamy spunk no longer. I grabbed hold of her warm, soft arse and jetted my load into her as she jerked to orgasm.

T.L. Birmingham.

Storing it up for Sally

Dear Linzi,
I split up with my wife about six months ago, and to be honest have been a bit of a wet fish ever since. I suppose because she ran off with another bloke, it knocked my confidence a lot. I can tell you that six months without a fuck was driving me to distraction. That all changed when a new rep called on my shop the other week.

I own a hardware store and most of my customers are 'old dears' needing a new plastic bucket, or greasy young men requiring new tools, so meeting a new woman at work looked to be a nonstarter. Until Sally the representative for the copper pots and pans company came a calling. She is a very sexy looking woman: twenty-eight years old, shoulder-length red hair and big, firm tits. That'll do for me, I thought, as she walked through the door! Still I didn't really think she'd be interested in me, although I'm not a bad looking bloke, I suppose it's just that I was feeling a bit sorry for myself.

Anyway we seemed to hit it off straight away, and as it was approaching lunch time I plucked up the courage to ask her if she'd like to join me for lunch. Actually I was quite taken aback when she agreed.

We went to a cozy little pub just around the corner from my shop and had a bite to eat. She told me all about herself, including the fact that she was single and didn't have anyone special in her life at the moment. I suppose it was because I'd been out of women's company for so long combined with her fabulous legs, but I don't know what came over me. As she crossed her legs for the umpteenth time, I reached under the table and stroked one, just above the knee. Withdrawing quickly, expecting a good slap round the chops, I looked at her and offered a mumbled apology, but was delighted when she gave me a winning smile and told me how nice it felt.

An instant later my hand was back on her leg, but this time placed a little higher. She sat back in her seat and spread her legs a little. I could feel my heart beating quickly, not to mention my cock which was pumping in my pants. God I felt so randy that I just had to have her.

'What are you doing this evening?' I ventured. My trembling hand still stroking her leg.

'What are you doing this afternoon?' she answered breathily.

I gulped and said, 'Half-day closing!'

It wasn't, but we both knew what we had in mind, as we hurried back to the shop.

In the small storeroom at the back, I grabbed her and crushed my lips upon hers. She tasted of strawberry lipstick and her neck smelt of sweet perfume as I licked her face, her cheeks, her nose and her eyelids. There was a mad struggle with clothing as our frantic hands stripped each other. I squeezed one gorgeous breast that popped free from her bra. I sucked on her swelling bud as she unbelted my pants and took my cock in hand: one hand snaked the length of my stem, while the other concentrated on the head, gently teasing it with her fingernails.

'Suck me!' I implored.

Her greedy tongue encircled my knob before she sucked me deep into her throat. I could almost feel her tonsils. I knew I would spunk in seconds, so I withdrew and grunted, 'Let me taste your pussy?'

She dropped her skirt to expose black panties that bulged with a mass of thick, ginger pubes that escaped over the top and out of both sides. I sank to my knees, pulled down her knickers and parted her dense bush with my tongue, breathed in her delicious juices, then pursed my lips and sucked on her little button clitty. She squealed with delight and gasped, 'Ooh that's nice, but fingerfuck me too!'

Immediately I stuck two fingers in her ginger minge and plunged them in and out. As her hot cunt squelched before my very eyes, and she shuddered to climax after climax, I thought I'd died and gone to heaven.

It was sometime later when I finally reached my ultimate goal. Both now stripped naked in the sweaty storeroom, Sally lay back on boxes and cartons as I entered her dripping cunt. I could feel the walls of her pussy contracting as I rode her. Her ginger cunt lips slid up and down my stem. I had to pause now and again to watch my cock thrust in and out because it not only felt so good, but it looked so good as well!

I rode her faster and faster, gorging on her swollen nipples, biting those pink buds until with one final violent thrust I shot my come right up inside her. She screamed at the top of her voice as she trembled to yet another climax.

She's quite a girl, my Sally, and every time we fuck, it's just as hot!

Gordon. Northumbria.

Alone At Last

Dear Linzi,

Cathryn was a petite blonde with a sexy figure, and big, innocent blue eyes. She was a college girl in her late teens and used to make a little extra money by calling once a week to help my infirm mother with the housework. Those Saturday afternoons were the highlight of my week. Cathryn was always very hard working, but she always took the time to give me a pleasant smile and a cheery word.

One Saturday afternoon in winter, it was absolutely pouring with rain when Cathryn had finished her chores, so I offered her a ride home. As she settled in the front seat of my car and removed her damp coat, I realized that this was the opportunity I had been waiting for. It was the very first time the two of us had been alone together. The heavy rain had made her long hair moist and tousled and her jumper was splattered with drops of rain. I couldn't help but notice her firm nipples sticking out through the jumper as I started the engine, put the car into gear and drove out of the drive.

We'd only travelled a couple of hundred yards when the rain got so heavy the wipers could hardly cope with the downpour. Cathryn suggested that we pull over for a moment. In the darkness with the lashing rain beating down outside the car, there was a sense of intimacy. Then without pausing to think, I reached out and took hold of Cathryn's hand. She didn't push it away; instead, she gripped it tightly, and then brought our clenched hands up to her mouth and started to kiss my fingertips. Within moments she was licking my fingers suggestively.

I unzipped her jeans and gradually slipped my fingers down her warm belly. She wriggled her bottom around so as to enable me to slip her jeans from her hips and get my first glimpse of her golden quim. As she slumped down in the chair, she whispered, 'Please, oh yes, please!'

She let out a throaty groan as my fingers brushed the lips of her cunt. She lifted her jumper to reveal her mouth-watering breasts. I lost no time in cupping them and licking her erect, sweet nipples as she lowered the passenger seat, lay down and closed her eyes.

By the time I had her jeans off she was begging me to fill her with my cock. She wrapped her legs around my bare back and gasped ecstatically as I mounted her, my cock sliding all the way in, my spunk-laden balls slapping against her creamy slit. She held me tight, her fingertips scratching up and down my spine, her warm breasts pressing against me as I made love to her smooth, furry pussy in the darkness surrounded by the pouring rain.

E.K. Scotland.

Tempting Trade

Dear Linzi,

Petticoat Lane, that's my patch. I only trade there on a Sunday, and sometimes trade ain't all I do! I've been told I'm a good looking bit of stuff. Nineteen years old, blonde hair, nice tits, long legs and me boat race ain't bad either. Most of the market traders I work with are geezers, or right dodgy boilers, so I can usually take me pick if I'm in the mood, and being a rampant little cow, I usually am!

The reason I thought I'd write to you is because one of the blokes down 'the lane' was chatting about you. Says you like to hear about right dirty goings-on. So get a load of this:

I was working at me stall feeling right randy when this tasty bloke was having a look over me gear. I sell shirts, ties, jumpers, trousers, all for blokes. Most of me customers are geezers, but this one was something special. Bit of a toff, but right good looking with it. He bought loads of stuff and then he asked me what I was doing later. I told him I pack up at four, so if he'd like to come by and pick me up then he could take me for pie and mash.

It was pissing down with rain when he came back. I had almost finished clearing me clobber away, so I told him he could keep dry by slipping out the back with me. I've got this tiny curtained-off bit at the back where me customers can try on the strides if they want to. I had my back turned to him out back while I was packing the last of me gear away, and when I turned back round to him he had his chopper in his hand! Bloody lovely it was! I took off me woolly gloves and grabbed hold of it. It was nice and fat and throbbed in me hand. He stuck his hand up me skirt and started to finger me fanny. Made me cunt all juicy. Then he stripped me naked, handed me a rubber johnny and told me to put it on his dick, because he intended to fuck the arse off me. Posh bloke like that talking all dirty to me got me cunt all twitchy!

I slipped the johnny on his fat dick, then he grabbed me, turned me around, bent me over the chair and slammed his rubbery dick right up me in one big shove. He rammed it in and out, fucking me faster and faster, fucking me like a bloody steam train until I started coming. I was screaming and shouting like crazy, cos I'm a noisy little bitch when I have a good shag, and that definitely was a good shag! I reckon he'll be back for more this Sunday. I bloody hope so!

Sharon. Rainham.

Going Up!

Dear Linzi,

I have followed your career for more years than you'd probably think prudent to mention. Let's just say at least a decade of excellence with your good self has been enjoyed. Now I have never written to you before but last night you were so vivid in my dreams that I felt compelled to tell all.

I visited a friend in a flat in Putney. He lives on the top floor and has a lift. I got in on the ground floor and just as the lift doors were about to close, you rushed in. I pushed the buttons so the doors slid back to let you in. You looked fabulous in a leopardskin dress slashed to the waist, and skintight on your voluptuous body. I could hardly believe I was that close to you. The lift doors shut and the lift moved upwards. It moved very slowly, then even more slowly and ground to a juddering halt. You looked at me in bewilderment, your eyes wide and scared. I pressed the buttons, trying them all, but it was no good we were stuck.

You shook your head with disgust then took a portable phone out of your handbag. It appeared to be working, so you called your friend on the seventh floor and asked her to call someone to get us out. In the meantime I rang the alarm bell. That done, we sat down in the corner and made small talk. You bunched up your knees in front of you, and just for a second I got a glimpse of your panties. You sensed that I was staring and gave me a little smile, and told me that we might as well use our time wisely and enjoy ourselves. With that you spread your knees to reveal your panties. With your thighs wide open I just stood there drooling, seemingly nailed to the floor.

It's only when you pulled your knickers off to the side, rubbed a finger all over your pussy lips, then offered it to me, that I sprang into action.

Lying on my tummy, I feasted on your honey-flavoured cunt. You took hold of my head and rubbed my face all over your cunt. My cock was positively boring a hole in the ground as I licked you to climax.

The lift had a kind of rail all the way around the wall, so when you recovered, you climbed up on that, spreading your legs wide against the side and back walls of the lift. You released my cock and demanded that I fuck you. And of course I did! Standing on tiptoes so as to be able to reach your cunt, I plunged it inside your hot hole. You felt even better than I ever imagined. Your lips sucked me in, holding my cock as I pounded into you until I spunked all over your smooth brown tummy.

It was another hour before we got out of the lift and by that time my cock was red raw from having pumped you relentlessly. You were every bit as animal as you appear in the mags. You seemed completely insatiable and just loved having my cock inside you.

Micky. Catford.

Any Time, Any Place, Any Where

Dear Linzi,
My wife is one of those hell-horny bitches who loves to fuck. Anytime, anywhere, anyplace, that's her motto. So, as you can imagine, I am one happy man. She is not only incredibly sexual, but she is also very beautiful. She is twenty-five years old, has a perfect figure with long, slim legs, slender belly, fabulous bouncy breasts and a glorious hairless cunt. We've fucked in alleyways, over the bonnet of the car, in graveyards, in cupboards, in railway stations, you name it, we've done it. Last week she made me fuck her on the top deck of a double-decker bus!

She plans it out so meticulously. While I'm at work, she works part-time, as a typist, then comes home, races around doing the housework, then sits playing with herself thinking of

133

new sexual games to play. I never know what's going to happen when I get home from work. Last week she came up with the bus scenario. She checked out a particular bus service and found out that a good venue for this fantasy of hers was on a bus that terminates at Worlds End, Chelsea. That was where she set her heart on getting fucked, so naturally I obliged.

We parked the car and boarded the bus at around nine-thirty in the evening at Knightsbridge. We selected the seat at the very front of the bus up on the top deck. She had dressed carefully for our premeditated fuck. She was wearing a loose-fitting dress with no undies and a long wrap-around coat. There were quite a few people on the bus behind us, but that didn't stop her resting her head on my lap, releasing my prick and engulfing it in her warm, wet lips. A few swift sucks and my hands were up between her thighs making her snatch good and wet. As usual her cunt was soaking. My probing fingers encouraged her to ease over on to my lap. With one hand she guided me inside her. Her cunt muscles awarded my prick a delightful squeeze as I entered her. I rolled her fat cheeks gently up and down, while her hairless minge caressed my shaft. I thrust my hips up to meet her, giving her every inch of my rod. I wallowed in every squelch of her pulsating pussy as it grew hotter and tighter.

All too soon I felt my cream bubbling in my balls. She reached behind her and grabbed my legs hard. I felt her long nails gouge my flesh through my trousers and knew that she too was climaxing. In the nick of time really because behind us I could hear a cheeky cockney voice saying, 'Fares please!'

Nicholas. Fulham.

Late Night, Open-Air Screw

Dear Linzi,

My boyfriend Colin and I are avid readers of *Penthouse* magazine and big fans of yours. I am a nineteen-year-old girl who is regarded as quite a looker. Colin is every single girl's dream – tall, lean, with shoulder-length hair and a cock like an oil rig. He only has to look at a picture of you to get an instant hard-on. Our screwing has always been great, but recently we engaged in a session that was the best yet.

A friend of mine was throwing a twenty-first birthday party and invited us both. I dressed like a complete tart in a short, black, leather skirt, black stockings and a white, loose-fitting top. I had no bra or panties on.

The party was okay. I had lots to drink, but Colin didn't touch a drop because he was driving. We left quite early as I wanted a good screwing. So on the drive home I leaned over and took out my fella's cock and began to wank it up and down and lick the end. It became too much for him, so we pulled over on to the grass verge. By this time I had a mouthful of come and expected Colin to screw me in the car as soon as he was hard again. However he pulled me out of the car to the grass, pulled down his jeans and pants and pushed his cock into my mouth again.

'Suck it again and this time use your nails,' he said.

I had done this many times as I have very long fingernails which Colin likes me to rub into his arse cheeks as I suck him off. I did as I was told until he was rock hard. At this point Colin led me to the back of the car. I took off my top and skirt. I was cold, but I didn't care, I wanted my pussy to be screwed hard and fast. Colin pushed me over the boot and squeezed hard on my tits, and then screwed me like a dirty dog on heat.

We went home soon after and sucked and fucked all night. Linzi, if you fancy a late night, open-air screw, Colin is your guy!

L.L. Coventry.

Wild in the Woods

Dear Linzi,
I hardly believe the sexual antics that some of your correspondents say they get up to. It's probably sour grapes because nothing that exciting usually happens to me. But last week it did. There's this girl at work that I've fancied for months – Kate. Kate looks like a dream with long, strawberry-blonde hair, pouting lips and gorgeous big tits, and she's only eighteen. I

135

finally plucked up the courage to ask her out for a picnic last Sunday and she agreed.

It was a sunny day when I picked Kate up. She was wearing a skimpy top and denim shorts. Her bouncing breasts looked magnificent pressing against the thin fabric of her T-shirt, and her legs looked brown and slender. She looked good enough to eat.

We set off to a beautiful wooded retreat, a local beauty spot that still is quiet and unspoilt. We parked, chose a spot and made ourselves comfortable. I started to open a bottle of wine, and Kate, stretching out on the blanket beside me, asked if I minded if she sunbathed topless. I nodded and grinned at her as she unfastened her top to expose these amazing bristols. She grinned back at me, noticing, I suppose, that I couldn't stop staring at her bosoms. Taking her left tit in her left hand, she leaned towards me and offered it to me nipple first, saying, 'Like to try?'

I wasn't exactly sure what she had in mind, but before she could utter another word I had that gorgeous nipple in my mouth. I undid her shorts and wriggled my fingers inside. I let my fingers explore her soft pubic hair, before moving lower and finding her wet opening.

'Take them off,' I urged.

She nodded, then closed her eyes and threw back her mass of golden hair. I pulled her shorts off her plump bum then slipped my fingers into her hot honey pot once more. She felt so juicy as I found her clit and flicked it gently.

'Let me feel your tongue,' she murmured, opening her legs wider.

Clamped between her hot little thighs I was awash with her juices and her sexy smell. I parted her red-blonde fur with my tongue and licked up and down her slit. She grabbed my head and pushed me hard towards her, riding my face, smothering me with pussy and trapping my head between her legs when she wrapped her legs around my shoulders.

I came up for air and asked if I could fuck her. She was speechless, in an orgasmic stupor from the efforts of my tongue. She nodded her head and closed her eyes again as I positioned my pink knob at the entrance to her lovehole. Her cunt welcomed me in and she moaned with every thrust of my cock. We rolled over onto our sides so that my cock slid in her sideways at an angle and I could feel every bit of her smooth wet cunt. I pumped her long and hard, changing positions frequently, finally ending up with her on top, her bouncy breasts slapping up and down as the last few thrusts sent us both to heaven and back.

So next time I promise I won't be so cynical!

Ian. Sussex.

9. MOUTH-WATERING MAMMARIES

The fortunate girlies who possess these valuable assets enlighten us to how much fun they can have with their big, bouncy boobies. And, the guys who are so enchanted by heaving, hefty hooters explain why they get turned into quivering jellies by the mere sight of them!

PROUD POSSESSIONS

MORE THAN A GENEROUS
   HANDFUL

EROTIC ENCOUNTER

PLEASE SEND ME YOUR
   TITS

A PERFECT PAIR

GETTING YOUR OWN
   BACK

FANTASYGRAM

I WANT

BIG BREATHS

Proud Possessions

Dear Linzi,

I suppose you could call me a late developer. One moment I was as flat as a pancake, and then within a few months I had been dealt a glorious heaving bosom. Not that I was aware just how valuable these hefty assets were going to be, never conceiving just how much fun I could have with my mammoth mammaries, gigantic jugs, mighty melons or titanic tits. But, call them what you will, when my breasts swelled out to a 38DD cup, I had the boys queuing up for a quick feel.

Unless you're the proud possessor of big, heavy tits, you'll never really know the pleasure they can give a girl. But I know you weren't at the back of the queue when it came to tits, Linzi! Perhaps the guys reading this will also immediately recognize the unbelievable ecstasy generated when a penis is installed between two pleasure-filled pillows. That's one of my favourite sex games. You see, although my tits would almost certainly be placed in the enormous category, that doesn't mean they're not sensitive. Oh no, I've got very large nipples that stick out like bullets when they're squeezed and fondled in the right way. You know I can never understand these women who've got big boobs and despise them. I've got a pair of wobbling whoppers and I simply adore them. So do all of my men friends, which I can tell you is a pretty extensive group of fellas!

At the ripe old age of twenty-two I've been enjoying the luxury of playing the field. Aside from my hooters, I'm quite a sexy looking girl. Although my shape would always be described as buxom, I've a slim waist, long legs and shoulder-length brown hair. Quite a head-turner I've been called. One other snippet of information that I'd like to pass on to you, Linzi, is that like yourself I'm a raving nymphomaniac. I just can't get enough sex. I wake up thinking about it and if I'm alone I finger myself to climax in my sleepy, languorous state. And if I don't get a serious shagging every day, there's plenty of titty sucking and fingering to be done each night! Still, those days are few and far between because I'm lucky enough to have a stable of studs who give me exactly what I need.

I've got four blokes that I'm seeing at the moment. All of them 'tit' men, enamoured by my sugar-sweet swingers. You should see the expression on a guy's face when I slowly unbutton my shirt. I've got it down to a fine art. I reckon I could be a striptease artist. I get the guy to sit down somewhere very near to me, but just out of touching range. Then I seductively unfasten my top to reveal my bulging bra. Having such big boobies, I always have to have a good brassiere, an underwired one. I usually choose crimson red or just plain black, and I always go for a front fastener.

When I've removed my top garment, I then really go to town on my tits, caressing them through my bra, hooking one out over the top to let my man see my swollen nipple. It's usually at this point I thrust my exposed tit into my mouth. Yes I can do that. It's a fabulous feeling to be able to suck your own nipples. Of course I know just the way I like it. I roll my tongue all over my rosebud until it's sticking out all firm and hard. Then gasping, my lips all wet, I go to work on the other one. At this point in the proceedings I can usually detect a nice hard protrusion in my fella's pants!

When both my nipples are erect and strawberry pink, I finally release my breasts from my bra completely. I do this incredibly slowly, firstly, holding each breast in my hands before letting them swing free. By this time my sex partner should have his rock-hard dick in his hand ready for action.

Now I've told you all about my gorgeous globes, what I look like, what it is that I enjoy sexually, so now I want to turn your readers on, Linzi, by writing about some very intimate details of my sex life. I'm sure that you and your randy readers will enjoy the explicit information that I want to reveal. And besides if you're a man who's never experienced the joys of seeing bouncing breasts slapping together as a voluptuous woman straddles you to orgasm; or never savoured the delights of thrusting to and fro between two squelchy, sticky, giant boobies as you ascend to spunk time; or never feasted your greedy mouth on tits so gigantic that cramming them into your guzzling gob is just too big a task to tackle, then you are going to love this part of my letter. The readers who have sampled some or all of these delights will no doubt wallow in the memory!

Last week I had the best sex of my life with a guy called Rob. I was out on the town with a couple of mates of mine. We were doing a bit of a pub crawl. I was dressed up to show off my titties of course. It was a warm night and I was wearing a very slinky, tight, red dress made out of Lycra. The neckline plunged almost to my waist, making my copious cleavage look something like the grand canyon.

Well I'd only been in this bar about ten minutes when this attractive man sauntered over and offered to buy me a drink. I could tell he was trying desperately to avert his eyes from my devil's dumplings, so I leant over towards him a little and kind of thrust them in his face!

After that Rob changed tactics. He couldn't take his eyes off my bristols, and now he made no bones about it. As he steered the conversation in a sexual direction, I looked him up and down. I estimated him to be in his mid-twenties. He was around six feet tall, had short black hair, cut close to his head, big eyes, and a very sexy full mouth. He had a way of licking his lips when he talked that started to make my pussy dribble. Of course what he was actually saying helped.

Running his tongue all over his bottom lip, he told me, 'I've never seen or felt such a beautiful big pair of breasts before.'

'Would you like to?' I offered.

'I'd love to,' he said almost salivating. He went on in a whisper, 'I'd love to feel my balls, full up with juice, slapping against them.'

The mood had definitely changed!

Completely unshockable, I placed my right hand on my left breast and gave it a gentle fondle as I played along. 'So you want me to strip off and squeeze my fleshy, full melons together and permit you to penetrate the soft, sweaty . . .'

Before I could complete my sentence, Rob, hardly able to contain his excitement, uttered, 'Oh yes, please!'

'I suppose that means you'd like to spunk all over my face, would you? See your come trickling all over my chin? Or would you prefer to shoot your seed over these lovely suckable nipples?' I teased in a breathy undertone.

Rob was visibly trembling, 'Oh God, yes!'

'Well what are we waiting for?' I smiled. And taking him by the hand, I led him out of the public bar.

Outside the door lay a cobbled alleyway. There was not a soul in sight.

'Let me?' Rob begged.

I knew exactly what he wanted. What all the guys who crave my tits want. A quick feel and a quick taste. Having a quick glance around to check we were all alone, I leant back against the wall and told him we must be quick. I eased the dress from my shoulders, hooked my right tit from its place in my cherry-red brassiere and stuck out my tongue towards my bared breast.

Seconds later his hands were all over me. Our tongues entwined as we slobbered on my strawberry bud. My breathing came hard and heavy as I felt one of his warm hands move up between my parted thighs. I let out an excited squeal as his fingers traced my crack through my panties. He didn't waste any time, as he dragged my knickers off to one side and zoomed in on my clitty. The sensation of our mingling tongues, and the pressure on my burning clit was enough to send me right over the top. I bit hard on my nipple to stifle my cries as I felt spasms rippling through my body.

Still shaking violently, I felt Rob lovingly replace my breasts into my dress.

'I'd better get you home,' he said.

I could hardly wait!

Home for Rob was about a fifteen-minute drive away. All the way home we talked dirty to each other and Rob drove one handed for part of the way to enable him to caress my heaving bosom whenever possible.

By the time we made it to Rob's bedroom it was still only early evening so we had plenty of time to make this a night to remember. I told Rob to make himself comfortable on a chair a few feet from the bed. I went straight into my routine.

Rob sat down and fixed his eyes on my body as I knelt on all fours on his bed. I faced him and gave him an eyeful of my swinging tits still caged in my bra and dress. I moved from left to right to allow him to watch them sway from side to side.

'Want to see?' I teased.

Silently he moved his head up and down. His hands were already unzipping his flies.

I dropped both shoulder straps and, sitting back on my heels, started to squeeze my tits through my bra. My erect pink nipples peeked through the lace. Robert now had his big fat cock in his hand and he was stroking it very slowly.

'Nice and easy!' I murmured as I undid the clasp on my bra. Proudly I took out my breasts one at a time. As I did I could hear Rob groaning. I pushed both of my heaving hooters together and massaged them vigorously. Then I bent forward on to all fours so he could watch them hang down. 'Like to shove that big dick between these?' I asked.

Rob was on his feet. Together we discarded his trousers and pants and then I lay back on the bed as he got to grips with my tits. First he used both hands to push them together, kneading them enthusiastically, his tongue frantically licking them as he buried his face in my gigantic jugs. I could feel his stiff cock probing my tummy to remind me of the pleasures to come as he feasted on me like a starving man.

'Let me feel those balls slapping against my tits,' I urged.

Rob was there in an instant, holding my bouncing bazookas in position as he jerked his cock between them. His fat dick was already moist as it poked into the heavenly chasm fashioned from my wobbling tits. Now it was his turn to shake and shudder. I felt a hot gush of sperm slide between my sweaty slappers and come to rest on my neck. Robert in a frenzy, released his dick and let the last few spurts ooze over my engorged, pinky nipples.

Rob only had to play with my titanic tits for just a few seconds to get his cock on the up once more. Then, bending me over the bed on my hands and knees, he took one of my dangly boobs in each hand and rammed his cock between the lips of my lubricated lovebox. He pumped me hard and fast, his cock filling me up, making me scream with euphoria as I clenched him inside me. I craved his cock even deeper in my hole, so I asked him to change position. I straddled him, lowering myself onto his pole-like prick, my pussy lips gaping open, my knockers swinging from side to side uncontrollably. The expansive movement of my gigantic jugs, coupled with the thrill of bouncing up and down on his bone-hard dick had us both coming a few moments later. My tits slapped up and down and rocked from side to side until our hips met for the final time and with impassioned screams and squeals our sex juices mingled.

Linzi, if in reading my letter you can derive a mere fraction of the excitement that I enjoyed that night of lust with Rob, then my guess is you'll be a little bit wet between the legs?

Lorraine. Bath.

More Than a Generous Handful

Dear Linzi,
How does an average guy get a date with a dreamboat like you? Okay, I don't! Only playing with you, Linzi – I wish! Thought you might like to hear about my very horny girlfriend. We've been together for about a year now and sometimes I can't keep up with her. She wants it every night and every morning. Sometimes in the morning I miss my train because she won't take no for an answer. She is twenty-eight years old, has bobbed dark hair. She has one hell of a hairy fanny and a real protruding pussy mound. Her tits are 36C, so they're more than a generous handful. She loves to have her nipples played with and she can come by just having them sucked and kissed. Her favourite sexual position is riding on top. I love to watch her gorgeous tits swing free as she slips up and down my cock. You know I don't really want a date with you, Linzi, Carol is enough woman for me!

Tim. Sussex.

Erotic Encounter

Dear Linzi,

I thought that I'd never have an erotic encounter exciting enough to be able to write in to a magazine, but now I have, so here it is:

I work as a telephone engineer and although some of the lads muck around and tell stories about knocking off some of the horny housewives on their travels, to be perfectly honest, I never believed a word of it. But it does happen, well it happened to me last Friday anyway!

I was on call for a fault on the line, and so I turned up at this lavish country house in Surrey. I pulled in to the drive, thinking to myself I wonder what lucky bastard lives here, when the door was opened by a stunning buxom blonde who was no older than about twenty-two or twenty-three. I headed towards her and showed her my credentials. She flashed pearly white teeth at me and told me that she was Mandy, the lady of the house, and that I should follow her. I almost said that I'd follow her anywhere, but didn't bother as I didn't think she'd appreciate the joke, so I merely nodded and walked behind her into the house. Her back view was almost as appealing; her fluffy, golden hair hung down to her shoulders, she had a narrow waist, a wonderful round arse which was emphasized by the clingy material of her dress, long slender legs and a sensuous wiggle when she walked. Some lucky bastard not only lives in this posh mansion but he's got a gorgeous wife like this to come home to as well, I thought, as I followed her up the majestic staircase.

'I think you should check the phone in my bedroom first. I think that's the one that's playing up,' she told me in a sophisticated, yet husky voice.

'Fine,' I said and once again allowed my eyes to wander over her delectable body.

The bedroom was divine, decorated in pretty pink, with large billowing furnishings, a brass four-poster and creamy white, deep-piled carpets. She pointed to an ivory-coloured telephone on the bedside table and sat down next to me on the bed. I knelt down to the connection and went to work.

'You don't mind if I get changed, do you?' she asked in a sexy whisper.

'No, no,' I gulped still looking down at the socket. 'Candid Camera' and 'Game for A Laugh' flashed through my mind. Was this some sort of set up? I made a real effort not to look towards her, but soon the temptation became too great. I was trembling and making a right pig's ear out of the job, so I thought I'd just take one quick peep. My heart almost skipped a beat when I saw her standing stark naked just a few feet from me. Her tits were beautiful and huge. Her hands rolled over her pink nipples, down to her flat tummy and settled on her glorious golden mass of pubic hair. Her fingers combed through her fine curls. She saw me looking.

'Like what you see?'

'Yes,' I gasped, barely audibly.

This wasn't a joke. The next minute we were entwined on the bed. She made a beeline for my prick, flipping it out of my flies within a few seconds and clamping her pouty pink lips around my knob. I thought it was all some kind of wonderful dream as her lips slid up and down my rod, gently squeezing my balls and wanking me all at the same time. I'm not a bad-looking bloke but this was just too much. As she sucked me urgently I wondered if she really fancied me or if this was how she treated all the tradesmen. Who cares, I thought and then spurted all over her lovely face!

She asked me to fuck her in front of the mirrored wardrobes, so we lay down on the soft carpet and she rubbed my prick until it was good and hard again. I kissed her fabulous big tits, wriggling my tongue around her nipples. She bent over in front of me and I tongued her wet cunt and pink arsehole, before working my cock into her hot twat. I held a heavy tit in each hand and watched in the mirror. Her facial expressions were ecstatic; she loved watching me fuck her. Her giant tits bounced up and down with each jerk and she cried out loud as we climaxed together. Mandy was trembling and squealing, her eyes never leaving the visual image of sex in the mirror. I exploded, shuddering and shaking as a vibrant orgasm hit me.

After that she left me and went for a bath. I mended the phones, but I must confess I did it with my brain in overdrive, and my spunky cock tucked away in my overall not knowing quite what had hit it. Then she came out of the bathroom, all wet, gave me a big kiss and said she'd show me out!

Terry. Guildford.

Please Send me Your Tits

Dearest Linzi,

I think you're divine. I bet most of your letters start: 'Dear Linzi, I love your tits, can you please send me a picture?' My approach is different! Howabout: 'Dear Linzi, I love your pictures, can you please send me your tits?' You know I'm sure they would keep me amused for hours on end. I imagine just squeezing your big globes for a few minutes and then getting to grips with those lovely big nipples of yours. I'd slip them in my mouth, one by one, then I'd try to cram them both into my big gob all at once, slurping and guzzling on them like crazy. Perhaps then I'd get some baby lotion and spread that all over them, slowly working the cream all over your swelling nipples. Then maybe, I'd bury my head deep in them, only coming up for quick gasps of air, when I am really gagging for breath. But my ideal would be to slide my cock up in between them, as you so kindly squeeze them tightly together, so I could get a really good friction going up and down between those teasing titties of yours. My creamy come exploding all over them, would have me believing I'm in heaven!

A Linzi Tit Fanatic.

A Perfect Pair

Dear Linzi,

Two days ago I met this girl who's got the biggest tits I've ever seen. We've been inseparable ever since. We met at Brook Green, Hammersmith. I was happily walking along, just coming out of the pub, when out of the blue, Melissa ran past me. She was wearing a tight T-shirt and denim jeans. Her massive tits were out of control, bouncing up and down and from side to side as she chased after her dog. Like her knight in shining armour (well in jeans and T-shirt), I came to her rescue and helped her to grab her tiny Yorkshire terrier that was speeding off like some demented greyhound. As I handed the little chap back to her I tried to look at her face which as it happened is bloody lovely, but I just couldn't drag my eyes away from those tits. She didn't seem at all offended, just took hold of her nice little dog, smiled sweetly and introduced herself.

We went into the pub and I got her a drink. When I joined her at the table, I just blurted out, 'I've never seen boobs as big as yours!'

'Well you haven't actually seen them, have you?' she grinned.

'Well no . . .'

'Yet!' she giggled, placing a hand suggestively underneath one gorgeous giant breast.

That was how it started. I took her and her tits, and her dog home, and then the fun really got going. Just pulling off her T-shirt and feeling the hefty sway of her humongous jugs was enough to send my prick throbbing. I fingered a red nipple and slipped it over the top of her bra and guzzled on it greedily. Little by little she peeled her bra from her mighty melons. I smothered my face in them and ran my darting tongue over every surface, forcing a nipple into my mouth as my hands worked overtime kneading and massaging her wobbly breasts.

Of course when I stripped her, my dick was really hard. She lay on her back on the floor and took me in hand. Carefully she rubbed my knob end across her huge tits and puffed out nipples. I was already seeping, as Melissa used her elbows to squash her gargantuan tits together and I slipped neatly inside the wonderous gap between her warm knockers. The feel of those great bit titties engulfing my cock had me shooting what felt like gallons of come. The dirty little bitch only bent over and lapped up all my cream from her jutting nipples.

When I fucked her we did it leaning against the wall. I plunged in and out of her tight cunt, while holding a huge jumping tit in each hand. Sheer ecstasy! We've been at it for two whole days solid. In the first rest period I've had, I've written this letter.

Paul. Shepherds Bush.

Getting Your Own Back

Dear Linzi,

My husband loves big boobs but unfortunately I've only got little tiddlers. He never complains when we make love, but I know he likes big tits – his favourite wank magazines are always big-tit specials. Well I was under the impression that he was quite content playing around with my 34A breasts and looking at the biggies. That is until I popped home in my lunch hour and found him fucking the woman from next door. She's got whopping great tits!

My husband isn't working at the moment, as he was made redundant a few weeks ago. I work in the supermarket just up the road. Well I thought I'd nip home to see what he was up to, and I bloody wished I hadn't. There they were in my lounge cavorting naked on the floor, my husband Gerry swallowed up by Rita's big tits. I felt so jealous that I just slammed out of the house.

I was fuming all afternoon at work. I decided to get my own back, so before going home that night I called round at Rita's house to have it out with her. When she let me in, she was wearing a skimpy top and her big tits did look very inviting. I started off by giving her a right mouthful, then the next thing I knew I grabbed hold of her by the throat and started a fight.

We were fighting like cat and dog, and before I knew it one of Rita's great big tits was out and I was fascinated. I tweaked the nipple viciously and Rita shrieked in pain. Then I bit it, and she moaned softly. Her nipple started to swell in my mouth and it tasted nice. The very next minute she had her hands in my jeans and was reaching inside towards my cunt. I felt very emotional that this woman had just fucked my husband and she was just about to play with my cunt, but I could feel myself getting juicy and I gave in to my sexual feelings. I tongued her huge breasts while her fingers slipped inside me. Her vibrating fingers teased my clit and she brought me off in just a few minutes.

After that she told me that she was really very sorry about that lunch-time and that it wouldn't happen again. I said I didn't

mind as long as she was a bit more discreet, used a condom and
played with my clit again. She did, this time with her tongue!

Sandy. Manchester.

Fantasygram

Dear Linzi,
One of my favourite fantasies is to be seduced by lovely
Natalie Banus, dressed as a schoolgirl. It happens on my
birthday. I am alone in my flat watching TV when the door
bell rings. I answer it and Natalie is standing there in a
schoolgirl uniform trying to look innocent sucking a lollipop.
She asks me if I'm Ron. I am somewhat stunned, but I say I
am. She says she's from Fantasygram and that she's here to
give me a birthday to remember. So I invite her in. I'm
gobsmacked as I eye her shapely stockinged legs, her short
skirt and her straining 40-inch bust under a tight blouse. She
promptly sits on my lap and smothers me in sticky kisses, then
tells me she would love to bonk my brains out, but first she
wants to give me a blow job.

She goes down on her knees in front of me and feels the big
hard lump in my trousers, teasing me a little. She asks me to
stand up and proceeds to pull my trousers down. By this time
I'm in need of some relief. She kisses the bulge in my briefs,
then peels them slowly down. Kissing me gently up both legs,
she takes my now fully erect cock in her mouth and goes all
the way up to my balls. She starts to go up and down and I
moan and take hold of her head, running my fingers through
her long, soft hair. In a few minutes I explode in her mouth.

After a brief rest I feel myself getting hard again and I start
to kiss Natalie on her neck and lovely red lips. I slowly take
off her school tie, then unclip her skirt. It drops to the floor and
I run my hands up her nylon-clad legs onto her panties, and
squeeze her firm bum cheeks.

I turn my attention to her school blouse and unbutton it to
reveal her big, firm breasts which are nestled in a low-cut lace
bra. I squeeze and kiss them gently and take her bra off. She
pleads with me to screw her and I say, 'Don't worry, I'm going

151

to screw the arse off you!' I turn her around and bend her over the arm of my leather sofa and start screwing her from behind. I start off slowly, then my thrusts get more and more forceful as she grips the sofa and screams with excitement.

After about twenty minutes, I can tell that she is coming. Her body starts to tremble and she writhes around ecstatically. I withdraw my cock, turn her around and squeeze my erect cock between her breasts and I tit fuck her for a while, then explode all over her 40-inch tits.

Ron. West Midlands.

I Want

Dear Linzi,
Regarding breasts, I love red nipples on small or large breasts. I find them so arousing, and adore the feeling of my swollen knob against bullet-hard nipples and then spunking all over them. Also I like big-breasted girls pushing their breasts together with their fists or their hands to make them swell and puff out. The sight of a bare-breasted woman doing this gets my pants stretched to the limit. I'd really love to give a lovely, busty lady a good poke and feel her breasts rubbing against me. I'd also really like to find a nice girl with a big, fat bum. I'd pull her knickers down to her knees, get her to bend forward so I could wank my penis and spurt my warm, sticky cream onto her bare buttocks. I'd cry out with ecstasy as I ejaculated my come all over that fat arse of hers.

B.H.

Big Breaths

Dear Linzi,
I'm not embarrassed to admit that I'm a tit man. I love gigantic tits. Tits so big they almost look deformed! I love them. Here's my 'Big-tit fantasy':

One afternoon when the weather is hot and sunny, I drive out into the countryside just a few miles from my home in

Staffordshire. I pull into a picnic area and get out of my car for a stroll. Then all at once I chance upon this vision of loveliness, sitting alone at a picnic table. She is a buxom brunette wearing a cheesecloth top that is pressed tight to her beautiful bosoms and her lovely nipples are poking right through. I glance down her body and notice she is wearing a shortish skirt of the same flimsy material. She hears me approaching and turns around to face me. As she swivels she lifts one leg over the bench chair and I get a wonderful flash of her cunt. She is knickerless!

She smiles and invites me to join her. I waste no time at all, and once I am seated I can't take my eyes off her huge tits that are pressing against the nearly transparent fabric of her blouse, and pointing straight at me. The more I stare at them, the larger the nipples become. All of a sudden I feel a warm hand on mine. She grabs my hand and places it between her legs. Her thighs are dripping with her juices and she has a big, swollen clit. She shudders at my touch and starts to whimper as I caress her with my fingers.

She wants me to suck on her massive tits, so she climbs on the table and I fingerfuck her with one hand, while alternating the other hand and my mouth on her delicious breasts. My cock is set to erupt in my boxers, so I take it out and this horny woman obligingly allows me to slide in between her big breasts. She lays on her back and pushes them firmly together, leaving just enough room for my dick. The feel of her soft flesh on my cock is unbelievable. I thrust back and forth, all the while playing with her clit, fingering her warm, wet slit until I'm coming, my spunk splattering over her huge bosoms.

I greedily lick it all off before moving down her body and taking her tasty clit gently between my teeth. I suck on it until it becomes bigger and bigger and she is climaxing again and again. She screams out to me that I must fuck her. She turns around and kneels up on the table, her arse high in the air. I stand with one leg on the bench chair, the other on the table, and, grabbing hold of her bare buttocks, I plunge my cock deep inside her. Her cunt feels tight and hot as I bang her harder and harder. I take hold of her fabulous hanging tits, the harder I fuck her, the more they bounce. She is loving every minute of it, savouring every inch of my dick. Suddenly she is having one almighty orgasm. Her climax brings about mine and I squeeze her divine nipples and shoot my load right inside her lovetunnel.

Jim. Stafford.

10. ORGYTIME

Could you bear the thought of sharing your marital bed with your spouse and lover simultaneously? Or how does attending an orgy where you indulge in non-stop sex with whoever, whenever, grab you? Perhaps you have wild fantasies about taking on eight sex partners in a Jacuzzi? Believe me, the debauched bunch who sent me these letters have done all that and more!

Two Men and a Naughty Lady

Dear Linzi,

Just when you think life is becoming a real bore, some element of excitement seems to materialize just in the nick of time. Know what I mean? Well that's exactly the way I feel about my sex life right now.

Firstly let me put you in the picture and enlighten you as to the kind of girl you're dealing with here. I'm Deidre, Dee to my friends, I've just turned twenty-four years old, hail from south London and I work as a secretary for a large legal firm. I'm reliably informed that I'm something of a 'looker'. I stand five feet six inches tall in my stockinged feet (although I reach an impressive five feet ten inches in my spikiest high heels), have shoulder-length, honey-blonde hair, oval green eyes, pouty lips, full hips, a slender waist and a biggish, firm pair of tits, if I say so myself!

Previous boyfriends. Well there aren't that many that are worth mentioning, but I suppose I've had my moments. There was Tommy who had a very persuasive way with his tongue but disappeared to go and work on a bloody kibbutz. Then there was Greg who had a massive cock and loved to talk dirty when he fucked me. Unfortunately he exited my life when he teamed up with some dizzy 'Page 3' girl. And of course there was Michael. Now he was one of those men who unleashed an insatiable animal-like passion in me. Every single time I laid eyes on him I wanted to unzip his flies, whip out his cock and feel it probing between the folds of my pink, wet pussy. Michael caused me no end of problems though. The idyllic situation of carnal lust for each other being blighted only by the fact that we worked closely together. We even had our first fuck during a tea break in a stationery cupboard. Michael just pulled me inside with him, clamped his lips to mine and soon had my soaking panties round my ankles. However, this was not a situation that could continue. I take my job very seriously and was probably in grave danger of being given the sack if fate hadn't taken over. Michael, my fabulous lover, got transferred to Scotland and is now no doubt poking his pleasure-filled tool between the cheeks of some other lucky legal sec. as he bends her over his accounting system. So that was the end of another beautiful friendship.

But my motto is as one door closes, another should open and that is exactly the reason this story is being written. At the grand old age of twenty-four there are obviously some sexual avenues still awaiting my exploration. One particular sexual game that I was desperate to play was the concept of taking on, servicing, being fucked by, call it what you will, two men at one time. The idea of savouring two cocks at once makes my mouth water. One fat greedy dick slipped between the lips of my juicy cunt while another probes my mouth. I could just imagine the sensation. My tongue sliding up and down a rock-hard shaft, while delicate fingertips squeeze those bouncing hairy balls. All the while being on all fours, firm hands gripping onto my rounded arse cheeks, as a red-hot dick slams into my twitching pussy. The sheer thought of it makes me juice-up immediately as you've probably already ascertained!

And just last week I managed to fulfil that fantasy.

One of the girls in the office was leaving, so an after-work drinks do was arranged in a local wine bar. There was about thirty of us from the office, mainly girls, and we ordered up lots of wine and set about the process of a piss-up and a good time. Wearing a cool white suit adorned with gold buttons, and featuring a tight skirt that stopped short about four inches above the knee, I parked myself on a bar stool and chatted with two girlfriends.

Some time during the early evening we were joined at the bar by two guys who were dressed in dark business suits. I found both John and Chris very appealing. John was about six feet tall, had short dark hair cut close to his head, soulful brown eyes and a wicked lopsided smile. His buddy, Chris, was blond. He had long, flyaway hair, big blue eyes and pearly white teeth. He was a little shorter than his mate, about five feet eight inches or nine inches and looked as if he worked out. Something clicked in my brain when we got talking. The conversation was rife with sexual innuendo and the atmosphere oozed sensuality. My two friends just faded from my attention as I familiarized myself with these two attractive men.

By the time the three of us had downed a bottle of champagne, I was ready to leave with them, eager to take them back home to my flat. I knew what I was doing was perhaps not sensible, but I wanted them, I wanted them both so badly my pussy ached.

John drove. Chris sat in the back while I rode in the passenger seat up front. As we travelled along the Brighton road, Chris reached forward and started to massage my neck. I relaxed and slumped down a little in my seat. I felt a tentative hand brush against my inner thigh. Giving John the green light, I spread my legs and wriggled the hem of my skirt brazenly up around my hips. My white knickers were already damp as John started to stroke me through the sheer material. I could feel Chris nibbling on my ear, his hot breath on my neck.

'Stick it in me!' I squealed as the fabric of my panties was drawn aside and fingers sank into me. With two fingers buried inside my wet slit, John manoeuvred the car expertly, frigging me vigorously, all the time his thumb working my clit. I closed my eyes and screamed in ecstasy. 'Stroke my clit. Oooh just like that! Oh I'm going to come, I'm going to come!'

My eyes tightly closed, I had unbuttoned my bolero suit jacket, enabling me to play with my nipples through my lacy bra. I squeezed my breasts hard as a burning fire exploded in my quivering cunt and I shuddered to a euphoric climax.

Somehow or other we made it home safely. I brushed down my skirt and led the two men through the garden gate, all the while experiencing the warmth of the juices that trickled down my legs. As I put the key in the door John stated in a strident tone, 'You are going to get well and truly fucked, young lady!'

I reached over, and stroking the massive lump in his pants, I grinned at both men like a cat who has just got all the cream and whispered, 'I really do hope so!'

The threesome was all I could ever hope for!

Once inside they stripped me quickly, warm hands and soft fingers caressing me all over. The prospect of two dicks inside my mouth made me tremble with anticipation. Once both John and Chris were unbelted and unzipped, I held a cock in each hand. Alternating my greedy lips from first left to right, I sucked first on one and then the other. I was able to get quite a good rhythm going as I stroked them simultaneously, my slithery tongue ever active, my mouth feasting on their knobs.

Between mouthfuls I uttered in an urgent whisper, 'I want you both to spunk on my face. I want to feel all that hot come spurting in my mouth, dribbling down my chin.'

A matter of mere seconds later my desires were fulfilled. John let out a full-throated cry as he shot his creamy load right down the back of my throat. I gagged before swallowing every last drop.

'Suck me! Suck me!' grunted Chris as his sperm bubbled up out of his dick all over my face and oozed down my chin to splash on my pink-budded breasts. I felt four warm hands reach down to finger my swollen nipples.

Pushed back on the sofa with my leg thrust back by my ears, I now enjoyed the sensation of two tongues surrounding my bulging clitoris.

'Taste me. Lick it up,' I gasped. My voice thick with sexual excitement. As they slobbered over my cunt, I squashed my heavy tits together. My nipples felt like bullets as my whole body started to spasm.

'Oh my god, I'm coming!' I squealed as they lapped faster and faster drinking my juices.

A few minutes to compose myself and I was ready for the *pièce de résistance*. I bent over one arm of the sofa. Chris stood before me, thrusting at my face, his engorged cock still slippery from spunk and saliva. My full lips swallowed it all up, taking him deep into my mouth. My back was arched, my arse thrust in the air, not only was I ready to indulge in a little cocksucking, I was ready to be fucked. By this point in the proceedings, I was so horny I would have begged and pleaded to be fucked.

However that wasn't necessary. I could feel the tip of John's cock as it nuzzled the lips of my pussy. Holding his cock, John teased my hot slit with it, gently rubbing it all over my pussy. With Chris still pumping away in my mouth, I reached between my legs and opening my wet lips wide, I guided John's beautiful rock-hard prick inside my pulsating pussy. The first sensation of penetration sent shivers throughout my entire body and encouraged me to gobble with more enthusiasm on Chris's cock. The whole experience of controlling these two men, their two cocks thrust inside my body was a little too much for all of us.

Within a few minutes I released Chris from my mouth, his spunk splattering on my face as I once again felt my climax bubbling under the surface. This time I started coming like never before. My orgasm was so intense that it commenced at my toes and rippled through my body, manifesting its exquisite delights in my throbbing cunt. I felt a hot gush of spunk fill me up, my knees turned weak, and my tongue was a blur on a big red knob, although at this stage in my frenzied passion, I hardly remembered to whom it belonged!

That was just the first time. Then Chris politely put forward the proposition that I straddle him and impale myself on his fat cock while his mate sucked on my jiggling breasts. A suggestion that proved amenable to all three participants. Great stuff! A little later we three indulged in some interesting oral play before both men were ready, willing and able to fuck me again, and again and again! As you can imagine we continued on into the night.

So, in conclusion a fabulous time was had by all, and my sex life, since palling up with John and Chris, can be described as anything but mundane!

Dee. Croydon.

Wet and Wild Wednesday

Dear Linzi,
Being sandwiched between two women in bed has always been a dream of mine. I never thought it would ever happen, but it did, and your forum seems just the place to show it off.

I was getting a bit worried about my weight. I passed thirty a few months ago and so I thought it as good a time as any to join a gym, keep myself in trim, know what I mean? Anyway

I was all set to join a gym, when a leaflet was pushed through my letterbox. Scanning through the brochure, I noticed that my local club were offering a special price on aerobic classes. It appealed to me greatly and the following Wednesday night I was there eager and ready.

Well it is quite obvious that the usual attendants at such classes are female, and I'll go one further, they're females dressed in tight swimsuits, leotards and the like. I like a woman with a bit of meat on her as well, so I suppose deep down I saw this aerobics class as a chance to put me amongst the girls. I was surprised that there were a couple of other blokes there, but the class was predominantly female. Most of the women had quite trim figures, you know with nice gentle curves that look all the better for being dressed in crotch hugging leotards and leggings. I own a dazzling pair of electric blue cycling shorts and I cut quite a dashing figure in them. I was delighted to notice one or two interested gazes from my work-out mates.

The class was quite relaxed. The instructor, Marie, put us through the paces. She was an attractive woman probably about the same age as me. I jumped and danced around to the music finding it all quite exhausting but fun nevertheless.

After forty-five minutes of vigorous exercise Marie told us that we'd finished for the evening. I bent over the water fountain to get myself a drink and that was when I was joined by two hot, sweaty females, Sarah and Anne-Marie. The three of us clicked and I became so suggestive to them in a matter of minutes that they giggled like crazy and told me they knew a place we could go.

They took me to the ladies changing room. I sneaked in feeling somewhat sheepish but with an enormous horn. Taking over I got both girls into one shower cubicle and started to strip them. Sarah had lovely pert breasts with firm standy-out nipples, while Anne-Marie had full, ripe heavy breasts. In the confined space I was surrounded by beautiful boobs, all the while the girls stroked my Lycra-covered prick. Sarah was the first to release me and stick me in her mouth. Her mate soon followed suit and got down on her hands and knees to join her girlfriend in the cocksucking stakes. Two women sucking on your prick is something that has to be felt to be believed. I make no apologies for the fact that I shot my load over them in a matter of minutes.

After that we turned on the shower spray and squashed together, the warm water cascading over our nakedness. While Sarah and I exchanged feverish, wet kisses, Anne-Marie climbed aboard my prick, wrapped her long legs firmly around my back and slithered up and down my length until she was satisfied.

She climbed off still moaning, and no sooner was my prick free of her hot, twitching cunt, than I felt another one opening up for me. Sarah wanted it now. So while Anne-Marie slumped to the tiled floor of the shower room still whimpering softly I gave it to Sarah, rear entry. Whilst I thundered away, screwing for all I was worth, I could feel nimble fingers kneading my balls. That did it! I came and came and came!

So I got my dream, it wasn't in a bed and unfortunately it's only been the once. The last two Wednesdays neither of the girls have turned up for class, but I live in hope!

Norman. Canvey Island.

A Little Bit of What You Fancy

Dear Linzi,

I thought I would write to you and your readers about an experience I had last weekend. My wife and I are fairly broad-minded, but were getting bored with our regular sexual habits. Whilst making love one evening, I suggested inviting a friend of my wife's along. Sue agreed immediately, and I told her to organize it for the next night if Jill, her friend, would like to join us.

The following evening, on returning home from work, Sue told me that she had spoken with Jill and that she was coming around at eight o'clock. I was very excited at the thought of having two women together at the same time, and as eight o'clock approached, I couldn't wait to get started. I told Sue to take off her jumper and I reached out and stroked her firm, rounded breasts, rolling her nipples between my fingers. At that moment the doorbell rang, and I left Sue sitting on the couch and answered the door. It was Jill, as expected. She smiled at me as she came in saying, 'I hope you're ready for me!'

I replied that we were and showed her through to the lounge. When she saw Sue naked to the waist, she said, 'I hope I didn't interrupt anything!' and Sue said, 'Of course not, he just couldn't wait!'

I laughed, I was feeling very randy and my penis was getting larger by the second.

I asked Sue to take off the rest of her clothes and walked round in front of Jill. She took off her coat and dropped it to the floor, as I reached out and unbuttoned her blouse. She too was braless and I stood and gazed at her bare breasts for a few seconds before bending my head down to kiss them.

I broke away after a minute or so, and got undressed, as did Jill. She reached out and took hold of my erect cock and ran her fingers up and down my shaft. She licked her fingers then peeled my foreskin right the way back, exposing the red throbbing head of my cock.

Sue said, 'Suck him off Jill. He loves a good blow job!'

Jill got down on her knees and licked gently at the tip of my cock for a while before taking it right inside her mouth. I looked around at Sue. She was sitting on the edge of the settee, wanking her fingers in and out of her pussy. When she saw me looking at her, she stood up and came over to us. Jill was still sucking gently on my penis as Sue slipped a finger inside Jill's pussy, then ran it across my lips. I licked the juice from Sue's finger, which was the final straw. I shot my spunk straight down Jill's throat. She swallowed five or six times and then said, 'That was great, did you enjoy it?'

I said I had, and Sue said it was now her turn!

Sue told Jill to lie on the floor and spread her legs wide apart, exposing her succulent, wet pussy lips. Sue bent her head down between Jill's legs and began to lick her pussy lips. Slowly she moved her body around until her cunt was above Jill's face. Then she lowered herself down onto Jill's mouth and was met by her tongue which flicked in and out until Sue's cunt was pressed right up against Jill's lips. They carried on like this for about ten minutes, then Sue gasped, 'Les, fuck me from behind!'

I moved around behind her. Jill was still licking her out, and

163

as my cock approached its target, she reached around and opened my wife's cunt allowing me to slide right in to the hilt. With Jill's face still below me, I started to thrust in and out, but after a couple of minutes Jill asked me to stop, and with my cock still inside my wife's cunt, Jill kissed and licked my balls. This felt so good that I couldn't take it for long. I pulled my cock almost right out of Sue's cunt and then thrust in just four or five times before I came for the second time inside her. Sue gasped and moaned and I knew that she too had orgasmed.

I pulled out my cock and a line of spunk stretched from its end back to Sue's cunt. Jill broke it with her finger and then licked the end of my limp cock until it was clean. After that we had a little rest then carried on. I fucked Jill, Sue fucked Jill with a dildo, Jill sat on my face while Sue sucked me off, Jill and Sue both sucked me off at the same time, we just went on and on.

In the early hours of the morning Jill had to go home. I returned to bed with Sue and we discussed the night's events and swapped opinions on Jill's genitals and breasts, comparing them with Sue's. We got a bit of sleep and then made love twice in the morning, and Sue suggested I write to you, which I have now done, thoroughly exhausted from an eighteen-hour sex ordeal!

Les. Leyland, Lancs.

Four Men in a Jacuzzi

Dear Linzi,

I've just got back from my holiday visiting my sister in Australia. For twenty days out of my three week holiday I was a good girl, but on the last day I just went wild. My sister's got a houseful of children, so as my husband's well off, I decided to stay in a posh hotel.

All throughout my vacation I resisted the advances of the hotel manager who had the hots for me, but it was in the hotel's health club that I succumbed to temptation – and there were four of them. Actually there were eight, but I only managed to get fucked by four. They were all members of the Australian

National Sports Team. I won't tell you what their sport was or that would give the game away. I got screwed by four members of the team in the Jacuzzi. Sitting on those warm jets of water, always makes me feel so raunchy, and what with eight well-built, husky, sportsmen surrounding me, well I just gave in. One minute I was savouring the sensation of forceful water gushing against my swimsuit-clad mound, the next thing I knew my top was down and I was fingering my big brown nipples. Naturally the guys in the spa bath joined in.

Before long, I had hands all over me, squeezing my nipples, playing with my arse, and fingers slipping inside the crotch of my costume, poking in my hot snatch. There was one bloke that I particularly fancied, and it was him that I allowed to remove my swimsuit. I kept below the bubbles of the water and wriggled over onto his lap. His fat prick was soon exploring the opening of my rampant minge, ramming its way deep inside me as he gripped my waist and jerked me up and down his meaty shaft.

While I was bumping and grinding to seventh heaven, all the other team members played with me. It was unbelievable sex! After I came twice and he spunked inside me, I slid off of his meat, and clambered on to the next stiff pole waiting to penetrate my red hot cunt. I fucked four of them before other guests seemed to work out what was going on. Then I think I realized just how naughty I'd been, so I hurried back to my room, taking the first guy, who I fancied like mad, with me, of course!

Maureen. Essex.

Cornucopia of Sex

Dear Linzi,
Forget acid-house parties - last week I went to an orgy. I've never experienced such a cornucopia of sex acts. I was sucked and gobbled by at least a dozen females, young and old, and I got to shaft three of them. I've been invited to another next week. I only hope I have the stamina!

Bobby.

Three's Not a Crowd

Dear Linzi,

On a recent holiday in Spain with my husband Todd, I sampled troilism and lesbianism for the first time. We travelled to the Costa Blanca with a neighbour, Wendy, a merry widow who owns a holiday apartment there. The great sex all happened so naturally and it was the most enlightening sexual experience of my entire life!

The very first day on a deserted beach when my hubby went off in search of some cold drinks, Wendy suggested that I sunbathe topless. She also warned me to be careful that I didn't burn my nipples, and then proceeded to smooth oil all over my pink buds. As she rubbed the hot liquid onto my breasts I felt myself blushing, but I could also feel an amazing tingling sensation between my legs. I looked directly at her and she leaned forward and planted a big kiss on my mouth. She pushed me back onto the towel, and still kissing me, started to press her jutting nipples against mine. Soon she climbed on top of me and our slippery bodies rubbed together. Her tongue probed in and out of my mouth and I could feel her hot breath mingling with mine. Then, very precisely, she wrapped her legs around mine until our two pussies were scissored together, and holding on tight to me, she thrust her cunt hard into me until we were both damp and orgasmic.

That was the first time. I didn't tell Todd at this stage. Plenty of time for that. That night we all went to a posh hotel restaurant for a meal. I was still feeling horny, not for Todd, but for Wendy. Although I'm sure he could have persuaded me to enjoy his body, what I really wanted was a taste of Wendy's quim.

Halfway through the evening I announced that I was going to the loo and Wendy said that she would like to make a visit too.

As soon as we were in the ladies, I looked at her and said, 'I don't know what's come over me, Wendy, but I want to lick you!'

She grabbed hold of my hand and pulled me into one of the cubicles. She lifted her skirt and slid her hand into her knickers.

I could hear that her pussy was wet. When she removed her hand, she held her forefinger outstretched to me and I sucked on it longingly. She tasted wonderful. Her aroma was so sexual that I almost came at once. I felt completely overcome with passion. That's the only excuse I have. I sank to my knees and with Wendy squatting on her haunches above the toilet bowl, I started to lick at her gaping cunt hole.

Five minutes later her lovejuices were all over my face, dribbling down my chin, and I had fingerfucked myself to orgasm. We kissed each other's mouths hungrily before I asked Wendy if she fancied a night of sex with Todd and me. She did. And Todd was quite keen on it too!

By midnight it was all arranged and we were back in the apartment. I was feeling merry and very sexy as Todd took me in his arms and kissed me. I reached down and started to undo his flies. Wendy joined us, and between us we got Todd's trousers and undies off. Wendy went down on her knees and started to gobble the base of his cock and lap at his balls, while I kissed and wanked him just the way he likes it. When I could tell that he was on the brink of coming, I told Wendy and we both held his cock and wanked his foreskin back and forth until he was coming all over the place.

Then Wendy asked my husband if she could eat my pussy. He just nodded excitedly and sat back on the sofa. I lay with my head on his lap as his fingers caressed my breasts. Wendy slipped off my juice-stained knickers and spread my legs. At first she used her delicate fingers to slide up and down my slit, spreading my wetness all over my cunt. I mouthed to Todd to suck my nipples as I felt a hot tongue on my clit and a gentle finger slide up my cunt. Wendy fingered me, pumping two fingers in and out of my hairy cunt, while her other hand stretched open my lips allowing her ravenous mouth to feast on my clit. I was in ecstasy.

As the evening progressed it got better and better. By the end of the evening I had been sucked, fucked and fingerfucked to orgasm after orgasm. Todd had managed to spunk about half-a-dozen times. He didn't know what had hit him. The three of us finally fell asleep together at five a.m.!

Gilly. Dartford.

Addicted to Blondes

Dear Linzi,

I would like to tell you about this wonderful fantasy that I have about yourself and the delicious Dane Trine Michelson.

I adore blondes, I don't know what it is, but I can't resist them. I'm especially addicted to blonde pubic hair. I'd happily die smothered in it! Anyway, back to my fantasy. You and Trine are great friends and often when your busy work schedules allow, you spend an evening together. On one of these evenings you are at home relaxing with Trine, sipping wine and having a girls' gossip night, when I knock on the door selling double-glazing. (That's not what I do, by the way!) Firstly you peer through the crack, with the door on a chain, but I convince you that I'm only doing a job and you agree to spare me five minutes.

As I enter I notice that you are both dressed erotically. You are wearing a red minidress, bare legs and high-heeled shoes, while Trine is wearing a tight leopard-print dress with white stockings and high-heeled shoes. You tell me to sit down and Trine fixes me a drink.

I am just about to go into my sales pitch, when you both sit on the floor on either side of me and I feel two pairs of soft hands stroking my legs. As I glance down, your hands work up towards my thighs, moving up to what is now a bulge in my pants. I gulp down my drink and lay back as you both unzip me and release my knob from my pants.

I'm soon in ecstasy as I feel two tongues darting up and down my shaft, your two beautiful bodies leaning over me. As you both suck me, I manage to slide the top of Trine's dress down and squeeze her tiny tits between my fingers. She gasps with pleasure and continues to suck me even more enthusiastically. You lift up your skirt and give me a good glimpse and whiff of your juicy pussy. Then, pantieless, you climb across me and position yourself right in front of my face. Obediently I stick my tongue in your golden honey pot. This is usually my first climax in my fantasy.

The real climax to my amazing fantasy is when I bend you both over the sofa so that both your juicy pussies are ready for me. I take it in turns to slide my stiff knob first inside you, then just as you reach your peak, I pull out and shove my stiffie right up to the hilt in Trine's tempting slit. Absolutely mind-blowing stuff!

Gordon. Rochester.

Getting Along With Your Workmates

Dear Linzi,

This is my fantasy involving two women that I work with. I have never been with two women at once, but I'm sure I could handle it, given half the chance! I work in a car hire showroom and working alongside me are two gorgeous receptionists – Gail who is twenty-two years old with a great body, long dark hair and blow job red lips, and Yvonne who is in her mid-thirties, very slim and sexy with short blonde hair. The two of them are great mates and tend to wind me up as they are well aware of how much I fancy them both.

In my wildest dreams I take them both to a swish hotel. We dine in style and then take a bottle of champagne up to the suite. Gail puts on some music and we begin to dance. Slowly we strip each other out of our clothes and I press my hardness against her. Her big, pouty lips descend on mine, her tongue flicking around my mouth as she runs her fingertips through my hair and rubs her big, bare tits against my chest.

Meanwhile Yvonne is reclining on the sofa. She has her legs apart with a hint of pussy showing on one side of her frilly knickers. Her pert tits are poking over the top of her low neckline. She takes the half-filled champagne bottle and rubs the neck of it across her cunt. She starts to ease it into her hole, so I go to her, sink to my knees, place her legs over my shoulders and froth the fizzy champagne inside her. Thirstily I drink from her cunt. Gail kneels beside me, pokes out her tongue and joins me in a celebration drink of Yvonne's lovejuice. Together we work the bottle in and out of her slot, frigging and sucking on her dribbly crack until the randy blonde begins to shudder to climax.

Gail moves up to kiss her friend's mouth enabling Yvonne

to savour her own cunt juices. I elevate Yvonne's arse and then lower her juicy pussy onto my stiff eight inches. I hold her around the middle and bang her fiercely as Gail works on Yvonne's bullet-hard nipples. Yvonne's cunt is so wet that my dick slides in beautifully. She screams that she likes to be fucked hard, so I slam it into her. Gail who is determined to get in on a bit more of the action climbs on the back of the sofa and spreads her legs for me. She fingers herself frantically as I fuck her mate to climax.

I've got to close now, Linzi, as it's all getting too exciting. Needless to say I fuck both of my horny workmates until they can hardly walk. Got to stop now as I'm in need of a wank!

L.O. London.

11. SEXUAL CONQUESTS

In this chapter, lustful sexpots recount in detail some of their favourite and most outrageous sex. There's Tracey who screws four tradesmen in one day, Colin who gets treated like a sex object by a rampant stripper, and Natalie who prevented her husband from going to work, just because she wanted him to fuck her all day long. Read on!

Yellow Peril

Dear Linzi,

My friends call me the yellow peril when I'm zooming around in my racy Volkswagen Corado. I bought my dream car just a few months ago, saved up for it all on my own, so I'm very proud of it. It's a four-seater saloon car, but it's got that kind of sleek, sporty appeal, and it's quite a head-turner. I'm sure it was instrumental in helping me to pull this right good looking bloke the other day.

It was a lazy Sunday afternoon and the sun was shining gloriously in a cloudless blue sky. The perfect time to take the yellow peril out for a spin. I always like to look good when I'm driving my flash car. There's no point in having smashing wheels if I don't look the business as well, so I tarted myself up. I washed my long, dark hair, applied a little make up, sheathed my slender body in a see-through white dress and completed the enticing ensemble with suede boots. I was raring to go!

The engine purred as I turned the key. Once out of my garage and on to the open road, I put my foot down and revved up through the gear box. I opened both windows slightly, so I could feel the soft breeze ruffling my hair. My pink nipples swelled up like bullets and nuzzled against the fine material of my frock. I felt vibrant and alive driving my nippy little car along the windy lanes deep in the heart of the Surrey country-side.

I'd only travelled a couple of miles when I spotted him. He was conventionally tall, dark and handsome, decked out in skintight cycling shorts and a singlet vest. I certainly took my eyes off the road when I spied this gorgeous hunk of manhood leaning against a crumbling brick wall. I glanced hastily in my mirror, it was all clear, so I screeched on my brakes, jerked the car into reverse, and was very soon parked up on the grass verge alongside him. Close up he looked even more delicious. His bulging muscles rippled and his wavy, black hair was moist, and curled into his neck. He was exhaling briskly and his body appeared damp with sweat. He was obviously out for a run and having a breather. I hit the electric window switch and the remaining glass in the door buzzed and disappeared inside the door panel.

'Fancy a lift?' I ventured cheekily.

His face lit up with a broad smile. I noted he had dazzling, pearly white teeth. 'I shouldn't do really, but I've covered around ten miles already, so what the hell!' he said, making his way towards the car.

As he eased open the door of the Volkswagen, I could smell his fresh sweat. It made my nostrils tingle pleasantly. He settled himself into the front seat. I handed him part of the seat belt and introduced myself: 'I'm Sherrie by the way.'

'I'm Billy, pleased to meet you, Sherrie. Nice car you've got here.' He smiled, his hands brushing against mine as he accepted the belt strap.

'Thanks. I thought you runners aren't supposed to stop. You know, you have to warm up and warm down because of damaging the muscles or something?' I remarked.

'Yeah, that's right. I think I've just strained a muscle in my leg. How come you know so much? Do you run?'

'Only from blokes I don't fancy!' I laughed and slipped the car into first gear and was off.

'Where are we going then?' I asked.

'Anywhere you like, I'm not in too much of a rush. I'm staying with some friends of mine round here and they're not expecting me back at any special time. What did you have in mind?'

I smiled wickedly as all of a sudden what I had in mind suddenly hit me. It hit me right between the legs!

'I'll take you to a quiet country place I know!' I announced looking him square in the eyes.

He smirked naughtily as he told me, 'I'm all yours!'

What a pleasure!

Now I'm not usually that promiscuous, but Billy reeked of pure sex; it was all that sweat and power. I just had to have him. As I drove along I could feel the sexual tension building between us. It was as much as I could do to keep my hands off his lithe, toned legs each time I changed gear. I was very wound up by the time we reached the back entrance of Chorley Farm, a favourite fucking spot of mine. Now that makes me sound like I'm a right tart. Let me explain, Linzi. I usually take my regular boyfriends there, not good looking, sweaty joggers I've just picked up off the street!

Anyway, as we drove into the deserted gravel driveway, Billy reached over and grabbed my hand. He lifted it to his mouth and kissed it tenderly, then using his tongue he started to suck and nibble the tips of my fingers. I braked hard and leaned back in my seat to savour his butterfly kisses. In between running his tongue around the palm of my hand, his eyes met mine and he said huskily, 'Back the car into that big barn behind us.'

Using just one hand I did as directed, and manoeuvred the yellow peril into the vast outbuildings, pulled on the handbrake and cut the engine. Billy hurriedly unclasped my seat belt and started to explore my body with his hands.

'You want it, don't you?' he rasped.

'Yes I want you to fuck me,' I moaned ecstatically as his hands surrounded my nipples and squeezed my pink tips.

He peeled off the top half of my dress and started to caress my neck with his tongue. His mouth teased my throat and worked its way downwards to the curve of my bosom. His searing tongue sought out my erect nipple and circled it. He rolled his tongue all over one swollen bud before engulfing it with his wet lips. Shivers ran up my spine as I watched with delight as he released my enormous engorged nipple, which was bright pink and still shiny with saliva. With both hands he squeezed my cupcake breasts together in order to cram both into his hungry mouth.

'Spread your legs!' he demanded, and I willingly complied. His hands snaked inside my skirt and came to rest upon my transparent white panties. 'My, my, you're so wet. Are you going to let me take your knickers off?'

'Please, please!' I squirmed as I felt his firm hands tugging at my panties.

Hastily they were discarded and his paws were all over my

sex. My cunt was oozing like never before as he spread my lips and worked a finger in and out. As his finger slid easily into my juicy hole, I reached over and grabbed the waistband of his shorts. Without too much difficulty I wriggled them down his thighs. His beautiful long cock flipped out, standing up proudly against his taut, bare belly. I grabbed it at the base and used my other hand to wank his throbbing shaft.

'Want me to suck you?' I whimpered through gritted teeth, the movements of his probing fingers exciting me towards orgasm. I do so love giving head, and he had such a handsome cock that I just couldn't wait to fill my mouth with his exquisite length of meat.

In a tangled embrace, with Billy's rampant cock gripped in one hand and his fingers still embedded in my squidgy cunt, we scrambled out of the car. He rested his heavenly tight buttocks upon the bonnet of the yellow peril and I squatted on my haunches before him. I opened my mouth wide and welcomed him between my lips. I love to look a guy right in the eye when I blow him. Billy's blue eyes shone with ecstasy as I swirled my tongue all around his knob. Saliva dribbled from my mouth as I lapped his length, massaged his spunk-laden balls and sucked him, giving him everything I'd got. I was so turned on that I just had to reach down between my legs and finger my inflamed clitoris.

'I want to come!' Billy shouted loudly, obviously bubbling up to the boil.

'Spunk all over my face, let me taste it!' I screamed and moved up a gear, frantically licking and lapping at his knob, my hand wanking his phallus and my clit simultaneously, and with extreme vigour.

All of a sudden jets of spunk hit the back of my throat, I guzzled greedily, swallowed hard, then withdrew my mouth. A couple more blobs of spunk hit my face and trickled down my chin. Wiping my mouth, I smeared his sticky jism over my aching nipples. In a whiny, little girl voice I asked, 'Will you lick my pussy, Billy?'

A moment or two later I was laid on my back in the soft hay. My boots were wrapped around Billy's neck as he eagerly made a meal of me. He used both hands – one on top of my pubes, to grab handfuls of my cunt mound, the other to toy with my hothole as his persistent tongue licked every surface of my raging cunt. His nose rubbed against my clit hood, his teeth nibbled my slippery lips and I felt an orgasm erupting from within. I grabbed him roughly by the hair, shoved my pussy hard at his face and wriggled my climactic cunt all over him. By the time I'd finished with him his entire face was smothered in my lovejuices!

And then he fucked me! Now it has to be said, blokes who can run ten miles have the stamina to fuck for ages, even if they have strained a muscle!

Feeling the way I did that hot, sticky afternoon, I just wanted to have my pussy filled for as long as possible by this sensual stranger. I just couldn't get enough of him. I lay on my tummy on a pile of tickly straw and arched my arse up expectantly. Naked, Billy crouched over me and stroked my throbbing slit with tentative fingers.

'Fuck me, please,' I urged.

The next thing I felt was the burning tip of his prick sliding up and down my creamy crack.

'You want it?' he teased.

'Yeah! Slam it all the way in! I want to feel your balls slapping against my arse. I want to feel your cock filling me to the brim,' I breathed. As I uttered the final part of my plea, Billy was already mounting me. Separating my round bum cheeks with his hands, he gradually forced his red hot meat between my quivering cunt lips.

'Oh yeah!' I cried out euphorically as his full length plundered my pussy. He started slowly, pumping me with long, hard strokes. He was so big he reached the uppermost point of my lovetunnel with ease. My cunt tightened around his magnificent member as we picked up speed. Resting on his powerful arms, he shafted me harder and harder until bingo, I was clawing my fingers through the straw, squealing like a maniac and shuddering with orgasmic delight.

But not Billy! No, Billy kept on going. I must have come six or seven times before he finally let go. Let go with such a fountain of sperm that whooshed up inside me and mingled with my hot come.

The sun had gone down by the time we both lay spent beside the yellow peril. I told you, Linzi, that my marvellous motor assists me in having such a good time!

Sherrie. Surrey.

Second Time Around

Dear Linzi,

Having seen your picture in *Penthouse* magazine offering up your well-shaped bum cleavage reminded me of an experience I had when an ex-girlfriend of mine decided she wanted to see me again. We had been dating for about six months, when she telephoned me and told me she didn't want to see me anymore. Then, two months later she rang me up out of the blue and asked if we could meet. Being an easy going sort of chap, I agreed. It was a bright sunny day and so we decided to go for a walk in the woods near her house. We'd only been walking for a few minutes when Denise put her arms around me and we started kissing. At first it was tender little kisses, but soon we moved swiftly on to open-mouthed kissing.

Denise reached down and felt the bulge in my trousers. My cock was growing stiff and excited, so I helped her to undo them. She went down on my cock stick and I brushed her long hair to one side so I could watch her suck me, up and down. I love to watch a woman's lips sliding up and down the length of my shaft. Denise's hands were softly kneading my balls as her tongue trickled all the way up to the head and circled it. She let go of my cock and looked me right in the eyes and said, 'You know why I called you, don't you?'

'You want me to fuck you,' I answered.

Taking another mouthful of cock, she had a good slurp before looking at me directly and saying, 'I really miss your cock. I want you to give it to me good and hard, baby. I want you to fuck my brains out!'

Denise had always been an enthusiastic partner before, but I don't actually remember her ever demanding it in such a manner. I picked her up, turned her around, and in one quick movement, pushed her down on her hands and knees, ripped

177

off her panties and felt for her slit. Her fanny was wide open and soaking.

'Do you want me to lick you out first?' I moaned as I probed two fingers inside her.

'No, I just want your cock!' she screamed, so loud that I'm sure nearby picnickers would also be aware of her requirements.

My cock was good and ready, so I wasted no time and glided my knob end between her ultra-sensitive lips.

'Oh, I love that cock, give it to me, baby. I want every inch of your hard cock,' she shouted ecstatically.

I had to let my mind wander to some tedious problem at the office so as not to spunk in her immediately. It wasn't easy controlling myself, but a few seconds later I had it mastered. Denise was now completely out of control, digging her fingernails into the grass, her back arched, her arse thrust out and her cunt spasming around my cock. Then I just had to shoot. Wow, my burning hot milk just kept on shooting up inside her twitchy twat.

We're back together now. I never really understood why we split up in the first place but that fabulous outdoor session seemed to do the trick. I must admit though, Linzi, I don't think I'll ever understand women!

B.K.

Wet Blonde

Dear Linzi,

I should like to write and tell your readers about a beautiful wet blonde that I picked up the other night. Being a sales rep, I travel many miles a year, and on this eventful evening, I was heading for London when I met Anna. My headlights stretched out in front of me, I suddenly saw this figure appear, my jaw dropped open as I spied this vision of loveliness standing on the roadside beside a car with the bonnet raised. She was drenched from a heavy downpour of summer showers. Her thick, honey-blonde hair hung tousled and damp down past her bare shoulders and her pale pink off the shoulder T-shirt clung to her pointy breasts. Immediately I slowed the car to a halt, opened the door and offered to help. The sensuous blonde introduced herself and asked if I could give her a lift home.

How could I refuse? I escorted her to my car and helped her on with the seat belt. As I reached over to fasten the belt, my hands brushed accidentally against her firm breasts. As the seat belt clicked, we clicked too. Her eyes met mine, and I could see that she was smiling wickedly. I stole a glance at her damp top and noticed how swollen her nipples were, each stiff bud poking fiercely against the thin fabric of her T-shirt.

'This is very wet,' she said naughtily.

'I've got a spare shirt in the back. Would you like to put that on?' I offered.

'Lovely,' she grinned, and with that she unfastened her belt, tugged the T-shirt over her head and sat brazenly in the front seat of my car wearing only her jeans. I reached over to the back seat to grab my shirt, but as I did, Anna caught hold of my hand and placed it on her naked breast. Her nipple was like a gobstopper, rock hard, and I started to caress it. I sucked it into my mouth and feasted on both nipples greedily while Anna busily unzipped my flies.

'What a lovely fat cock,' she cooed as she released me and lowered her head to my groin. Using her warm, sexy mouth, she slipped back my foreskin and lashed her tongue around my bell end.

'Let me play with you?' I begged, as her hot lips devoured my shaft. Her lips still clamped on my throbbing cock, Anna helped me tug off her jeans. She spread her legs and flashed her golden, wet quim. I savoured her expert tongue sliding up and down my pole as I squelched a finger in and out of her hairy hole.

It wasn't long before I had Anna over the passenger seat of my car. She was stark naked aside from her socks, her peachy buttocks thrust high in the air as I split her pink pussy lips with my ramrod cock. My cock thrashed hard and fast within her moist lovelips as I pumped her vigorously, her tight cunt, gripping my cock. Very soon I could feel my seed rising. I filled that sex-starved blonde bitch full of my cream. Then I took her home and did it again and again!

Gary. Bucks.

Early Riser

Dear Linzi,

What a great summer we are having. Fabulous would be the right word. I feel like standing naked under a nice cool fountain. I wonder if you'd like to join me?

The heat has really got to me these last few nights. I toss and turn alone in my bed. My cock full of fun, but with nowhere to go! But one morning I managed to get the wife at it. My cock rose and rose all night majestically, and early in the morning when the wife peered in, I was stark-bollock naked and needless to say my penis was standing up. She asked me if I'd got the shopping list. I retorted, 'Shopping list? Send me a nice, leggy Swedish girlfriend!'

The wife smiled at me, then put her hand around my shaft and locked my knob in her plastic rubber glove. It felt fine, especially when her other hand started playing with my balls. Her rubbery fingers wanked me slowly and steadily. For a moment I thought it was my birthday or I was about to get the OBE. I could hardly believe it; it had been months and months. She was all of a tremble and moments later stripped out of her housecoat, spread her fleshy thighs and impaled herself on my cock. I quickly shot my load. Then we reversed positions for a second jump.

Big Horn John. Walsall.

Her Indoors

Dear Linzi,

When I finish my housework I'm bored, bored, bored! Sometimes I'll spend my afternoons shopping, but I soon get fed up of that, because I can't really afford to buy much. Then last week I had this brainwave. I got out 'good old yellow pages' and started to ring around a few companies for quotes. And for one very exciting day I had them calling round. I could say they've all been coming around my house, because that is exactly what's been happening!

The first to arrive on my doorstep was a young bloke in his

early twenties (I'm twenty-nine by the way). He was just the type I fancy for a toy boy – tall and lean with sandy-blond hair, dressed in tight jeans and a T-shirt. He worked for a company that installed built-in wardrobes, so I took him up to my bedroom to show him what I supposedly required. As I was only wearing a pink nightie, it didn't take him long to get the message. One flutter of my eyelashes and a good flash of thigh and he placed his warm hand on my bum.

Moments later he was on the bed and I was tugging at his belt. I had his cock hard in no time and was soon crouching above him, easing myself up and down, taking his cock to the hilt in my fanny. As my next appointment wasn't until midday, I had all morning to play with him. I had him on the staircase and over the kitchen table before he offered me a very good deal on a complete bedroom unit! Not a bad start!

I just had time for a quick shower, and to change into a tight, black dress before my next visitor arrived. This one was completely different but fanciable all the same. I suppose he was in his early forties, dressed immaculately in a dark blue suit; he had short black hair and a closely clipped black beard. I've always had a bit of a thing about men with beards. The new arrival worked in kitchen fitments, and as we sat down together at the kitchen table, images of his tickly beard rubbing between my legs, as he enthusiastically tongued at my cunt, flashed through my mind. I suppose I must have been smiling because he asked me if he'd said something amusing. So I just came straight out with it and told him what I'd been thinking about.

At first he looked at me in utter astonishment. I suspect he thought me a cockteaser, but I proved to him very quickly that I really did mean business. I dragged him by his silk tie into the lounge and got to grips with him on the sofa. He lifted my dress, tore my knickers off to one side, and quickly unzipping his flies, he fucked me doggy fashion. Then knickerless, I sat down on a hard-backed chair, thrust my spunky crotch at his face and wrapped my legs around his neck, while he sucked my cunt until I was jerking around like crazy. His beard and tongue brought me off again and again. Then he left me with a mere twenty minutes to have a wash and brush up before my two o'clock appointment.

Funnily enough I never imagined that two might turn up together. What an added bonus, I thought, as I opened the door, wearing a cream, silky dress, peach undies and high heels. My cunt was feeling slightly sore but itching for more action. The two men followed me into the lounge where they intended to give me an estimate for an artex ceiling. They were both well-built blokes. The boss was probably about thirty-five, with short brown hair and a 'tash'. His mate was no more than a boy, probably about nineteen or twenty and he was something else! He had long black hair, Roman features and bulging muscles. I knew I was going to have some fun with those two! I told them I wanted the bedroom ceiling artexed and made sure that I led the way up the stairs, knowing full well that my tight dress rode up and showed off my bum.

Three-quarters of the way up I stopped and looked around at them. The older bloke had his eyes riveted to my arse cheeks, and his young mate was craning his neck to get a better look. I asked them if they were staring at my bum, and then smiling I lifted my skirt to give them a better look. Very naughtily I thrust my arse out as far as I could and reached back and slipped the gusset of my panties off to one side. By now my cunt was drippy and my thick black bush was damp with my juices. I felt two pairs of hands. One slipped three fingers easily into my open hole, the other massaged my cheeks, firmly squeezing my buttocks and pulling them apart. I was already almost at the landing of the stairs, so I laid down on the staircase and arched my arse up to meet their eager fingers. The older one started to pump his fingers in and out, while his colleague slipped his hands beneath me and rubbed me up and down my crack.

Soon the stairs became too restrictive, so we adjourned to the bedroom. The pair of them stripped off my clothes, stroking my tits, biting my arse and generally playing with my wet cunt. Just dressed in a suspender belt and sheer stockings, I lay back on my double bed, opened my legs and asked them to eat me. I spread my lips open for them and felt hands and drooling tongues all over me, nibbling, biting, licking, slurping. It was unbelievable, I felt like my cunt was on fire it felt so hot.

Suddenly I was coming like never before, and as my body trembled from orgasmic spasms, I felt a thick cock slide easily inside me. I opened my eyes to note that it was the boss who was mounting me. Still riding on the crest of a mind-blowing climax, I looked up and noticed that temptingly within range of my mouth was the young one's dick. What a beautiful specimen it was too, I couldn't get it in my mouth fast enough. The boss was building up speed, pounding me harder and harder, his clammy hands massaging my breasts viciously as he slammed it into me one last time. A warm gush of cream hit the back of my throat, just at the same time as I felt the guy that was fucking me shoot his fountain of sperm inside me.

The young stud was far too gorgeous to waste on just a blow job. I wanted him to fuck me, so when the boss rolled off, I went to work on the young man's prick. I held it at the bottom and slowly wanked him. He started to swell in my hand, so I encircled his knob with my tongue, trailing globules of saliva all over his shiny purple head.

In no time at all he was hard and ready. His boss laying on the bed, stroking his cock and watching intently while his young mate fucked me. I put on my high heels and let this beautiful hunk of man lift me off the ground and sink his cock inside me as I wrapped my long legs around his waist. His powerful arms and thrusting cock banged me up and down. I kissed his sensuous mouth, scratched his neck with my long fingernails and screamed out that I wanted him to fuck me harder and faster. It was fucking brilliant!

A perfect end to a perfect day? Not quite. After showing that randy pair the door, I had to get washed and changed and return to being a suburban housewife again. I picked up the kids from school, gave them their tea and sat down to watch *Neighbours* waiting for Art, my husband, to come home. As we sat watching TV all evening, my mind was on other things as you can probably imagine.

Tracey. Middx.

Let's Get Personal

Dear Linzi,

I work as a personal trainer at a gym, so you can imagine that I get my fair share of crumpet, but this girl I started training a few weeks ago is something else. First off, she has a spectacular body – big, firm tits, a taut muscular belly, a lovely tight arse and long, toned legs. She uses the sun beds at the health studio so she's even got a smashing all-over tan. She's got long, brown hair, very sexy eyes, is twenty-four years old and well on the way to being a nymphomaniac.

She's just joined the gym, so as normal on her first visit I took her on an induction course to demonstrate how all the exercise equipment works. Every time she got on a piece of apparatus I couldn't help but notice how brazen she was about spreading her legs.

A couple of days later she was back to use the gym, but she only seemed to want to go on the machines that enabled her to spread her legs and show off. She was wearing this electric-blue striped leotard that cut tight into her and exhibited the curved shape of her cunt. My eyes kept being drawn to it, focusing on the trickle of sweat or wetness that appeared before my eyes.

'You're staring at my cunt, Roger,' she said matter of factly.

I thought shit, I'm in trouble now, but instead she glanced around to make sure that no one was watching us, then she clamped her legs around my body and pulled me to her. She rubbed her cunt against my body, shut her eyes and frigged herself to orgasm, while I stood there like some dumb fuck!

'Fancy a fuck in the shower?' I asked when she'd finished using my body as a sex toy.

'Yeah!' she said, and that was that!

By the time we got into the changing rooms she had half torn off my clothes. I kissed her hungrily and pulled the leotard off her tits. Her nipples were pink and puffy. I licked them excitedly as she stroked my cock. My fingers wriggled inside the gusset of her leotard and found her wet gash. She was panting as we made it into the shower, her tight bodice still on the lower half of her body. I got down on my knees and she turned on the water. I slipped the leotard from her body and came face to face with her hairy quim. As the warm water splashed over us, I parted her thighs and stroked her clit with the tip of my tongue. She was growling and making a hell of a noise as I used my fingertips to spread her lips, then sucked on her bulging clitty. I stuck two fingers up inside her and she asked for more. Pretty soon I had four fingers up her and my tongue squirming all over her clit. She wriggled her hips, screamed out loud and climaxed joyfully.

The warm water splashed over our nakedness as I lifted her onto my rock hard prick. She threw her head back, held onto my neck and gripped me with her legs crossed around my waist. She kissed my lips hungrily as I thrust upwards, hard and fast. Her nails scratched my back as I started to increase the speed of my powerful thrusts. She started talking dirty to me, telling me her cunt was going to squeeze out every last drop of my come, and that pushed me over the edge. I spunked up her hot tunnel.

This horny young woman had really got to me and I wanted to fuck her again. We found an empty squash court and tucked away in a corner, I lay down on my back on the hard floor and pulled the crotch of her leotard to one side and she climbed onto my prick. She squatted above me, her strong legs lifting up and down, her big tits bouncing free as she fucked me. Her cunt felt tight and soft as suede.

After that we went to the bar for a quick drink, and she still wouldn't leave my cock alone, she kept squeezing it under the table. So then I took her into the ladies loo and fucked her rear-entry while she bent over the bog.

She comes to see me at the gym almost every other day now, and on each occasion I get to fuck her at least twice. I don't know about being her personal trainer, I might be more aptly described as her personal prick, but I'm not complaining.

Roger. Berkshire.

Misbehaving

Dear Linzi,
Ohhh I've been such a naughty girl and I've just got to tell somebody! It all started when the video recorder broke. Tom, my husband, rang the repair shop and they said they'd send a man around that afternoon. A likely story, I thought, but I was in anyway, so I just hoped for the best.

Well at three on the dot, just as promised, the engineer arrived. A fine figure of a man, about twenty-five years old, he had a cute smile and curly brown hair. He showed me his credentials, so I let him in, then shot off to the kitchen to make him a cup of tea.

A short time later I popped my head around the door to ask him if he took sugar, and I was astounded to see that the video now seemed to be working, and that the tape he had put into the player to test it was a porno movie. One of my favourites! Mesmerized I watched as a stunning blonde starlet on the screen devoured a lovely fat dong.

I watched for just a few moments then hurried back to the kitchen. I didn't know what to do. Obviously the workman was interested in the porno movie, and I naturally felt too embarrassed to interrupt him, but, ooh, I could feel my fanny twitching!

Standing with my back against the sink, I hitched up my skirt and felt my moistness through my cotton pants. I closed my eyes and let my fingers trace the line of my slit. I could feel my clit hardening, so I pulled my pants down to my knees and fingered my burning bud of flesh. I was so engrossed in my own enjoyment that I didn't hear the video engineer enter the kitchen and sink to his knees. It was only when his warm tongue poked into my hot slot that I realized that I wasn't alone.

'Oh, you wicked boy!' I groaned as he feasted on my cunt. His tongue flicked up and down my swollen lips while his hands roamed my body. Hastily I unbuttoned my blouse and unclasped my bra to let my boobs swing free. He grabbed them roughly as his tongue lapped faster. 'You're going to make me come!' I breathed, then shivered as a sensational orgasm ripped through my body.

I was still twitching and coming as he dropped his jeans. His erection sprang out, and he pushed me over the sink.

'Madam, you're going to get fucked!' he growled excitedly as his big dong slid between my cheeks and headed for home. My cunt quivered with delight as he banged me aggressively until my come and his were mingling.

I told you I'd been a naughty girl!

Anonymous.

Life in the Old Dog

Dear Linzi,

I am fifty-five years old and the managing director of a large company. Over the last ten years or so my sex life has dwindled to nothing. I entertain myself sexually by the odd visit to a prostitute, or a striptease show and I read magazines like *Penthouse*, over which incidentally the wife would have a blue fit if she ever found out. Well my non-existent sex life changed dramatically when my long-serving secretary was taken ill and was replaced with a temp.

Carol, my temp, was wonderful. She was in her early thirties, terribly efficient and very attractive. She'd come into the office wearing a crisp, white blouse over her rather large bosom, a pencil-type, knee-length skirt and high-heeled court shoes, which set off her great legs. She wore her long dark hair up in a ponytail, and her sweet perfume used to drive me wild when she'd lean over my desk or stand close to me.

With my frustrated sex life at home, very soon my fantasies were running riot with Carol. I'd dream of slipping my hand up her tight skirt to discover that her tights would be cutting into her hairy pussy and would be wet from her juices. It was only a few weeks after I had that thought, that I was lucky enough to fulfil my fantasies about Carol.

There was a bit of a party on for one of the chaps that was leaving, so of course Carol and I attended. We seemed to get on well out of the office, so I invited her for a meal afterwards, firstly ringing the wife and telling her that I had to work late.

Well after we'd had a couple more drinks we loosened up and Carol started telling me how sexually frustrated she was since she split up with her boyfriend four months ago. With that knowledge, I bravely ventured a hand under the table, on her knee, then her thigh, and then I went for gold!

Back in the empty office block Carol sprawled across my desk, while I buried my head in her crotch. I had removed her panties and was now biting my way through the crotch of her tights. Her fanny was so wet by the time my tongue found its way through to part the thick black hairs and dip my tongue

187

inside. She tasted like honey and as I sucked on her minge, I reached up and undid her blouse releasing her voluptuous breasts.

At fifty-five I'm still pretty nimble and soon after she had unzipped my flies I clambered on top of her, eager to bury my cock in her juicy fanny. She lay flat on her back, her legs sliding off the table, fixing her feet firmly on the floor, she eased my cock inside her. Once I was in her, she seemed to tighten her muscles to squeeze my cock. It sent shivers throughout my entire body and made my balls ache. I was so excited that I came inside her almost at once.

Within seconds of finishing, she was on her hands and knees taking my cock in her mouth. The ecstasy I felt as her smooth lips parted and encircled my knob was mindboggling. She ran her tongue up and down on the underside of my shaft, concentrating on my knob and then taking my balls one at a time into her warm, gentle mouth. I reached down and cupped one of her breasts. Her nipple looked delicious, pink and erect as I fingered it lovingly.

As soon as my cock was fully hard again, Carol bent over the desk and guided me inside her doggy fashion. As I made love to her, I held onto her smooth buttocks with both hands, drawing her right on to my cock, sliding it inside her as deep as I could. She seemed to be loving every minute of it, thrashing about and moaning in a low, husky groan. When she started to tell me how good my cock made her feel, well as you can imagine, I just couldn't hold back. This time I withdrew and splashed my semen all over her bum.

After that wonderful sexual scenario Carol and I worked 'late' in the office once or twice a week. If my cock wasn't tucked away between her warm thighs, it was being sucked expertly in her sensual, sugar-sweet mouth. Unfortunately all good things come to an end, as did my affair. My regular secretary returned fit and well and my darling sexpot Carol went off to temp elsewhere. We did keep in touch at first, but you know how it is. Not that I'll ever forget her. So for now it's back to whores, strip shows and *Penthouse*, but at least I know there's life in the old dog yet!

Jim. Yorks.

Just What the Doctor Ordered

Dear Linzi,

My name is Natalie and I wrote to you recently and asked you to send some goodies to my husband who has been rather poorly. I am writing to thank you for the photos and for the pair of black silky stockings which you sent him (and me!). It was great to see his face when he opened the package, and also when I explained to him what I had done.

Your package seemed to have the desired effect, as his lust seemed to return, and his spell of ill-health was forgotten in an instant. As you can imagine it was a case of straight back to bed (we had both just got ready for work). I slipped the stockings on (out of his sight), under my smart grey suit which I wear for work. I then went into the bedroom. Andrew was already lying naked on the bed, his cock slightly swollen in anticipation. I then stripped out of my skirt and jacket in front of him and gently fondled my breasts through my blouse. With my other hand I rubbed my pussy through my panties. Andrew got up off the bed and, kneeling before me, he ran his fingers up the back of my stocking-clad legs and rubbed my buttocks. He then slid his tongue up from my ankles to my stocking tops, taking in your body scent from your stockings. He nuzzled his head in my juiced-up sex before plunging his tongue deep inside my pussy. I let out a series of primitive grunts and groans as I became highly aroused. I honestly felt like Eve when she first tempted Adam in the garden of Eden. Needless to say we had the most incredible and erotic sex, and ironically we both had to ring in work and say we were ill, so as to be able to prolong our ecstasy. Thanks, Linzi!

Natalie.

Angel

Dear Linzi,

The other night I went along to a stag show at my local village hall with a couple of mates. It was the first time I'd been to that kind of thing. I'm sure you know the kind of evening I mean. There was a couple of comedians telling blue jokes, and there were three strippers.

The evening was really entertaining. The jokes were old, but still funny when you've had a few drinks, and the strippers were really horny, especially Angel, but I'll get to her in a minute. The first girl was black and was dressed in a PVC tight bodice, a Gestapo hat and thigh-length boots. Her bodice was crotchless and she seemed to get quite a buzz out of walking amongst the audience giving them a flash of her wiry black muff.

The next girl was very young looking. Only around eighteen, I reckon. She was dressed as a schoolgirl and wandered around the blokes posing provocatively and licking a big, red lolly. She stripped slowly down to virginal white undies and then returned to the centre of the stage. The best bit of her act was when she was just wearing her stockings and suspenders and she started to wank herself with her tie, pulling it up between her legs and manipulating her pussy lips. I was convinced she had an orgasm for real – if not she must have been a bloody good actress!

Angel was definitely the highlight of the night. She was the final stripper and a real stunner. She came on dressed in a slinky yellow dress and a black feather boa. Her long, blonde hair fell down her back and fluffed out sexily as she shook her head about and paraded around. At a guess I'd say she was in her late twenties. She had big, blue eyes and thick lips covered in red lipstick. She seemed to make a beeline for our table, and we all joined in cheering and trying to grope her. She came and sat on my lap, hoisted up her skirt and asked me to feel her stocking tops. My hands trembled as I touched her smooth, tanned skin. Just as she got up to move off, she winked at me and said, 'Meet me later.'

My mates were really taking the piss when I told them. They said she probably said that to one guy on each table and we'd all turn up at the dressing room like a right load of nerds. I was unsure what to do, so I shut up about it, sat back and watched Angel's show.

By now she had got rid of her boa, stripped out of her dress and was just wearing yellow undies and sheer-black seamed stockings. She bent forward and unclipped her bra; her scrumptious tits cascaded out and she looked straight at me as she toyed with her nipples. Then, taking a bottle of baby lotion, she squirted the white cream all over her tits. She walked towards me purposefully, then she spread her legs and straddled me. She took my hand in hers and put it on her creamy tits. She felt fantastic as I rubbed it into her nipples. They started to grow hard as I massaged them with my thumb and forefinger.

She grinned and was off. I looked at my mates as if to say, 'I told you so!' but they still weren't impressed, they still reckoned it was all just part of her act. Now I was getting a bit more confident and was sure she really did fancy me. Meanwhile her act was getting better and better. This time when she squirted the lotion she let it trickle down between her tits, run down over her bellybutton until it was moving towards her panties. She gripped her yellow knickers and held them away from her body so the cream could continue its journey. Suddenly Angel jerked her body excitedly. Although the audience couldn't see it, it was obvious that the cream was seeping through her pubic hairs. I could almost imagine my spunk mingling with her golden bush. Then Angel licked her big, red lips, stuck her hand down her knickers and started to finger herself frantically.

She lay down, facing us centre stage, and opened her legs wide. Her fingers were still in her knickers and she was wanking, seemingly oblivious to the crowd, just having a good time. Her knickers were so wet they had become transparent and you could actually see her sliding her fingers in and out of her cunt. My cock was getting bigger and bigger in my trousers as she thrashed about, the music building as she masturbated to orgasm.

Pretty soon she was there. She let out an animal cry and her body jerked up and down in spasms. Her eyes half-closed, she scrambled to her feet, slowly turned around, and with her back to the audience she bent forward and lowered her knickers. I could see how swollen her cunt was as her pink sex peeked out through her bum cheeks. Her clit was so big, I just wanted to lick it. She was no actress. Angel had definitely just wanked to orgasm in front of a hundred rampant men. Now my mind was made up, I was definitely going back to try to meet her.

She turned towards the crowd who had quietened down, they all seemed transfixed by this sexy woman. She grinned and walked towards me, then pushed her cunt soaked fingers into my mouth. Her aroma was sheer nectar. I sucked on her fingers and didn't want to release them. I wanted to start licking her cunt out there and then. She winked at me again and said, 'I'll see you later!' Then she was back on the stage, bowing, and then gone.

Ten minutes later, I was outside the girls' dressing room. There was a big bloke on the door, but he took one look at me and then waved me in. The other two girls were just leaving, but Angel was still undressed. She was wearing a pink towelling robe and was smoking a cigarette. I felt a bit of a jerk, but then she beckoned me over. As soon as I was near enough to touch her, she crushed out her cigarette and pushed me to the ground. She spread her legs and raised them up on my shoulders. Her golden pussy was bare and she told me to lick her. I parted her lips with my tongue and flicked my tongue along her slit. She was so wet and her cunt lips were ultra-sensitive and quivered at my touch. Her clit was still huge, so I took it between my teeth and nibbled on it gently. She told me that she hadn't been fucked for almost a week and that she was desperate for some dick. She wanted me and she wanted me now!

No woman had ever expressed their desire for me so forcibly. So I wasted little time. She took out my cock and I grabbed her by the arse and pulled her right towards the front of her chair. I raised her legs up onto my shoulders again and slammed it in her. As I fucked her she screamed wildly and played with my spunked up balls. She came twice before I let go inside her.

A minute or so later she told me to leave. Funny girl, treated me just like a sex object, but I couldn't give a shit. You should have heard me boasting to my mates about Angel, a real nice bit of cunt!

Colin. Norfolk.

12. RANDY REQUESTS

Over the years I've received in my mailbag all kinds of weird and wonderful requests – proposals of marriage, offers of torrid threesomes, applications from prospective porn studs who wish to be pointed in the right direction, cries for help and sexual advice, correspondence from inquisitive magazine readers who have a quest to find out more about my personal sex life, and of course naughty boys who crave my wet panties! Here are a saucy selection, complete with my replies.

Recurring Dream

Dear Linzi,

Please forgive me for I have sinned. I have not bought a copy of *Penthouse* for three months and have not written to you since April. Sacrilege! How can I ever repay you? I will accept any form of punishment you give me, my dearest, sweetest, sexiest person I know. Linzi, if you can forgive me I would like to share this fantasy that I've got about you, which by the way came about after several recurring dreams.

The setting is a really exquisite restaurant where I work as a waiter. One evening I notice that table fourteen is reserved for Miss L. Drew and her three guests for 8.45 p.m. Number fourteen is one of my tables and the manager has instructed me to cater for all your requirements and to treat you like royalty as you are a regular and popular customer.

At 8.30 the very best champagne is on ice and there are candles flickering away slowly on the table alongside a dozen red roses, courtesy of the management. Then it happens. In walks this stunning blonde who looks to be in her mid to late twenties. This has to be you, and you look absolutely superb. You are wearing a navy blue wrap around dress which is a touch revealing about the cleavage, and is showing off your stocking-clad legs to their full potential. I know that I am going to enjoy waiting on table fourteen tonight!

I help you into your seat, enabling me to get a good eyeful of your splendid boobs, and I can just make out a lacy bra. You instruct me to call you Linzi as you sexily cross your legs revealing plenty of firm thigh. As I move away you reach out and gently touch my bum, I can tell it's going to be a hard night ahead.

As I serve you the first course I notice while sipping your champagne you leave a cherry-red lipstick smear on the rim of your glass and I watch and enjoy as you run your elegant fingers up and down its stem.

As the night goes on, I cannot help but notice that your dress is opening up ever so slightly around your waist giving me a stunning view of your dark stocking tops and creamy thighs. I lean over to take your plate and one look at your heaving boobs gives me an instant hard-on, which nudges your right elbow. You know! With that knowledge you discreetly move your left hand over and slowly brush your hand against my cock through my tight trousers. Plates in my hand, I head off to the kitchen – bulge first!

All four of you get up and head towards the loo, but you catch me up to whisper that you are off to discard your knickers, and you blow me a sweet kiss.

Well, Linzi, this is where things get really funny. You know how weird dreams are. All of a sudden I am sitting at table fourteen in your seat. It is now your turn to serve me and as you stand next to me to take my order I slowly slide my right hand up the back of your nylon-clad leg and along a suspender. I caress your beautiful arse before slipping a finger into your soft, golden pussy, flickering it over your clitoris. You respond by unzipping my trousers and easing out my cock. Gently rolling back the foreskin to expose my purple end, you teasingly begin to wank me off.

I manage to pull your dress open, to take off your bra and gently fondle your magnificent boobs. You now lower your head down onto my lap and my cock enters your mouth, your teeth clasping my helmet, and your tongue darting over its eye. Wow!

Meanwhile as my left hand gently cups one of your tits, my fingers squeezing its erect nipple, two fingers of my right hand are thrust into your wet pussy, going in and out at the same pace as your distinctive head movements. I'm now fighting hard not to shoot in your mouth, but you raise your head and move away. You slip your dress off completely and reach towards me, easing down my trousers and my boxer shorts. From nowhere you produce a condom which you roll down over my stiff shaft, and positioning your right leg over mine, you lower yourself down, pussy first straight onto my shaft.

We now seem to kiss for an eternity as you wriggle your bottom around my lap as things start to hot up. You raise and lower your arse, my cock firmly gripped by the tight walls of your experienced pussy. I know that I'm about to come, but I try to hold out as long as possible while your hips are grinding down on my cock.

Next I lift you up onto the table, my cock still engulfed in your blonde lovebox. I fuck you quicker and quicker as your nails rip down my back and over my arse while you moan and groan, louder and louder. Then it comes. I call out your name, 'Oh, Linzi! Linzi!' as what seems to be gallons of burning, creamy spunk shoots out of my cock, until finally the last drop oozes out and my cock twitches one last time.

Then you are gone, but I awake with the memory of you fresh in my mind. The sight of your face as you come is something wonderous to be seen by any man or waiter! I'm left with a satisfied smile and sticky, wet sheets. I can hardly wait to get to sleep tonight to see if I meet up with you again. You know, Linzi, I haven't had a good shag in ages. I've nearly forgotten what it's like. I was wondering if you could remind me?

Martin. Avon.

Nice try Martin, but no!

Linzi X.

Is Size Important?

Dear Linzi,
Please answer a couple of questions for me. I've been a follower of your fabulous form for some years now and there are just a couple of questions that I'm desperate to ask you. Firstly, there is so much emphasis on a man's member. I'd like to know if you think dick size is important and could you tell me what turns you on most when making love? Only two, Linzi, please, please, please, pretty please, do tell!

Gary.

Of course I'll tell you Gary, because you know I love talking about dicks! You didn't say whether or not you had a whopper, but honestly for me I don't really have a specific preference, although men with small cocks often have a hang up about it, so that can be a real turn off! Big dicks are wonderful to suck on for hours, but for prolonged sex they can make a girl feel a little uncomfortable. Guys with medium-sized dicks, who can keep it up for ages, are probably best for hour upon hour of screwing. As for my favourite sexual turn on, it's having my pussy licked for hours by a man who knows exactly what to do or does exactly what he's told! Enough said!

Linzi X.

Fancy a Threesome?

Dear Linzi,
I am writing to you for a few reasons: my boyfriend, Shane, and I were so turned on by some pictures of you dressed as a cheerleader. The main reason being that Shane plays American football for one of the leading clubs in England and I can imagine you and I clad in cheerleader gear, making love to each other and then to Shane in our humble abode. Before, I had always been turned off by other girls, but you can make me come on sight. I would love to have a threesome, but only with you. I know it's a lot to ask, but do you think you could help us? I'm eighteen and Shane is twenty and we both love sex. Both of our goals are to sleep with you. Please could you fulfil two peoples' dreams in one go? If not, could you please send us a vibrator that you've used, that would really make me wet.

Anyway, Linzi, I think I've said enough, please think about it and write and let me know what your answer is. And remember to send your favourite vibrator.

Toni. Middx.

Love to help you and sexy Shane out, but I'm a bit too busy to dash over to Middlesex for a torrid threesome right now, and I couldn't possibly part with my trusty vibrator, it's like a best friend to me!

Linzi X.

Trevor

Dear Linzi,
My name is Trevor. I stand six feet tall and have a healthy body of medium build. I am in my thirties but look younger which is mostly due to my astrological star sign, Capricorn. I have many interests, and I am a superduper cook. A mouth-watering pizza is my speciality. On a more intimate level I am the perfect lover, as defined by Masters and Johnson, who are the leading researchers into sexuality. I am very well-endowed with a thick eight inches and I know how to use my body to give a woman the maximum sexual pleasure. Women don't need to fake their orgasms with Trevor, as I use my body to make them orgasmic, so that simply by touching or kissing them they have multiple orgasms. I like to spend approximately two hours with a lady getting to know her body and her erogenous zones, through caressing her and using my very versatile tongue. Then, finally, I use my cock to slowly massage the inside of her vulva until she comes, while holding back on my own climax; then I let her recover before taking her in another position, until she comes again, then another position until she is ready for the ultimate orgasm, which will sub-sequently bring about my own.

Well, Linzi, now you know all about my sexual prowess, I would request that you pass my details on to someone who would like to meet me, or to a video company that could offer me work making love to sex starlets?

Trevor.

Oh do piss off, Trevor!

Linzi X.

Tempting Proposal

Dear Linzi,
Will you marry me? I'd take you away to a remote paradise island and worship your body. While sunbathing, I could rub suntan oil over your firm breasts, squeezing and holding them.

Next I'd cover your flat tummy, working my way down to your hips and lovely blonde fanny hair. I'd cover your legs, and the insides of your thighs. I'd kiss your greasy body all over and then slide on top of you rubbing myself slowly up and down before entering your warmness. We'd make love on the beach all day in the sun, falling asleep in each other's arms, completely satisfied.

So what about it, Linzi, will you marry me?

Stephen. South Shields.

It's a tempting offer Stephen, I love the oily honeymoon bit on the beach, but sorry I don't believe in marriage. I think it's all bollocks!

Linzi X.

Up Yer Kilt!

Dear Linzi,

I am a twenty-two-year-old Scotsman who would like to know what an ordinary guy like myself has to do to get you between the sheets. I want to dip into your gorgeous, golden honey pot and fill you up with gallons of steaming, hot spunk. Could you possibly answer these questions for me?

1. Can you tell me what, if any clothes you like to wear when you're fucking?
2. Can you tell me your favourite place to fuck?
3. What makes you come?
4. Have you ever been fucked by a man in a kilt. If not, do you want to, as I'm volunteering!

Stewart. Dundee.

So you want me to open up for you, Stewart. Okay. You've got it! The first question is not one I can answer in a couple of words. What I wear to make love can vary so much depending on where I am and who I'm fucking. If I'm at home with a boyfriend I usually like to dress in silky undies and either have

199

my knickers ripped off or pulled off to the side when I get shafted. But if I've been out for an evening and I come home with my date and we're so horny we can only just make it inside the front door, then I usually get fucked with my posh frock hiked up around my arse, and in my stockings and suspenders and high heels. On the other hand, if I do it in the bath or the shower, I'm in the buff!

My favourite place to fuck is a difficult one. The other night I did it for the first time in the passenger seat of a Ferrari. I never actually thought there was room, but there was and it was great. The best place of all to fuck is wherever you are at that moment when you really want it! I like doing it on beaches, and in public places where there's a chance you might get caught!

What makes me come is a humdinger of a question. So many things; being on top, being fucked very hard doggy fashion, delicate fingers, experienced tongues, shower nozzles, dirty talk, my lovable vibrator and of course men in kilts!

No seriously, Stewart, I've never been fucked by a man in a kilt, but if I feel like it I promise to bear you in mind!

Linzi X.

Copious Emissions

Dear Linzi,
During my frequent masturbating sessions, your bottom is the most favourite of my fantasies. How I long to spurt my stuff over your beautiful bottom, annointing both cheeks and the delicate wrinkles of your bumhole. How I long to watch my copious emission trickle down the seams of your black, silk stockings. I know I never will, so could I please have a moment of you? It would make my wanks so much more enjoyable if you could send me a pair of your knickers or a snippet of your pubic hair or maybe a signed photo? Please. With love and a stiff willy,

Bobby.

I've never heard it called a copious emission before, I'll have to remember that one. As to your request, I'm all out of knickers,

200

*and my golden blonde muff is neatly trimmed so I have no
surplus snippets, but I've got plenty of rauchy photos, so I'm
signing and kissing one and sending it off right now!*

Linzi X.

A Little Gentle Persuasion

Dear Linzi,
I felt I just had to write to you to let you know how hot
and horny I think you are. Photos of you even make the wife
wet between the legs. I'm sorry to say that she has never tasted
another girl's lovehole, but she did give me a great blow job
while I looked at your perfect 36-inch breasts. My wife's tits
are 40 inches, and the thought of you and her in a 69 position
gives me such a hard on that I need a good wank just thinking
about it.

Any suggestions, Linzi, how I can persuade the wife to get
into some wet and willing pussy? I'm sure she would enjoy it,
as would I, using my full 10-inch cock on the two of them
afterwards.

Ian. Great Yarmouth.

*If your wife is as horny as you say then she'll probably come
around with a little gentle persuasion, but if she doesn't, don't
push it, or it could all end in tears!*

Linzi X.

Kinky Games

Dear Linzi,
I have been married to John for over twenty years now and
our sex life is pretty good. We enjoy kinky activities, but
generally it's my husband who comes up with all the ideas.
We do both enjoy bondage and I thought it would be rather
nice if I could surprise him one night with some kinky games.
Any suggestions?

P.L.

I certainly have. Why not try these outrageous ideas?

*Before he's due to arrive home, put on as tarty a dress as
you dare, and leave a note for him telling him that tonight you
are on the game and will be working in such and such a pub
from 8.30. Tell him he'd better get there to make you a good
offer, or someone else is bound to. Then leave the house and
arrive at the pub at 8.40. Act like a complete tart and even
charge him a fee.*

*Or get yourself some really sexy PVC or rubber underwear.
Be ready and waiting in it when he comes home from work.
You are now his dominatrix and he must do whatever you tell
him. Perhaps have a cane and swish it around a bit to let him
know you mean business. Then strip him naked, blindfold him
and tie him to the bed. Stand over his nude body on the bed
and masturbate with some baby oil. As you play with yourself
let all the oil and your juices run down on him, then massage
him to a climax with the oil.*

*Those couple of ideas should keep you both well entertained.
Have fun!*

Linzi X.

Goddess of British Sex

Dear Linzi,
You adorable little Goddess of British sex. The erogenous parts
of your shattering anatomy hold no secrets for me, thanks to a
French invention – the photograph. However, what holds the
highest price in my eyes is your moving face, a mirror to your
soul. Please send me a picture, face only, of course!

Paul. Paris.

*You French are so romantic with your words, and not so bad
with your tongues either! Now Paul I wonder if you're really
sure you want a picture of my moving face? Howabout a
close-up shot of my moving fingers on my swollen, pink clitty?
No? Okay, you win. Here's a pretty headshot from your 'Little
Goddess of British Sex'. (I like that!)*

Linzi X.

Little Willy

To Linzi Drew,
Who is deliciously delectable, and so beautiful, gorgeous, sexy, elegant and horny. And oh what legs! So long and shapely. How I'd like them wrapped around my neck, holding my head between those strong thighs and forcing my face into that juicy cunt. I would lick your sweet honey pot out for ever and I'd love to drown in your sticky juices. What a way to go! I would have loved to make love to you as well, but my willy only stretches to two and a half inches at best. I'd doubt you would even know I was there, so I'd be quite content having your pussy engulfing my head, drinking your come, plus anyone else's if it's there.

I've got many photographs of you and I think you knock spots off your younger rivals. I wish I could get a picture of you in a sexy short skirt and stockings flashing a bit of thigh and in various stages of undress. Good luck and enjoy your humping with your big-cocked friends.

Your humble servant John.
P.S. I think you should be Queen of England.

After all that flattery and your misfortune of having such a little willy, how could I refuse? I'll send you some sexy snaps right away!
Linzi X.

Question-time

Dear Linzi,
Being a fan of yours for a long time I feel I know quite a lot about you, but I would like to know more, so I have compiled a few questions, which I would be so grateful if you could answer for me.

1. What is your favourite fantasy at the moment?
2. How many boyfriends do you have on the go (ones you make love with)?
3. What turns you on in a man?
4. What turns you on in a woman?
5. Could you describe the last time you had sex?

Larry.

Well Larry you really do want to know all my intimate little secrets. But as I suspect many of my other readers will also be interested, I'm prepared to reveal all!

1. As I've just returned from my holidays in Antigua, my favourite fantasy is screwing on a deserted beach in the heat of the late afternoon. The water is warm as my man and I wade out into the clear turquoise sea and we embrace. We both know what we are about to do as our hands explore each other's oily bodies. I jump up onto him, my long legs wrapping around his slim waist, as he teases me with the tip of his stiff cock. It nuzzles against my hot lips, and the warm water swirling around our bodies makes the moment seem very intense. Pretty soon I want him inside me, so he slides his rock-hard dick in me to the hilt, lifting me up with it as I grip tightly around his shoulders and feel every inch as he shafts me to climax.

2. I have two regular boyfriends keeping me sexually satisfied at the moment.

3. Lots of things turn me on in a man. I like men who are very erotic and highly sexed. I like men who enjoy talking about sex and who like to spend hour upon hour making love. You know the type who just can't keep his hands off you, and halfway through a meal in a restaurant he wants you to nip out to the car for a quickie. Or boyfriends who ring me after boring board meetings and tell me exactly what they'd like to do to my breasts and pussy. I adore men who enjoy hours of foreplay, which I do! I also like men with nice hands, because I suppose I know how good those hands are going to feel when they're playing around with my pussy!

4. I haven't had as much experience with women as men, of course. The kind of women I find physically attractive are petite blondes with slim, tanned bodies, small pert breasts and short pubic hair. I find very hairy pussies a complete turn off. I like them nicely trimmed. I also love girls with long fingernails.

5. The last time I had sex was yesterday afternoon in my office at home. My home office doubles as my dressing room as well, and one entire wall is covered with mirrored wardrobes. Just perfect for screwing in front of! If I tuck both chairs in under my two desks, there's plenty of room to romp around on the thickly carpeted floor. I love to watch myself at it! I was wearing a black lacy bra and French-cut matching panties, when my boyfriend arrived late in the afternoon. He gave me a long, deep kiss and told me he had to make one phone call. When he had finished he came up to my office. I was kneeling on all fours in my undies, with my knickers pulled off to one side fingering myself and watching myself in the mirror. You can imagine it didn't take him long to join in!

Linzi X.

Ode to Linzi

Dear Linzi,

No doubt you've already been told loads of times, but I'm going to tell you again. You are without doubt, the most gorgeous sexiest girl to walk the face of the earth. Linzi, you are two hundred and one per cent woman and I love you. Well now you know how much I think of you, howabout showing how much you think of me by sending me a signed photo? Before I go, here's a poem I've written for you. It's not very good, but I hope you like it.

> My dearest, darling Linzi,
> You will never know,
> Just how much I love you,
> And long to hold you so.
> I'd like to lie down next to you,
> On a bed of feather and down,
> To plant a kiss upon your lips,
> And breasts so soft and brown.
> I'd like to kiss your cheeks and neck,
> Then kiss your breasts some more.
> Then kiss where only lovers go,
> Then fuck till you were sore.
> I'd kiss your lovely stockinged legs,
> I'd kiss your lovely bum,
> I'd love to kiss you all over,
> Then fuck you until you come.

205

But I know that this will never be,
Cause we will never meet,
Oh yes and while I'm at it,
I'd kiss your lovely feet.

John. Bromley.

I'll have to agree with you there, John, it isn't very good. Shakespeare you're not, but I'm sure the thought was there. I'm sending you a naughty photo to give you some inspiration!

Linzi X.

Blind Date

Dear luscious, voluptuous, gorgeous, lustful and fuckable Linzi, You have a really fuckable body. You have an excellent figure and a golden fuckable pussy. Do you work out to keep your figure in trim? Whose cock or pussy do you work out with? That's what I'd like to know!

I'd like to watch two women enjoying each other. If I was a good boy they might even let me join in. I'd like to put my eight-inch cock between your ample and plenteous tits. You would rub me up and down. My cock would throb so much that I wouldn't be able to hold back any longer and I'd shoot my spunk over your chin and face. Your tongue would reach out and lick the come around your gaping mouth. Then you'd give me the best blow job I could ever imagine.

Some come would still be on the tip of my knob. Your tongue would run up and down my cock making it harder (with your presence alone, Linzi, my cock would be rock hard!). Then you'd lick the tip of my cock, swallowing the come before putting it deep into your mouth.

To finish off I'd fuck you until your cunt was so sore, sex would be the last thing you'd want for a week. How about it – can we meet?

James. Clydebank.

You have got to be joking, James. A man that wants to fuck me until I'm sore holds no appeal for me whatsoever!

Linzi X.

206

Do You Swallow?

Dear Linzi,

I am a Royal Marine currently serving in Norway. I am writing to you simply to tell you how much I think of you. I am sure you get plenty of letters from servicemen in my position. You are, I can assure you, a great morale booster, and the closest thing to home comfort we get is to open the pages of your magazine and dream of what it would be like if you could be here. I have followed your career for the last few years through the various magazines. The promise of seeing your gorgeous tits pushing out at me and your lovely legs slightly spread to reveal your inviting pussy is enough to secure a sale with me and many of my mates. I have many fantasies about you, but the main one is when I imagine your mouth slowly sliding over the end of my eager, waiting cock and giving me a fantastic gobble, while I fondle and squeeze your perfect tits. Then as I am about to come, you stop sucking and lick my big, heavy balls until my spunk shoots over your chin, neck and tits. I'd turn you over so I can give you a long, hard screw, doggy position.

I don't suppose you have time to reply to all your letters, but if you do could you please answer these questions?

1. Do you enjoy oral sex, and if so, do you prefer it if the man pulls out instead of expecting you to swallow his come?
2. In what sexual position did you lose your virginity?
3. Does the thought of all those men wanking over your pictures turn you on?

Mark. B.F.P.O.

Well Mark I think it's amusing how you ask if I like oral sex when you are obviously only referring to fellatio! We females do like to be tongue-teased as well you know! As it happens I do love cocksucking and whether or not I swallow depends entirely on the cock I'm sucking, but I do like the taste of come!

2. I lost my virginity in the back of a transit van and it was in the missionary position.

3. I simply adore the thought that men all over the world are wanking over my photographs!

Linzi X.

Wet Panties

Dear Linzi,

I have had three similar dreams about you. They go like this: I went to see you in a nightclub. I'm afraid you were only stripped to bra, panties and stockings. So as you left for your dressing room I followed you secretly, full of anxiety and spunk. You turned around and saw me, not looking surprised. You took off your stockings and bra. Then I looked in wonder at your gorgeous body. You smiled and slipped your hands into your knickers and fingered yourself. Then your pants turned wet. You masturbated until your juices were running down your legs onto your red high-heeled shoes. I couldn't stand it any more. I got out my cock and you walked up to me smiling, slithered down my cock and sucked hard. You sucked me dry, then removed your knickers, picked up your bra and stockings and gave them to me still wet. Then you softly kissed my lips and showed me out. What a dream and what a present that bra, stockings and wet panties would have been! Do you have any worn panties that you could send me?

S.B.

I'd love to send you a pair of my wet panties, but if I were to post a pair of my perfumed frillies through the Royal Mail, one whiff of my sweet pussy juice would undoubtedly send those posties crazy and disrupt the entire postal service. I just couldn't do it!

Linzi X.

13. SHAVEN HAVENS

If you've got a muff that you're proud of girls, would you let your man shave it off? This chapter is full of ladies who have, and there's a naked cock and balls thrown in for good measure!

Bald is Beautiful
Filled With You
Sexy Women Who Bare All
Quite Remarkable!

Spanish Lessons
A Couple of Baldies
Have You Tried It?
What a Surprise!

Bald is Beautiful

Dear Linzi,

Bald is beautiful, well when it comes to my cunt it is anyway! Since shaving off all my luxuriant pubic bush, I am having a wonderful time sexually. Everytime I get fucked I feel delicious, decadent and dribbling wet. My naked mound seems to be so much more sensitive minus my curly, brown thatch. When my boyfriend, Richard, goes down on me and rubs his face all over my smooth twat, I seem to feel every square inch of his tongue, licking and lapping at my shaven lips.

Actually it was Richard's bright idea to remove my pubic hair. In fact he'd been going on about it for months. One night he started to tell me exactly how he'd shave me. I got so horny listening to his graphic sexual descriptions, that I told him to hurry off and find his disposable razor and make my cunt smooth and bald, and quick please!

It was the early evening and we were relaxed and sitting together on the sofa. Richard was playing with me at the time. My lemon-coloured cotton dress was up around my waist, my white panties were pulled down and hanging off one ankle, and my bare legs were well spread. Richard was using the tip of his forefinger to trace the furrow of my pussy lips. I was becoming juicy and I started to thrust my crotch towards him in an effort to feel his fingers inside my lips. My clit was beginning to throb and I could feel my nipples tingling in my bra. I pulled the front of my dress from my body and exposed my large, up-turned breasts, stroking them and squeezing them hard. With my thumb and forefinger I tweaked my strawberry-pink nipples fiercely and then used my long thumbnail to flick them as they began to swell to twice their normal size.

Running his fingers through my bushy cunt hair, Richard began to fantasize.

'I'd love to shave off all this hair and see your beautiful cunt when it's bald,' he groaned.

Still kneading my tits with both hands, I answered huskily, 'Tell me what you want to do to me.'

'I'd like to smother your beautiful cunt with creamy shaving foam and rub it into every inch of you.' As he spoke he was grabbing handfuls of my cunt. He continued, his voice becoming gravelly and excited, 'I want to take off all this lovely soft hair and then when you're smooth and naked, I want to lick it all over and then when your whole pussy is slippery and wet from my tongue, I want to sink my dick in you and feel your baldness engulf my rock-hard shaft.'

I squirmed on the sofa as his fingers probed the fleshy folds of my sex and penetrated my pussy. He worked two fingers in and out of my sopping hole, all the while using his thumb to stimulate my clitoris. I was well away as he swiftly brought me to orgasm. Still yelping and trembling, my pussy hot and twitchy, I stroked a languid hand across my swollen lips, gave him a wicked smile and told him that I wanted him to shave me!

By the time Richard had returned from the bathroom, armed with a disposable razor, a can of shaving foam, a bowl of warm water and a towel, I had stripped out of my dress and was on my back on the living-room floor. I was feeling very randy and so was keeping myself amused by sliding a finger up and down the length of my wet slit. Richard fell to his knees and licked my cunt long and hard. I love having my pussy licked. Once he'd started on me there was no way I was going to let him stop until I was good and ready. I grabbed his hair and thrust my public mound hard at his face.

'Lick me until I come and then I'll let you shave me.'

Richard came up for air and smiled sexily at me, 'You, young lady, are going to get seriously licked, then shaved, then fucked!'

'Yes, please,' I murmured as Richard used both hands to open my labia lips before homing in on my clit.

After another wonderous orgasm, the delicate shaving operation began. Richard spread the large towel beneath my bottom as I propped my back against the sofa. As he pushed my legs wide-open, I glanced down at my damp pubic hair one last time

211

and wondered if I was doing the right thing. My doubts were swept from my mind, when I felt the cool foam hit me between the legs. The mere sound of it squirting from the can made me quiver with anticipation. Richard smeared the cream all over my pussy, his fingers exciting me as they travelled all over my cunt, seeking out every hairy area. Positioning the razor on the highest part of my pubic line, he began with gentle, stroking movements. I kept very still as little by little my dark bush disappeared before my very eyes.

I opened my legs even wider and Richard told me to lean back and to thrust my crotch forward. Quick as a flash he shaved off all the hair from my inner thighs, all around my pussy lips and beyond. A splash down with some warm water and my new bald pussy was revealed in all its glory. It simply looked so rude! I ran my hand over it and savoured its smoothness. Richard covered my hand with his and together we cupped my naked pussy.

'Bend over and let me see how pink and exposed it looks from behind,' Richard suggested.

I was up on my knees at once, thrusting out my arse and exhibiting my bald pussy proudly. Richard wriggled beneath me and stared at me hard. His thick cock started to jerk visibly as his mouth closed in on my bald beauty. As his tongue went to work I was overcome with a completely new sensation. I felt so naughty, so horny and so wet. His tongue slid deliciously all over my pussy, licking my bald mound, poking into every hidden crevice, sliding up and down my hairless inner lips until he found my clit. The feel of his tongue and his soft, warm flesh against mine made me tremble with desire.

'Move around so I can suck you!' I gasped.

Richard crawled beneath me and positioned his monster dick for my eager mouth. Using my tongue I teased his helmet, gently rolling my tongue around its circumference. Saliva dribbling from my lips, I ran my tongue up and down the length of his shaft, before taking his swollen knob between my slippery lips. All the while I was being licked and fingered from below. I was rubbing my shaven haven all over Richard's face as he guzzled greedily on my naked quim. As I started to come I released Richard's knob from my mouth.

212

'Oh lick me!' I yelped, as I felt a searing orgasm traverse my sensitive body.

Still on all fours I was ready to be fucked and Richard was desperate to be inside me. He gripped his cock at the base and wanked his knob up and down my bald slit.

'Oh fuck me now!' I begged, my shaven cunt eager to be filled up with his dick.

He made me wait, teasing me with his hot helmet, sliding it up and down and from side to side across my crack, circling my clit and caressing my bald lovelips.

Eventually and agonizingly slowly he sank his hot meat into me. I felt every glorious inch as he gingerly entered my ecstatic cunt, until finally with one firm thrust he was in me to the hilt. Every stroke of his thick cock sent a shiver throughout my whole being. My nipples burned with excitement, while my tits bounced up and down with the force of our sexual rhythm. I could feel his wiry pubic bush slamming against my baldness as he plunged it into me time after time. His hairy balls banging on my hairless twat felt so good. He rode me slowly at first, picking up speed gradually. Each time he slammed his cock all the way in, I felt the slap of his balls on my hairless quim and it felt wonderful. So good that I was coming again in no time.

'Fuck me hard. I'm going to come!' I cried out euphorically.

With that Richard gripped both my buttocks hard and fucked me hell for leather. I was coming like never before, my pussy was erupting like a volcano and my legs turned to jelly. Somehow or other I found myself rolled over on my back with Richard kneeling between my legs holding his bulging cock. Creamy blobs of spunk spurted from it and splashed over my beautiful bald puss. Still trembling from my orgasm, I reached down between my legs and massaged my fiery, hairless cunt with his come.

Well that was the first time I experimented with my sexy shaven haven. Since removing all my pubic hair my sex life gets better and better! It's a bit of a drag shaving almost every day, but designer stubble on the pussy is not an attractive sight! So I get out the razor, lather up and keep my cunt smooth and free of hair, because believe me it's worth it!

K.L.

Filled With You

Dear Linzi,

The other night I saw you on the James Whale Radio show. You looked fantastic. How did you get into that dress? As the programme is on so late at night, I usually watch it in bed, so after the show I drifted off to sleep. But you must have made quite an impression on me because my dreams were filled with you!

I dreamt I was in this local nightclub and you walked in with a lot of showbiz people wearing that same tight, black dress. It looked so good, I could barely resist reaching out and stroking you as you walked past. You positioned yourself at the bar only a few feet from me. With difficulty you climbed up onto a high, bar stool, your gorgeous legs swinging to and fro as you sipped your cocktail. I couldn't take my eyes off your cleavage, and then your lips as you suggestively sucked on a straw. I suppose I was really staring because it was at this point you looked at me and winked. I nearly fell off my bar stool, but, determined to get to know you, I went up to you and asked if I could buy you a drink. You accepted my offer and told me to pull up a chair.

We got chatting and got on like a house on fire. Then they put on some smoochy records and I asked you to dance. Taking you by the hand, I felt like a king as I led you to the dance floor. With your body pressed so close to mine, I had real difficulty not poking you with my stiffening penis. Now that would have been really uncouth! But, I couldn't stop myself from becoming hard, and this seemed to please you as you pushed your body firmly against mine. I started to stroke the part of your back that was left bare by your revealing dress. You nuzzled into my neck and then it happened, you tilted your head towards mine and out lips met in a wonderful kiss. Suffocatingly deep, with our tongues exploring wildly, my hands running all over your wonderous body as you held my head and really kissed me.

Moments later we jumped into a cab and headed for your hotel. It was a penthouse suite complete with a giant circular bed, surrounded by bronze tinted mirrors, a huge Jacuzzi and champagne waiting on ice. The tease was to strip you out of your fabulous dress. You stood posed like some sort of fabulous goddess as I knelt behind you unlacing the ties that crisscrossed across your delicious back. I couldn't take my hands off you, and with each tiny piece of bare back that was revealed, I had to stand up and kiss the beckoning skin, and rub my hands all over it.

I was trembling with anticipation by the time you were completely unlaced and all I had to do was wriggle the skintight frock over your beautiful rounded arse. I gasped with delight when the dress came off. Your legs were even longer, leaner and more sensual than I'd ever imagined. You were a vision before me – your back arched, your legs splendid and only wearing high heels, and sheerest black stockings.

Very slowly you turned to face me. I looked up at you in awe, being afforded a breathtaking view of your large breasts and bald pussy (I've no idea why I dreamt you had a shaved pussy, Linzi!). I stared hard at your naked quim, it looked so neat and inviting, as did your sensuous, large breasts. From my position they looked enormous and I reached up and cupped them, taking each breast one by one into my mouth, sucking on those delicious hard nipples, running my tongue all over them as I rubbed my hands all over your body. As I feasted on your tits I could feel your hairless pussy pushing against my chest. You felt damp and that sent a shiver up my spine. I was so excited I abandoned your breasts, and moving lower, I breathed deeply, taking in your delicious sexual aroma. Then taking the plunge, I placed my forefinger on your pussy and very gently started to massage you. I located your clitoris almost immediately and you let out a tiny gasp of pleasure and grabbed my head and pulled my face into you. I ran my tongue along the length of your slit. This was driving you wild and you collapsed back onto the bed and spread your legs wide open, demanding that I suck your bald pussy.

You watched me in the mirrors as I moved in on your beautifully spread thighs. I kissed, tongued and nibbled you, and then I probed a finger inside you. This sent you into delirium and soon I was tasting your sweet lovejuice and sneaking a look at your beautiful face to watch your expression when you shuddered to a climax.

215

After that you stripped me naked, and taking the champagne, we moved into the bathroom. In a swirly bath full of bubbles, we sipped champagne and played with each other. Your nimble fingers wanking my cock up and down and squeezing my balls, while I played with your pussy which was hot and quite swollen. I dribbled some champagne on your nipples and delighted in sucking it off. Then you clambered out of the bath and ordered me to pour champagne on your bald pussy. Your glistening wet body looked amazing as you lay at the edge of your sunken bathtub, your legs open slightly. I shook up the bottle and watched with delight as the frothy champers fizzed around your pussy. You giggled excitedly as I knelt up to lap up every last drop. Your pussy was sizzling as I slipped my tongue into your hole.

Soon you were so excited you told me to make love to you. You pulled me over to you and positioned yourself on top. I found your opening, then spread your lips and little by little I thrust inside you. Your bald pussy was hot and tight. It clung to my cock as I bounced you up and down on my shaft, fingering your nipples, kissing your neck until we came together, shouting and screaming as a breathtaking orgasm ripped through our bodies simultaneously.

Unfortunately, Linzi, that was just about the time I woke up with sticky semen all over my boxer shorts. Still I continued in a half-sleep dreaming of how I would make love to you on that big bed, seeing your facial expressions of ecstasy and watching those wonderful bouncing tits of yours. I still don't know why you had a shaved pussy in my dream!

Gary. Aldershot.

Sexy Women Who Bare All

Dear Linzi,
My wife, Kate, and I have been fans of yours since we saw you consumer testing dildos on an early Electric Blue. Kate is an American, thirteen years my junior (lucky for some), and since we met have embarked on a full and varied sex life. We have a large collection of video tapes which always get us in the right

216

mood, particularly those with women who have shaven pussies. Sadly, these are a rarity. There's something incredibly sexy about a woman who bares all and I often shave Kate because this always results in a prolonged bout of lovemaking. It's so much more exciting licking a pussy that's shaved. One problem though. Kate always gets quite sore a few days after, despite the applications of creams and powders. We have noticed that all the model girls we see in magazines are always shaved so clean and smooth. Probably touched up with make up!

Gary. E 9.

Quite Remarkable!

Dear Linzi,

I finally persuaded my horny girlfriend Carol to shave off her cunt hair. What a night we had! There was nothing on the TV so we were sitting around quite bored. I told Carol to take her knickers off so I could play with her black hairy snatch, and then I jokingly said, 'I bet it would be nice to see your cunt bare.' I must have caught her just at the right time because she immediately agreed, and not long after her wet fanny was covered in soap. I carefully shaved off every last bit of her wiry hair, patted her down with water, then splashed her with my aftershave. It didn't sting her, and it stopped her from getting an ugly shaving rash. Her cunt looked quite remarkable!

Licking that beautiful shaven haven was a new experience for me. Carol talked me through it as I went down on her bald beauty. She told me where she wanted to feel my inquisitive tongue as I explored her squelchy cunt to the full. I had the horny little bitch rubbing herself all over my face. And then my prick!

I bent her over on all fours and ogled her bald slit. It looked so tasty. I grabbed her bum and pulled her towards me, then rubbed my helmet all over her bald, twitching lips. Her cunt was so hot that I just had to fuck her. She was screaming wildly as I fucked her nice and hard. The feel of her smooth shaven haven had both of us coming very quickly. What a satisfying fuck!

217

Carol's pubic hair has grown back now, but I know that every now and then we'll shave off her hair and have some fun!

Ronnie. London.

Spanish Lessons

Dear Linzi,

I attend the adult education classes at my local college where I am taking a course in conversational Spanish. A few weeks ago a new student joined the class; a beautiful, sultry looking woman in her early twenties. I was smitten at once and managed to get chatting to her after class. I invited her for a bite to eat in a restaurant and she accepted my offer. We had a great time. I found her witty, amusing and very sexy. When we parted company, I gave her a kiss. I didn't know whether to plant it on her lips or on her cheek, but I went for her mouth and she accepted the kiss, parting her moist lips as they met with mine.

The musky smell of her perfume and the taste of that kiss stayed with me all week. By the time the following week's class arrived I was in a near state of panic. What if she didn't turn up for class? Or what if she wouldn't accept my offer of another dinner date?

However, my fears were unfounded, she did turn up for class. All through the teaching period I could only concentrate on her. Our eyes kept meeting across the classroom, her dark eyes smiling at me invitingly. When eventually it was time to leave, I hurried to her and asked her to dinner. She took hold of my hand and said, '*Sí, sí!* '

During dinner the sexual tension between us built. Her lovely legs brushed against mine from time to time and she was very tactile, touching my hair and hands. When we'd finished our meal and drunk two bottles of Spanish wine I offered to escort her home. She stroked a delicate hand across my face allowing her fingers to creep into my mouth. I ran my tongue around her fingertips as she nodded her head in acceptance.

In the taxi to her flat, I struggled with an erection. I wanted to reach out and caress her beautiful neck, stroke her pert breasts and ease a hand up between her legs. I did none of this, I just sat there holding her hand while my cock throbbed in my pants. Just as the taxi came to a halt her gaze moved slowly down to my crotch and then back up to meet my eyes. All she said was, 'My, my!'

Once inside the lift, riding up to her flat, I cradled her in my arms and kissed her hard on the lips. My cock pressed against her and her eyes rolled excitedly. In the time it took to travel the seven floors, she climaxed. My hand reached up inside her knickers and stroked her wet, wet pussy. I was excited to find out that she was completely shaved. My fingers probed the insides of her sex and soon found the entrance to her hairless hole. As I pushed two fingers in and out, she whimpered softly that she was about to come.

In the privacy of her comfy flat, she stripped me. She confidently showed off her gorgeous slim body, her firm, small breasts and smooth shaved cunt. When she stood before me naked, she unleashed my cock and still standing, guided it between her exposed quim lips. I wrapped my arms around her and lifted her up onto my raging cock. Her quivering, hairless pussy surrounded my prick. She was no weight as I lifted her from the ground. I slipped into her wetness with ease, my rock-hard penis pounding away, fucking her long and hard as she scratched her fingernails into the skin of my back, and screamed out in climax. Her face a picture, we came together, our hot sticky bodies, shaking and convulsing as our lovejuices intertwined.

D.L. West Country.

A Couple of Baldies

Dear Linzi,
I have shaved off all my pubic hair! You wouldn't believe how sensitive my cock and balls are. When my girlfriend sucks me, the sensation is simply wonderful. Fucking too is sheer delight. My girlfriend, Sher, has removed all her pubic hair as well and our sex life has improved. I would strongly recommend depilation to enhance every sexual encounter!

Bald Bill.

Have You Tried It?

Dear Linzi,

I'm writing to you about something you may or may not have tried before, but if you haven't, you don't know what you're missing, darling! I'm talking about pubic shaving. I tried it a few months ago and the feeling was absolutely fantastic. To be fucked with a totally bald pussy is bloody amazing. But the funny thing is, before I defuzzed my puss, I wouldn't have dreamed of shaving my pubes. It was my boyfriend who convinced me to do it. He just loved the idea of shagging me with a bald fanny and so I reluctantly agreed. You see, I had such a lovely black pussy forest that I didn't want to see it go. As a matter of fact I was proud of my curly bush and I know that many cocks have risen at the sight of my hairy pussy. I hadn't dreamt of shaving it until Mark (my boyfriend) mentioned it.

It was a strange and rather pleasurable experience watching my black hairs being cut off by Mark's razor and seeing a bald patch in my crotch for the very first time. I looked in the mirror and stood in awe of my bald puss. It looked so sexy. I lay down in front of the mirror and the totally soft, smooth, hairless pubis made me juice almost instantly. Before I knew it Mark was up me giving me my first hairless shag. It was an absolutely fantastic feeling, his wispy hair tickling my bald skin. He must have thought it fantastic too because he spunked much quicker than usual.

Pleasurable as it was being bald, I eventually gave up keeping myself in trim and allowed the black hairs to slowly break through again. I'm pleased to say I have my full black forest again, but I'm sure I'll fancy a shave again one day soon. Try it, Linzi. You'll love it! You've got a gorgeous hairy pussy, but the guys love it soft, smooth and hairless! May the spunk flow for you!

Claire.

What a Surprise!

Dear Linzi,

The other night my girlfriend surprised me by shaving her hairy cunt, and we had an explosive night of sex. Let me tell you about it. I'm twenty-four years old, not bad looking, have quite a good-sized cock, not fat, but long and lean, and I work as a carpenter. I've been dating Julie for about six months now, and we've been living together for about six weeks. She is just twenty years old and a highly-sexed shagging machine. Now I don't mean that detrimentally, no she is one hell of a girl; she's got thick black hair, a right sexy mouth, big eyes, big tits and a big arse. Lovely! She's also a very nice warm human being who happens to fuck like a steam train!

Anyway being so dark she's also incredibly hairy. I battle bravely through her thick bushy cunt hairs to reach her pot of gold to bring her orgasm after orgasm. She's very demanding, my Julie, she won't allow me to fuck her until I've made her come at least twice with my fingers and my tongue. Not a bad deal as I love the taste of her cunt. Still I do keep getting a mouthful of her muff, so one day I suggested she trim her pubes a little. She smiled and told me she'd think about it.

The next day when I got home from work I'd forgotten all about it. I went upstairs to wash and change. When I came back down to the lounge, there she was sitting on the couch, stark naked with her legs spread, fingering her hairless cunt! I couldn't believe my own eyes! She was already swollen up from her fingering. Her cunt looked so exciting, I couldn't stop looking at it! Her clit looked huge!

I told her how beautiful her cunt looked as I dropped to my knees and crawled towards her. I rubbed my face into it and experienced its new exciting smoothness. I let my hands stroke her outer lips, savouring the new sensation. Then my tongue touched it, but I didn't penetrate her bald fanny for a long, long time. I had such fun licking every inch of her lips, sliding my tongue all over her clit, until she started to spasm. When she came, she was in a frenzy like never before, thrashing about, gripping my hair and really screeching. My long prick was so hard that I had to take it out of my tracksuit pants.

I moved to get up and fuck her, but she roughly pushed me back down between her legs and told me that before I could, I had to bring her off one more time. So this time I stuck my tongue all the way in and worked it in and out, like a tiny

221

clockwork prick, while I manipulated her squeaky clit with my thumb. I know just the way she likes it, so I had her coming again in about five seconds flat. Now I was going to get to fuck her!

I first slapped my prick into her hairless minge while she was bent over the back of the sofa, then she lay spread-eagled on the living room table while I licked her out some more, then I climbed on top and fucked her on the table. I damn near broke it! Next we fucked on the living room floor with Julie sitting astride me, slithering her bald cunt up and down my pole until I shot my seed like never before!

The hair's growing back a little now, but Julie's promised me another bald session at the weekend. I can hardly wait!

Lawrence.

14. THE FIRST TIME

They say you never forget your first time, as losing your cherry is the beginning of a very special voyage of discovery. This chapter is full of keen first-time travellers; there's one guy who feels up a sexy stripogram, a virginal college girl with 40DD breast measurements, a sophisticated older woman who takes advantage of a student and a complete nerd who expects me to meet him outside the lifts on the fourth floor of some hotel, to initiate him to the joys of sex!

CHEEKY CHARLIE
DIVINE DAVINA
SHOW ME THE WAY, LINZI!
STRIP, STRIP HOORAY!

VERGING ON THE RIDICULOUS!
VOLUPTUOUS VIRGIN
RANDY RITA
SUCK ME DRY

Cheeky Charlie

Dear Linzi,

I've just turned nineteen years old and I've only just lost my cherry. Going all the way always terrified me. I'd let a guy feel me up, even lick me between the legs and I'm getting quite good at blow jobs, but actually screw me, well I always said no. Until last week at a party when I lost my virginity. I'd always heard that the first time was a bit of a let down, so that's probably one of the reasons I'd been putting it off, but to my delight it was wonderful, beautiful, fabulous. I only wish I'd been at it for years!

I met my new boyfriend, Charlie, at the party. He's a real charmer, mature and very sexy. I was wearing this little off-the-shoulder number and he kept putting his hands on my neck and stroking my baby-blonde hair as we stood talking. When there was a lull in the conversation it seemed so right that we should start kissing. His kiss was such a turn on. The way he held my face and tenderly parted my lips with his tongue, then French kissed me, that was terribly exciting. He pressed his firm body against mine and I could feel a hardness in his groin which pulsed in time with mine. Again the thought went through my head, shall I or shan't I? Will he be the one that fucks me for the first time? It was a foregone conclusion really. Charlie was turning me on like no man had done as his hands roamed over my body, gently caressing me. I just knew that it was about to turn into a real night to remember.

We found a deserted room upstairs and continued our passionate kissing. Charlie pulled me down on top of him on the bed and we rolled over until he was lying on top of me. With a gentle tug the bra part of my dress came away and my small boobs sprang free. Charlie stopped kissing me and looked at my breasts, he licked his lips in approval and then lowered his mouth to my red nipples. He made an appreciative moan as he sucked them into his mouth one by one. By now my whole body was trembling and I was keen for him to touch me between my legs, but I was also apprehensive that I wouldn't know how to behave if he went one stage further. I grabbed his shoulders forcibly and made him look at me. He still had a mouthful of my nipple as I told him, 'I'm a virgin. You'll have to take me through it gently.'

My nipple almost fell out of his mouth as he looked hard at me for a moment or two, then he reached behind my back, took hold of my zipper and undid it.

I lay on the bed naked, aside from a tiny pair of white panties. Charlie knelt in front of me and smiled as he looked me over.

'You are beautiful,' he said in a sexy whisper.

I felt myself blush, but I also felt my pussy start to throb.

'I'm going to take real good care of you,' he said softly as he started to ease my knickers off. He ran his fingers through my golden-blonde pubes, then with one finger he carefully traced a line down the front of my lovebox. I could hear my sex moisten as he continued to slide his finger up and down on the outside. My pussy was beginning to feel like it had just caught fire. I actually felt myself opening up in readiness for his penis. But first he licked me and that was unbelievable. He knew exactly where to find my lovebutton, and he pursed his lips and sucked it into his mouth. Just a few moments later I started to come. It was almost the most intense orgasm of my life! The best one came when he made love to me!

My pussy was so wet and open. He told me we should do it with me lying on my back first of all as that would be easiest for me. His penis looked so big, but he was so careful. He spread my legs and slipped two fingers in me.

'You're ready, Danni,' he said, his voice thick with sexual excitement. He removed his fingers and replaced them with the tip of his cock. It felt sensational.

'Push it in me,' I whispered.

Inch by inch he entered me. I could feel the walls of my pussy spreading open as he mounted me gently and with rhythmical thrusts.

'How is it?' he asked when he was almost there.

'Oh God, yes!' I screamed. 'I want it all!'

With one final thrust he was in me fully. It was a tight squeeze but it didn't hurt at all.

'Wrap your legs around my waist,' he directed.

So I did and it felt even better as he pumped his whole penis in and out, in and out until suddenly my head felt like it was exploding. My pussy was bubbling over with an intense heat, which sent me wailing and shuddering. It was just the best!

'Are you coming?' Charlie asked.

Was I coming! I shook my head enthusiastically and carried on moaning. Moments later Charlie came too, spunking up inside me. The whoosh of his hot come shooting up inside me felt magnificent.

Charlie broke me in gently, but after that first time he fucked me from behind. That hurt initially because Charlie has such a big penis, but we've been practising it a lot. I'm sure I'll get the hang of it soon.

Danni. London.

Divine Davina

Dear Linzi,

They say you never forget your first time and I know I never will. But I suspect most virgins don't have the pleasure of having a woman like Davina to initiate them to the joys of sex. To an eighteen-year-old student like me Davina is a dream – cool, blonde, sophisticated and worldly. I would never have dreamed that she'd have given me the time of day, but she did and that sensual woman has been a great teacher.

In the summer break I've been doing a little part-time labouring work. By sheer fluke I ended up working at Davina's elegant manor house, and it all began. I suppose I was quite a late starter where sex was concerned. I've had my fair share of blow jobs, pussy-eating and feeling girls up. I'd done just about everything with a girl except screw her, and then I met Davina and learnt there was so much more.

Late one afternoon when I was last to leave her house, I had just finished clearing away the tools, when Davina slinked into the room looking sensational in a cream button-fronted dress with patent high-heeled shoes. Her fluffy, honey-blonde hair was piled on top of her head and she was elegantly made up. She's one of those upper-crust types that it's difficult to guess the age of, but she's got to be in her mid to late thirties. Nevertheless all the young men working on the house had the hots for her. Me included! She strode briskly towards me and stopped a few feet in front of me. I smiled at her politely and then stood mesmerized as she started to unfasten her dress. I stood rooted to the spot as she allowed her dress to slip from her bare shoulders. In a flash she was stripped down to a bronze, silk camisole, sheer stockings and high heels. She stretched a hand out towards me. I gulped and grabbed it and then she led me on a voyage of sexual discovery.

In the bathroom she stripped me and fondled me with her warm, sensitive hands, my young cock standing up to the challenge like a majestic flagpole. I was surprised to discover that the tub was already filled as though she had meticulously planned the scenario. I obediently climbed into the sunken bath and she reached beneath the surface of the water and soaped my body. Her silky lingerie got wetter and wetter from the bubbles as she lathered up my firm shaft. The sight of her pert, pink nipples revealed against her damp underwear made my seed rise. She could tell that I was reaching the point of no return, so she gripped my prick firmly and whispered, 'Not yet!'

We moved in to the sumptuous bedroom. She patted me dry with a towel and then told me in a breathy undertone, 'Now you're going to learn how to lick my pussy.'

She unbuttoned the gusset of her camisole to reveal a beautiful golden cunt, then lay on her back on the grandiose four-poster and spread her long, lean legs. Using just the tips of her exquisitely-manicured hands, she parted her glorious muff.

'Lie between my legs and look at my cunt,' she directed.

I crawled up onto the bed and positioned myself between her splayed thighs. Taking hold of her lovebutton, she whispered, 'This is my clit. Suck it gently, lick it with long, slow sweeps of your tongue. Use lots of spittle and do not use your teeth! When you've made me climax three times, I'll allow you to fuck me.'

That said, she lay her head upon the pillow, slipped the shoulder straps from her, and languorously caressed her breasts. With closed eyes she delicately spread her bulging lovelips in readiness. As she did so, her delicious sexual smell wafted under my nostrils, and like a starving man, I buried my face in her mouth-watering pussy and commenced with my challenge.

Her cunt tasted marvellous. She squirmed on the bed and talked to me in a husky whisper as I pleasured her. Sometimes she wanted the touch of my fingers and tongue to be soft and light, and then every few moments she'd be almost overcome with passion and grind her cunt hard against my face. Davina is one of those lucky women who has multiple orgasms. Waves of crashing orgasms seemed to be hitting her every few seconds. I had completed my task many times over in just a few minutes, but I was having such a good time sucking on that sweet clit of hers, that I kept on at it until my face was soaked with her juices and her clit was swollen and bright pink.

Finally she grabbed me by the hair and dragged me up her heaving, sticky body. She kissed me on the lips, her tongue darting all around my mouth. She told me how to excite her breasts and nipples. My stiff cock was nestling in her moist pubic hair and I was already dribbling a little, my cock desperate to be inside her. I caressed her nipples with my tongue and cupped her gorgeous breasts while awaiting further instructions.

Davina decided the time was right to fuck her. I tried to calm myself, but it was no good, I was so wound up and anxious to feel the inside of her breathtaking pussy that I knew I would come too quickly. She told me to lie flat on my back as she wanted to ride on top. The mere sight of her gaping pussy sinking slowly onto my cock made me start to come. As soon as I felt her hot heaven grip my shaft, I was spunking, my milk shooting up inside her. Davina didn't mind, she just kept on milking every drop, and then carried on riding my prick. I didn't even get really soft.

I was soon rampant again. I thrust up hard into her hairy pussy and watched her beautiful small breasts jump up and down as she fucked me. Her tight cunt muscles gripped me and sent tremors of excitement racing through my body. Davina started to tense, her expression turned to one of sheer joy as she began to climax. The sight of this sophisticated blonde coming on my prick was too much. I was at it again, spurting like crazy.

We spent most of the evening screwing. I had the time of my life. I've managed to be a good boy and keep my secret, although I've been dying to boast to the other blokes. If I did, though, it would be the end of it, and as she lets me make love to her once a week when her husband is out of town, there's no way I'm going to blow it.

Brad. Suffolk.

Show Me the Way, Linzi!

Dear Linzi,
I'd like to share a fantasy with you now if I may?

This particular fantasy begins after we've had a day out together. We arrive home and as it's a hot, sticky evening we decide to change before we do anything else. You leave me to watch a blue movie on the video whilst you go to take a shower. When I think it's safe to do so, I take out my straining erection and gently stroke myself as I watch the two pretty girls giving each other climax after climax in the sixty-nine position, absorbing the vivid close-ups of tongues darting in and out and around shaven pussies. The girls are so obviously enjoying themselves as can be heard from their pleasurable moans and seen from their glistening tongues. I hear a door banging and quickly stuff my stiffness away. God, it wasn't easy to do, Linzi.

'Shower's free now,' you say with a grin on your face. 'I can see you've enjoyed the video,' you say patting my crotch as I walk by with an embarrassed look on my face.

It's a relief to get into the bathroom to get out of my clothes and set my stiff penis free. I hear a few odd noises but think nothing of it and shampoo my hair. My eyes are tightly shut to keep soap out. I feel a slight draught and start to clear my eyes to see what's happening. Before I can see, I feel what must be your sensual lips close around my stiff cock. My eyes are now open. The feelings are new to me and I love them. I watch you tease my length and circle my glans with your expert

229

tongue, and finger your pussy lips with your knowing hands. I am a bit embarrassed and I think you can tell because you stop and ask what's wrong.

'Nothing,' I reply quietly.

You must realize and ask, 'Are you a virgin?'

Well you've hit the nail on the head, Linzi, so I say, 'Yes, but, Linzi, I don't want to be. I want you to take it. I cannot think of anyone more desirable. I really like you, Linzi, I hope you don't mind that?'

'Of course I don't mind, but let's do this properly,' you say.

We get out of the shower and dry one another off, then you lead me to the huge bed. You pull back the sheets and climb in, beckoning me to join you. After a little hesitation I do, and the next hour is spent kissing and cuddling and exploring your body. I place the palm of my hand on your breasts just to get to know the feel of them. Your nipples become erect and I want to suck and lick them. I must be doing the right thing because you are moaning and panting.

'Linzi, I want to fuck you now. I really want to be in you now before I come from just looking at your beautiful body.'

I then position myself between your raised knees and taking my eight inches of stiffness in hand, guide it into your wet pussy. I am determined that this isn't going to be over in a flash and we take it slowly. I know how much I can take from my own masturbation and am going nice and steady whilst kissing you and fondling your breasts. But a hand and a vagina are two completely different things as I discover when your vagina starts to tighten, then loosen quickly around my penis. After that it isn't long before I come inside you.

I don't want to leave you disappointed so I give you a quick orgasm with my fingers. You know, Linzi, losing my virginity to someone as attractive as you would be the perfect way to be introduced to sex!

Barrie. Bolton.

Strip, Strip Hooray!

Dear Linzi,
The reason for me writing this letter is that I'd like to tell you

about a twenty-first birthday surprise I had a couple of weeks ago. It regards a stripogram my mum lined up for me.

The stripogram girl arrived late in the evening whilst mum and I were chatting in the sitting room, with nobody else in the house. She eventually came into the room, and she was wearing a big coat that she soon slipped off to reveal her outfit, which was a basque, silk stockings and suspenders and high heels. She was about thirty years old and had about a 36-inch bust. When she slowly took off her basque to reveal her breasts, her nipples were like big strawberries. I found this very exciting. She undid her suspenders and took down her stockings, lifting each leg up. Then she was just left with her knickers on. She came right up to me so that I could take them off for her, which of course I did, sliding them down over her legs with shaky hands. She was completely naked and she sat on my lap and put her arms around me. I then, quite nervously worked my hands over her breasts, fingering her lovely large nipples. At this point my mum coughed, gave me a wink and went to put the kettle on.

My hands left her big, strawberry nipples and slid down her flat tummy. She obviously could feel my stiff dick pressing against the side of her left buttock, which made her comment, 'Don't worry, it's only natural!' She eased open her legs a little more. This was my chance to get my first real feel of pussy. My hands moved slowly up her legs to her parted thighs and I rubbed a finger along her hairy slit. She felt nice and juicy as I rubbed my fingers up and down her. She was wriggling around on my fingers and squeezing her nipples. I could hear my mum bustling about in the kitchen as I inserted two fingers into the stripogram's cunt. Her breathing started coming in big gasps as she jerked her body up and down. I knew I was running out of time as she started to move faster and faster and then she came with a short, sharp shudder. She gave me a big kiss, thanked me and said she'd love a cup of tea.

I knew what I would have loved, Linzi, I would have loved to have had her upstairs in my bed! My mum is understanding, but not that understanding!

Neil.

Verging on the Ridiculous!

Dear Linzi,

Well they usually say third-time lucky, so here goes! Just a few points first to jog your memory. Sorry there's no address as this could cause problems. I am a twenty-three-year-old virgin; I am clean, smart, and have a good sense of humour. The last time I wrote to you I was unemployed, but good news, I have at last got a job. But this still leaves me with one problem. As you may well remember the last two times I have written to you I have asked you if you could come up to Bromley and help me with my virginity problem. My next suggestion may be more convenient for you. The job I am employed in is sales, but I am not a travelling rep. In September we are at an exhibition in London, and I hope that this will make it more convenient for you to meet me and help me with my problem.

We will be staying at the Wembley International Hotel, Empire Way, from the 16th to the 19th of September. Not knowing anywhere in London, the best place for us to probably meet would be at the hotel. Let's say on the fourth floor by the lifts at 8 p.m. on the 16th? I'm almost certain I will be attending and would really appreciate it if you could possibly help me.

If you do decide to come please bring some sexy underwear, high-heeled boots, fishnet stockings etc. My main ambition is to shave your fanny and then for you to shave my prick, hopefully I won't come while I'm doing it. Then, with you lying on the bed with your legs spread as wide as possible, I would slip my six-and-a-half-inch virgin dick into you and at last pop my cherry. After this you would teach me all the different sexual acts including oral sex.

I would prefer to fuck you rather than a prostitute, not because I won't have to pay you, but because I know you would be more understanding and spend more time with me. This is a genuine appeal, Linzi, and I would really love to come in your cunt and mouth, so please, Linzi, do help me. Every time I see your pictures I fall more in love with you. You have a superb body, lovely tits, a nice round bottom and no words can describe your cunt. With those lovely looks you are the ideal woman. I hope you turn up on the 16th.

Peter Hampton. Bromley.

Voluptuous Virgin

Dear Linzi,

I want to tell you about my first sexual experience. My name is Maggie, and I'm an eighteen-year-old student studying at Cambridge. Until three months ago I was a virgin and I didn't have a boyfriend. There didn't seem much likelihood of that changing, but things did change one Saturday afternoon.

It was quite a warm day and I was out in the high street doing some shopping. As on most Saturdays it was pretty crowded, but despite all the people around, one boy caught my eye. He had the most gorgeous thick black hair and was wearing skintight denims and a T-shirt which emphasized his delightfully proportioned body.

Soon I found myself walking behind him. My mind completely diverted from doing any shopping. I began to feel quite aroused when I noticed he kept stopping, turning around and smiling in my direction.

Eventually he came to a halt and as I walked alongside him he spoke to me. All he said was, 'Hi my name's Alan.' But that was enough for me, my legs turned to jelly and I tried to reply coolly, 'I'm Maggie.'

He was looking me up and down. I was holding my jacket and was just dressed in a pink jersey, a black leather miniskirt and my legs were bare. Most people tell me I have a good figure. I do have good, long legs, but personally I think my boobs are too big. I take a 40DD-sized bra. I glanced down at myself and because I was so excited, my nipples actually seemed to be poking through my jumper. I think he realized his staring had unnerved me, so he apologized and then said he thought I was the most beautiful girl he'd ever seen! Thinking back I suppose it was a bit corny, but at the time it was like music to my ears. Before I knew what was happening Alan had taken hold of my hand and we were crossing the road together.

For the next hour or two we just wandered around chatting and getting to know each other. It turned out that he too was at Cambridge and had lodgings nearby.

Early in the evening we went to the pub for a snack and a couple of beers. It was great and the time just seemed to fly. When we left it was dark outside so Alan walked me home. On our way home, for some reason I turned to Alan and said, 'Would you believe I'm a virgin?'

I don't know what made me utter those words, but it stopped us both in our tracks.

'Yes, I believe it,' he said and kissed me on my lips. We both burst out laughing, deep down knowing the situation was about to change.

I invited Alan in when we got back to my place and he accepted without the slightest hesitation. After hanging our coats up, I went into the kitchen to make some coffee. As I was in the middle of my task I felt Alan's hot breath behind me as he deftly slipped his hands around my waist. I squealed momentarily then turned to face him and gazed into his eyes. We began to kiss passionately, our tongues thrusting and probing. I could feel the whole of my body tensing in anticipation. We stood there in the tiny kitchen kissing and cuddling, our bodies pressed tightly together as one. I wanted to take him off to my bedroom, but I didn't want to let go. So still keeping tongue to tongue and pelvis to pelvis contact, I backed out of the kitchen taking Alan with me.

In my bedroom we fell together on the bed, his body covering mine. We squirmed around, our two bodies rubbing against each other. His feverish hands made their way between my legs and he started to smooth me on top of my pants. I felt myself getting wetter and wetter as he used his other hand on my big boobs. He carried on stroking between my legs with one hand while I helped him to undo my bra. He stared in wonderment at my boobs, squeezing them before licking all around my nipples, biting and nibbling them until they stood out proud and hard.

I was a bit embarrassed as to what to do next, so I decided to leave it all to Alan and just lay back on the bed and enjoy myself. Still rubbing and kissing my boobs, he frantically ripped off my knickers and then started to touch my bare pussy. Gently he stroked me, gradually opening my lips and sliding a finger inside. He moved it around until he found the right spot, then bingo, I started to shake. I grabbed hold of him and told him he was hitting the right spot. With that he let go of my breasts, yanked my leather skirt up higher and crawled between my legs. He took his finger away and very gently touched me with his tongue. I had never let a boy do this to me before, and I knew almost instantly that I'd been missing something very good! Seconds later I wrapped my legs around his shoulders and was climaxing.

But the best was still yet to come. As I lay back on my bed still trembling, he said to me, 'Can I make love to you now?'

'Yes, Yes!' I moaned.

And he did. Very carefully and with much tenderness he pushed the end of his cock inside me. I felt it enter me and the head felt very large within my lips. My pussy began to tingle and shivers ran up and down my spine as slowly but surely his cock penetrated me. I could feel every inch as he slipped it all the way in until I had taken the lot. We rolled around on the bed thrusting at each other. I was really taking to this like a duck to water and within a few minutes I had changed positions and I was on top. I felt a bit self-conscious at first, my big boobs swaying around when I moved my hips in rhythm with his, but I was soon too involved to care. He reached up and supported my boobs, intermittently flicking my nipples which felt sensational as did his big cock pumping away inside me.

The harder he thrust inside me, the more excited I became. I reached over and pushed my boobs against his body, cradling him close to me as our bodies rode up and down, faster and faster, harder and harder. All the time Alan was talking me through it, asking me if I liked what he was doing to me, and if I was about to come.

Suddenly I felt a jolt through my whole body and I knew it was going to be like no orgasm I'd ever had before. At the top of my voice I cried out, 'Now Alan, I'm going to come, I'm going to come!'

We clung together and moved faster and faster, both crying out as we climaxed together.

Well, Linzi. I hope you enjoyed my story. Alan and I are going steady now and the sex just gets better and better.

Maggie. Oxford.

Randy Rita

Dear Linzi,

My name is Rita, I'm thirty-five years old and a housewife. I've been married for twelve years and have two children. My husband is the managing director of a local company and on the whole I enjoy a very comfortable and safe lifestyle. That's not to say I'm entirely content with my lot. There always seemed to be that little something missing, until recently that is.

You see during the last couple of weeks I've done something that's very daring. Something that if my husband found out about could put an end to my comfortable lifestyle. You've probably already guessed that I've been unfaithful to him, Linzi. Well I have and I loved every minute of it. In fact, I've already done it with two different sexual partners. I'm not sure if it's the actual sex that's given me so much pleasure or the fact that for once, it has brought an element of risk and danger into my life.

First off, both incidents took place in my own house and they were both with men my husbands knows.

The first time was on a damp Monday morning. Gerald, a friend of ours, had called round to do a spot of building work. It wasn't especially that we needed too much doing, but Gerald was down on his luck and my husband felt sorry for him and had found him a day's work. Now to be honest I can't stand the bloke. He's the same age as me and I've known him since before he or I was married. On virtually every occasion we meet, Gerald has chatted me up and on some drunken occasions actually attempted to grab my breasts. He's the sort of man I've only tolerated because my husband is so friendly with him, and his wife is a good friend of mine.

As I said earlier I was feeling a bit restless and dissatisfied with my lot, so I decided that if Gerald made a pass at me while he was in the house I would take him up on it. I must admit I gave him plenty of encouragement. To start off with I answered

236

the front door only dressed in my nightie. It was cold and my nipples were standing out like organ stops. As I leaned over to pick the milk up from the doorstep I could feel Gerald's eyes penetrating my cleavage. I think he was a little lost for words, as I offered him a coffee.

As we sat at the breakfast bar drinking our coffee Gerald passed some vulgar comment about the inside of my thigh. I was sitting with my legs slightly open, so I expected him to make such a remark and when he did I began to feel randy.

After about five mintues it was obvious from the bulge in his trousers that I was having a pretty dramatic effect on him. His hand rested on my knee and began sliding ever upward. I cooed seductively, 'Oh Gerald, we shouldn't be doing this, should we?'

That comment was like a rag to a red bull!

Gerald now thought he was totally in control as he told me to take off my nightdress. I played along as subserviently as possible. After I discarded my nightie I was left naked, but for a pair of brief panties, standing in my kitchen at 9.30 in the morning with my husband's best friend drooling all over me. It felt very strange, but I could feel myself getting even more worked up, particularly when Gerald started talking dirty to me. My husband would never dream of saying anything as crude and descriptive, but I found I wanted to hear much more.

Soon we moved into the lounge. Gerald's trousers were off and it was action time. In fairness to him he was very well-endowed and I wasn't sure if I'd be able to cope with him. I didn't get much chance to protest as he turned me around saying he was going to take me from behind. I gasped as he thrust himself at me. I had one knee on the sofa, the other on the floor as Gerald made the most of what he'd been waiting for for almost twenty years! It turned out to be a wonderful session and I was very pleased with my new seductress role.

A week later I began to feel the need for a repeat performance. There was a ring on the doorbell, it was the young man from next door. I'm very good friends with his mother. His mother had sent him around to borrow some milk. Within twenty minutes I had his lovely young cock in my mouth, then he pulled my pants down to my ankles, played with my tits, then fucked me doggy fashion. He told me he had been a virgin!

So, Linzi, I really am playing with fire but I'm having fun. I've got Gerald, and Johnny next door and I'm still on the look out for others. I'm beginning to like this game!

Rita. Dagenham.

Suck Me Dry

Dear Linzi,

There are a few words that describe you – beautiful, horny and delicious. You have the most gorgeous hair I have ever seen. Both on your head and your cunt. Blonde pubes give me a ginormous hard on. You have a breathtaking face and I would give anything to kiss those soft lips. Also your tits are nice and round. But the best is your tanned, long legs and perfect pussy. I've had quite a few daydreams about you. One is when I meet you on a bus. We talk and I invite you back to my house. When we get indoors I need a slash, so I pop to the loo. When I return you are stripped off lying on the floor with your legs wide apart, wearing only slim panties, a bra and stockings. I feel my dick increasing in size. You ask me to undress in a silky voice. Then I sink to my knees, pull your knickers to one side, open the sides of your lips and sink my tongue into your juicy pussy. The taste is superb and then you start having an orgasm over my face. Finally before leaving you give me an amazing blow job and suck my cock dry. I would give anything for a dream like this to come true as I am an eighteen-year-old virgin.

B.L.

15. TOYS THAT PLEASE

Strap on dildos, vibrators, fresh fruit salad and red, spiky, high-heeled shoes are just some of the playthings used for tittilation in this stimulating section. I just hope you're ready for this!

SLAVE TO LOVE

WANKER IN THE WILD

PUMPING FEMALE
   PLEASUREMAKER

MAID FOR EACH OTHER

FEELING FRUITY

SLAM IT IN ON THE STAIRS

SHINY, RED SHOES

UP THE CRACK

WATCH ME WANK,
   HONEY

Slave to Love

Dear Linzi,

After reading in *Men's Letters* magazine how much fun you had when you became a sex slave for the day, I thought that you would be interested to hear about my sex-slave games. Like you, I am highly sexed and I am very lucky with attracting men. That is probably because I am quite a good-looking girl. I am twenty-six years old, stand five feet nine inches tall, have a slender figure, big breasts and very long, blonde hair. I like to dress up in sexy, exotic clothes when I go out and when I play around at home. I also have a vast collection of sex toys.

My men friends don't often last long. I prefer to have a lot of variety with my sex slaves. If they're really good then maybe they'll be allowed to stick around for a couple of weeks before I move on to the next man to please me. I'm amazed how many women don't realize the power of their own sexuality. In certain situations I know I can make a man do anything.

My most recent slave conquest is a managing director of a company. I work as a sales rep so I do get to meet lots of men. This particular man, whom I shall call Barry, is a lot of fun. There had been some sort of problem with an order, so I had to see the boss. As soon as I saw him looking so powerful behind his massive desk, I wanted him. I wanted to have him on his knees begging to put his hand up my skirt or pleading with me pitifully to taste my cunt. It was a piece of cake. I waited until his secretary brought us in some coffee and had left the room, then I took a large black dildo from my briefcase and asked him if he minded continuing our meeting while I fucked myself with a rubber prick. He almost choked on his coffee but he said No! I relaxed back in the swivel chair, hiked up my tight miniskirt and stroked the rubber dicky against my cunt on the outside of my knickers.

'I bet you'd like to watch this big cock sliding inside my hole, wouldn't you?' I teased as I started to turn myself on. In an instant he was on the phone telling his secretary that he didn't want to be disturbed.

'Get down on your knees and come and take a closer look,' I ordered as I wrenched my wet panties off to one side.

On all fours he crawled towards me until he was between my knees.

'Not too close,' I groaned and then excrutiatingly slowly inserted the dildo inside my lubricated lovelips.

'Hold it for me,' I moaned. Barry nodded and gripped the end of the sex toy obediently.

'Now work it in me nice and slowly,' I breathed. 'That's it, slide it all the way in. Get nearer my cunt so you can smell it. I bet you love it, don't you?'

The next minute Barry was only inches from my squelchy pussy breathing heavily and drinking in my aroma.

'I suppose you'd like to lick me, wouldn't you?'

'Oh please, let me please!' was his immediate reply.

Using a long fingernail to expose my pink clitoris, I whispered, 'If you ask very nicely I might let you tongue my clit.'

'Oh please, please!' Barry whined, his face only inches away as he worked the dildo in and out of my sopping slit.

'Make me come with this fat, rubber cock and I might just let you,' I rasped, gritting my teeth as I felt my first climax building.

I allowed Barry to fuck me to two orgasms with my sex toy, then he fingered me to yet another, before I ordered him to smother my ecstatic, hot cunt with cold cream from the coffee tray and slowly lick it off. Soon after he was begging me to let him fuck me. I pushed him away and told him to be at my house in one hour. As I left, I heard him cancelling all his appointments for the afternoon.

We had a whale of a time at my place. After a number of hours of being a good slave and doing exactly as he was told, I eventually gave permission for Barry to fuck me. Barry is a very, good and obedient slave, so I might allow him to stay around for a while.

Janet. Manchester.

Wanker in the Wild

Dear Linzi,

I thought it would be nice to write and tell you of an experience that happened to me last summer. I am twenty-two years old and enjoy cycling. It was a sunny day, so I went for a ride.

After an hour or so I was taken short, so I clambered over a stile into a field for a leak. To my amazement and delight, I spotted this completely naked woman sunbathing in the far corner of the field. She appeared to be quite a bit older than me, probably in her late thirties, early forties but from the look of her, she had it all in the right places!

I had my leak, abandoned my bike and sneaked around the perimeter of the field to get a better look at this naked woman. I was lucky to find a big tree just to the side of her, so I stationed myself there and started to watch her. She was a big woman with soft, heavy tits and a really hairy fanny. As I watched her she seemed to be pretty restless, moving about an awful lot, opening and closing her legs. Because of this I was able to get a good view of her hairy fanny. She started to stroke her big tits. I watched fascinated, already feeling a bulge in my trousers as she slid one hand down her body. She was spreading her legs and I could see her pushing her finger up inside her. I was getting so excited my cock was throbbing in my pants and I was rooted to the spot.

She took her fingers out of her cunt and started sucking them. The next thing I knew she had taken some sort of vibrator out of her bag and was sliding that in and out of her hairy, wet minge. The vibrator was moving really fast and her legs were closing and opening up very slightly. She bent her head and bit on her pink nipple as she fucked herself with the sex toy. I have to admit it, Linzi, it was at this time that, checking there wasn't a soul around and certain that the coast was clear, I took out my dick. It was rock hard as I began to wank my shaft.

I think I came before her. I was spunking in a few seconds, while it took a few more minutes until she was rolling around and crying out, alone (or so she thought!) in the field.

Then I cleaned myself up with my hanky and got back on

my bike leaving her to her multiple orgasms and her sunbathing. It has been a fantasy of mine to screw an older woman ever since!

D.N. Ireland.

Pumping Female Pleasuremaker

To my cock-throbbing, fantasy-girl Linzi,
I have yet another of my fantasies which I would like to share with you. For a number of years now I have had great pleasure in tasting the great wines of the world. After finishing each bottle I find myself licking the top so as not to waste a single drop. My fantasy begins with you, Linzi, stretching your legs across my bed (which by the way is a king-sized double), while I start to thrust the whole neck of my empty white wine bottle in and out of your luscious cherry-red cock stimulator (your cunt) until you reach an almighty orgasm. You replace the wine bottle with my almighty eight-inch drilling rod (my cock), and I guarantee you the pleasure of my pumping female pleasuremaker, which will release all your juices making them run down over my pubes for you to lick off. By now, of course, I would be fingering and tongueing your saturated pussy and erect clitty.

Being a man of the world I must admit I've tasted the best in women so my fantasy would not be complete without me licking your anus whilst you masturbate with a dildo and wank my tool to near orgasmic eruption. I'm a man who also believes in the saying 'waste not, want not', so obviously your firm, rounded, pert-nippled titties would have to be tasted. I'd pour French white wine all over them, allowing the cold liquid to trickle down your navel into your even tastier pussy. I guarantee you that by the time we've tasted each other's beautiful bodies for this long, the fantasy will turn into reality, which will keep us together for a long time.

Antony.

Maid for Each Other

Dear Linzi,

I'd love to watch two beautiful women get it on together. Here's my ultimate fantasy:

I work as a landscape gardener, so I meet many women while working in different gardens. In my fantasy I am working in the garden of a manor house. It's very hot indeed and so the lady of the house suggests that when I need a drink I just go to the fridge and help myself. That's exactly what I do do, and while I'm pouring myself a glass of fruit juice, I hear a loud moaning coming from the next room. Feeling curious, I open the breakfast hatch and peep through. There before my very eyes is the lady of the house sitting back on the sofa completely starkers with her legs spread and resting on the shoulders of her maid, who is on her knees engrossed in plunging a massive vibrator in and out of her boss's pussy.

Both women are gorgeous. The maid is around eighteen years old, dark-haired and sultry, and dressed in a cute uniform that shows off her big tits, tiny waist and long legs. Her mistress is a sophisticated blonde in her early thirties. Her small tits are jumping up and down as her maid works the lovetoy in and out of her blonde, fuzzy cunt. Neither woman notices my intrusion so I continue to spy on them as the lady of the house starts to wriggle and writhe in orgasm.

Then it's the maid's turn. Her mistress strips her slowly, cupping her hanging melons, fingering her soft skin and running her gentle fingertips over her peachy arse and thick bush of black pubic hair. The maid is whimpering continuously as she gets down on all fours and spreads her legs right in my line of vision. Her cunt is dribbling and my heart feels like it is about to stop. The lady of the house opens her lesbian lover's hairy crack with both hands and I get a glimpse of her pink, wet cunt. I can almost smell it. She inserts a manicured finger and screws it around in her maid's hole. She fucks the finger in and out then licks it greedily. She takes hold of a golden, buzzing vibrator and from behind runs it all over her maid's cunt, centring on her clitoris, rotating it round and round.

244

The maid starts to scream out loud when she sees what's coming next. The mistress straps on a black, plastic prick and swiftly rams it in her maid's hot cunt. As she thrusts hard inside her, the young maid's big tits are swinging and slapping around. She is fucked hard and fast, her mistress fingering her nipples, slapping her bouncing buttocks until her maid starts screaming wildly and they collapse on top of each other.

The lady unstraps the plastic cock and lies on top of the maid, grinding her blonde fuzzy cunt into her lover's dark hairy one. They wrap their long, lean legs around each other and ride their wet cracks until they are coming again and again. Linzi, it looks like my fantasy has got the better of me, time to go!

Dave. Sussex.

Feeling Fruity

Dear Linzi,

My sex life is pretty good and I've a steady boyfriend who I'm very fond of. I suppose on average he fucks me about three or four times a week, but a lot of the time he works away and that is when my kinks take over. Of course you're dying to know what kinky games I get up to! Well, I play all sorts of games by myself. Fruit cocktail is one I especially enjoy. I cut up all different kinds of fruit into small segments. I usually choose plums, oranges, grapes, apples and melons and then I test how each fruit feels inside my cunt – for sensations or slipperiness, durability, messiness, but most of all overall ecstasy content. If I get the opportunity I try all sorts of exotic fruits, but of all the ones I've tried I must admit the banana suits me best.

Another game I enjoy is to get my Polaroid camera, loaded with flash and film, and hold it at arms length. I begin to gently squeeze and caress my naked body with one hand while holding the camera with the other. I then proceed to take photos of my various stages of arousal, capturing a dramatic display of my fingerwork on my cunt and ferocious manipulation of my clit. It gives me a great deal of personal satisfaction if I am able to capture an orgasmic expression on my face, or better still catch my cunt coming!

I remember once sending a batch of these photographs to an ex-boyfriend who had just rejected me. With the photos I enclosed a note saying, 'Wish you were here!' He telephoned me a few days later, but I told him to get lost!

Michelle. Tonbridge Wells.

Slam it in on the Stairs

Dear Linzi,

Like most sensual women I enjoy experimenting in bed. My boyfriend has a vivid imagination and together we have some great sex. He loves to watch me masturbate, and I used to be a little embarrassed by this, but seeing how much this turns him on makes me really enjoy it. It's not just in the bedroom he likes to watch me wank, sometimes he'll ask me to do it while I'm sitting watching TV, or in the bathroom after taking a shower. He even gets me at it out in the garden when it's warm enough! I've got a couple of vibrators with variable speeds, and I also like to fiddle with my fingers. I've got very long nails and I love the feel of them on my juiced-up pussy.

The other night was very special because he asked me to sit halfway up the stairs and play with myself. He lay flat on his stomach on the stairs in front of me and observed closely as I pulled my tight black knickers to the side and showed off my cunt. With my long nails I parted my honey-blonde pubic hairs and gave him first sight of my pink. I was already wet and my clit was popping out. Very slowly I used one finger to slide the length of my slit, rubbing it up and down until my finger was smothered with my juice. Then I offered it to his mouth. He sucked on it urgently and then tried to tongue my cunt, but I told him he had to wait.

I wanked myself to climax three times, twice with my fingers and then with my favourite vibrator, then I let him lick me out, turn me around on to my knees and fuck me hard on the staircase. I loved every dirty minute of it.

Carol. Thornby.

Shiny, Red Shoes

Dear Linzi,

My husband, Ernie, and I have a fetish for high-heeled shoes. We use them as our sex toys to stimulate us and add that extra dimension to our sex life. He likes me to parade around naked for him just wearing thigh-length boots, or shiny, black, patent court shoes or ankle boots with a high heel and padlock. I've got some fabulous footwear because he's always buying it for me. I look good in ridiculously spiky heels. I've got slender, long legs, a tight little arse, long red hair, bright blue eyes and a big wide gash of a mouth. I've got full, firm boobies and my right nipple is pierced. My cunt is always moist and covered in a layer of fine ginger hair.

Ernie gets off on wanking over my feet encased in shiny shoes, or by watching me run my tongue over a pair of shoes, especially when I tongue the heels. I never wear my best ones out of the house, I just keep them for playing around with at home. Last week Ernie bought me a present and we had so much fun with my gift that I felt I just had to write to you, Linzi.

Ernie came home from work with a parcel. When I opened the box, I was turned on immediately by the cherry-red, patent, high heels inside. The heel measured around six inches and there was an ankle strap that made the shoes look amazing. I asked Ernie to go upstairs and get undressed. I stripped off, oiled up my voluptuous body and placed a chair from the kitchen in the centre of the room. I took some silky stockings from the cupboard and then called my husband.

He was stark bollock naked and his penis stood to attention when he walked in the room. I told him to sit down and then taking the stockings I fastened his arms behind his back and secured them to the chair, then bound one leg to each front leg of the chair.

When he was totally tethered and helpless, I placed one spiky heel between his open legs, just a few inches from his cock and told him I wanted to feel his spunk all over my red, shiny shoes. Ernie was squirming and his cock visibly twitching as I steadily rubbed the toe of my shoe along the underside of his dong.

Then I lay on the floor with my ginger fanny facing him. With one hand I fingered my open gash, the other I used to stroke my shoes. Ernie was starting to wriggle around frantically and pleading to be set free. I dragged another chair alongside him and stood on it. My wet fanny was just inches away from his face as I slid two fingers inside. Then, balancing carefully I raised one leg and allowed Ernie to lick at my shoe.

By now we were both so fired up that fucking was the order of the day. I like to be on top, so I straddled my husband. I allowed his pink cockhead to touch my cunt lips, then jerked away for a few seconds to savour the tingling in my cunt. Then I gradually sat down, fanny first on his thrusting phallus, my cunt so lubricated his pole slid in me with ease. I started to control him by setting the pace, moving up and down and leaning forward a little. I love to feel Ernie's cock in me at an angle. That night neither of us could hold back and within a few minutes the come was flowing.

Maria. London.

Up The Crack

Dear Linzi,

Hello. I hope you're fine. I am a twenty-year-old virgin who wanks a lot. Recently I finally got my fingers up the crack of a girl I've fancied for three years. On the night Jenny came round to my house and I unbuttoned her jeans, she was wearing black, brushed-cotton knickers. I would have given anything to fuck her. Anyway, she let me rub her. I pulled her knickers off to the side and tried to stick a finger in her pussy. I wasn't very experienced at this, so she showed me how to do it. As I fingered her she told me that I should take my trousers off. I did. I knew she wouldn't let me fuck her, so I bought a vibrator especially for her. I eased it into her as she laid back. I kissed her hard as I rammed the plastic cock inside her. She was still wearing her tight, wet knickers. She seemed to love what I was doing to her, crying out loud as I shoved it in and out.

Linzi, I have a kink that I'd like to share with you and you only. I love wearing women's nylon knickers. I don't dress up in women's clothes, just women's knickers. I told a friend of mine this and he gave me a pair of his mum's, they're pink, silky nylon. I like to sniff them while I'm wanking.

Tony. Dorset.

Watch Me Wank, Honey

Dear Linzi,

I am thirty-eight and have been married to the same man for fifteen years, so as you can imagine my husband and I like to try new sex games for variety. One of Lloyd's favourite pastimes is watching me masturbating. I'm a real exhibitionist and his eagerness to spend ages ogling me, turns me on no end. I like to lie on our bed while he sits in a chair at the end, and I talk him through it. I like to dress in stockings, suspenders and tight briefs or sometimes crotchless knickers. Lately I've started wearing a bright-red, one-piece teddy that unbuttons under the crotch, and I can really put that bit of underwear to good use.

I've got small tits, but my nipples are very special, they cover over half the area of my tits and they can increase in size to almost an inch in length. I make myself comfy on some pumped-up pillows and start off with my tits, fingering my nipples and talking dirty to the old man while I frequently open and close my legs. Lloyd usually takes his cock out and wanks as soon as I get going.

When I've got my nipples looking just the way I like them, I rub my hands up and down my body and play with myself through my pants. I start to get wet and a damp patch is soon evident. I love to taste my cunt when I'm turning myself on, so I slide my fingers up inside the gusset of my panties and cover my fingers with my lovejuice. I keep very quiet at this point so that Lloyd, can hear just how wet I am. As I suck each juicy finger, Lloyd is always wanking furiously.

Now I pull open the buttons of my outfit and reveal my hot pulsing sex. With both hands I part my pussy lips and give Lloyd a good, wide-open look at me. Then I play around with my clit, all the while licking my lips and telling him how much I want his cock. I take hold of my vibrator, it's black and about ten inches long and nice and thick. Slowly I force it into me, pushing it in and out, in and out, occasionally removing it completely to wank over my clitoris. I talk to Lloyd as I get more and more turned on, and it never takes me long to come when I'm playing this game. Just as I'm in the first throes of orgasm Lloyd usually jumps on me and replaces my ten-inch dildo with his massive nine-inch shaft.

Anyway, Linzi, that's how I keep my sex life interesting!

Peta. I.O.W.

16. VULGAR VOYEURS

Peeping Toms with binoculars, amorous exhibition-
ists and cock-loving housewives and their voyeur-
istic spouses are just a horny handful who have
contributed to this particularly carnal chapter. Take
a peek, I bet you'll love reading their randy
relevations!

A ROOF WITH A VIEW   JUICED-UP JENNY

FOXY FLASHER   KEEP IT IN THE FAMILY

PERK UP YOUR SEX LIFE   SEX QUEEN WAITING FOR

A ROOM WITH A VIEW   A STUD

A Roof With a View

Dear Linzi,

I thought you might be interested in a very sexy happening that took place at my place of work a few days ago. Now sex in my line of work is particularly unusual as I'm a roofer by trade, and as you can probably imagine, screwing on slated roof tiles has got to be one of the most difficult locations for lust. As it happens this wasn't the case. The sex took place in a bedroom of a house, and my roof where I was busy at work, just happened to be the best viewpoint.

The day began as normal with my young assistant and I busy on our roof by about eight-thirty. We were working on the back of a small two-up, two-down terraced house. The back garden ran to meet with another house, similar in proportions. I'm not sure how my eyes were attracted to this particular house at the back, or the bedroom, but I was drawn somehow. I spied a very well-built blonde in her mid-twenties strutting around with the curtains drawn back and she was totally naked. I tell you, Linzi, I almost slid off the roof. Excitedly I told my helper, Joe, and we both scrambled a little lower to get a better look.

The woman knew that we were watching her and she was in her element. A real show off. She had lovely, full breasts, probably about 38's and she loved flaunting them. We watched mesmerized as she sat on the edge of the bed, spread her thighs open wide and then started to play with her tits. After pinching and squeezing her nipples a great deal, she even managed to slide the nipple of her left breast into her mouth.

Well by now Joe and I had steaming great erections and she knew it. I made sure I was safe on the roof as I continued to stare at her. I didn't know where to look as she kept on sucking on her red nipple while one hand strayed down between her thighs. Even from the distance of about thirty feet, I knew her pussy was soaking wet.

As she slipped her fingers inside her blonde, hairy snatch, she released her bosom and threw her head back ecstatically. I almost came in my overalls as she removed her finger and slowly sucked on it, all the time looking over in our direction.

From then on the spectacle just got better and better and I must confess that I took out my cock and started to stroke it as I watched the entertainment before my very eyes. I thought what the hell, we were in a very secluded position, so there was little chance that anyone would know or believe what was going on up there!

Joe took my initiative and before long we were both beating our meat like crazy and watching this horny bitch in action. Now she seemed to be in such a frenzy, she was on all fours on the bed, her arse thrust out towards us, her fingers moving feverishly on her clit, all the time her ample bosom bouncing and swaying.

I really thought it couldn't get much better, and then it did. Another girl, a different type altogether, but just as pretty, walked into the bedroom to join the blonde. The newcomer was also naked. She had short, dark hair, an impish face and small tits with great big, brown nipples. She looked about eighteen or nineteen years old. As soon as she sat down on the bed, the blonde took her fingers away from her fanny and stuck them straight into the brunette's mouth. Then they started attacking each other's mouths with their tongues, their hands groping hard nipples and fingering hairy pussies.

As I'm relating this story to you, Linzi, it seems too amazing to be true, but I swear to you it is. I just lay there with my swollen dick in my hand calling out encouragement like, 'Suck that pussy, you horny little bitch!'

Joe was also calling out to the girls, egging them on as they manoeuvred into position to perform a sixty-nine. At this point, we couldn't see too much, but we knew what was going on alright, and the excitement of those hot, eager tongues had me spunking like never before.

The girls must have come soon after because they were making a hell of a row. After a moment or two they stood up and took a bow, then spread open their fannies to show us their swollen clitties. From our rooftop viewpoint we could just make out how pink and bulging they were. I tell you, Linzi, it was sheer magic!

John. Bristol.

Foxy Flasher

Dear Linzi,

My wife is such a wild one. Whenever we go out she winds the blokes up something rotten. She never wears knickers and is forever flashing at men. The other night in a country pub she went even further and picked up this young bloke and let him fuck her.

We'd just gone out for a quiet, early evening drink in a country pub, but as usual Marie was on top form. She was wearing a thin cotton dress that buttoned up the front. Marie purposely left the top three buttons undone to show off a hint of her big bosom and because she is, of course, such a randy little flirt. It gives me a right buzz watching men ogling my wife, but them actually getting their hands on her is another story. That is until the other night when I let her fuck a complete stranger.

I got a couple of drinks from the bar and when I got back to the table, I noticed this young bloke, who couldn't have been more than about twenty, eyeing my missus. Marie was loving every minute of it. I handed her her drink and sat down next to her. She took a large gulp of her cider and let some of the liquid seep out of her mouth and dribble down her chin. Staring over at this young man in the corner, she deliberately stuck out her tongue and slowly licked her wet lips. The cider had also trickled down her neck and made the front of her dress wet, so Marie started to rub at the material, cleverly caressing her nipples at the same time.

'You're driving him crazy Marie!' I told her.

'Wait until I give him a flash of my hairy cunt!' she laughed. Then her face turned quite serious as she asked me, 'Would you mind if I fucked him?'

I could feel my cock stirring in my pants as I stared at her open-mouthed and answered: 'Only if you let me watch!'

Well one flash of her minge and John joined us at the table.

254

Marie started to wind him up immediately and before too long he had one hand up her skirt playing around with her fanny. Marie wriggled around in the chair moaning softly as he stuck his fingers inside her pulsating pussy. I could hear the slurpy noise of his fingers sliding in and out of my wife's hot twat and it was making my cock bone hard.

Five minutes later the three of us were outside the pub, screened from prying eyes behind a wall of bushes. Marie was on her back, her skirt pulled up to her waist and John was between her legs slurping at her hairy hole. Marie squashed her heavy jugs together and tweaked her rosebud nipples. She was loving it, panting and puffing and sliding her hot cunt all over John's face as he licked her greedily. I stood just a few feet away, my stiff tool in my hand and watched my wife have her cunt eaten.

It wasn't long before John's long, thin meat was slapping into my wife. She was kneeling on the grass, her arse cheeks wobbling as he vigorously fucked her, each thrust causing Marie to scream loudly. It was such a turn on seeing my wife fucked that I wanked faster and faster. All of a sudden Marie started to thrash about wildly. My randy, cock-loving wife was coming. Suddenly John withdrew and splashed his sticky cream all over my wife's bare arse. I jerked my dick a few more times and spurted my come all over Marie's lovely bum cheeks.

Bob. Oxford.

Perk up Your Sex Life

Dear Linzi,
A few months ago my sex life was non-existent, so me and my husband, Jerry, sat down to talk about our problems. Jerry is an avid *Penthouse* reader and he suggested that we both browse through an issue together, to get some ideas to get us both excited. On your letters page we came across one particular letter about a guy who liked to watch his wife having it off with other men, especially well-endowed black guys! Well, anyway, this letter got us both thinking about trying something a little bit different.

My chance to make events occur happened very quickly when we had two burly workmen around to mend the road outside the house. I took a shine to them and said to Jerry that I'd like to have them both in for a cup of tea. By the glint in my eyes, he knew I had designs on them. So Jerry positioned a mirror on the landing to have a bird's-eye view of the goings on!

I invited them in and they accepted. One of them was a tall blond boy of about nineteen, the other man was perhaps in his mid thirties, thick set with dark, curly hair. They sat in the kitchen while I prepared the tea, all the time I exaggerated my movements, leaning over them, offering them a biscuit and sticking out my firm bosom at every opportunity.

I sat in a chair opposite them and I could see that they were both getting a bit hot under the collar, especially the younger man. I was only wearing a small dressing gown, and as I got up to get them some more tea, I let the flap fall open, revealing that I was completely naked underneath it. As I handed the blond his cup of tea, I thrust my bare crotch towards him and immediately he started caressing my thighs. The other guy stood up and started to kiss me, his tongue probing in and out of my mouth. Being starved of a really good sex session for so long, my juices were running from me as blondie slipped his fingers inside me and started to frig me.

I slid the other guy's cock into my mouth and sucked it firmly between my wet lips. Blondie took his fingers from me and filled me up with his hot cock. The harder he pumped, the harder I sucked until we all came together in a shaky climax.

Then they laid me on the kitchen table and both screwed me again. When they left Jerry came into the kitchen with his cock still out, limp from wanking himself silly. So thanks to *Penthouse* we are happy again!

Mrs Y. Cumbria.

A Room With a View

Dear Linzi,

I want to tell you about an amazing experience that has happened to me. It began one evening as I was going to bed.

I was in my bedroom about to pull my curtains when I noticed a light on in the flat directly opposite mine. The curtains were not drawn and the lady who lived there was undressing. I was glued to my window as this tall, dark, beauty gradually began to strip out of her clothes. She had a lovely pair of perky tits, a round bum and soon to be revealed glorious thatch of thick black pubic hair. As I watched her, I could feel my prick hardening inside my pants, and as soon as she got into bed and turned out the lights, I pulled the curtains, took my prick out and beat my meat.

The next morning I spotted her at the bus stop as I set off to walk to work. Seeing her standing there made another bulge appear in my pants, especially when she smiled at me.

That night I kept a vigil in my bedroom and right at 11.30 she came into her bedroom. I was ready for her armed with my binoculars (I usually use them for horseracing). That night she really went to town. She slipped out of her skirt and blouse revealing bright red undies, which she took off incredibly slowly. I had a distinct feeling that she knew I was watching her and was enjoying every minute of it. As she squeezed out of her half-cup, push-up bra, I undid the zip of my trousers. She started to rub her nipples with the palms of her hands, closing her eyes in ecstasy. I stood behind my curtains, my binoculars in one hand and my growing member in the other. She turned her back towards me, stuck her rotund bottom out, and with a little wiggle, very slowly eased down her panties. With my binoculars I managed to home in on her pussy as she thrust her bottom towards the window and lay on her tummy on the bed.

As soon as she lay down her hands went behind her to her bottom and she began to fondle her cheeks, squeezing at the delicious, curvaceous mounds of flesh. Then she reached into her beside cabinet and pulled out a shiny, silver vibrator which she slid between her lips and sucked on eagerly. As I could see her lovely mouth working on the vibrator tip, I shuddered to my first orgasm, but I was far from finished yet!

Completely naked, she rolled over on to her back and for the first time I got a great view of her black, bushy puss. Zooming in there with my binoculars, I could almost smell her cunt as she opened her legs and moved the vibrator down her body. It came to rest on her pubic hair and she started to rub it along her hairline, her body slithering and sliding all over the bed as she did. By now my cock was stiff and excited once more, especially when she took the tip of the vibrator and made contact with her cunt. I could almost imagine the taste of her sweet clitoris as she started to rotate the vibrator between her lips, obviously in search of her lovebutton. Her body started to buck up and down, and her lovely head with her fabulous dark hair shook around wildly. That time, I honestly believe we came together!

I was still not sure if she was putting on this show for me, even when she placed the vibrator in her mouth and started sucking her own lovejuices. But I was sure when she walked over to the window to pull the curtains, and she blew me a kiss!

Well the next morning I stopped to talk to her at the bus stop and she asked me outright (in a whisper!) if I had a good wank over her last night. When I told her frankly that I did, she smiled and invited me over to her flat. I did, and naturally I stayed all night. She is an expert cocksucker and just loves to watch me wank. We screw together regularly now and I wouldn't change my neighbour for the world!

Al. West Midlands.

Juiced-up Jenny

Dear Linzi,
I finally talked my wife, Jenny, in to allowing me to watch her wank herself off. She's always at it, and up until recently she never let me get a look in. It happened after we were looking at a copy of *Men's Letters* magazine. She loves reading the dirty letters and also seems very taken with the girlie photosets. She seems to have a fascination with the girl's pussies, as I must confess I do! Anyway it all started when Jenny said to me that she thought it funny how these girls could quite happily spread their legs like that and not feel embarrassed. I answered her by saying that I thought pussies were so beautiful they

deserved to be shown off. With that she whipped off her knickers and lay back in the armchair. When she asked me in a sexy voice if I thought her pussy stood up against the model girls, I told her she had a beauty and made a move to touch her. She giggled and told me too look, but not touch, just as if she was a girl in a magazine.

She began to comb her fingers through her curly bush. I could tell she was getting turned on, so I asked her to let me watch her make herself come. She was really into it by now and she nodded her head. She raised one leg so that it was resting on the edge of the chair and then she wriggled her bum forward and thrust out her bare cunt. I could see from her juiced-up crack that she was starting to get wet already. She parted her soft bush and used a forefinger to trace a line up and down her slippery sex. Breathing heavily, she started to move her hips in time with her fingers. Her fingers were creeping closer and closer to her hole as she began to whimper. She inserted two fingers and slipped them in and out, while she used her thumb on her clit. I could smell her sweet juices as she flicked her thumb on her clitty, faster and faster, until she cried out that she was coming. It was at that point I just had to get my mouth on her wet pussy.

After drinking her juices I just wanted to bang her. Jenny was dying for it too. I bent her legs back by her ears and rammed my mammoth erection up her to the hilt. Her pussy was wetter than ever when I fucked her, hard and fast until we both came and she licked the sticky cream from around my throbbing knob.

Now Jenny adores me to watch her wank and I've got *Men's Letters* to thank for that!

Brian. Scotland.

Keep it in the Family

Dear Linzi,
Many times I've read letters printed in men's magazines which relate to wife swopping, or in particular just watching your wife get screwed by another bloke. I always thought it kinky and

something that I'd probably not try as it would only end up in rows and bothers, but to my great delight, me and the missus have tried it and we both get off on it!

Babs, my wife of seven years, is a very sexy lady. She loves to be fucked and is never afraid to make the first move. In fact I think she is probably more highly sexed than I am. If a couple of days go by when I don't service her, then she gets the right needle.

It just so happened that we'd had a few problems within my family which resulted in my brother-in-law coming to stay with us. All fine and dandy until Babs starts telling me one night while we're in bed making love, that she would like to fuck my brother-in-law. The thought of it made me spunk instantly!

But it wasn't until a few days later that she told me the same thing when I was having my tea. She was deadly serious about it and wanted to know if I would mind. So I asked her exactly what she had in mind. She told me she wanted to sneak into his bed that night and see how he would react. I told her that I didn't object just as long as I could watch, and I suggested that instead of creeping in on Tommy we should confront him when he came in from work.

So, all agreed, aside from Tommy that is, Babs went into the bedroom and got dressed up in a slinky knitted dress that buttoned down the front. She put on her best, matching undies, minus the knickers, with stockings and high heels, prettied herself up with make up and perfume. That done, we waited for Tommy.

Tommy came in wearing his overalls. He's a mechanic so he gets very grimy. He commented on how nice Babs looked and then went upstairs for a wash. Babs was beaming. He returned a short while later, and when he walked into the room, Babs patted the sofa and invited him to sit beside her. Still having no comprehension of the situation, Tommy sat down and asked what there was to eat. That was the opportunity Babs was waiting for. She dragged her skirt higher up her thighs and exhibiting her stocking tops and hairy cunt told him he could eat her if he was hungry.

You should have seen his face, Linzi. He looked from Bab's cunt to me and back to her cunt again. I asked him what he was waiting for and then he dived straight in, opening her hairy lips with both hands and licking her. Babs whimpered ecstatically and I could see his long pink tongue sliding in and out of her wet pink slit. Babs is one of those women who gets very wet and I could actually see the juice oozing from her cunt.

'Fuck her Tommy!' I urged.

Babs scrabbled over on to all fours as Tommy wrestled out of his clothes. As he slid his stiff tool into my wife's open cunt, I felt a slight twinge of jealousy, but it soon passed as I took my dick out and hurried towards them.

'Do you want my dick as well, you horny little bitch?' I asked.

But she didn't answer me. Oh no, she just grabbed it and sank her lips around me.

You know it was quite bizzare. Tommy, who due to his marital problems hadn't had a jump in months, slapped it into my lovely wife, while she sucked me off. Weird, but mind-blowing nevertheless! That was the one and only time with Tommy. Babs and I decided that it's best if we don't get attached as a threesome, but just grab the moment when it happens. We've had half-a-dozen sessions so far. Sometimes Babs takes us both on at once and other times I wait until the other fellow has finished with my wife before I take my turn. Babs is very, very happy!

R.P. Kent.

Sex Queen Waiting for a Stud

Dear Linzi,

I am one of those lucky guys who has a really randy wife. She's always keen to try out new tricks and her latest sex game is fucking other men. This arrangement suits me down to the ground, and as long as these studs wear a condom and I can watch, I'm all for it. She's got three blokes who service her regularly. They weren't hard to find because she is a very good-looking girl, the wife. She's twenty, five feet nine inches tall, has a lovely figure with big tits and she has long, chestnut-coloured hair. The studs just can't get enough of her ginger minge!

We usually make an evening of it. She invites one of her blokes round. Before they turn up, she dresses up in some sexy undies (her favourite colours are red and black), then she sits up in bed like some sort of sex queen and waits for her fuck to turn up. I let them in and then take up my position on a chair at the end of the bed. She always makes them go down on her first, makes them suck her wet pussy for ages before she lets them fuck her. I love to watch their tongues flick all over her nipples and clitty. I usually sit wanking and watch them at it. By the time her stud gets to fuck her I've usually come, so I stop wanking because I like to save the next lot of come for her. As soon as she's had enough of her stud, she asks them to leave and then lets me have my go!

Donny. Milton Keynes.

17. WHAT A MOUTHFUL!

Oral sex. It kind of rolls off the tongue, doesn't it?
Well in this closing, climactic chapter it certainly
does! There's plenty of pulsating pussy getting a
good tongue-bath, and throbbing members galore;
twitching and coming and splashing and spurting.
Sounds like good fun, eh? Read on, it is!

Oral Paradise

Dear Linzi,

I am an eighteen-year-old girl who is quite naive about sex. I am still a virgin, and did intend to remain that way for a while. I wanted to take things slowly, but I've met a thirty-five-year-old man who is such a skilled lover that he awakens new sexual desires within me.

I met Brian in a wine bar. He isn't my type at all really, but for some reason his body language excited me. I left my friends and went off to a restaurant with Brian, and throughout the evening I felt myself being wound up so tight that I felt I might burst. By the time he drove me home in his car I was desperate for him to kiss me, to feel his hands all over my body, but he behaved like a perfect gentleman.

When we got to my bedsit, I invited him in for a coffee. He accepted. As the term bedsit suggests, my humble abode is quite small and the bed is quite a main feature. Brian took my hands and pulled me down to sit beside him on the bed. Then he kissed me tenderly. His lips were so soft and moist and his tongue probed into my mouth urgently. I felt shivers run up and down my spine as this older man's hot breath and warm tongue made me all of a tremble.

I had no control over myself after that. Brian undressed me, his fingertips and tongue lingering on every curve and crevice of my body, his sensuous mouth teasing my nipples, sucking them, using his teeth to bite on them gently. I was whimpering softly and breathing heavily as Brian slipped my wet knickers easily down my thighs. It was then that I told him I was a virgin. My knickers were discarded as he parted my thighs with his strong hands and told me not to worry. He kissed my bare belly and told me that he was not going to make love to me with his prick, but with his tongue. As he uttered the words, I trembled with excitement and anticipation.

Brian's tongue was lashing across my inner thighs. I spread them wide and looked down at my glistening pussy. He raked his fingers through my soft brown pubic hairs and his finger travelled up and down the length of my slit. My cunt was throbbing and I could smell my sexual juices. His mouth was moving closer and closer to my wet lips. I had never allowed a man to lick me before, but at that moment I have never wanted anything as much. I craved to feel his sensual tongue flickering around my lips, my clit, and I wanted to feel its wetness slide deep inside me.

Brian lifted his eyes to mine and told me to relax. I nodded and wished he'd get on with it. The very next second, he did. He used both hands to open my cunt slightly and then his tongue made contact. When his slippery tongue probed the folds of my sex, an involuntary spasm ran through my body. He licked his way to my clit and gently he lapped at it, his saliva washing over it, his tongue swirling around every crevice of my aching cunt, making my body jerk and giving me an immediate orgasm.

My cunt was throbbing, pulsating as his tongue licked me with long, tender strokes, concentrating on my clit yet taking time to penetrate me orally. I felt another orgasm build as his darting tongue slithered up inside me and he buried his nose in my cunt. This time I clung on to him, grabbed his head and pulled him hard onto my climactic cunt, grinding myself into him, screaming and hollering as I began to come again and again.

Brian spent almost two hours making love to my pussy. I've never experienced sex like it. I'm not sure about not wanting to lose my virginity now, because if Brian wants to lick me for hours, then fuck me for hours, I've got a feeling that I'm not only going to let him, but I am going to be in absolute paradise.

Janey.

Fancy a Lick?

Dear Linzi,
Love your letters page in *Penthouse* and the whole magazine

for that matter! Just thought I'd like to see my favourite fantasy about you in print. So here goes:

I am an amateur photographer and attend weekly camera club meetings. Every Wednesday we have a model pose for the fifteen or so regulars who turn up. The models are usually housewives and part-time girls, who are on the whole quite pretty and don't mind flashing their pussies for a tenner an hour. And, the men who go do their best to get some adventurous shots.

Well in my fantasy I turn up one Wednesday and see a poster outside the club advertising a guest appearance by yours truly, Linzi Drew. I am absolutely thrilled as are all the other blokes. You are just as stunning in real life as you are in all your pictures, and we all get down to work when you strike up a pose, wearing just a skimpy black garter belt, fishnet stockings and high heels. As you pose on the backdrop I get the distinct impression that you are focusing your attention on me as your big, green eyes seem to be watching my every move. As you change from one position to the next, I become aware that you are actually staring at me. I can hardly believe it, but I snap away getting the best possible shots and more importantly I also get a great view of your pussy!

I keep on taking my pictures, well and truly aware that I am getting a hard-on underneath my jeans. Naturally I try to control it, but the more photos I take, the more I am convinced that you know exactly what you're doing to me. When I glance around the room at the other photographers, I realize that none of the others are looking hot and bothered and none of them seem to have noticed my predicament.

Anyway I manage to keep my swelling cock under control until the end of the hour session. You take your leave of the set, and another model takes over, but I'm not interested in her. My eyes are firmly fixed on you as you drape a robe around your shoulders. You wink at me, beckon me over and say, 'I wonder if you've a minute to help me with something in my dressing room?'

Of course I agree enthusiastically and then I follow you trance-like to a tiny curtained-off area at the other end of the large studio.

Once inside you slip the robe from your shoulders and gently run your hand over the crotch in my jeans.

'I see you have a bit of a problem with your cock!' you giggle, and quicken the speed of your hand, which is now squeezing and massaging my ever-swelling member.

I gulp and say nothing as your red-tipped fingernails trace a step up to my top button which you release.

'Sit down,' you order, and offer me a high stool.

I do exactly as I'm told as you slowly unzip me and slide your hand inside my pants, finding my hard cock and easing it out through the gap in my trousers.

'I fancy a lick. Would you like me to suck on it?' you ask, licking your lips and starting to wank me up and down.

I nod my head, still unable to find any words. Then your hand moves much faster, stroking firmly, until suddenly I feel your hot, slippery tongue on my helmet.

All the time you are almost naked, but I know I can look but not touch because you are completely in control with those lips that surround my cock. As the tip of your tongue slides all around my knob end, you use one hand to stroke my hard length while the other hand toys with my bollocks. My final ecstasy comes when you release my cock from your sensuous lips, and, still wanking me ferociously, you suck both my balls into your mouth.

Then you damp your full lips with your juicy tongue, give me another wink and say naughtily, 'That's better!' which I take as my cue to grab a wad of tissues and leave.

Simon. Clapham.

Deep-Throat Delight

Dear Linzi,

I have heard of many couples experimenting with deep throating, none too successfully because of the girl gagging and choking. My experience fairly recently seems to have overcome the problem and I thought it may be of interest to you.

First of all let me explain that until recently I was not a dedicated cocksucker. In fact I would never suck my husband's prick at all, as he was uncircumsized and I did not find it attractive enough to take between my lips. At the age of twenty-five he was circumsized, not totally because of my preference, but due to medical reasons as well.

Within a month of his operation I started to lick and suck his penis. I had actually tasted his spunk before when licking my fingers after wanking him, but now I was able to get the real feel of his lovejuice as I swallowed his hot cream eagerly. Now the rolls of his foreskin were gone, I found I was hooked on sucking him at every opportunity. His naked tip is irresistible to my lips. I spend hours on my knees with his smooth, nine-inch dick in my hands, holding him firmly by the base and sliding my tongue up and down his shaft, swirling my tongue into the eye of his knob and welcoming him into the warmth of my mouth.

Taking fellatio one step further was my ultimate desire. I started to practise deep throat by sliding my fingers down my throat, which was awful and made me feel sick. So I moved on to a banana which was much softer and pretty quickly I found I could insert it very gently and remove it without gagging. I was keen to try it with Gary, my husband.

Taking things slowly at first, I allowed him to touch the back of my throat with his knob, and then push very gently. I find it works best if I lie on my back on the bed with my head hanging off the edge, while Gary lowers his cock into my throat.

I've got my wish and I must say I'm something of a deep-throat expert these days. There really is nothing like that creamy whoosh of hot jism spurting straight down the back of the throat!

F.P. London.

A Cornucopia of Cocksucking

Dear Linzi,
I couldn't believe what happened the other night. I went out for a bit of a rave at a local nightclub and ended up having my dick sucked by more women than I could count. No, this is the truth!

Thursday night is the night for pulling at my club. You see

it's the night when all the girls celebrate their hen nights. The place is usually packed and the mix of men to women is about three girls to every bloke. I'm surprised more blokes haven't caught on to it. In my experience a girl's night out can get pretty rude. I've had loads of gropes on the dance floor with a pretty girl whose about to become hitched on the following Saturday. I've even had two or three of them in the back of my car, but what happened last Thursday was nothing short of mindboggling.

It started when I spotted this girl I took a fancy to and I asked her to dance. She was a real looker; short, blonde hair, pretty eyes and a divine smile. She was wearing a glittery, black dress that showed off her shapely curves. As I danced cheek to cheek with her my hands dropped to her bottom, I could feel the elastic of a suspender belt.

'What's your name?' I asked, feeling the beginnings of stirrings in my loins.

'Sharon,' she replied.

Coming from these parts I might have known! I tried the well-used line,

'Come here often?'

'Nah, it's my first time. My mate, Karen's, getting married, so we thought we'd bring her here to get her pissed and laid!'

Taken aback by her directness, I hesitated momentarily and then jokingly said, 'Well if you need a volunteer!'

She stopped dancing, dropped her arms from around my neck and said, 'Why don't you come and meet her?'

It was too good an offer to refuse.

Karen was, in fact, just as tasty as Sharon, as were the half a dozen or so other girls in their party. I was introduced to them and then I joined them at their table and we all got chatting. I couldn't believe that it was really possible, but I just had this inkling that if I pushed it I could hump any one of the horny bitches!

Things started to develop in that direction when Sharon leaned towards me and rested her cupped hand on my cock.

'Why don't we take a little walk outside?' she suggested.

To my amazement all the girls stood up and grinned at me. So, followed by about eight attractive young women in their late teens or early twenties, I went out into the car park. There, in the moonlight behind a brick wall I thought I'd get the proceedings moving, so I unzipped myself and flopped out my dick. Like a flash they were on it. I felt a dozen hands stroking me, playing with my arse and fingering my balls. Tongues galore tickled my prick, my balls and nibbled at my pubic hair. In ecstasy I glanced down and saw Karen take the lead.

Kneeling in front me, she held my cock firmly and encircled my knob with her tongue, before accepting me deep into her throat. I could almost feel her tonsils. While she sucked me fiercely I felt fingers and soft fluttering tongues all over the base of my shaft, around my arsehole and spunk-filled balls. I felt a pair of firm, young breasts and a couple of pairs of right big knockers thrust against my chest, and squashed into my hands. The sensation was totally unreal. Soon my seed was rising.

'Suck him Karen!' urged a number of girly voices.

Karen was doing just what was asked of her and very nicely too. She was an experienced cocksucker. No doubt she'll make some lucky bloke a very nice wife. As my come raced through my tubes, her fingers wanked my shaft faster and faster and the tempo of her tantalizing tongue became even more energetic. She gorged on my helmet, drinking down every drop of my jism as I started to spunk. She was smiling broadly and licking her lips with glee as she gulped it all back. As you can imagine I was pretty happy, too!

Lawrence. Essex.

A Blow Job in the Backrow

Dear Linzi,
I just had to write to tell you of a dream that I've been having about you. I've been an ardent admirer of yours for years and lately I've been dreaming about you so regularly that I feel I know you very well.

Naturally as you're such a sensuous woman my dreams have been of rather a wet nature and I just know you'd like to hear about my favourite one.

I'm a bit of a film buff and go to the cinema as often as I can. Often I go alone. In my dream we meet up in the back row of a darkened cinema. I squeeze along in the back row and sit down to watch a latest release. Moments later you arrive. You settle yourself in the seat next to me and we both begin to watch the movie.

Within ten minutes or so the screen fills to the brim with a love scene; a thick-set, handsome actor carries a beautiful blonde woman to his bed. As their lips meet I feel a warm touch on my thigh. Their embrace becomes more passionate and I feel your long, pointy fingernails at work on my zip. Moments later my semi-erect cock is in your hands. I lay back in my seat and close my eyes, forgetting the movie and everything else around me except your expert hand as it wanks me. Your delicate touch, making my cock swell monstrously as I bristle with desire.

Then you wriggle down onto the floor space in front of me and start to blow me. Your big, thick lips are smeared in strawberry-pink lipstick and it sticks to my cock as you ease me between your hot lips. Your tongue starts to do an erotic little dance all over my tip and your hands are constantly tormenting me by squeezing and massaging my balls. My cock is pumping blood and is throbbing ecstatically by now. I can't take much more of it, and then all of a sudden I feel your creamy, fleshy tits surrounding my cock as you finish me off with a wonderful titfuck and my spunk explodes in your beautiful, sexy face.

It doesn't half make a mess of my sheets!

Reg. London.

Party Pooper

Dear Linzi,
I've been in a stable relationship for a couple of years, and although I love my partner very much, I've fancied some sexual variety for some time now. I just wanted to do something wild and dirty. Not a full-blown fling, or even a fuck, I knew that some heavy petting and multiple orgasms would keep me happy for a while.

So, at this party a couple of months ago I was a very naughty girl. I got chatting to a good-looking bloke and we were flirting like mad. Out of the blue I asked him if he would like to eat my pussy! He readily agreed!

We sneaked off to a small cubby hole next to the payphone and I hoisted up my dress. Seconds later his fingers were on my hot clit, wanking me faster and faster until my whole pussy felt like an erupting volcano. As my creamy crack was still spurting my lovejuice, this fella (whose name I didn't even know!) was getting down on his knees and sliding his tongue into my hot hole. I was such a tease. I allowed him to lick me to orgasm after orgasm, but I wouldn't even take his prick out!

When I returned to the party, my boyfriend wondered why I had such a big grin on my face!

Lisa. Putney.

Oral Sex Fanatic

Dear Linzi,

I am a confirmed oral sex fanatic. My every fantasy involves women with pouting, painted, sticky lips sliding tightly up and down my tool.

I'd like to have a gorgeous huge-tittied blonde dressed up in a yellow bikini crouching before me. Her huge melons would be hanging out of her bra as she welcomes my throbbing prick into her warm, wet mouth. She'd use one hand to steady my cock, while the other would be tweaking and rubbing her gobstopper nipples. The gusset of her bikini briefs would be tugged off to one side to reveal her slimy, hairy hole. And, in between fingering her nipples, she'd be frigging herself to climax while she sucked me. I'd slide my prick in and out of her ruby red lips and feel her pearly white teeth nibbling on my bell end before I'd spunk all over her pretty face.

I wonder if you enjoy sucking cock, Linzi, or is that rather like saying do bears shit in the woods?

Terry.

Festive Fellatio

Dear Linzi,

Having been a reader of your magazine for some time, I have always found it very exciting, and it occurred to me that your readers might find my story interesting. Over Christmas I went away to stay in a hotel in the west country with my brother. The hotel was very plush and had a great indoor swimming pool.

After much gorging and boozing on Christmas day and Boxing day, I got up bright and early the following day and took myself along to the pool. It was only seven-thirty and the pool was deserted.

After fulfilling my set task of swimming thirty lengths, I clambered out feeling quite smug and ready for a good breakfast. I wandered into the changing rooms and was just giving my penis a good rub down when I noticed that the person on the other side of the room drying themselves was of a different gender. I bent down and peered through a gap between the wooden slats and my hanging clothes to take a closer look. Yes, she was definitely female! She had a pair of full, pink-tipped breasts, and a black-haired, closely-trimmed fanny. Now either she had come into the wrong changing room or I had. I glanced around and saw three pairs of large trainers on the floor near me, and various kinds of men's clothing hanging up on pegs. Having confirmed in my mind that it was she that had come into the wrong dressing area, I wrapped my towel around my waist, emitted a gruff, manly cough and set off in her direction.

As I approached her she looked at me wide-eyed, but to my surprise she didn't cover her nakedness.

'This is the men's changing room,' I told her.

She let out an excited giggle and said in an American drawl, 'Oh my!'

After that I didn't know quite what to say. I just stood for a few seconds with my eyes fixed on her breasts; they looked such an inviting mouthful. She seemed totally unfazed by the situation. Pulling a robe around her elegant shoulders, she said, 'Well I'd better get the hell out of here! Hey do you fancy some breakfast?'

I guessed this was a definite invitation, so I graciously accepted and agreed to meet her in the restaurant in ten minutes.

Over breakfast it was obvious that we had a mutual attraction. Her name was Tammy and she openly admitted she had a voracious, healthy appetite for food, sex and life. The way she behaved at breakfast seemed to confirm all three. She ate heartily, smiled all the time and flirted outrageously with me. Then she took hold of my hand and grinned, 'Let's go up to my room!'

She certainly did have a hearty appetite for sex. She undid my flies and grabbed my cock immediately after shutting the bedroom door. She had incredibly long fingernails which she slid back and forth on my foreskin.

My cock was getting harder and harder, but what really made me bone hard was when she closed her fat lips around it. Tammy looked me right in the eyes as she sucked me. She used one hand to grip my cock at the stem and the other to reach down between her legs and sink one of those talons inside her pussy. She was very, very wet. I could hear her squelch. She drew me further and further into her mouth like she was trying to swallow me all up, then she let go and with her soft tongue dribbling all over the head of my cock, she looked at me and asked, 'You like deep throat?' I'd never before been lucky enough to try it, but I was eager now, so I nodded my head in the affirmative.

With that she got onto the bed and lay flat on her back with her head hanging right off the edge. She told me to lean over her and push my cock slowly into her mouth and ease it right down her throat. I did exactly as she told me and it felt amazing. Words fail me to describe it. Inch by inch I felt this hot mouth engulfing my cock until all of a sudden my balls were resting on her slippery wet bottom lip. Holy shit! I just couldn't control myself and I was coming, shaking and shuddering with this new unbelievable sensation as my thick cream disappeared right down the back of her throat.

We had a great morning of it. After my first deep-throat experiment I fucked her doggy fashion over the edge of the bed and then she straddled me while sitting on a hard-backed chair. Tammy was certainly the type of woman you'd leave home for.

Perhaps I'll spend next Christmas in her hometown of Wisconsin? If all the girls there behave like Tammy, it surely must be a hedonist's paradise.

Harry. Leytonstone.

Sit on My Head??

Dear Linzi,

Ooh the girls, glurp, chuckle! The pictures in your mag make me mad, each one of them makes me come. I enjoy masturbating while looking at them. I do not get *Penthouse* regularly over here, but whenever I come across a copy, I leave no stone unturned to acquire the same.

With *Penthouse* in my hands I often fantasize and get lost in the heaven of sexual pleasure. I often imagine myself in your company with the beautiful *Penthouse* girls pictures around me, while you're sitting on my lap. Your beautiful body is covered with lots of pink, lacy lingerie and stockings. I am fondling your boobs and this prick of mine is getting harder and harder. Suddenly you jump up out of my lap and I am disgusted. But then you start releasing your boobs enticingly. You place your fingers beneath your panties and inside the crevice, and slowly but maddeningly you remove them. Ahh ooh, chuckle, what a pretty, flowery pussy you have!

I watch you masturbate and see your beautiful pussy getting pinker and pinker as juice oozes from it. You catch it and start fucking it into your boobs. Ooh, ooh what a pleasure! Ah what are you doing now? You are sucking me dry! I'm deep in your throat, I love it, I love fucking your mouth.

I adore your beautiful long legs. Ooh I'm jealous of those stockings. How intimate they are in touch with your thighs. All this juicy pink pussy is mine, all mine. So here is my tongue ready to fuck your rosy, lovely cunt. Would you please arrest my head firmly between your plump thighs? Can you engulf my head inside your pussy? I would love that, glurp, chuckle. Ooh I love the taste of your juice. I love to eat it, I want to lick it, bite it and breathe it. I love to work on it with all of my tongue, my teeth, lips and nose. Oh god, let the time stop! Let me remain in this ecstasy for ever. Why on earth do I have to ejaculate! Linzi, can't I extend my durations of ecstasy?

B.K. India.

Changing Room Cunnilingus

Dear Linzi,

I'm blonde, pretty, twenty-seven years old, bisexual and run my own small boutique in the high street. You'd be astounded by the amount of uppercrust, frustrated housewives that call on me regularly. I suppose the word is out that the proprietress is a raving lesbian nympho and it's very good for business!

It all started one day when I was called into a private cubicle to assist one rather elegant, middle-aged lady with the cups of a delightful, expensive swimsuit. As I slipped my hands into the front of the costume for adjustment, my fingertips brushed against her breasts and I could feel her nipples harden to my touch. The lady stood very still as I took one nipple between my thumb and forefinger and rolled it around slowly. I felt her body tense with excitement, so I squeezed it a little harder while my other hand reached for her pubic mound. She thrust it forward to meet with my cupped hands, and through the silky material I grabbed a handful of her warm pussy.

Up until that point she hadn't uttered a word. She emitted a tiny whimper of excitement as I bent my head to her breast and sucked her red nipple into my mouth. As I teased my hot tongue all round her areola, I gripped the crotch of her cozzie and yanked it off to the side.

'Oh no!' my customer cried out feebly.

I removed my lips, looked into her eyes and challenged, 'Do you want me to stop?'

'No, no, don't stop,' she whispered.

One hand squeezing her breast, the other running through her silky thatch, I asked, 'Would you like to buy this swimsuit?'

'Yes, please,' she breathed.

'Would you like to take it off so I can suck on your sugar

276

sweet pussy?' I giggled naughtily finally parting her pubic hair and feeling the furrow of her sex lips.

She merely shook her head emphatically and wriggled out of the costume.

'Kneel down then,' I said firmly, positioning this fine, upstanding pillar of the community, naked on all fours away from me.

I lay on my back and squeezed beneath her. All the time she used her fingers to play with her pussy. She spread her lips wide and gave me an amazing flash of pink.

'Watch me suck you in the mirror,' I urged.

Her eyes were already fixed to the mirror as I flicked her clitty with my long tongue. She was dying for it. Her pussy was sopping with her juices, and her milky-white thighs reeked of expensive perfume as I gripped hold of her legs and licked her sex. I lapped her faster and faster until she actually spurted in my face.

That was the first. I haven't had another spurter yet, but there is plenty of time, and as I've said business is booming.

Ang. Surrey.

These Boots Were Made for Walking

Dear Linzi,

I really have done my best to be a good boy, but it seems hopeless. When I saw you in your leather paraphernalia I went completely to pieces. You could have walked all over me in Nazi jackboots. I was hardly able to sleep all night.

When I first got married, the king-sized bed needed clamping to the floor. We gave the springs such a rocking and of course the bed clothes ended up all over the place. We had it in no end of different positions. She loved to squeeze my penis until it was hard and throbbing. We kissed all over our bodies in a very personal way. Sometimes in an untamed manner. To hell with the rest of the world. It was a good job the mother-in-law was never about!

In those days the wife didn't keep her fanny under wraps. She bleached it two-tone blonde and wore very short skirts so that when she squirmed in the chair I could get a good view of her fanny. No wonder my eyeballs nearly popped out with all that arsehole hassle! She always used a powder puff and plenty of perfume between her thighs. What fun we newly-weds had! She loved being pampered, petted and indulged. She knew my weakness for garter belts, suspenders and fine stockings with wide tops. She looked glorious in the larger suspender types. She loved me to suck rhythmically on her clitoris. Fanny licking is such exciting behaviour!

John.

Long Ones, Fat Ones and Spunky Ones

Dear Linzi,
If guys ask me what I love best about sex I have to answer that it's cocksucking. It seems to prove a popular answer and I am constantly to be found on my knees with a rock-hard prick filling up my mouth. I like cocks with foreskins and cocks without. I like long, slim cocks that I can deep-throat, fat ones that make me gag, and I adore cocks that shoot warm come straight down my throat. As I'm such a fan of fellatio, I thought you might like to hear about my fantasy. Here goes:

One night after a serious sucking session with my current boyfriend, Rick, we get talking. I tell him how much I would love to be surrounded by stiff dicks, so I could wank them and suck them in an orgy of throbbing meat. Anyway he's not the jealous type so he tells me he can arrange it for me.

The very next night he rings me from work and tells me that I'm to expect him and three of his mates at about eight. Receiving the good news that I'm going to have four stiff dicks to chew on makes me feel so sexy. I have a bath and all the while I'm laying there in the soapy water I can't leave my cunt alone. The sheer thought of sucking on all those cocks makes me go weak at the knees. I struggle out of the bath and get dressed in underwear only. My thinking is that that way I can get into the action quicker and I can have all that lovely cream shooting all over me. I put on black stockings and undies and don't bother with any knickers.

When Rick lets himself in with his key, I am stretched out on the floor of the lounge with my legs wide open, my fingers embedded in my cunt. I'm immediately up on my knees and within seconds I've unzipped and unbuttoned all their flies and taken out their cocks. They are all beautiful and hard. I cram two in my mouth at once and take one in each hand as I suck greedily on a pink, swollen knob. Rick removes his meat from my mouth and kneels behind me, his cock nudging at the entrance to my cunt. I raise my arse to enable him to fuck me and he slams it in me hard as I wank two dicks and suck on another. One huge, long prick is filling my mouth to the brim as Rick pumps in and out. He fucks me hard and fast, squeezing my tits as he rides me.

Suddenly the spunk is flying. Great blobs of it hit my face and dribble down my chin. Another lot splashes on my tits and even more spurts down my throat. I'm coming in spasms now, the sensation of all that hot dicky is bringing me off like never before. I am still trembling and crying out as Rick grips my shoulders and suddenly fills me up with his hot milk. I lose control, but I am one very happy girl!

In reality Rick would never let me do that!

Grace. Bristol.

A Taste of Honey

Dear Linzi,
As a long-time admirer of your body, your writing and your magazine, I feel compelled to tell you of an experience that makes me an even bigger fan of yours. Seven inches in fact and that's just when I hear your name!

I was in bed last night, asleep, after having spent a delicious hour licking wildflower honey from my girlfriend's pussy. Lisa is a terrible tease. She makes me watch, but won't let me touch as she takes honey from the jar with her fingers and then puts them inside herself. It's only after I've watched her massaging herself for ten minutes, manufacturing a delicious perfume of honey and pussy cream that she lets me drink her mouthwatering concoction. Not that I'm complaining, mind you!

Not surprisingly my dreams were of a sexual nature. A lorry

load of *Penthouses* were delivered to my house and emptied in my bedroom. Unable to believe my luck, I leafed through one of them. The first page was entirely devoted to your creamy, pink nipple. As a connoisseur of your body from thousands of angles, I'm sure it was the left nipple. If you look closely you'll see it's slightly lighter in colour than its equally beautiful companion. Every exquisitely attractive detail was visible.

The next page showed two fingers of your left hand poised over a golden thatch of coiffeured pubic hair. A hint of pouting red pussy lips was visible. Page after page revealed knob-hardening glimpses of your sexy body. On one, your rouged, moist mouth was open, with the tip of your tongue wetly curling out of one corner, as if in anticipation of an imminent blow job.

It was all too much for me. I shot a wad of spunk over the magazine, and in reality over Lisa's back – when I found the page revealing your pussy in all its glistening, honeyed glory. I wanted to drive my tongue into that dripping love tunnel and have you howl with pleasure as I teased your quim and clitoris with my tongue and teeth.

I realized that this was a *Penthouse* special. No ads, no other models, just hundreds of pictures of you, which when assembled made a life-sized photo of you, nude, caressing yourself to an explosive orgasm. If such a magazine were possible I'd sell my house to buy it! Please, please, is there any chance of my dream becoming reality? If not, I'd settle for a close-up pussy shot or a centre-spread entirely devoted to your tits!

Dave. Ilford.

Double Dicky

Dear Linzi,

I've just discovered the joys of sucking dick. I'm twenty-two years old and quite a horny little handful, but I've always felt so self-conscious about giving a man a blow job. But now I've got the hang of it.

It was at a party that I finally got my lips around a swollen knob. Well two in fact! It was at a girlfriend's twenty-first and there were some really great looking men there. I was wearing an off-the-shoulder, tight, red dress, black stockings, suspenders and high-heeled shoes. Two guys, Derek and Ian kept me supplied with wine, so by about ten in the evening I was feeling a little tipsy.

I really fancied both Derek and Ian, although I couldn't decide on which one I preferred. Both men seemed very attentive towards me so I assumed I could take my pick. I'm not sure how it happened but we got on to the topic of blow jobs. I think it was at this moment that I placed both of my hands on bulges in their pants and they in turn started to smooth my legs and play with the nape of my neck. I admitted to them that I'd never had a dick in my mouth before and that I would very much like to try it, like nowish! Then I waited a couple of seconds to let them digest that, and then I said that two would be much more fun than one!

We sneaked upstairs and found an empty bedroom, I unzipped their jeans and eagerly took out their pricks. I didn't feel at all nervous as they took off my dress and rubbed my tits. I was becoming more and more turned on as they started to play with my pussy through my knickers. I was dying to taste their cocks. I'd heard that everyone tastes different and I soon found that to be true!

I knelt on the floor and took a cock in each hand. Wanking them gently, I alternated my tongue from one to the other, swirling the tip of my tongue around the swollen heads, before running my mouth up and down the length of their shafts. When I started to really get a rhythm going, my mouth was a blur, swopping from one thick prick to another, saliva dribbling from my wet lips as I guzzled on their throbbing members. The guys were grunting and groaning noisily as simultaneously they started to come. Derek shot his load straight in my mouth. It was my first taste of spunk. It tasted sweet and I licked it all up greedily. Ian came just seconds after, his warm sperm splattering over my face and trickling down to soothe my burning nipples.

I'm seeing both Ian and Derek now, although we don't go out in a threesome as I prefer to suck one dick at a time these days. But if the mood takes me I know it can be arranged!

Pauline. Aberdeen.

Lives to Suck Cocks

Dear Linzi,

On holiday in Greece I had the pleasure of meeting Carol, a dark-haired, petite woman in her early thirties, who had an insatiable desire for giving head. I met her in a beach bar, we clicked and she suggested we go for a walk on the nude beach. Well you can guess what that led to?

Carol couldn't take her eyes off my willy, and I too had difficulty averting my eyes from her ripe, swinging tits and hairy cunt. My prick was beginning to rise as she turned to me and said, 'Mind if I suck your prick?'

She was already on her knees homing in on my helmet!

Of course I didn't even answer. I just shut my eyes and wallowed in the pleasure of her tongue exploring between my arse cheeks, wriggling up and down my long prick before finally swallowing me up in her cavernous mouth. Her hands were all over me as she gobbled me so enthusiastically and expertly that I came in a matter of seconds.

After that first sensational suck-off Carol would do it at every possible opportunity. She didn't give a damn who saw us, she just wanted to suck me all the time! She was the sexiest woman I've ever met. Holiday romances have to end, but I'll never forget Carol the woman who just lives to suck cocks!

Brian. London.

NEXUS BACKLIST

Where a month is marked on the right, this book will not be published until that month in 1994. All books are priced £4.99 unless another price is given.

CONTEMPORARY EROTICA

CONTOURS OF DARKNESS	Marco Vassi		
THE DEVIL'S ADVOCATE	Anonymous		
THE DOMINO TATTOO	Cyrian Amberlake	£4.50	
THE DOMINO ENIGMA	Cyrian Amberlake		
THE DOMINO QUEEN	Cyrian Amberlake		
ELAINE	Stephen Ferris		
EMMA'S SECRET WORLD	Hilary James		
EMMA ENSLAVED	Hilary James		
FALLEN ANGELS	Kendal Grahame		
THE FANTASIES OF JOSEPHINE SCOTT	Josephine Scott		
THE GENTLE DEGENERATES	Marco Vassi		
HEART OF DESIRE	Maria del Rey		
HELEN – A MODERN ODALISQUE	Larry Stern		
HIS MISTRESS'S VOICE	G. C. Scott		Nov
THE HOUSE OF MALDONA	Yolanda Celbridge		Dec
THE INSTITUTE	Maria del Rey		
SISTERHOOD OF THE INSTITUTE	Maria del Rey		Sep
JENNIFER'S INSTRUCTION	Cyrian Amberlake		
MELINDA AND THE MASTER	Susanna Hughes		
MELINDA AND ESMERALDA	Susanna Hughes		
MELINDA AND THE COUNTESS	Susanna Hughes		Dec
MIND BLOWER	Marco Vassi		

Title	Author	Price	Date
MS DEEDES AT HOME	Carole Andrews	£4.50	
MS DEEDES ON PARADISE ISLAND	Carole Andrews		
THE NEW STORY OF O	Anonymous		
OBSESSION	Maria del Rey		
ONE WEEK IN THE PRIVATE HOUSE	Esme Ombreux		
THE PALACE OF FANTASIES	Delver Maddingley		
THE PALACE OF HONEYMOONS	Delver Maddingley		
THE PALACE OF EROS	Delver Maddingley		
PARADISE BAY	Maria del Rey		
THE PASSIVE VOICE	G. C. Scott		
THE SALINE SOLUTION	Marco Vassi		
STEPHANIE	Susanna Hughes		
STEPHANIE'S CASTLE	Susanna Hughes		
STEPHANIE'S REVENGE	Susanna Hughes		
STEPHANIE'S DOMAIN	Susanna Hughes		
STEPHANIE'S TRIAL	Susanna Hughes		
STEPHANIE'S PLEASURE	Susanna Hughes		Sep
THE TEACHING OF FAITH	Elizabeth Bruce		
THE TRAINING GROUNDS	Sarah Veitch		

EROTIC SCIENCE FICTION

Title	Author	Price	Date
ADVENTURES IN THE PLEASUREZONE	Delaney Silver		
RETURN TO THE PLEASUREZONE	Delaney Silver		
FANTASYWORLD	Larry Stern		Oct
WANTON	Andrea Arven		

ANCIENT & FANTASY SETTINGS

Title	Author	Price	Date
CHAMPIONS OF LOVE	Anonymous		
CHAMPIONS OF PLEASURE	Anonymous		
CHAMPIONS OF DESIRE	Anonymous		
THE CLOAK OF APHRODITE	Kendal Grahame		Nov
SLAVE OF LIDIR	Aran Ashe	£4.50	
DUNGEONS OF LIDIR	Aran Ashe		
THE FOREST OF BONDAGE	Aran Ashe	£4.50	
PLEASURE ISLAND	Aran Ashe		
WITCH QUEEN OF VIXANIA	Morgana Baron		

EDWARDIAN, VICTORIAN & OLDER EROTICA

ANNIE	Evelyn Culber	
ANNIE AND THE SOCIETY	Evelyn Culber	Oct
BEATRICE	Anonymous	
CHOOSING LOVERS FOR JUSTINE	Aran Ashe	
GARDENS OF DESIRE	Roger Rougiere	
THE LASCIVIOUS MONK	Anonymous	
LURE OF THE MANOR	Barbra Baron	
MAN WITH A MAID 1	Anonymous	
MAN WITH A MAID 2	Anonymous	
MAN WITH A MAID 3	Anonymous	
MEMOIRS OF A CORNISH GOVERNESS	Yolanda Celbridge	
TIME OF HER LIFE	Josephine Scott	
VIOLETTE	Anonymous	

THE JAZZ AGE

BLUE ANGEL DAYS	Margarete von Falkensee	
BLUE ANGEL NIGHTS	Margarete von Falkensee	
BLUE ANGEL SECRETS	Margarete von Falkensee	
CONFESSIONS OF AN ENGLISH MAID	Anonymous	
PLAISIR D'AMOUR	Anne-Marie Villefranche	
FOLIES D'AMOUR	Anne-Marie Villefranche	
JOIE D'AMOUR	Anne-Marie Villefranche	
MYSTERE D'AMOUR	Anne-Marie Villefranche	
SECRETS D'AMOUR	Anne-Marie Villefranche	
SOUVENIR D'AMOUR	Anne-Marie Villefranche	
WAR IN HIGH HEELS	Piers Falconer	

SAMPLERS & COLLECTIONS

EROTICON 1	ed. J-P Spencer	
EROTICON 2	ed. J-P Spencer	
EROTICON 3	ed. J-P Spencer	
EROTICON 4	ed. J-P Spencer	
NEW EROTICA 1	ed. Esme Ombreux	
NEW EROTICA 2	ed. Esme Ombreux	
THE FIESTA LETTERS	ed. Chris Lloyd	£4.50

NON-FICTION

FEMALE SEXUAL AWARENESS	B & E McCarthy	£5.99	
HOW TO DRIVE YOUR MAN WILD IN BED	Graham Masterton		
HOW TO DRIVE YOUR WOMAN WILD IN BED	Graham Masterton		
LETTERS TO LINZI	Linzi Drew		
LINZI DREW'S PLEASURE GUIDE	Linzi Drew		

- -

Please send me the books I have ticked above.

Name   ....
Address   ....
            ....
            .... Post code ....

Send to: Cash Sales, Nexus Books, 332 Ladbroke Grove, London W10 5AH

Please enclose a cheque or postal order, made payable to **Nexus Books**, to the value of the books you have ordered plus postage and packing costs as follows:

UK and BFPO – £1.00 for the first book, 50p for the second book, and 30p for each subsequent book to a maximum of £3.00;

Overseas (including Republic of Ireland) – £2.00 for the first book, £1.00 for the second book, and 50p for each subsequent book.

If you would prefer to pay by VISA or ACCESS/MASTERCARD, please write your card number here:

Please allow up to 28 days for delivery

— — — —   — — — —   — — — —   — — — —

Signature: _____